MYSTIC VISION

Nina knew many things that could not be explained. She had known about the deaths of the warriors at the hands of the Others even before Phoenix told the Council, she had known the instant the Sky Ship had been destroyed. Most important, she had known what had happened to Coconino, when no one *could* know.

"He is not dead," Nina had asserted quietly. "He was in the Magic Place That Bends Space, but something went wrong and it bent Time as well. He has gone before us, to the Times That Are to Come."

"How far?" Phoenix had pleaded.

To that Nina only shook her head. "He sleeps," was all she would say. "He will come again."

D1010202

By Catherine Wells
Published by Ballantine Books:

THE EARTH IS ALL THAT LASTS
CHILDREN OF THE EARTH

CHILDREN OF THE EARTH

Catherine Wells

A Del Rey Book
BALLANTINE BOOKS • NEW YORK

Sale of this book without a front cover may be unauthorized. If this book is coverless, it may have been reported to the publisher as "unsold or destroyed" and neither the author nor the publisher may have received payment for it.

A Del Rey Book
Published by Ballantine Books

Copyright © 1992 by Catherine Wells Dimenstein

All rights reserved under International and Pan-American Copyright Conventions. Published in the United States of America by Ballantine Books, a division of Random House, Inc., New York, and simultaneously in Canada by Random House of Canada Limited, Toronto.

Library of Congress Catalog Card Number: 92-90623

ISBN 0-345-37463-0

Manufactured in the United States of America

First Edition: October 1992

To Errol, my in-house editor,
April, my proofreader,
and Joanne, my cheerleader

ACKNOWLEDGMENT

Thanks to Stephen Stein for being my resource person in the physical sciences.

PROLOGUE

"In the Days When Coconino Walked the Land, the Mother Earth was pleased with her children and caused them to prosper. The corn grew tall and the cotton flourished, and in the Valley of the People it was always warm. The river that watered that place ever flowed, and all the People gave praise to the Mother Earth. Even the Men-on-the-Mountain respected the Way of the People and did not trouble the Mother Earth in their habits."

Thus began the Legend of Coconino, told in the evenings around the Elvira, the ceremonial fire of the People. It was a dream of Camelot, a dream of David's Israel, the shining memory of a time that was never quite as golden as the stories painted it. But it had been a time of contentment for the People. Then came the Others, descendants of those who had fled Earth's wrath centuries before. The Others did not respect the Mother Earth, and the Way of the People was threatened.

"And so the Mother Earth raised up her favorite son, a man of great stature: strong of limb and cunning of both mind and tongue. He was the best of the People, the finest hunter, the most devoted child of the Mother Earth. He was Coconino." To him fell the task of protecting the Earth from reinfestation by a careless people. But the Earth did not set him to his task alone.

The legend also told of the Witch Woman who came from the Mountain to be his hunter-companion. It told of Tala, the great one-horned beast that flew through the skies with Coconino on its back. It told how together they fought to keep the Others from returning to the Earth in great numbers, "for the Earth would have no traffic with those who had abandoned Her."

"Then did Coconino ascend to the Father Sky and tear the great Sky Ship from its place," the People said, "so that the Others could speak no more with the Sisters of the Mother Earth." For

1

them it was all that had happened. The People did not know of the lie that had been told, the tale of a deadly plague reported to the spacecraft's home world before communication was lost. They did not know how Coconino had conspired with the detested Derek Lujan to keep the secret that Earth was once again habitable, that plant, animal, and human life had survived on a planet once believed to be self-destructing.

But they knew the price Coconino had paid for his service to the Mother Earth. They had paid the price as well. "Then Coconino entered a Magic Place, and it cast him into the Times That Are to Come." The People were left with only the querulous Witch Woman to pilot their course. She had loved Coconino, and for his sake she loved the People, but she had come from the Mountain, from that other surviving culture that used machines and kept strange ways. She never learned to hear the voice of the Mother Earth.

Still she tried. And even as she tried to protect the People from the Others who had been trapped on Earth with them, beyond the stars were those who wondered at the fate of their lost ship and its crew.

The People knew nothing of that, either. They knew only the cold of the haven to which the Witch Woman had led them, the Village of the Ancients that Coconino had found. There they waited. " 'Where is Coconino now?' the People cry. And the Mother Earth replies, 'He sleeps. He will come again.' "

In the Times That Are to Come, Coconino awoke to find that the Earth he had defended had cast him up among a people he did not know. All those he loved now lay cradled in the bosom of the Mother Earth: his friends, his family, his Witch Woman. Only one had been cast forward with him, and of that one Coconino tried not to think. To Coconino it seemed that he had been abandoned.

But the Earth had not removed her hand from him yet.

CHAPTER ONE

Coconino could hear his enemy approaching—clumsy still, though he tried to move stealthily through the shrubby mesquite and creosote. Where Coconino stood, on a rocky piece of ground high above the canyon, there was no shelter, no place to hide, nothing to do but wait for his enemy to come. Heart pounding, sweat beading his coppery brow, he stood facing the approach, feeling at his bare back the watching eyes of those who believed in him. *Spare me your belief!* he thought. *Do not lay that burden upon me....*

Overhead, the sun beat down from its zenith, leaving virtually no shadows on the parched earth. Coconino brushed his coal-black hair back from his face with a sweaty arm and waited, knife in hand. He would have welcomed a thick stand of cholla, a spreading prickly pear, an outcropping of any size on this rock shelf to shield him from his enemy, from the sun, from the watching eyes of those who believed he would save them....

Who asked you to? he demanded silently. *Who asked you to place your faith in me, to make me a god when I am not? I am only a man, a sorrowing man, a man who has already given all that he held most dear in the service of the Mother Earth. I want only to rest and to grieve, but you—you will not let me be. Neither will he, this one who comes after me—*

On a small rock just in front of Coconino a banded lizard sat, its brown and buff tail curled around nearly to its snubbed nose. "Can you make him go away?" Coconino implored the lizard, but the creature only bobbed its brown head and looked to the south.

And then he was there, striding out of the high desert scrub, a mocking smile on his cruel, handsome face. His eyes were blue, his short hair a light rippling brown, his skin a pale shade unseen among the People. *Alien,* it shouted. *Other. One who would take*

3

*the Way of the People from them. One who had already stolen
more than that from Coconino.*

*Coconino met him, black eyes flashing. "Where is Phoenix?"
he demanded. "What have you done with my Witch Woman?"*

But Derek Lujan only stopped and smiled his infuriating smile.

*Then Coconino saw that the ground at Lujan's feet was littered
with bones—dried bones, bones of those who had died seven generations before. Seven generations! Gone, all gone: Juan, Falling
Star, Two Moons, Tala, Phoenix . . .*

*With a roar Coconino launched himself at his enemy. It is your
fault, he thought. You did this to me. You did this to her. It was
you who tore us apart—*

*But Lujan had grown stronger since their last encounter. With
a deft movement he turned Coconino's lunge, and suddenly the
young primitive found himself pinned to the ground, his knife useless in a hand he could not move. From Lujan's throat came a
strange animal sound, half snarl, half growl, and terror gripped
Coconino. Mother Earth, help me, he prayed. Send Juan, send
Tala, send—*

"Phoeni-i-i-i-x!"

"Husband," Hummingbird whispered, shaking his shoulder.
"Husband, hush. It is a dream. You are dreaming again."

Coconino woke, sweating, in the utter darkness of his wickiup.
It smelled strongly of dust and dried grasses even over the scent
of wood smoke and newly tanned leather. The patter of tiny claws
told of an adventurous squirrel scampering across its top. Coconino raised himself on one elbow and lay panting, staring into the
darkness until his senses oriented. Then slowly he sank back down
on his mat. He was still here. He was still here.

Here was the island canyon far north of the Valley of the People,
the canyon he and Phoenix had found together nearly two hundred
years before, years he had skipped over when a spray of electricity
from Tala's horn had done something to the Magic Place so that it
bent time. It had coughed him up near the Well, there to be found
by the People of that Time, by Climbing Hawk and his band of
traders.

"Are you all right?" Hummingbird asked, an anxious voice in
the darkness.

A foolish question. But she was a dear, foolish girl, and he had
no right to trouble her with the truth. "I am all right, Hummingbird. I am sorry I disturbed you. Go back to sleep."

He could hear her then, settling down on the mat next to his.

On the other side of the wickiup was a similar sound, and he knew Ironwood Blossom had been awakened as well. Of course, awakened; he had called out in his sleep again. Called out for Phoenix . . .

Tenderly he touched the pendant that hung from a thong around his neck. It was a blue-green stone, set in silver, in the shape of a bird, a bird rising from the ashes of its nest. Once he had given it to Phoenix; here he had found it again at the Well, marking the place where the heroine She Who Saves had descended to the bosom of the Mother Earth. "It is a good day to die," he had told himself on the day he had entered the Sky Ship to carry out the Mother Earth's mission. But here he was alive, and it was his Witch Woman who was dead, gone to dust generations before anyone now living had been born. Anyone save himself.

It had stripped him of purpose. Climbing Hawk and his band had brought Coconino back with them to their village, in awe of the great Coconino who had returned to the People as legend foretold. They had not yet discovered that instead of a hero, they had brought back an empty husk. He had lost Phoenix, lost Tala, lost Juan and all his friends—there was only the Mother Earth, and she seemed to be done with him. He had rescued Her from the Others by banning any more of their kind from Her soil; and now she told him, rest. Rest.

But he could not rest.

When he had been with these People a handful of days, when he had talked to Twisted Stick and learned all he could of what had happened in the time from which he came, when he knew at last that there was no hope of going back, he plunged into deep and utter despair. In anguish he had scaled to the very top of the island, a rocky nub salted with cholla and yucca and tufts of juniper. The slopes of that mountain fell in choppy rock ledges to the canyon floor, that deep crevice of verdant green so foreign to his desert-born eyes. A swift stream coursed through the cleft on the western side of the island, swollen with snowmelt, while the eastern cleft was dry.

It was toward that dry channel that Coconino had turned his face, toward the silent, relentless sun that rose toward the vaulted heights of Father Sky, and there he had wailed out his grief. It was a terrible, mournful chant that made the People below shiver in their adobe houses. He wailed all that day and into the night, crying out for all those he would never see again. In a mighty voice he sang the praises of his hunter-companions, of the mother who had borne him, of the powerful beast who had joined in his fight to save the Earth. He sang of the sweetness of the Valley of the People, of the pleasant stream that flowed through its fields, of the blessed Village of the Ancients that graced its cliff wall. And finally, as the moon retreated from its starry realm and the sun rose again to warm the land, his voice hoarse now and his strength waning, he sang the praises of his Witch Woman. He sang of her courage, her strength, her strangeness, and her will. He sang until exhaustion overcame him and he slumped to the ground, to the sweet, sun-warmed bosom of the Mother Earth.

Climbing Hawk had found him there, as he had found him unconscious on a hillside west of the Well. Feeling both sorry and responsible for the young god-man, he had carried Coconino back down the mountain and into the shade of one of the mud houses built into shallow caves in the butte. When Coconino had finally awakened, he had offered the older man no thanks but had gone to build himself a brush shelter on the canyon floor, far from the rest of the People.

Much of Coconino's grief had been purged in this ritual, for the ways of the People were wise in such matters. Afterward he tried to go on with his life, for that, too, was the manner of the People. He was a young man, having seen only twenty summers, and as it had before his bereavement, his body continued to torment him with its need for a wife. Phoenix was gone, and with her all hope of marrying his *moh-ohchi*, the companion of his spirit, and despite his loud and lengthy mourning, he still felt an emptiness so vast that it threatened to swallow him whole. So he resolved to take a wife of these People, someone to whom he could cling in the endless, vacant night, hoping in marriage and mating to find some measure of peace.

Listening to Hummingbird's gentle breathing now, Coconino remembered how he had carefully, dispassionately looked over the available maidens. At fourteen, Hummingbird was the brightest, the comeliest, with a clear round face and sparkling eyes. Little things delighted her, and she would bounce up and down on her toes, her infectious laughter touching even his barren heart. He needed such light and joy in his life.

So he went out to hunt—not on the lands just above the island canyon, though there were deer and bighorn sheep to be found. Instead he went miles to the northeast, to the Old Black Lands where once he and Phoenix had searched for Tala, and there he found a herd of Great Antelope. They were twice the size of a deer, with majestic racks of horns. His arrow found the heart of a fine young buck, and he labored long and hard to drag it back on a travois, down through the canyon and up the steep island slope to a cluster of mud houses on its southern face, to the door of Hummingbird's mother.

The old woman, whose name was Night Comes Quickly, had been dumbfounded. She had stared in disbelief from the antelope to the young god who had brought it and back again.

"A gift for you," he had begun, the traditional opening. "For a mother of such good fortune."

Understanding crept into her black eyes, and they began to shine. "I perceive, señor," she responded, "that you are a young man who appreciates good fortune and a man well able to provide for a wife."

"A wife, indeed," he confirmed.

Then Night Comes Quickly had hesitated, and he had wondered what was wrong. Perhaps she did not want so illustrious a son-in-law.

But that was not her dilemma. She bit her lip and lowered her voice. "Señor, I have *two* daughters," she said.

He looked beyond her then, to the open area beside the house, where two young women knelt in the sun, industriously grinding corn and pretending not to hear. Hummingbird did, indeed, have a sister—an older sister. An older, ugly sister. Well, not ugly, but not beautiful. Her body was large and blockish, not small and round. Strong, no doubt. Her hands were large and strong as she plied her *mano*, the stone pestle used in grinding corn and beans. She had a high forehead and features without delicacy.

Coconino's heart pounded against his ribs. She looked to be seventeen or eighteen; she had been passed by many times. Now her younger sister had come of age, a beautiful, fetching young maiden, and she was about to be passed by again. It wasn't fair; what difference did it make to him, anyway, which woman bore his children?

As he watched them, side by side, he saw a tear escape from the older girl's eye and trickle down her cheek. She knew. She already knew.

"It is Hummingbird I desire," he whispered hoarsely, and hated himself.

So the People had made a great feast and built a Marriage Wickiup—backward, he thought, from the way things used to be. In the Valley of the People everyone had lived in wickiups, and the Village of the Ancients high on the cliff wall above them had served for ceremonial purposes such as weddings. Many things had changed since then. But when he retired with his bride and sought solace in her arms, he discovered that some things had not changed.

"You are a great husband," she told him afterward.

He laughed softly, pleased with his choice. If anyone could restore his spirit, it would be the spritely Hummingbird. "How would you know?" he teased her. "Have you had so many?"

"Oh, no," she protested, "but you give me such joy—I am sure no one could do better."

Someone could love you, though, he thought. I don't.

"And you are such a great hunter," she continued, "I know you will bring home more food than two people could eat."

"Then we must have many children to help us," he replied. Children were the wealth of the People, and Coconino intended to be rich.

"But they will be little babies for a long time," Hummingbird persisted. "I am so fortunate to have so much. More than one woman needs."

It occurred to Coconino then that he did not want to hear any more, so he kissed her to quiet her and found that his body had not expended all its energies. It seemed, at the time, a good way to distract her.

But in the aftermath she said, "See? I knew you were more than enough husband for me. I would be selfish to keep you all to myself."

Coconino sighed and rolled over onto his mat, staring up at the ceiling. He began to understand some of the jests his friend Juan used to make about married life. With a great sigh he heaved himself up onto one elbow and looked down at the round, soft-featured face of his bride. It glowed in the moonlight that streamed through the uncovered door, and the long black hair was a shadowy veil across her upper body.

"Is this truly what you want?" he asked. "To be only one of two wives? To be forever the younger? To listen to—to the sound of your husband with another woman?"

"I love my sister dearly; there will never be any jealousy between us," Hummingbird promised, and added, "She's a better cook than I am."

So the next day Coconino had gone out and shot two deer, a comparable gift, and brought them back to Night Comes Quickly's door.

That had been the previous spring. It was late fall now, and they still lived in the wickiup, the three of them. There had been some murmuring over the wickiup, but he was Coconino, and the People let him do pretty much as he pleased. As for the second wife, they were only glad that someone had taken pity on Ironwood Blossom.

Yet it is you who have taken pity on me, he thought as he lay in the darkness now. Both of you. For how many wives would keep silent when night after night their husband called out in his sleep for another woman?

Phoenix flung herself over the hill and hauled up short, a cry on her lips. Too late! She was too late.

Five bodies lay at the river's edge, five men of the People burned and bloody from the fusion weapons of the Others. Damn you! she raged silently. Damn you all. In five hundred years couldn't you find some better use for your technology than in weapons of destruction? What chance did they have with their frail wooden bows and their flint-tipped arrows? What chance against your centuries of diabolical inventions?

Weeping in despair, she stumbled down the slope toward the bodies. There was no chance that life lingered in any of those mutilated men, and reason demanded that she go on after those who had survived, to see to the destruction of the fearsome weapons they had stolen. But reason had no sway here, only grief and anguish and the desperate need to know who it was that had died so violently.

One corpse lay stretched out face up, apart from the others, the leader of the group. Juan! Phoenix's heart wrenched within her. Never had there been a more good-natured companion, a man with an easy manner and a ready jibe. Now he lay with his mouth agape, bearing no trace of the crooked smile that had ever graced those lips. He had come forward to meet the Others, to explain to them that the People meant them no harm. Their response to his outstretched arms had been to burn a hole through his midsection. Phoenix dropped to her knees beside him and tried to cradle his head in her lap, but that gesture threatened the fragile integrity of his body. Tears streaming, she closed his sightless eyes and turned to the others.

Seeing their friend cut down, the remaining four men had drawn their bows and fired. Their deadly marksmanship had cost them their lives in turn. The acrid smell of burnt flesh turned her stomach as Phoenix moved among the corpses, trying to identify them. It was not easy. Runs Like a Fox and Two Lizards—or was it his brother, Always Hungry? She would not know until she found the survivors.

But here—ah, Mother Earth, how could this happen? The broad shoulders, the scar on his left leg—it was Falling Star, her other hunting companion. He of the droll stories and the lazy smile. Were it not for the scar, she might not have known him now: his head was gone.

Falling Star was seventeen.

There was one body left. It had been hit by multiple shots and was mostly blackened flesh. The smell nauseated Phoenix, but she drew close enough to see that it was a smaller corpse, perhaps only a boy— Her heart crashed against her ribs. Coconino's half brother had been with the band of raiders who had gone to steal away the fireshooters of the Others. Flint was only twelve and about this size— Phoenix backed away from the charred mess that had once been someone she knew, the enormity of the possibility squeezing her lungs and robbing her of breath. Not Flint. Please, Mother Earth, not Flint, not Flint, not Flint—

Phoenix woke with a cry, drenched in sweat, her stomach a knot of fear and revulsion. The smell of burnt flesh seemed to linger in the air, but it was only a faint trace of smoke from the fire in her stone house. Soon even that faded.

Sinking back on the adobe floor, Phoenix tried to drive the dream from her mind. It had been six months since the massacre, six months since the People had fled from the wrath of the Others, six months since Coconino had disappeared. . . . Mother Earth, will it ever end? she pleaded. Will I ever stop finding their bodies, ever stop smelling that awful, acrid stench and wondering if Flint is the final victim of this outrage?

Flinging back her sleeping furs, Phoenix forced her body to its feet and staggered toward the door of her house. She stooped low, for she was a tall woman and it was a small door. She pushed past the hide covering to where the cold of the winter night slapped her, bringing her wide awake. Quickly it penetrated her leather tunic and leggings, raising gooseflesh beneath, but Phoenix did not care. She stood on the ledge outside her house and gazed across the deep river canyon to the far wall. It was obscured by darkness now, but it, too, housed a line of crumbling stone dwellings. Ah, Coconino, she thought, how excited you were to find this Village of the Ancients, sheltered high in the rock wall! How insufferably proud to return to the Valley of the People on the back of Tala, the alien flying antelope, and tell them of this place that none had seen before. You wanted so much to be part of their legends. Well, you have your wish, my arrogant friend. If only you were here to enjoy it. . . .

The scuff of a moccasin reached her, and Phoenix peered into the darkness on the narrow path that encircled this island butte and connected several clusters of mud houses. Overhead the stars were sharp points of light in the clear black expanse of Father Sky. Let it be him, Phoenix prayed. Mother Earth, let it be Coconino, come to find me, come to relieve me of this responsibility—

"Witch Woman."

It was his name for her, but it was not his voice. A tear of disappointment welled in her eye; she brushed it away angrily. She had had enough of tears. They did no good.

Nina's form took shape in the darkness. She was a full head shorter than Phoenix and growing into the roundness that was characteristic of the People. For Nina, naturally bony, this required some help: the warm furs wrapped around her were part of it; the constant supply of food Phoenix brought to the younger woman was another part. But mostly it was due to the best reason a woman of the People could imagine: Nina was pregnant.

"Nina, you should be inside," Phoenix admonished gently. "It's cold."

"I'm all right." Her face came into view now as she stood beside Phoenix on the ledge. Her hair and eyes were black, her cheekbones high, but even among her own Nina was considered ugly for her large nose and the gap between her front teeth. When, at seventeen, she'd still had no husband and no prospects, she had gone to an upper chamber in the Valley of the People to make her plea.

It was the Way of the People that even if a woman had no husband, she was entitled to a child. When Nina had taken up residence in that ancient cliff dwelling, it had been an invitation to any man so inclined to visit her chamber and give her a child.

And Phoenix knew who had gone.

Nina was watching her now. Phoenix could feel those clairvoyant eyes on her, peering through her to her very soul. "You have dreamed again," Nina said gently.

Phoenix did not reply. She only drew a deep, stinging breath and looked away to the south, to the sunbaked river valley where the People had lived in peace for five hundred years. And beyond it, to the camp of the Others, where geodesic domes squatted rudely out of place, an offense to the People and to the Mother Earth.

A breath of breeze shot through Phoenix, and she shuddered convulsively. I hate this cold place, she thought. But it was safely removed from the Others. And Coconino would know to look for them here.

When he came back.

Beside her, Phoenix heard Nina's furs rustle, and she tried to pull herself back to the present, away from the haunting dream. "What are you doing up in the middle of the night, anyway?" she asked Nina. "Is that young hunter keeping you awake with his kicking?"

Nina's smile was a spreading shadow in the starlight. "No, he sleeps quietly," she replied. "Would that I could say the same!"

"Only two moons left," Phoenix encouraged. "Soon he will be running wild, and you will wish for the days when you always knew where he was!"

Nina did not smile at that, and Phoenix's heart jumped. What did the younger woman know about this child's future that she did not smile at the gentle jest?

Nina knew many things that could not be explained: She had known which hunters had died by the river even before Phoenix could blurt out her painful news; she had known that the Mother had died at the very instant that the Sky Ship was destroyed; and most important, she had known what had happened to Coconino.

"He is not dead," Nina had asserted quietly to the Council. "He is gone from us, but he is not dead."

Phoenix had clutched at the girl's testimony, which corroborated her own interpretation of the fantastic events. "He was in the Magic Place That Bends Space," she explained urgently, using the People's words for the warp terminal that provided transport between the orbiting ship and the base camp. "But something went wrong, and I think time was bent as well." It had to be; she could not face the alternative.

"He has gone before us," Nina had agreed, "to the Times That Are to Come."

Forward, of course; accidental time warps always went forward. Phoenix knew that. But how far? "How far?" she had pleaded.

To that Nina only shook her head, maddeningly calm and at peace with the situation. "He sleeps," was all she could say. "He will come again."

Now Nina stirred. "You must not stand here in the cold with no blanket," she told Phoenix. "Go inside." She turned to do likewise.

But Phoenix caught at her arm, engulfed as it was in the antelope hide. If Nina knew something now . . . "Tell me about the child," she pleaded.

Nina was startled. "How did you know?"

Phoenix gave a confused laugh. "How did I know? You've been thanking the Mother Earth for six months—and that bulging belly tends to give it away, too."

"Oh, *this* child," Nina said with some relief, and tried again to leave.

But Phoenix still detained her. This child? "What other child might I mean?" she demanded.

Nina hesitated. "It does not concern us."

"Oh?" There was a suspicious edge to Phoenix's voice. Despite her dark coloring and hunter's garb, she was not of the People. She came from the Mountain, where suspicion and deceit were second nature and little was taken on faith.

Nina debated how to respond. "It is not a child of the People," she said, hoping that would be enough. It would have been enough for anyone else.

"Who, then?" Phoenix persisted, determined to know what had disturbed the younger woman, what it was that she would rather not share.

Nina saw now that Phoenix would not be put off. The tough older woman seldom was. Nina sighed and told her. "A child of the Others," she explained. "There is a woman in their camp who will bear a child in the summer." Then, in a voice barely audible, "Coconino's child."

Phoenix stood dumbstruck. Another child of Coconino . . . Karen. He had spent one night with Karen Reichert, part of their scheme to get aboard the spaceship *Homeward Bound*. Could it be that Karen—

It seemed too cruel. That a woman could spend one night with a man and become pregnant, when Phoenix had spent seven years with her ex-husband without a flicker of life in her womb. . . . But that was the hand she had been dealt. Her Fallopian tubes were blocked, and Phoenix would never conceive. It had devastated her, destroyed her marriage to Dick McKay. It had kept her from seeking the fulfillment of her desire with Coconino, for she made herself believe it was a crime against him that he should waste his seed on barren ground; by the time she realized the foolishness of her protest, it was too late. When the lack of his presence, when the lack of his child within her womb, was a constant ache, could it be true that this woman who spent only one night with him now bore that child?

But even as Nina slipped away into the darkness, Phoenix knew it was true. Nina was never wrong. Whether it was communion with the Mother Earth or some other psychic experience, Nina had not been wrong in the six months since they had moved the tribe north, out of the Valley of the People, away from the deadly firepower of the Others.

Another child of Coconino? Phoenix remembered his words only too well as they sat on the riverbank in the Valley of the People. "I want to marry," he had told her. "I want to marry and leave children. . . ." How Phoenix had wished then for a starship to come, bringing back the medical techniques that could correct her barrenness! And she'd had her wish: the ship came. Phoenix saw the prospect of renewed contact with the stars as her salvation, but Coconino had seen it as something else, and Coconino had been right.

Now, in the perpetual chill of his absence, two things drove Phoenix, gave purpose to her daily life. One was the safety of the People, which she had struggled to purchase with words and distance. The other was to see that Coconino's legacy was preserved among the People.

Phoenix looked out again from the fearful height of her mountain ledge and saw the faint graying of dawn in the southeast. You left me here, Coconino, she thought bitterly. Left me alone to watch and ward over the People, and that I have sworn to do. When you come back, beloved, you shall find the People safe here in this canyon. You shall find that they honor and respect the name of Coconino and the passion he bore for the Mother Earth. You shall find that the Way of the People has not been violated and that your children have been brought up in it. *Both* your children.

Phoenix's eyes narrowed as she studied the sky to the south. Overland as the hawk flew would be too difficult a journey at this time of year. But up the canyon to the river's source, across to the marshy lakes, and down through the Red Rock Country . . .

Both your children, Coconino, she resolved. I will see to it.

Chelsea Winthrop stared in horror at the blood dripping down the woman's arms, trickling off her elbows, staining the pale blue skirt of her expensive garment. She would have been a beautiful woman, with honey-blond hair and perfect skin, her body well proportioned and graceful, if only it weren't for the blood.

At the beautiful woman's feet lay the crumbled body of Oswald Dillon. Dillon: founder of the Interplanetary Museum of Art, corporate magnate, wealthiest man on Argo, bloody corpse . . . He had been run through with a crude stone-tipped spear. Its wooden haft still protruded from his chest, bloodstained and grim. His legs were bent where they had folded beneath him when he had slumped down to the marble floor of the museum. The front of his crisp gray garment was soaked with red, and on his face was a look of mild surprise, as though he had been asked an unexpected question. Perhaps the question was—

"Why?" Cincinnati demanded. Chelsea looked up at her older brother, at the handsome face of a young man behind which lay the mind of a child. And the child demanded of the beautiful woman, "Why?"

She turned to them, she whose scream had brought them running back into the Earth Room, running from their own personal tragedy into this bizarre, enigmatic one. Her face was ashen, her eyes glazed, and she worked her jaw several times before she could answer Cin's question, if answer it was. She said only, "He promised me no one would die."

No one would die?

Suddenly alarms shrieked, locks hissed menacingly into place, and panic gripped Chelsea. They were trapped in this place, locked in this gallery with a corpse and a murderer, and she realized with a jolt that Cincinnati's fingerprints were on that spear. Cincinnati, whose mental deficiency might be viewed as instability— No sooner had the thought occurred to her than there were uniforms everywhere. Museum guards, police, enforcers—there were weapons raised and orders shouted. Someone grabbed Cincinnati and forced him to the floor. "Stop it!" Chelsea shrieked. She tried to run to him, but they held her back. "He didn't do it!" she shouted at them. "He didn't do it, it was her, it was her, it was her—"

"Good morning, Ms. Winthrop."

Chelsea woke with a gasp and a fierce rage seething inside her, rage against fools who assumed that the developmentally disabled were more capable of violence than other people. Her stomach still churned with the anger and frustration of that day. An artificial voice filtered through to her, and the blare of sirens became only the gentle gurgle of the coffeepot going to work in the kitchen. "It's five forty-five A.M., Argoan Standard," the artificial voice told her. "This is Tuesday, the twenty-sixth day of February, and you have an appointment—"

"Wyatt: stop," Chelsea snapped at the computer, fighting to control the frustrated fury the dream had left her with. Six months earlier she had not controlled it well at all, struggling and shouting at the guards, who had simply immobilized her as though she were a querulous child. Why didn't they ever think it was me? she wondered. I was the one carrying on. But no, they went straight for Cincinnati: tall, strong, terrified Cincinnati. They had him down on the floor, sobbing like the child he is, calling for me, and they wouldn't let me *go* to him.

Chelsea drew a deep breath and blew it out. Well, it was over now. In truth, it hadn't taken the guards long to reassess the situation, to realize that the blood covering Camilla Vanderhoff was Oswald Dillon's and not her own. Then it was Camilla they immobilized, and Chelsea and Cincinnati were released. All they had wanted then were statements, and Chelsea had swallowed back her rage at last and told them what she could.

It was then that Camilla's enigmatic statement began to haunt Chelsea. "He promised me no one would die."

A grayish light filtered through the simulated window of Chelsea's bedroom now, the colorless light of Argoan day. She could have programmed it for something cheerier, but why remind herself of home with yellow sunlight and blue skies? She was a young professional in the corporate realm of Argo, next in line for the position of chief technical investigator for Inverness Financial. Chelsea grimaced and took several more deep breaths to clear the dream from her mind, irritated with herself for having dreamed it again. She had put it behind her, put it behind Cincinnati, too, and propelled them both into their new condition: orphaned. Strange, she thought, to be an "orphan" at twenty-three, but she was. And now she was a mother, too, because Cin was her responsibility. So forget the murder, forget the shock, forget the rage—

And then she remembered.

With a groan, Chelsea rolled over and hunched her shoulders against the inevitable. As the computer had reminded her, this was the twenty-sixth of February, and Chelsea was giving her deposition in the Dillon murder case.

"Ms. Winthrop," the computer began again, "it's time to get up now. This is an important day—"

"I'm up!" she groused, struggling to get her feet onto the floor and effectively squelch the program. "What are you, my mother?"

Then what she had said hit her, and Chelsea gave a bitter laugh. I torture myself, she thought. Every time I think I've gotten used to it, I say something or do something, and suddenly I think of Mom or Dad.

It had been September—summer in New Sydney—when Chelsea had left Cincinnati strolling through the Interplanetary Museum of Art while she went to the Terran Research Coalition offices to get the latest word on their parents' expedition. Something was wrong; she had been reading it in the faces of the TRC personnel for days. A navigational error, a probe that malfunctioned—they all smiled and told her everything was fine, but she knew they were lying. That was why she had gone in person, tired of being put off, intending to cut through the red tape and make someone *talk* to her.

But by the time she arrived they were through talking. They simply handed her a printout of the latest dispatch. A landing team, a virulent disease, a dedicated doctor—and now it was up to Chelsea to tell her brother, Cin, that their parents wouldn't be coming home again. She had found him in the Earth Room with Dillon and the beautiful Camilla Vanderhoff and had drawn him away into another gallery where they were alone.

Cin had read it in her eyes even before she got the words out. He was clinging to her, weeping, when they heard that soul-rending scream—

"Wyatt: start shower," Chelsea commanded, forcing herself to her feet. Maybe a good hot shower would rinse this sense of dread from her and revive her enough to meet the challenge of the deposition head on. After all, she was a Winthrop; the daughter of Clayton and Jacqueline Winthrop could handle a simple deposition with dignity and decorum. She could handle almost anything when she had to. Pioneer stock, her father would say. Ornery, her mother would add.

But dear God, what she wouldn't give for one friend who could understand.

"Wyatt," Chelsea commanded briskly as she shoved her feet into slippers. "Status on attempts to reach Zachery Zleboton."

"Mr. Zleboton is still on special assignment for his law firm," the computer replied. "His office has relayed your request but regrets that Mr. Zleboton may not respond at this time."

Cursing softly, Chelsea stumbled toward the open door of her bath, where steam was rolling up from the shower. I've been tough, she thought petulantly. Since that day I've kept calm, kept control of myself for Cincinnati's sake. I've put up with lawyers and clerks and infinite bureaucrats. Is it too much to ask that on this one day, the day when I must live the whole nightmare again, before witnesses, the one man who might understand should give me a call?

They had been the only young people at the memorial service for the crew of the *Homeward Bound*; only the Winthrops and Chief Rita Zleboton had had children. It was only natural that they had found each other, found a common bond in their sorrow, found a quiet bar afterward and told stories and remembered and laughed and wept. When Cincinnati had returned to the center with his girlfriend, Susan, Chelsea and Zachery had stayed on, talking quietly until the pale Argoan sun rose in the murky sky.

"You should see the sunrise on Juno," she told him. "Brilliant colors! Crimson and rose and amber and delicate shades of peach . . . Someone told my father sunsets were like that on Earth, and so he bought a ranch there and called it Terra Firma."

"I wish I'd known your father," he murmured, his voice a rich rumble in his broad chest. Somehow she had wound up leaning on that chest; she wasn't quite sure how, but it felt good, so she stayed. "Of all of them, it seems almost . . . appropriate that he should end his days there."

She took his hand, a broad black hand that dwarfed her own pale one, long-fingered though it was. "Zach, something was going on," she confided, "something the TRC never told us about. I could see it in their eyes every time I asked for news. Even before they reached Earth, something was not right on the *Homeward Bound*."

He twisted his head to look at her face, to see, she imagined, if she was drunk, or delusional, or dim-witted. He was a striking man, his face wide-browed with strong features and penetrating hazel eyes. "Oh, it's probably just me," she responded hastily to his unasked question. "But—but when Camilla said . . ."

"Who is Camilla?" he asked.

So she told him about the murder, about finding Dillon gored in his own museum, in the Earth Room. She omitted her own fury at the initial treatment of Cincinnati—that was over, and nothing could be done about it. Instead she told him about the beautiful woman, Camilla Vanderhoff, standing over Dillon with blood dripping from her arms and how she had answered Cincinnati's desperate question.

"He promised her no one would die," Zachery repeated thoughtfully. "And you think she meant the crew of the *Homeward Bound*."

"I have no reason to think that's what she meant," Chelsea replied. And yet she knew she did think that. "It was only because we had just found out, and because I was sure something had been wrong on the ship. . . ."

Zachery had held her close then, never questioning, never chiding. It was as though her belief were enough for him, but of course it was only the moment and their mutual need for companionship. He was only humoring her, only being supportive—

"Supportive, hell," Chelsea muttered to her image in the bathroom mirror. It was the image of her mother's face—high forehead and strong, horsey jaw—but softened by masses of blond curls cascading past her shoulders. What beauty nature had failed to give Chelsea, she had achieved by other means. "He was just there, that's all. I needed someone to talk to, and he was just there."

And where are you now, Zachery Zleboton? she wondered. Now that I must dredge it all up again for the deposition, must relive that scene in the Museum and all its attendant emotions—where are you, who might understand how I feel? And why do I really care?

CHAPTER TWO

Coconino heard the scuffing of a moccasined foot behind him, and his already tense body grew more rigid still. Turn around, he willed the approaching figure. Turn around and go back up the trail to the village. Or go on down to the stream, whose quiet gurgle mocks me with its peacefulness. But do not come to my wickiup, you with the weighty step. Do not invade this sanctuary I have created on the canyon floor. Do not intrude on my thoughts, my recollection of the dream of my enemy, and the banded lizard, and the unprotected rock shelf . . .

But the footsteps came inexorably on. Coconino closed his eyes and took a deep breath.

He sat outside his wickiup, enjoying the warm fall afternoon and carefully smoothing the shaft of a new arrow. It was barberry, an excellent strong wood for arrows. Beside him lay four similar shafts ready to be hardened in the hot ashes of the cook fire. The mindless work was what he needed after his restless night, and he had been content in it and his brooding until he heard the step behind him. Now he wished that he had gone hunting instead.

Some twenty yards downstream from him Hummingbird knelt and scooped moist clay from a deposit in the silty ground. She had drawn her long black hair to one side, and it dangled down into the mud, but that didn't seem to bother her. He sometimes wondered which she liked better, fashioning her pots or digging in the mud for the clay from which she made them.

Just a breath of wind pressed her loose leather tunic against her, outlining the slight swelling of her abdomen. Coconino smiled in spite of himself and wondered briefly if having a baby would slow her pace at all. He doubted it. He hoped not; she was a pleasant distraction.

Unlike the shadow that loomed up over him now. Coconino did

20

not stir from his task but continued running the shaft through the stone smoothing tool. Perhaps if he ignored the man . . .

"Pardon, Coconino."

Sighing wearily, Coconino put down his work and looked up. His father-in-law, Pine Pitch, was a stocky, heavy-limbed person who walked ponderously. Large protruding lips and slightly angled eyes gave his face an officious expression, but his tone to his son-in-law was always polite.

"Yes, Pine Pitch?" Coconino responded, wondering what new scheme the man had dreamed up to capitalize on his elevated status.

"The Council is concerned," the older man began with great dignity, "that the harvest is so small this year. It has been very dry, you know, and—"

"Yes, I know," Coconino interrupted impatiently. "I have been living here, too."

"Pardon, Coconino," Pine Pitch said. "It is just that newlyweds often have other things on their minds besides the weather and the crops, and I thought—"

"Please go on, Pine Pitch," Coconino prompted, trying to hurry the man to his point so he would go away again.

"As I was saying," Pine Pitch backtracked maddeningly, "the Council is concerned that the corn and vegetables may not last until spring, so I told them I would speak to you."

Speak to him. Coconino picked up his arrow and studied it thoughtfully. A bird chattered in a nearby tree; the water gurgled in the stream; a hawk soared in the air above them; and still the sense of Pine Pitch's statement escaped him.

"And here you are speaking," he said. "What is it you have to say?"

The man seemed surprised. "Why, I am asking for your help," Pine Pitch said, as though that were perfectly obvious.

Coconino's jaw tightened painfully; he forced himself to relax it. "And what is it you want me to do?" he persisted irritably. "See, I am preparing new arrows for hunting; perhaps I will be able to bring you many deer and some of the Great Antelope. Is that what you meant?"

"That is very good," Pine Pitch said, "but if you could do something about the harvest . . ."

At that Coconino's irritation turned to anger, and he leapt to his feet. "Am I the Mother Earth, to change the way plants grow? Can I give or withhold rains and floods? Can I make the sun shine in Father Sky? I am only a man, Pine Pitch!"

Pine Pitch looked startled. "A man, yes, but you are Coconino."

That was what he said, but what he meant was, You are the great god Coconino.

Coconino paced furiously in front of his wickiup. "Yes, I am Coconino!" he snapped. "Yes, I come from the Time That Was. Yes, I tore the Sky Ship from its place. But I am not a god! You would ascribe to me power that rightfully belongs to the Mother Earth; will you call down Her anger on us all?"

He came to a halt in front of his father-in-law. "I cannot make the corn grow, Pine Pitch. I cannot make the squash swell. I cannot make the trees bear more nuts. The People must do as the People have always done; they must pray to the Mother Earth to feed them from Her bounty. They must go forth upon Her bosom and search for the fruits She supplies."

Reaching down, he snatched up the half-made arrows. "As for me, Pine Pitch, I will hunt and share my kills, giving thanks to the Mother Earth for all that She supplies. And I will pray with you that She will be merciful"—though why, he thought, She should be merciful to a thick-headed, faithless person like you is beyond me!—"and grant us a mild winter with no sickness. But I can only do what any other man of the People can do!"

Then he added, as salve to his own pride, "What any other man of my hunting skill can do."

As he glared into his father-in-law's disappointed face, Coconino saw Hummingbird running toward them. She had heard their raised voices and had come to intervene. "Father!" she cried out gaily. "Father, did you see the fine, fat duck my clever husband brought home yesterday? It had the prettiest green head; I wanted to make a rattle from it for the baby, but Ironwood Blossom said it wouldn't look very pretty in a few days. So I saved the feathers instead, and I'm going to use them to decorate a shirt for the baby." She caught Coconino's arm and beamed up at him.

Coconino looked down into her shining eyes and round face, and it did, indeed, leech some of the bitterness from him. If only the rest of the People could accept him as Hummingbird did, making only those demands which were reasonable to make. He touched her cheek and gave her a small, reassuring smile.

Then he turned back to his father-in-law, who was still smoldering at the rebuff. The man would never believe him. No matter how many times Coconino explained that he was only human, that he had no mystical powers or undue influence with the Mother Earth, Pine Pitch would continue to think that Coconino was holding back. The older man would return to the Council now and tell them that Coconino had refused to do anything more than pray to the Mother Earth.

"I am sorry, Pine Pitch," he heard himself saying. "I wish I could do more. I wish I could do half the things the legends say I can. But all life still rests in the hand of the Mother Earth, and I cannot tell Her what to do." If I could, he thought miserably, do you not think I would tell Her to bring my Phoenix back to me?

The apology softened his father-in-law's hurt expression somewhat, but still Pine Pitch seemed disinclined to leave. "Perhaps," the older man suggested, "If you would sit with us on the Council . . ."

"I will not sit on the Council," Coconino repeated, as he had repeated each time he was asked. "I am a hunter and a storyteller. Let me be what I am, Pine Pitch."

"Come, I will go back up the hill with you," Hummingbird volunteered, dragging her father away from her moody husband. "I want to speak with Mother about how big I should make the shirt for the baby. I have never sewn for a baby before, you know."

Coconino watched them go, and a small guilt nagged at him as he saw Hummingbird struggle up the steep path to where the rest of the village lay nestled in the shallow caves of the island. It was unfair to his wives to keep his dwelling down here on the canyon bottom, away from the rest of the People. It was especially unfair to Hummingbird in her condition to make her climb so far just to visit her mother or join the other women grinding corn in one of the common areas.

But he could not build a wickiup on the steep slope of the butte, nor was there room on any of the rock shelves to construct such a dwelling. And wickiups were where the People were supposed to live. They were constructed of wood and earth, grasses and leaves; they were round, making the floor a circle as all of life was a circle. They were domed as Father Sky was a dome above their heads. It was *moh-ohnak* to live in such a place.

How had the People come to forget that?

Coconino heaved a great sigh and turned his gaze to the south, toward the village where he had grown to manhood generations ago. So much had been lost since then. Cotton would not grow here; the People went about in leather and in clothing made of yucca fibers. No one spun yarn or operated the great looms that had dotted his village. The ceremonial ribbon shirt he had been wearing when they found him had been a great oddity to these People, though now they imitated it in buckskin.

Ah, Mother Earth, why did you do this to me? he asked desperately. Why did you cast me up here, so far from all I know and love? Why did you take me from Phoenix?

And in the quiet murmur of the brook, in the sigh of the breeze through the juniper and the pines, he heard the answer he had heard each time he asked these questions. To save you, Coconino, the Mother Earth whispered. To save you from the wrath of the Others, for you would not have survived it. The Witch Woman was enough to save the People, but she could not have saved you. I had to do that.

Ah, Mother Earth, Coconino thought as his heart ached for the village that no longer existed, for the People who had been dead nearly two hundred years. I would trade the rest of my days . . . I would trade—

But Coconino knew he wouldn't. Each time he tried to make the complaint, he knew that he treasured the rest of his days and wanted to spend them . . . somehow. Doing something.

In a fit of restlessness he seized the five arrows he had been working on and thought to snap them in his hands, but such waste appalled him. Instead he paced the short distance to the cook fire and placed the arrows carefully in the ashes to harden. Then he snatched up his throwing club and headed for the trail that led out of the canyon. Woe be to the rabbit or squirrel that crossed his path today!

Mother Earth, make them leave me alone, he prayed as he trotted toward the canyon wall to pit himself against the steep trail there. I am tired of being a hero. I am tired of their demands. I am tired—

I am simply tired.

Hummingbird found her sister in the common area just outside their mother's house. Ironwood Blossom was grinding corn, always grinding corn, preparing the meal that would see them through the cold winter ahead. Hummingbird was afraid sometimes that constant work had made her sister even more unattractive, for her wide shoulders seemed to stoop forward more these days and her large hands were callused to the point of being misshapen. Yet their mother had the same wide, work-worn shoulders and callused hands, and she did not seem unattractive to Hummingbird.

"Good morning, Sister," Hummingbird called out.

Ironwood Blossom looked up and smiled, flicking her long black hair back over her shoulder with one hand. "Good morning, little one," she replied. "How are you feeling today?"

Hummingbird flopped down beside her, postponing the moment when she would have to take up a *mano* and join her sister in the monotonous work. "Oh, I feel wonderful. I can feel the baby squirming around inside me; it's so exciting! I can't wait for it to be born. I hope it's a boy."

Ironwood Blossom's smile became a grin as her sister's exuberance infected her. "A fine, healthy boy," she agreed, not missing a beat in the rhythm of her grinding. "To grow up and be a hunter, like his father."

Hummingbird laughed and shifted onto her knees, reaching for the stone *mano*, which lay close at hand. "Did you ever think that we would marry a hunter?" she asked gaily. "I always pictured myself as a farmer's wife, going out into the fields every day, chopping up the ground with a hoe."

"You will spend your share of time in the fields," Ironwood Blossom assured her. "Everyone does."

"Yes, but we have such fine hides to tan," Hummingbird persisted. "And always plenty of meat in the stew pot. I like meat, you know. And of course—" She patted her protruding stomach. "—I didn't have to help with the harvest at all this year. Do you suppose I can arrange to be pregnant every time they need help in the fields?"

"Pregnant women work in the fields all the time," Ironwood Blossom reminded her. "It is only because you had those false pains that Mother wouldn't let you go."

"I've decided about that," Hummingbird went on airily, tossing a handful of grain into the *metate*, the large dished stone in front of her. "I've decided the Mother Earth sent those pains to warn me what it will be like to deliver this baby. She wants me to be prepared. But Sister—" Hummingbird reached out and put a hand on Ironwood Blossom's wrist, and finally the older girl paused in her grinding. "—did you ever dream that Coconino would awake in our time and that he would want us for his wives?"

But instead of responding in joy, Ironwood Blossom's face grew sad. She managed half a smile, but it was a sad half. "No, little one," she replied softly, "I never dreamed it."

Hummingbird was confused. "You are happy, aren't you?" she asked anxiously. "He is a good husband and so kind, and it is such an honor—you are happy he chose you, aren't you?"

"Of course I am happy," Ironwood Blossom assured her, reaching over to hug the smaller girl. "There can be no better husband in all the village. But Hummingbird, I know I was not his choice. I would never have been anyone's choice."

"That's not true!" Hummingbird exclaimed, drawing back. "No one forced him to take a second wife. And even if he hadn't, I'm sure someone else . . ." But her voice trailed away; she couldn't carry it off. Ironwood Blossom wouldn't believe it, anyway. "But he did choose you," she persisted. "A man like Coconino does only what he wants."

"Or what his new wife asks."

Hummingbird applied herself to grinding with sudden intensity, her mouth drawn into a small pout. "You make too much of my influence. Coconino is a god—" The word died on her lips, and she looked around quickly to make sure he had not heard that. "Coconino is a great man, a wise man, and he does only what he thinks is right."

"Such as taking pity on a poor, ugly girl who has no prospects." There was no bitterness or irony in Ironwood Blossom's tone; it was a fact she had grown accustomed to.

"You're not ugly!" Hummingbird cried, and did a poor job of fighting back tears. "You're—big, and that's better for having children. And you have strong hands; you work very hard. And . . ." Hummingbird brushed moisture from her cheek, then pursed her lips into a sly smile. "And I don't believe I have heard any complaints after the nights Coconino has spent on your mat."

Ironwood Blossom reached out a hand to brush the hair away from her sister's face and to touch her cheek. "I'm not unhappy, little one," she soothed. "The Mother Earth has been, oh, so kind to me. As has Coconino. But I hold no illusions as to my own part in the matter. I am grateful, and I feel myself blessed beyond any woman in the village. Even you. Because I had no reason to expect such good fortune."

Hummingbird clutched her sister impulsively. "It is my good fortune that you are with us," she whispered fiercely. "I would be a bad wife if you weren't there to help me."

Ironwood Blossom laughed gently. "Well, be a good wife now and help me grind this corn."

Laughing and brushing tears from their eyes, the two sisters returned to their work. But after a moment Hummingbird spoke with her usual authority. "Soon you will have a child, too."

Ironwood Blossom's lips twitched slightly. "Yes, soon I shall."

Hummingbird stopped in midmotion and stared at her sister. "Are you . . . ?"

Suddenly bashful, Ironwood Blossom nodded. "I think so. It

has been a full two moons since my last moonflow time. And my stomach churns like a muddy brook in the mornings.''

Hummingbird jumped to her feet. ''Oh, that's wonderful!'' She grabbed her sister's hand and tugged her up also. ''Come, we must tell Coconino! He will be so pleased. Two moons? Oh, then yours will be a spring baby— Mother, Mother, guess what!''

And off Hummingbird went with her older sister in tow.

From the corner of his eye Coconino watched the two brothers approaching. Both were scrappy, sinewy boys, one fifteen and the other eleven. The older one was catching at the younger one's arm, trying to restrain him, but the younger tugged free and marched on resolutely. Now the older one bent and put his mouth close to the younger's ear, urging something—caution, most likely. Perhaps threatening dire consequences. Then he looked up and saw Coconino seated on the path, his feet extending down the steep rocky slope that fell to the canyon floor, and he hesitated.

The younger one came on, his tousled hair glinting blue-black, his coppery face set. But even he slowed his steps as Coconino looked up, as though having second thoughts.

It would be amusing, Coconino thought sadly, if it were only these boys who approached me with awe. But they all do it. The other young men, the village elders—even my own father-in-law. Unconsciously, his brow darkened.

''Good day, Coconino,'' the younger boy ventured, his voice still high-pitched.

''Good day, Red Snake,'' Coconino replied gravely. He shifted his eyes to the older boy, who hung back two or three paces on the path. ''Good day, Tree Toad.''

Tree Toad murmured a response but came no closer. Unlike his younger brother, who had not undergone his manhood ceremony yet, Tree Toad wore a headband of woven yucca fibers around his black hair. Both boys wore loincloths of the same material and leather moccasins.

Coconino returned his gaze to Red Snake, who shifted from one foot to the other. Coconino waited.

''A pleasant day, isn't it?'' Red Snake tried.

''Very pleasant,'' Coconino agreed, beginning to take some pleasure in the boy's discomfiture. At least he was a bold boy. Coconino glanced again at the older one. ''Don't you agree, Tree Toad?''

''Yes, very pleasant,'' Tree Toad replied hastily, and his voice cracked embarrassingly. Coconino kept his straight face with difficulty.

"A good day for hunting, wouldn't you say?" Red Snake blurted.

Now Coconino lounged back on his elbows and studied the brothers. Was that what they were after? The honor of a hunting trip with the great Coconino? Well, that was what Red Snake was after, at any rate. Tree Toad would never have presumed to suggest it. But the subject having arisen, there was hope written all over the older boy's face. Hope and trepidation.

Should I growl at him? Coconino thought. No, the poor boy would probably go running in terror. I will never get rid of this noxious image of godhood if I act the part. Better to play the ordinary man. The *humble* ordinary man.

His teeth gritted. Coconino had never been humble.

"An excellent day for hunting, yes," Coconino agreed, sitting back up and dusting his elbows. "I think I will get my bow and go farther up the canyon. Oh!" He paused in the act of rising to his feet. "Would you like to join me?"

A wide grin split Red Snake's face. "Oh, yes!" he exclaimed. Behind him the quieter Tree Toad was also smiling, though it looked more like relief than unabashed joy. "We were thinking of going hunting ourselves," Red Snake dissembled. "It would be good to go together."

Coconino could not help smiling himself at the cavalier remark. "I will stop at my wickiup," he said, "to pick up my bow and—"

"Coconino! Coconino!"

Coconino turned to see Hummingbird running up the path from her mother's house, dragging Ironwood Blossom by the hand. "Coconino, guess what!" she gasped, stopping directly in front of him. She came only to the middle of his chest, her shining face turned upward to meet his eyes. Even among the People she was petite. Ironwood Blossom, on the other hand, was several inches taller than her sister, an average height.

Ironwood Blossom was blushing. Coconino took note of the fact; he couldn't recall ever seeing the older girl blush.

"Coconino, Ironwood Blossom has something to tell you," Hummingbird giggled, pulling her sister forward and changing places with her. Ironwood Blossom seemed mortified; she hid her smiling face in her hands and tried to escape, but Hummingbird held her in check.

"What is it?" Coconino asked, his curiosity piqued.

"Tell him!" Hummingbird urged.

Ironwood Blossom forced the hands down from her face—and saw the two boys behind Coconino. She gasped. "I can't tell him *now*," she protested with a meaningful look at the brothers.

Coconino looked over his shoulder and found himself caught. Obviously, his wives needed his attention now. But there waited the two eager boys, wanting him to go hunting with them. Could he ask his wives to wait? Of course not. Could he send the boys away?

"Red Snake," he said, "can you and your brother go to my wickiup and find my bow and quiver? I will meet you at the foot of the trail in a few minutes."

"Certainly, Coconino!" the boy said quickly, thrilled to be entrusted with the responsibility of entering the great man's wickiup and handling his weapons. He turned on his heel and headed for the trail that led down into the canyon, his brother close beside him. Coconino watched the two boys pushing and jostling each other, venting their joy in playful antics as they hurried away.

Turning to Ironwood Blossom, he put his hands on her sturdy shoulders and looked into her brown face. "Now tell me," he commanded with mock severity. "What is it?" And say it quickly, he thought. I want to go hunting with those two young rascals.

Blushing furiously, she stared at her toes. "I think—no, I know," she corrected, and managed to lift her chin just a little. "I am carrying your child."

Coconino jumped, a motion that was transmitted to her through his outstretched arms. She stopped smiling and looked anxiously into his face.

Coconino knew he needed to say something and say it quickly, but his mind was dizzyingly blank. He looked beyond Ironwood Blossom to where Hummingbird danced with excitement on the path.

"It's true, it's true!" Hummingbird sang, throwing her arms around her sister's shoulders and squeezing her gleefully. "Now we are *both* carrying babies! Isn't it wonderful?"

"Yes," Coconino managed. "Wonderful."

Two babies. He had not yet accustomed himself to the idea of one, and now there would be two. At nearly the same time.

"Oh, look, there's Father!" Hummingbird cried, spying Pine Pitch seated in the shade in a common area just down the pathway. "We haven't told him yet. Come, Ironwood Blossom; he's going to be so surprised."

But Coconino recovered enough to grab his older wife as the younger one started to haul her off in this new direction. "I *am* pleased," he told her sincerely, knowing she needed that reassurance after his initial reaction.

A gentle smile warmed her face, and her dark eyes softened. "So am I," she whispered back. And then Hummingbird whisked her away.

Stupefied, Coconino stood staring after his two wives, the one so lively and irrepressible, the other so somber and insecure. Then he sank heavily on the path once more and gazed out over the empty air of the canyon. Its far wall was striped with rock layers and scrubby vegetation, buff and green, buff and brown. There were the ruins of other houses there, too: high on the wall in shelves that corresponded to the ones here on this butte. They had been built by the Ancient Ones long ago, before the Before Times.

Some of these houses had been repaired like the ones on the island, and families lived over there from time to time. But as space became available on the island, those families always moved back. None of the women seemed anxious to live so far away from their mothers and sisters and aunts. Often they all crowded in together, extended families in a single house twelve feet deep by fifteen feet wide: parents, grandparents, babies . . .

A second child. Coconino swallowed as he tried to take it in. As long as he could remember he had wanted children, wanted sons and daughters to nurture, to teach, but somehow, now that the moment was imminent, the reality of it escaped him. A tiny child, wrapped in its leather swaddling, lying in his wickiup? *His* tiny child?

Two tiny ones?

Coconino shook his head dazedly. He could picture Hummingbird with an infant cradled in a sling against her body. He could even picture Ironwood Blossom grinding corn with a babe slung across her back. But himself? Holding a child? He stared at his hands.

It was incomprehensible.

Mother Earth, is it always this way? he wondered, and he thought back to his friend Juan. How had Juan acted when he knew he was about to become a father? Nervous. Giddy. Boastful.

Boastful. Now, that was something Coconino could do. He puffed up his chest now and tried it out. Yes, I am expecting *two* children. One late this winter, and one—when? He hadn't asked. In panic, he looked around for the two women.

There they were, excitedly relaying the good news to their father. Hummingbird bounced up and down, while Ironwood Blossom tried to restrain her. It is good their children will be so close in age, he decided. They will help each other and share their joys and their frustrations.

Only where do I fit in the picture? he wondered suddenly, and knew that that was the true source of his uneasiness. It was not that he feared fatherhood or wondered how to deport himself. It was that he had not yet come to feel like a husband.

Ah, my Witch woman, he mourned. Life with you, in a single wickiup—that is no stretch for my imagination. Sitting companionably by the fire on long winter evenings, talking of where to find game and how to season roast javelina—that is an image that wears as comfortably as an old cotton shirt. But this, what I have now: I feel as if I am living with two strangers. Who are these women? What should I say to them? Do they truly believe me when I say that I am just a man, or do they, too, persist in thinking me a god?

Below him in the canyon a flash of motion through the trees caught his eye. It was Red Snake racing his brother to the wickiup. Soon they would be headed back to meet him at the foot of the trail.

Coconino fairly bolted down the path. It suddenly seemed like a wonderful time to go hunting.

But as he drew near the joyous knot that was his new family, Pine Pitch stepped out and approached him. "Great news, Coconino!" the older man beamed, clapping his son-in-law on the shoulder. "The Mother Earth has blessed you, indeed!"

"Indeed," Coconino replied, and couldn't resist adding, "I am her favorite son."

Pine Pitch roared as though that were the funniest thing he had ever heard. "So you are! And this proves it. I am overjoyed for you and for Ironwood Blossom." Then the stocky man leaned confidentially toward Coconino and lowered his voice. "I don't mind telling you, it was a great relief to me when you asked for her as well as Hummingbird. I was beginning to think I would have to take her to the Camp of the Others for her Fulfillment. Or perhaps even to the Southern Village."

Coconino forced a smile at the tasteless remark. "I am so overjoyed, Pine Pitch," he lied, "that I am going out right now to shoot rabbits so that my two children will have warm, soft furs when they are born."

"Oh, yes, very good!" Pine Pitch approved, allowing Coconino to escape toward the trailhead. "Rabbit furs are the very best."

Coconino hurried away before someone else could stop him, seething inside at Pine Pitch's insensitivity. Take Ironwood Blossom to the Camp of the Others, indeed! She was not so ugly or loathsome a girl that some man of the People wouldn't hear her Plea and give her her Fulfillment. It was unthinkable to allow a man of the Others to—well, it was unthinkable. And as for the Southern Village—

Southern Village? At the trailhead now, Coconino hesitated. Of course, he had heard the Southern Village mentioned before. But he had thought it a myth, a fable, some imaginary place where the weather was always perfect and food was always plentiful. Pine Pitch had spoken of it now as though it were a real place, with real persons who could mate with the People.

Red Snake was waiting below, brandishing Coconino's bow. Tree Toad stood more sedately beside him, inspecting his own bowstring. Coconino waved at the boys and started down. If the Southern Village were a real place . . . He hurried his steps and arrived somewhat breathless at the bottom of the butte.

"Thank you, Red Snake," he said, taking his bow and quiver. He checked them over with a careful eye, then nodded his approval at the lad. "Come. Let us go to the south."

The boys fell in beside him as he started along the canyon bottom. "I have just heard a curious thing," he began casually. "Pine Pitch was just speaking of going to the Southern Village." He waited for a response.

Tree Toad snorted. "No one goes to the Southern Village."

"That's what I thought," Coconino murmured.

"It is not a place to go," Red Snake chimed in.

"My father-in-law has some . . . fanciful . . . ideas," Coconino agreed darkly.

"It is not *moh-ohnak* for the People of this Northern Village to visit the People of the Southern Village," Red Snake continued. "Old Pine Pitch says many things that are only talk."

"Besides, I have seen some People from the Southern Village," Tree Toad added airily, "and they are no different than we are, except that they dress in cotton, of course."

Coconino missed a stride and slapped at an imaginary insect to cover his error. "You saw them, you say?" he asked conversationally.

"Oh, yes," Tree Toad bragged. "When I was at the Camp of the Others two years ago. It was my first trip there. They had also come to trade with the Others. They brought the skin of an animal I had never seen before, but of course," the boy added hastily, "it was only an animal."

"An animal from the south, no doubt," Coconino observed. "How far south is their village, do you think?"

"Oh, far beyond the camp of the Others," Tree Toad invented. "Farther to the south than we are to the north, most likely. But no one really knows, since no one has ever been there."

"Do the Others know?" Coconino asked.

Tree Toad shrugged. "They might."

They walked in silence while Coconino phrased his next question.

"Why do you suppose it is not *moh-ohnak* to go there?" he asked in his best philosophical tone.

Red Snake shrugged. "No one ever says." Then he looked up at the tall man walking beside him. "But what is *moh-ohnak* for one is not *moh-ohnak* for another," he observed in his own best philosophical tone. "Perhaps it would be *moh-ohnak* for you to go, Coconino."

Coconino felt a sudden and unexpected surge of his spirit. To travel alone to an unknown place, to set out on an adventure, finding another thing of legend, as he had found Tala, to leave behind his stranger-wives, if only for a little while . . .

But he would have to ask directions in the Camp of the Others, and the specter of his dream loomed large. Derek Lujan. If Phoenix had not come through the Magic Place with him, if Karen Reichert had stayed behind, then there was only one other person who could have made the time journey with him. Derek Lujan had to be the second man Tree Toad had seen "fall from the sky." And being a resourceful man, Lujan had undoubtedly found his way back to the Camp of the Others.

Coconino's skin crawled at the very thought of clever, cruel Lujan strolling through that place with its artificial white buildings whose very presence was an affront to the Mother Earth. Did he now lead the Others? Climbing Hawk claimed that the Others were now friendly, though very strange. But how friendly would they be once Lujan took charge? Coconino had no wish to find out.

"Will you go, Coconino?" Red Snake prompted.

"I will think on it," Coconino promised. It was *moh-ohnak* to make the journey south; he could feel it in the thudding of his heart, which had not rejoiced so since he had arrived in this time. But to approach the Others, to risk coming face to face with Lujan . . .

Are you truly there, my enemy? he wondered. And if so, do you know that I am here?

* * *

Janine Thornton put the spoon in the bowl she held, sat back, and flexed her shoulder blades to ease the ache between them. It was such an awkward position, leaning forward to feed the stranger sitting in the chair opposite her. But what kind of person would she be if she refused to help a soul in need because of her own discomfort?

Setting the bowl aside on a small table, Janine brushed crumbs absently from her cotton blouse and gazed sadly at the stranger. He might be a handsome man if there were any sparkle of life in his features. But there he sat, vacant-eyed, slack-mouthed, his hair grown overlong and his beard thick and curling. She thought now and then of shaving him, but although Janine had a husband and four grown sons and had tended them all through some sort of illness, she'd never touched a razor to one. She couldn't quite bring herself to start now.

From the other room the door creaked, and she heard her husband, Casey, knocking the dust from his boots before he stepped into the house. A moment later he appeared in the bedroom doorway, his graying hair all awry from the hat he had just pulled off. Across his forehead was a telltale band of pale skin, attesting to long days of wearing his hat in the scorching sun. It was a universal mark in Camp Crusoe; everyone's tan stopped at the hat line. Janine had it, too.

"All through?" Casey asked her.

"I think so," she replied, standing up and adjusting the waistband of her cotton trousers. "He ate all the stew. Even picked up a roll again today, but it fell out of his hand like yesterday."

"Still, that's an improvement," Casey observed, looking down at the stranger seated in a chair by the bed. It had been his idea to bring the man home; if anyone could love life back into him, Janine could. "Last month he wouldn't even reach for his food. Month before he wouldn't drink from a glass. He's going to pull out of this, I'm sure of it."

The stranger heard them, but his mind was somewhere else. On a hilltop. Looking down at the cluster of white geodesic domes with a shuttle in their midst. *Only something was wrong. . . .*

Casey leaned closer and examined the face of the man in the chair. "His color looks better. I think I'll try taking him outside again tomorrow. Maybe I can get him to walk a step or two on his own."

Wisps of fog clouded the man's mind. *Log cabins. Why were there log cabins with the domes? And those cultivated fields along the river—they hadn't been there. Not when he went up to the ship.*

There was an edginess in Casey; Janine could hear it in his voice. She felt it in herself, too. Collecting the empty dish from the small table, she slipped one arm around his waist, and they walked from the sick man's room into the common room of their cabin.

A sturdy metal stove sat in the center of one wall, a dry sink under the window. Casey had wanted to make a drain to the outside for Janine, but she'd declined. "Heaven only knows what would be crawling up that drainpipe," she pointed out. "I'll just throw the water out when I'm ready." Janine was content with her house. It didn't have the convenience of one of the old dome houses, but none of those appliances still worked, anyway.

In the bedroom the stranger's mental fog grew thicker. *He was no longer on the hilltop. He was in a shallow valley, and his head hurt. Someone lay beside him on the ground. His enemy. He took one look and set off running, running back toward the camp, only which way was it? He didn't know. But there was someone, one of those primitives, and he ran away to the south. It seemed like a good direction.*

Back in the common room Janine laid the empty bowl in the sink with the other dirty dishes and put a kettle of water on the stove to boil for washing. A sigh escaped her. "All this time I was so sure," she confessed at last. "I was so sure he was from the Mountain and that his truck broke down and he got sunstroke or something."

Casey had held the same idea. But today traders from the Mountain had come and put an end to the notion. He was not one of theirs.

The stranger scrambled up and down hills in his mind, finally recognizing the Valley of the People with its stone cliff houses. But they were empty—deserted. No wickiups stood among the trees below. Where were the People? Where were all the People? And how had such tall trees overgrown the place where the wickiups had been? Dazed, confused, he followed the river downstream toward his own camp.

"Do you suppose he could be from some other part of Earth?" Janine asked her husband. "That there are other settlements that survived somewhere and no one's known about it till now?"

"Anything's possible," Casey replied doubtfully.

The stranger struggled up the hillside from the river, at the end of his strength. He crested the hill and looked down on his base camp. People! Yes, there were people there. And log cabins. And cultivated fields. And, my God, the shade trees—

"There's only one other option," Janine said quietly. It was what they had both been thinking ever since the traders had arrived, but neither of them could say the word aloud. There was too much attached to it, both of hope and of fear. Neither could say: offworld.

The stranger stood panting on the hilltop. There were shade trees planted beside the log cabins, on the west sides mostly. Large shade trees. Trees that had to be thirty, forty, or even a hundred years old. A hundred years!

Oh, God! the stranger screamed in his mind. Oh, God, oh, God, it didn't just send us to the wrong place, then. It warped time. The terminal malfunctioned, and it's thrown me into the future—decades and decades into the future! I'm lost! My way home is lost, Dillon is lost, everything I know is lost, lost, lost—

"Those clothes he wore when we found him," Janine reflected. "The fabric was odd, but they looked almost . . . military. Don't you think?"

Casey lowered himself heavily onto a wooden bench near the stove, reaching automatically for the wooden spoon he was carving. It was a large wooden spoon meant for the soup kettle he had just bartered from the traders from the Mountain. "Not necessarily," he replied finally. "From what I know of . . . previous cultures, lots of professions wore white uniforms. The health professions, for instance. It wouldn't have to be a . . . a *military* uniform."

The fog and the panic cleared slowly from the stranger's mind, and he knew he was in a room in a log cabin and the couple who lived here had taken care of him for many months. He thought about getting up from the chair and going outside, but the act would not manifest itself.

It was Coconino, he thought bitterly. It was that crazy aborigine and his unicorn, that unicorn with the sparks coming out of its horn. I saw them; I'm not crazy. It destroyed the bridge; it took out the comm system before I could send a distress signal, ravaged the propulsion controls. And then in the warp terminal, when I tried to escape—

Electrical charges can foul up warp transmission, can warp time as well as space. And that's what's happened. That creature, that monstrosity, and his master have sent me far, far into the future. I'm trapped here—yes, trapped. Trapped here forever and ever and ever and ever . . .

The fog slipped back over his mind, but it was not as thick now, hadn't been as thick for several weeks. It's your fault, Coconino, he thought. You brought the beast onboard and commanded it; you chanted your mystical chants and called up all the demons of hell to attack my ship. You destroyed it! And you destroyed me. All the plans I had made, all the power I had achieved, all the wealth I had stored, gone—gone to some unknown idiot a hundred or more years ago, and I am trapped here with nothing. . . .

Fire burned bright in the steely blue eyes of the stranger. I will make you pay, Coconino, he vowed. For all you've taken from me, I will require double from you. For all the anguish I've suffered, you will suffer ten times more. I will hunt you down and demand of you more pain than you knew it was possible to feel.

Watch for me, Coconino. I am coming.

CHAPTER THREE

Phoenix stalked along the narrow trail, wrapped in deerhide and puffing steam in the crisp February air. Heads turned as she passed house after house, and she heard the murmur that followed her: "There goes the Witch Woman. There goes She Who Saves."

They never called her Phoenix anymore, never called her "the sister-brother of Coconino." That had been a ruse, of course, the ruse she and Coconino used to fool themselves, to pretend they loved each other only as *compadres*. She ached to think of the time wasted, of the nights spent sleeping alone when she had only to beckon and he would have come. . . .

Phoenix shook herself and drew a sharp breath of the cold air. That was past. This was now, and she had something to do. For Coconino.

Two Moons' house was halfway around the mountain from hers, on a lower tier that was more convenient to the river path. Once men of the Before Times had installed steps up and down the steep slope to the north, but the Mother Earth had removed them with her floodwaters. The People did not try to restore them. Instead, they made their own trails from one cluster of houses to another and down the hill to the water.

Smoke curled through the ventilation hole above the door of Two Moons' chamber. The door itself was covered with a large tan and white hide, that of a Great Antelope of the eastern prairie. Phoenix stopped just outside and called the old woman's name softly.

In truth, the woman who bade her enter was less than ten years Phoenix's senior, perhaps thirty-seven or thirty-eight. But the People aged quickly, and as Phoenix stooped and crawled into the warm adobe chamber, she thought the round face of Coconino's mother was more deeply lined than the day before, her gray hairs multiplied overnight. Two Moons had taken the Mother's place as leader of the People, had supported Phoenix and Nina's proposal that they should move north. There was still grumbling over that.

Now Phoenix needed her support again. The Council advised Two Moons, and she listened closely to them, but it was she who made the decisions. Phoenix must convince Two Moons of the worth of her plan or have it die aborning.

"Good morning, Witch Woman," Two Moons greeted her, her round face placid and dignified. "Do you want something to eat?"

Phoenix refused politely. There was seldom an abundance of food in the widow's pot. Since Coconino's disappearance, Two Moons had only her youngest son to provide meat for her, and he was a boy barely thirteen. Flint.

Glancing around the tiny chamber, Phoenix noted the boy's absence and surmised he must be out hunting already, driven less by hunger, she knew, than by the responsibility of filling his half brother's role. And Phoenix's heart was warmed just knowing that he lived to try. Thank you, Mother Earth, she prayed silently. Thank you that the fifth body was not Flint. She was sorry for the family of Broken Arrow, but she would never be sorry that it was not Flint who had died. How could she face Coconino and tell him that his young half brother had died in bloody battle? Bad enough to have to tell him about Juan and Falling Star.

When he came back.

"How is the hunting?" Two Moons inquired next. It was impolite to move too quickly to the point. Phoenix chafed at the delay but knew she must mind her manners. The Way of the People was her way now and would be until Coconino returned and beyond.

"The hunting is . . . not bad," she replied. "We saw tracks of many deer yesterday, to the east. Feathers Are Loose and Strong Hand were going back this morning to see if they could find them. I think soon there will be meat in every pot in the village."

Two Moons smiled at that and nodded approval. "My pot is never empty," she said, "but there are others less fortunate who sometimes go for two or three days with only a handful of roots. The winter is very long in this place."

Phoenix nodded and knew that the days would be much warmer where she was going, with no snow or freezing nights to worry about. She looked forward to that part of the journey.

"You do not go with the hunters," Two Moons observed.

"No, Two Moons, I do not. I have other business."

"Ah." The older woman poured herself some tea and wrapped her cotton blanket closer around her. It was a blanket the Mother had woven; Phoenix recognized it. "And what is this business of yours, Witch Woman?"

Phoenix drew a deep breath. Now that she had permission to begin, she was not sure how. "Nina told me something," she said finally. "Something that—concerns the People. It seems that there is another child of Coconino to be born."

Two Moons looked up sharply, and Phoenix hesitated. It was not the Way of the People for men to be indiscriminate with their seed. To tell this woman her son had planted arbitrarily was to accuse him of mocking the Mother Earth.

"You know that we visited the Camp of the Others," Phoenix went on. "While we were there, they offered Coconino the Right of the Chosen Companion." It was only a small lie. "Nina says that his Chosen Companion now bears his child."

For a long moment Two Moons was silent, sipping at her tea and staring into the distance. Finally she put her cup down. "That is good fortune for the woman," she said.

"It should be good fortune for the People," Phoenix replied.

Now Two Moons lifted her eyes to study Phoenix. She was shrewd, this new leader, schooled at the Mother's knee. The Mother had angered Phoenix at first, terrified her at the end. If Two Moons did not sanction Phoenix's mission, there would be no point in carrying it out. But you must, Phoenix willed her. Don't you see? It's your grandchild; it's Coconino's child—

"The child belongs to the mother," Two Moons decreed. There was no room for argument in her tone.

Phoenix's heart raced. This couldn't be the end of it. It couldn't be over just like that. There must be something further to say, something to— "But would you welcome the mother into our village?" Phoenix asked, carefully keeping the desperation from her voice and her face.

Still Two Moons' eyes rested on her—not with clairvoyance, as Nina's did, that saw into her very soul, but with careful judgment, weighing factors, testing possibilities, calculating good and evil results.

Eventually Two Moons picked up her cup again. "She who has been my son's Chosen Companion," she said, "is always welcome in this village."

Phoenix felt an explosion of relief. It was not a blessing, but it was not a curse, either. It would allow her to proceed with her plan. "Thank you, Two Moons," she said sincerely.

Just briefly it occurred to Phoenix that Two Moons might have more than one Chosen Companion in mind.

"I will leave today for the Camp of the Others," Phoenix said, rising awkwardly. The roof was scarcely five feet tall. "I will be gone perhaps two weeks."

"We will see that Nina is cared for," Two Moons promised. It was generally accepted in the village that Phoenix had taken on that responsibility. "Walk carefully, She Who Saves."

She Who Saves. Phoenix pushed aside the door covering and escaped into the cold outdoors. There she stretched her thin body to its full height, her joints popping and cracking. Did they have any idea how she hated that name? She Who Saves. Phoenix snorted in disgust. She Who Was Crazy Enough to go roaring into the Camp of the Others after that massacre, after she found those five bodies on the river's edge.

She hadn't even balked as armed guards came at her. "Put those damned things down," she snapped. "If I cared about my own life, do you think I'd be here?" She had come from the village, from the wails of mourning, from Talia gone into premature labor when she learned her husband was among the slain. That put another life of the People in jeopardy, and Phoenix had had enough. "We have to talk, and we have to talk now. Who's in charge here?"

Tony Hanson had stepped forward, a squat pig-eyed man with a belligerent arrogance. "Acting Captain Tony Hanson," he said. "You are to surrender the men who—"

"I'll surrender nothing!" she snarled. "You will do no more violence against the People, do you understand me?"

Hanson bridled. "You're not in a position to give orders," he warned her.

But Phoenix was too far gone to make rational demands, only emotional ones. She felt no threat from the weapons trained on her, felt no fear at the fact that she was in the enemy camp, surrounded by people who had suffered loss of life themselves. She felt only rage, unequivocal rage at the absurdity of the violence, the uselessness of the killing. "No position!" she hooted, pushed almost to morbid laughter. "And what do you think *your* position is? Do you know where you are? Do you have any idea what kind of situation you and your merry band are in at this moment?"

And he had hesitated—they had all hesitated—because in truth everything was chaos. No one knew what messages had been sent, or what had happened to Lujan and Coconino, or whether anyone had survived on the ship above them. So she told them. "Your ship is gone, Mr. Hanson. Your home planet thinks you have all died of a plague that infests the Earth, and there is going to be no rescue mission."

"You're a liar!" Hanson flared. "I don't know what you and your friend did up there—"

"Not half of what Derek Lujan did," she retorted. And she could see it in their faces then: they knew. They knew that ultimately it was Lujan who had betrayed them.

But Hanson wasn't satisfied, could never be satisfied to give an inch with half his crew gathering to watch him. He stiffened, straightened his blockish form, and glared menacingly. "Your people broke into our supply huts, stole our weapons. They killed Sebi Chaku."

Phoenix knew about that. Flint had told her when she had arrived, breathless and sobbing, back at the village, fresh from the scene of the massacre. "We did as Coconino told us," he said, his voice choked with tears he dared not shed. "We forced one of the Others to open the wickiup where they kept the fireshooters, and we started to carry them away. But a man saw us. He was going to give the alarm. Falling Star shot him through the heart."

The pain on the boy's face was vivid. He had never seen one human being die at the hands of another; it was unknown among the People. That his own brother-in-law had had to do such a thing— "The People only wanted to get your weapons away from you," she grated at Tony Hanson. "They were terrified that when you found out you were stranded, you'd take it out on the closest scapegoat. They knew they couldn't stand against your weapons. They were right."

He bristled. "We acted in self-defense!"

"You acted in stupidity!" she hissed. "Did you ask those men at the river what they were doing? Did you even know if they were the same ones who took the weapons? Did you see one of them was a fourteen-year-old boy?"

"He shot his bow like a man!" Hanson fired back. "Three of my crew died at that river, too!"

They were edging closer; she could feel them now, beginning to hem her in. Phoenix forced herself to take a long, deep breath and tried to see a way around the impasse. "So you have dead. We have dead. That's not the question, Mr. Hanson. The question is, What do we do now?"

For that he had no answer.

"Will you kill us all?" she pressed. "Will that get you off Earth? Will that restore your ship? Will that bring back your dead?"

There was an uneasy shifting in the crowd around them. Hanson shifted his weight from one foot to the other, indecision written on his sweaty face. It was as though he had to have something, some victory over her. "Give us back the weapons you stole," he said finally.

She stepped back, suddenly tired—very, very tired. Weapons in the hands of a man like this? It was the very reason Juan and Falling Star had given their lives, to make sure such firepower was not in the hands of men like Tony Hanson. "You're welcome to them," she told him. "They're at the bottom of a lake, about fifteen miles northeast of here."

"A *lake*?" he howled.

Phoenix almost sneered with satisfaction. "The People consider them a desecration," she explained, and she thought, Not in vain, Juan, my *compadre*. Perhaps your sacrifice was not in vain.

"How are we supposed to defend ourselves?" he demanded.

"You've got half a dozen left," she said, indicating the guards, who even then held her in their gun sights. "That's enough to keep off snakes. I guarantee you have nothing to fear from the People."

"Oh, you guarantee," he mocked. "You've destroyed our ship, you've taken our weapons—"

"If I were you, Mr. Hanson," she cut in, "I'd be less concerned about weapons and more concerned about how I was going to plant corn and squash in this valley. About where I was going to dig a pit trap for deer and javelina. About which of these native plants was poisonous and which was good to eat. If I were you, Mr. Hanson, I'd be a lot more concerned about how I was going to fend off starvation than about how I was going to fend off the clubs and arrows of a handful of people who only want to be left alone."

Then Rita Zleboton had come out of the crowd, shouldered through, and laid a hand on Tony's arm. She was an ominous presence, dark of skin and eye, powerfully built. She was bigger than Tony, older by years, wiser by worlds. "So you're suggesting a truce?" she asked.

"I'm suggesting a peace," Phoenix replied. "No more killing. Neither of us can afford it."

"That's it?"

"I don't bother you, you don't bother me."

Hanson snorted. "Nice in theory."

"Better in practice," Rita said. "Take the offer, Tony. We've got better things to do."

"I'm in command here!" Tony snapped. He shook off her arm, straightened himself, and turned back to Phoenix. "For our part, we're prepared to cease hostilities," he told her. "But I warn you, we're going about armed, and if one of your people so much as sneezes in the wrong direction—"

"I'll do you one better, Mr. Hanson," she interrupted. "I'll take the People away from here. We'll finish the harvest, and we'll head north. Just so there won't be any accidents."

Now Rita looked alarmed. "Tony, no! We're going to need them. They know how to survive here; we don't!"

But he brushed her off. "Don't need savages like them," he muttered, and to Phoenix, "You just take your people and go, hear me? Stay out of our way."

Phoenix's eyes flashed, and she bit back a harsh reply. Let it go, she told herself. Let the little man blow smoke in front of his own. They'll be sorry soon enough.

So Phoenix had turned, turned her back on them all, the people she had once thought were Earth's hope and salvation. But Rita called after her.

"Phoenix! The captain . . . the doctor . . . ?"

A genuine anguish touched Phoenix, and she turned back. When they'd first come to the camp, she and Coconino, she had promised Rita she'd tell her where she had last seen the Winthrops. "There's a mountain. Southwest of here."

Rita nodded. "The captain's mountain, yes. There was a beacon there."

I helped make it, Phoenix remembered. Would that I never had! "Look for them on the mountain. But I don't think you'll find them. I hope I'm wrong, but I'm afraid Derek Lujan got to them first."

Now, retracing her footsteps to her own house, Phoenix wondered if the Others had found their missing leaders or just what they had found on the Mountain. What had Lujan done there to keep the Men-on-the-Mountain from coming to look for the crew of the *Homeward Bound*, whom they knew had landed?

The Others were still in their original camp; Nina had told her as much. But how had they fared these past six months? Did they still blame Coconino for their plight? Had they managed to retrieve any of their weapons from the bottom of the Well? Had their anger abated or increased?

The trip south would take her three days. She would know soon enough.

Jacqueline Winthrop pocketed her scope and stood eyeing the young woman on her examination table. Pale—not enough iron— and thin, but healthy enough. Short brown hair that had once been trimly cut was now shaggy, as the rest of them were shaggy in this place. I know a good barber on the Mountain, Jacqueline thought, but they won't let us come there. Not after what Lujan did to them.

The thought of Lujan brought her again to the woman on the examination table. Karen was twenty-five, with a small and delicate bone structure, almost too small to deliver the child she now carried. Of all the things Lujan had done to the poor woman, this was potentially the most damaging.

"I'm out of iron supplements," Jacqueline told her. Their infirmary had been set up to last two months, not six. "You need to eat more poultry."

Karen nodded dully. There was no sparkle in her eyes, no glow to her complexion, but there never had been. She had been lovely in a haunted, fragile way, but so quiet—almost listless. What had a dynamic person like Derek Lujan seen in her? Submission, most likely. Someone to dominate, someone to use. Karen had been their chief communications officer on the *Homeward Bound*; as they found out later, he had used her to alter their transmissions back to Argo. He had used her to weave his web of lies about the Earth expedition. Some of the crew had turned spiteful toward Karen, but most, like Jacqueline, realized that she was as much a victim as the rest of them—perhaps more so.

"Do you sleep?" Jacqueline asked, and remembered another woman with dark-rimmed eyes whom she had met on the Mountain. It was a man who haunted that one, too. Why? Jacqueline wondered. How can they love someone who hurts them so much? It had never been like that with Clayton. Clayton had been calculating at times, but waggishly so. He'd been obdurate, yes, and demanding, but no more of others than of himself. And heaven knew there were nights aplenty that she'd missed sleep on account of him, but never out of pain. No, never that.

Not until he died.

Jacqueline sighed deeply and tried to bring her mind back to her patient. There was something here she was missing, something about the young woman that was affecting her health. What had she just asked? Oh, yes, about sleep. And Karen had shrugged. What approach to take next? What question was going to touch the nerve, spring the trigger that popped the secret out into plain view? "What kind of work does Tony have you doing?"

Again the shrug. "Not much," Karen replied without interest. "He thinks I'll break."

Yes, that was like Tony, Jacqueline thought. When the Mountain dwellers had refused to take in the castaways, refused to integrate them into their mechanized if antiquated society, Second Officer

Tony Hanson had huffed and puffed and set himself up as the leader of this community.

Leader! Ha. Clayton Winthrop had been a leader. Even Derek Lujan, manipulative bastard that he was, had been a charismatic leader. Tony Hanson was a petty bureaucrat.

Perhaps she should have taken over when she got there. They had wanted her to, Rita and other members of the crew. "You outrank him," they assured her, though it was a civilian operation. "We need your wisdom guiding us, Jacqueline. We need your leadership."

But she had been too depleted, too numb from Clay's death to want anything to do with it. She ached for her husband, ached for the two children she would never see again, ached for the quiet country estate that had been their home between voyages. No, she could see to the castaways' health, advise them on nutrition, even act as liaison with the suspicious Mountain dwellers. But she could not lead them.

"I feed the ducks," Karen volunteered, and Jacqueline covered a start. Where is your mind, woman? she chided herself. Pay attention! "And I tried my hand at sewing on that machine they gave us. But I kept breaking the needles."

That machine they gave us. The Mountain dwellers had refused them sanctuary but had not abandoned them to their own ignorance. Seed grains and some animals, bolts of cloth and a sewing machine, other necessities to help them harvest the land and see them through the mild desert winter. She had even convinced them to share some of their medical supplies, although the Mountain dwellers would be hard-pressed to replace them now. At one time those resourceful survivors had flown to deserted cities, to abandoned pharmaceutical plants, and found or produced an amazing array of drugs. That had ended when Derek Lujan destroyed every machine they had that was capable of flight.

Blast it, Clay, why did you have to get on that aircraft? Why did you leave the Mountain one way and let Derek Lujan go another?

"Exercise," Jacqueline admonished her patient. "Never mind Tony Hanson. You need to walk, twenty minutes or more, get your heart pounding. Labor's no picnic, and you need to be in shape."

Again the nodding head.

"Your first baby?" Jacqueline asked suddenly.

Karen flinched.

That was it. That was the question. But Karen's medical file mentioned nothing about a previous pregnancy. "What became of the first one?" Jacqueline continued.

Karen's lower lip trembled a little. "I had an abortion," she whispered.

That should have been in the file. Someone had kept it out. "How old were you?"

"Thirteen."

Incest. The word screamed through Jacqueline's mind, though she had suspected as much, the way the man had come storming into the Terran Research Coalition's headquarters demanding the return of his daughter. Rage boiled inside Jacqueline, but there was no point dwelling on that. At least the man could not reach Karen here. "Why did you decide to keep this baby?" she asked.

Karen's arm slid protectingly around her stomach. "It hurt," she said softly. "The first time. I was terrified. I bled. I didn't want to go through that again."

Jacqueline bit her lip; that was not good news. With the perfection of the Genetti Technique some four centuries earlier, even a shady clinic that specialized in keeping certain procedures out of a patient's medical records could have performed a simple abortion with almost no discomfort or bleeding. Either someone had botched the procedure—possible—or Karen was susceptible to complications. For Karen's sake, Jacqueline hoped it was the former.

"Well, I doubt childbirth will be easy for you," Jacqueline told her honestly, "because of your size. But I promise you one thing: You won't go through it alone. I'm here for you; there are other people here for you. Just because Derek Lujan abandoned you, don't think you're in this alone." With that Jacqueline stepped back and gestured toward the door.

But Karen continued to sit on the table. "It's not Derek's baby," she said softly.

This time Jacqueline jumped visibly. "Excuse me?"

"I said it's not Derek's baby," Karen repeated a bit louder, a bit firmer. "Derek always used protection, always. He was afraid of disease." The corner of her mouth twitched. "Isn't that ironic?" Lujan had reported to the TRC that the crew was overcome by an unknown plague; he and his friends planned to return as the only survivors. But Coconino had disabled the spacecraft so that Lujan himself was stranded with his crew, with no hope of rescue.

Jacqueline took one breath, then another. "Whose baby *is* it?" she asked finally.

"Coconino's," Karen replied. "He's the only other one. It's Coconino's baby."

* * *

Phoenix knelt to drink from the fast-running creek. A plump lizard sat on a stone at the water's edge, sunning its brown and green body. For a moment it seemed to be staring at her, its snub-nosed brown head fixed on a neck ringed twice in black. Phoenix stared back; then, impatient, she waved her arm and shooed it away. Kneeling on the stone where it had been, she cupped her hand and brought water to her mouth.

The creek was getting shallower quickly as she approached its source in the high volcanic lands west of the village. It was time to fill her gourd canteen and strike out toward the marshy lakes that skirted the Black Lands, then west to find the next river. It would take her to the one she wanted, the one that flowed past the camp of the Others, just south of the former Valley of the People.

As she rose, however, Phoenix felt eyes watching her, a hunter's instincts in a woman who twelve months before had never touched a bow. Cautiously she searched the landscape on all sides, trying not to move. Was it a puma looking for prey in a winter that had offered too little of that? Or just a curious coyote wondering what this two-legged creature was doing in his domain? But Phoenix could see nothing.

Finally she moved on, more carefully this time. "The Mother Earth has put many creatures within her bosom," she could hear Coconino telling her. "You cannot walk through the world as though you were its only inhabitant, or the Mother Earth will surely show you how weak and insignificant you really are."

I'm learning, Coconino, she thought. Truly I am. If I learn to be a good daughter of the Mother Earth, then will She send you back to me?

I tried to make a bargain with Her once. I promised I would do what was required to keep more Others from coming if only She would give me one night with you afterward. One night! But you can't bargain with the Mother Earth. She holds all the cards.

The day was growing warmer; by nightfall Phoenix would have lost enough elevation that her single blanket would provide warmth enough for sleeping. For all the sleeping she was going to do, at any rate.

How should she approach the offworlders' camp? Walk boldly in and announce that she was taking Karen back with her? No, that would never do. Brazen nerve had gotten her in to negotiate the peace, but it wouldn't work for this. She would approach stealthily, survey the situation, and probably sneak in at night. Talk to Karen, see if she would be reasonable. "It's Coconino's baby," she would say. "It belongs to Coconino's people. *You* belong to them. You'll be well cared for, better cared for than you've ever been in your life. You'll be like a goddess to them, you see, because Coconino was like a god. Ask Nina. Nina can tell you. Honor and respect, as the mother of Coconino's child. You'll live like a queen.''

And if that didn't work, she'd tie her and gag her and drag her out of there. But she was going to get that baby.

Your child! Oh, my love, if only it had been me. . . . But it wasn't. It was Karen. Does she even want your baby? Not the way I do, that is certain.

Suddenly a trumpeting filled the air, a harsh sound in a harsh land. Phoenix jerked her head toward its source and saw the proud animal standing on the ridge above her.

Tala! There was no mistaking the huge stature, the single horn of his silhouette. His deep barrel chest seemed even larger because of the rippling ridges of his wingsock. A hoofed foreleg pawed the ground impatiently, and he tossed his head with regal arrogance. He trumpeted again, imperiously, as if making a demand, and looked down at her with his odd, slightly telescoped eyes. "Where is he?" Tala seemed to ask. "Where is Coconino?"

"I don't know," Phoenix answered helplessly. "I don't know where he is. He's gone. Some other place, some other time. I wish I could tell you—oh, God, how I wish I could tell you!"

Tala stamped his feet and shook his head, as though the answer were unacceptable.

"You could help me," Phoenix called out to him. "You could help me get Karen, bring her back to the People. If you would let me ride on your back the way he used to. We could pretend, you and I. We could pretend that he is only gone hunting—just over there, in the Red Rock Country. And that we were going to meet him. Would you let me do that? Just ride you that far, to the Red Rock Country?"

But Tala trumpeted angrily and turned away.

You never would, Phoenix thought sadly, bitterly. *You only tolerated me for his sake, never for my own. If he was riding, you'd let me come, too, but never by myself. And you always dumped me, every chance you got. Well, go on, then. Go on back to the Old Black Lands or wherever it is you spend your time. If he shows up, I'm sure the Mother Earth will tell you.*

When he shows up. When.

Phoenix turned and set her face once more to the south.

CHAPTER FOUR

"Before you go in there," Dee Fitzsimmons warned, "you should be aware that the defense has changed strategy."

Chelsea Winthrop sat back in her chair and studied the middle-aged prosecutor, wondering again whose side the woman was really on. The state's, of course; it was her job to protect the interests of the Government of Argo. Normally that meant prosecuting suspected criminals with the utmost fervor, but the interests of Argo were complex and varied.

The truth was that Oswald Dillon's vast corporate holdings were temporarily being administered by the state until the execution of his will, and the will could not be executed because one of the witnesses to it was Camilla Vanderhoff, whose sanity was currently in question. If the defense convinced a jury, as they had first planned, that it was a temporary insanity, occurring at the point of the murder only, then the will was valid. If, however, they did not convince the jury, the question of insanity would linger. And while it lingered, the state would happily run Dillon's empire to its own advantage, taking—as Argoan law permitted—a lucrative fee for its services.

Chelsea had determined at her first meeting with Ms. Fitzsimmons that she and Cincinnati were mere pawns in this investigation and trial and that the noble prosecutor would not hesitate to throw either one of them to the proverbial wolves if it served her purpose.

Chelsea was not worried for herself; she knew her testimony would help the state. She had seen the suspect standing over the body with blood on her hands. Cincinnati's testimony, however, was another matter. He had spoken with the suspect only moments before the murder. Questions of sanity and premeditation swung on his story. What would they do when it was time to depose him?

Chelsea reached over to her brother now and gave his hand a

reassuring squeeze. "It doesn't matter to me," she said pointedly, "what the defense's strategy is." That wasn't quite the truth, but it would serve the purpose. "I'm going to tell exactly what I saw and heard no matter what they are trying to prove. Right, Cin?"

"Right," he said sullenly. Cincinnati had inherited all of their father's chivalrous notions of justice without the intelligence to temper them with reality. He was not happy with the notion that his testimony might be used against the "nice lady" he had met in the Museum. That was part of the reason Chelsea had insisted that she be deposed first and that Cin be present—to see not only what was in store for him but also that the facts did not change no matter what issues were raised or how questions were worded. It would mean she'd have to curb her temper, but that was good for her, anyway. No point in decking the defense attorney.

But the prosecutor shared none of the noble sentiments Chelsea had expressed for her brother's benefit. "Well, it's going to make a difference," she replied tartly. "They've got a new lawyer in on the case, and he's decided not to go for temporary insanity."

At that Chelsea's eyes blazed. "Does he think he can prove that woman *innocent*?" she demanded. "We found her standing over the body, covered with blood. Her handprints were on the weapon. The height of the wound, the angle, the—"

"Calm down," Dee instructed, one gray eyebrow arched in a gesture vaguely reminiscent of Chelsea's mother. "This new boy's not foolish enough to plead not guilty. No, it seems he will contend that Ms. Vanderhoff's insanity was not temporary and that she is now unable to assist in her own defense."

It took Chelsea a moment to assimilate that. If Camilla were unable to assist in her own defense . . . "Then all this is unnecessary," Chelsea realized. "The depositions, the trial—we don't have to do this."

"He has only announced his intent to file a motion," Dee told her. "Until he does, and until it is ruled on, we must proceed." She glanced at her wrist chrono. "It's time, Ms. Winthrop. Shall we?"

For a moment Chelsea balked, strongly tempted to refuse to give the deposition today. If she could delay things until it was unnecessary for either of them to be deposed . . . But it was a rash idea, and she discarded it. She had to set the example for Cin, to be the epitome of cooperation with authority while staying true to one's principles. With Clayton and Jacqueline gone, it fell to her alone to be the role model.

So Chelsea smiled rather convincingly and rose to her feet. "I'm ready. Are you ready, Cin?"

Cincinnati, though mentally retarded, was not unobservant. "You don't want to do this, do you?" he asked Chelsea as they started down the hall.

Chelsea sighed. With Cin, honesty was always the best policy. He was terribly adept at seeing through lies. "No, I don't, Cin," she replied. "But it's the right thing to do, so I'm going to do it."

"Will Ms. Vanderhoff be there?" Cin asked hopefully.

Chelsea's blood chilled at the prospect. She had no desire to see Camilla Vanderhoff again, even without bloodstained hands.

"No, you won't see Ms. Vanderhoff till the trial," the prosecutor told him. "Today there will only be the monitor, who runs the recording equipment, the defense attorney, and myself."

"Who is the defense attorney?" Chelsea asked as Dee stopped in front of a sliding door.

"Some wunderkind the family brought in from offworld," Dee grumbled as she palmed the door open. "Come in, I'll introduce you," she said, leading them into the conference room. "Chelsea Winthrop, Cincinnati Winthrop, may I present—"

"We've met," a familiar baritone interrupted. "How are you, Chelsea? Cincinnati?"

And Chelsea found herself looking up into the handsome face and smiling hazel eyes of Zachery Zleboton.

"Thank you, Ms. Winthrop," the prosecutor concluded. "We'll gather again tomorrow to depose your brother." She rose to lead the way out, Cincinnati following obediently.

But Chelsea sat seething in her chair, glaring across the table at Zachery. He was strikingly dressed in rich gold tones that set off his ebony skin, though they could not match the effect of the white mourning robes he had worn at the memorial service. But he was in his professional role now: Zachery Zleboton, advocate—not Zachery Zleboton, the proud and grieving son. It irked her that she had been so taken in by his sincerity at their first meeting, that she had confided in him, that she had thought to call on him for support— "Is this why you wouldn't answer my messages?" she demanded.

He smiled, an infuriatingly bemused sort of smile, the kind he had been giving her all morning. "You're a witness for the prosecution," he told her. "I'm an attorney for the defense. It would be . . . inappropriate."

She continued to glare at him, trying to see through this public mask, trying to find the real Zachery underneath, but apparently this was the real Zachery. Had the other, then, been a false persona? Would she ever know? Abruptly she rose, sending her chair skittering back toward the wall, and made for the door.

"Unless, of course," Zachery called after her, "you were my client."

Startled, Chelsea spun back to face him.

"Counselor!" Dee Fitzsimmons hissed. "That's conflict of interest. You can't—"

"Prior association," Zachery quoted at her. "The Argoan bar's code of ethics ruling 26895. If Ms. Winthrop chooses to retain me, say for a fee of one redback universal . . ."

Without hesitation Chelsea opened her handbag and slapped a red universal note on the table.

"Ms. Winthrop!" Dee protested.

"I accept," Zachery said, smoothly scooping up the bill. "If you'll excuse us, Ms. Fitzsimmons, I wish to confer with my clients in private."

"Your client, singular," Dee snapped, her hand instinctively closing on Cincinnati's arm. "Code of ethics be hanged, you're not talking to the boy until after he's been deposed!"

Zachery shrugged. "Do you mind, Cincinnati? She really is right, and if we want the court to trust what you say, you and I shouldn't have any private conversations right now."

"Well . . . I have to go back to work, anyway," Cincinnati said reluctantly. "Chelsea . . . ?"

Chelsea looked at her brother, saw the confusion in him. From long habit she forced every trace of concern from her face, brought her temper under control, made herself calm again. "It's all right, Cin," she told him, hugging him so he could feel that the anger was gone and that there was no cause for alarm. "I'll come over to your apartment tonight and tell you everything that happened."

"Okay." Relieved, he kissed her forehead and went out the door with Dee.

Silently Chelsea turned back to Zachery and waited.

"You're angry," Zachery guessed.

"I'm beyond angry," Chelsea snapped. "A person I hoped could be a friend to me in a difficult time turns up across the table defending a murderer!"

"An alleged murderer," he corrected, leaning back in his chair and smiling that infuriating smile at her. "And anyway, it's your own fault," he told her with a twinkle in his eye. "You told me about the murder, and I was so intrigued, I had to have this case."

Chelsea drew back. "You deliberately *sought* this case?" she screeched.

"Deliberately, doggedly, and with great passion," he assured her. "I convinced Camilla's family that a temporary insanity plea was playing right into the government's hands: If they lost, Camilla would be summarily executed in a highly publicized display of swift and immediate justice, and if they won, the state would move for a mistrial and start the whole proceeding all over again."

"Mistrial?" Chelsea was caught off guard. "On what grounds?"

"Inadequate counsel. Withholding evidence. Any number of things. Chelsea—" He leaned forward, and suddenly he was no longer bemused but terribly, terribly earnest. This was not Zachery the advocate; this was the man she had known before, the wounded young man who begged her companionship with unspoken words, who made simple, passionate accolades to their lost kin, who spoke bitterly of the legal maneuverings of the Terran Research Coalition to avoid responsibility for the deaths of the crew. This was the Zachery she had wanted in her corner. "Camilla is not rational," he said quietly, sincerely. "The state should have ordered a psychiatric examination, but they chose not to. They're stalling, Chelsea, dragging this out—"

"Because of the will." She sat, finally, in the chair directly across the table from him. "And they'd have put Cin and me through this whole circus when they knew it was unnecessary, just to use up time, just to hang on to Dillon's estate awhile longer."

"I'll contend that she snapped at the time of the murder," Zachery explained. "That will not reflect on her sanity at the time she witnessed Dillon's will. The probate court will have to act, though God knows it will take them five or six years anyway, simply because Dillon's holdings were so complex. But this trial would have added several more years, not to mention the revenues it would generate for the government-owned broadcasting company." He sat back again, and the smile returned. "They're not happy with me."

Serves them right, Chelsea thought. But she wouldn't give Zachery the satisfaction of her approbation—not just yet. "Why did Camilla's first lawyer contend temporary insanity?" Chelsea wanted to know.

"Grandstanding, probably," he responded. "Going for big fees; Camilla had legal insurance. At any rate, he was acting in his own interest—not Camilla's." He propped his chin on one hand. "Ask me a different question."

Chelsea blinked, not understanding. "Like what?"

"Like why I wanted this case."

Why should I care? Chelsea wondered, and yet she did, she cared terribly. The image she had formed of Zachery was one of a person who hated injustice, who used the letter of the law to achieve the spirit of the law. The image she had of Camilla was that of a brutal killer—and now, it seemed, a maniacal one. "Why *did* you want this case?" she demanded. "Did you know her before? Did you have something against Dillon? Why would you want to defend a woman you *know* is guilty, especially—" Especially when I'm the one fingering her, she wanted to say. But she couldn't admit that. "Especially of such a heinous crime?"

His eyes never wavered from hers. "Because," he said softly, "you felt there was a connection between this murder and my mother's death."

For a moment Chelsea just stared at him; then she shook her head. "Zach, I told you it was probably a non sequitur."

"But what if it wasn't?" he asked. "You were right about something being amiss on the *Homeward Bound*. The TRC refused to release the unedited log recordings to me, and they wouldn't do that unless they had something to hide. What if you were right about this, too?"

"They wouldn't give you copies of the logs?" Chelsea asked in surprise.

"I even tried to subpoena them and found out that on this planet you can't do that without tangible evidence of wrongdoing." He snorted. "The proverbial judicial dodge and dance—I can't prove a connection to the Dillon murder unless I can prove a connection to the Dillon murder. Anyway, I decided the only way I'd find out if there was one was to talk to Camilla Vanderhoff, find out how much she knew. And the only way I could do that—"

"Was to serve as her attorney," Chelsea finished. She gave a mirthless chuckle. "You're a devious SOB, Zachery Zleboton."

His answering smile was wry. "But I protect my client's interests," he pointed out. "Better than that made-over civil attorney she had before."

That was not hard for Chelsea to believe. There was little violent crime on Argo; virtually everyone on the planet was employed by some corporation or other and lived above the poverty that historically bred violent crime. There was white-collar crime aplenty, and it was severely punished, but those proceedings were more closely allied to civil law than to criminal. No wonder Zachery, coming from Darius IV, where murder and mayhem still brought a decent living, had been tagged by Dee Fitzsimmons as a wunderkind. In its own pathetic way, it made sense. "So what did you find out," Chelsea asked, "when you talked to Ms. Vanderhoff?"

The smile faded into one of deep poignancy. "I found out," he said sadly, "that she's crazy." He reached his hands across the table toward her, and Chelsea found herself sliding her own hands into them, drawn by the same magnetism she had experienced in their first meeting. "Chelsea, come and talk to her," he urged. "Maybe seeing you will trigger something in her."

Immediately Chelsea's eyes grew cold. "I don't think that's appropriate for me at this point."

"Not now, no," he agreed. "But after my motion's been ruled on. Please, Chelsea."

And there was in his tone a quiet despair that made her wonder. Was it for his mother, this despair? Was it that he couldn't lay the ghosts to rest believing there might have been foul play aboard the *Homeward Bound*? But no, there had been no trace of that in him before. At the memorial service his grief had been like that of a victor, someone who, while he felt the loss keenly, had no regrets for the life that had been or the way he and his mother had parted.

Whence, then, this despair? For whom? Chelsea studied him a long moment so that he turned away and let go of her hands. He had not meant for her to see it, or if he had, he was not going to let her witness it for long. He rose to his feet and prepared to leave.

An incredible thought filtered through to Chelsea. Camilla. His despair must be for her, for the beautiful woman lost now in her own mind. Who is she, Zachery, that she could have done this to you?

"We can talk about it later," he said with careful indifference in his voice. "A ruling is weeks away, anyhow. I'll see you tomorrow, won't I, when we depose Cincinnati?" He started around the table for the door.

"Zachery."

At her quiet call he stopped and looked at her from a sideways stance, a guarded look that asked her not to pursue what she had seen.

She came and stood in front of him, pausing a moment to enjoy the feel of his towering height. He was six foot five at least, and she was scarcely over five feet tall. "I'll go," she said quietly. "When it's appropriate. But I have my price."

Zachery drew a deep breath.

"Dinner by Chef Zleboton," she finished with a twinkle in her eye. "You bragged enough about your cooking last time we met; now put up or shut up."

"Wyatt: messages," Chelsea called when she had dialed into her home system from the mobile unit in Zachery's flivver.

"You have three messages," the musical voice chimed. "Message one is from Cincinnati, marked 'not urgent'; message two is from Mr. Clifton of Armgold Memorial Pylons; message three is from Indigo Lawrence."

Chelsea gave a low growl. "Wyatt: hold Cincinnati's message," she instructed. "Tell Mr. Clifton I have a suggestion for what he can do with his memorial pylons. And tell Ms. Indigo Lawrence to go to hell."

She glanced over at Zachery, who was calmly piloting the flivver along New Sydney's major aerofare toward a very old-money suburb called Outback. Does he get these calls, too? she wondered. Do these vultures prey on everyone who suffers a death in the family? Or have they singled me out for special harassment?

Feeling her eyes on him, Zachery glanced up, smiled absently, and lifted the vehicle to a higher-altitude route over Flatsville. He didn't even hear, Chelsea realized. He isn't really with me now. He's already with her. He's already with Camilla.

Zachery's motion for dismissal had been approved with as little delay as was possible in the Argoan legal system. It seemed he had not exaggerated Camilla's madness, and since the state was more interested in the nonexecution of Dillon's will than in the execution of a lunatic, it did not protest the psychiatrist's evaluation with any vigor. They were now, Zachery had informed Chelsea, seeking evidence that her mental illness had begun before she had witnessed the will. "They won't find it," Zachery had snorted contemptuously. "She snapped at the moment of the murder, and that's a plain fact. But they'll take as much time as they can to come to that conclusion."

Cincinnati had been much relieved that Camilla was not to be prosecuted. "She was a nice lady," he maintained. "That Mr. Dillon must have done something real bad for her to get so mad that she killed him." Something like arranging the deaths of thirty-seven people aboard the *Homeward Bound*, Chelsea thought, but she couldn't tell Cin that. It would be unfair to burden him with her suspicions.

But Zachery was another matter. "Why can't we get the log reports from the *Homeward Bound*?" she had demanded several weeks ago. "You're a lawyer; can't you do something?"

"Not without evidence of wrongdoing on someone's part," he'd replied. "The TRC, its staff, the crew—someone. Technically, those logs are corporate records, and on this planet the corporation is sacrosanct. If they don't want to give them up and I can't show just cause, I'm out of luck. You should know that; you're an information investigator."

"That's not my realm," she had hedged. "I can only access public records: public personnel files, government reports, private purchase records." But there were ways, she knew—back-alley ways that as a professional she knew about but shunned. At least until now. No doubt Zachery knew about them, too. "I suppose that's why the TRC decided to set up headquarters here on Argo, where everything favors the corporation and the individual is incidental."

He had favored her with one of those bemused smiles she found so infuriating. "You live here, too," he had pointed out.

Yes, I live here, too, Chelsea thought as they dropped down to an airway that skimmed along over the tops of turkabee trees. Here in this land of murky skies and plascrete buildings, where even the cultivated vegetation is a dull ash green. Is there anywhere on this planet you can ride a horse, just get in the saddle and ride for miles and miles with the wind in your hair and the sun in your eyes?

Suddenly, below them, the trees disappeared and they were sweeping over a broad expanse of green lawn. Hallelujah! Chelsea thought. There's someone else on this planet who appreciates open space and more than a token amount of grass.

Then she realized they had reached Mountain Springs Mental Hospital.

"Pretty plush," she commented to Zachery as they made their way from the parking lot to the chateau-style administrative building.

"It caters to the high-level executive," he replied. "For some reason you don't have too many criminally insane on this planet, and they didn't quite know what to do with Camilla. But her benefits package through the Museum included, as most Argoan contracts do, very generous coverage for mental illness. So they sent her here."

"The Cuckoo Clause," Chelsea responded. "Paid vacation in a burnout bin." She suppressed a shudder. "I've got it, too."

In the early days of colonization Argo had been only marginally habitable. The air was breathable, but there was virtually no animal life because the vegetation was so nutrition-poor it would not sustain much. Sprawling ranches of incredible acreage were required to provide food for the early settlers who came to mine Argo's sketchy mineral deposits.

Yet as old Earth's corporations bought up colonial rights to everything that did not have to be terraformed, several Australian firms had formed a joint venture and moved their corporate headquarters to Argo. It was a risky venture, for they were the first to remove their administrative offices from the comfortable security of Earth and out into the burgeoning galactic frontier.

It had been a stroke of genius. Planted smack in the middle of five other colonized worlds, Argo was an obvious central processing point for the raw materials its neighbors produced. In no time numerous industries sprang up that produced consumer goods for the managers and accountants and other intelligentsia peopling corporate headquarters. A government was formed that, though deeply rooted in the Anglo-Saxon judicial code, catered to the specific needs of corporations. Even before the Evacuation forced the last remnants of Earth's population out to the stars, Argo had become a corporate world.

Over the centuries, however, corporations had learned the value of taking care of their own. High-quality education was the inalienable right of every Argoan; high-quality medical care was a foregone conclusion. Benefits packages included luxury vacations, family counseling, clothing and transportation allowances, and health and recreation club memberships. But the stresses and strains of intense commercial competition and personal career building always took their toll, so programmer and designer and manager alike had generous coverage for any form of psychiatric wellness or rehabilitation program.

Still, as they crossed the verdant grounds toward a magnificent and imposing entrance, Chelsea felt the unease of one entering a foreign realm. She hoped sincerely that she would never have to use her Cuckoo Clause.

"G'day" the receptionist greeted Zachery as they entered the lobby. "Here to see the little lady, are you?"

"Yes, I've brought a friend," Zachery replied. He flipped the man his ID, and Chelsea did likewise.

"Wish I had friends like yours," the man commented in a strong twang that after seven centuries was still called "down under." He glanced at Chelsea's ID. "Resident of Juno. A country girl, eh?"

"And a service brat," she replied. "I take it you're one of those rare specimens, a native-born Argoan."

He grinned broadly as he ran computer checks on their IDs. "Stamped all over my vocal chords, is it?"

It's not just your speech, Chelsea thought. To run a computer check on a man you obviously know on sight—now, that's a genuine Argoism.

"Is Camilla in her room?" Zachery asked with a trace of impatience.

"Solarium, it looks like," the receptionist replied, consulting yet another computer panel, which showed the location of all patients. Then, "Good job getting her off, mate," he confided as he handed the IDs back. "She's a nice lady."

Nice lady, nice lady, Chelsea grumbled silently as they passed through an energy gate onto the grounds of the hospital. Hasn't anyone noticed that this nice lady ran a spear through her employer? But Cincinnati, the receptionist, and Zachery all seemed able to ignore that little defect.

So let's see this woman, Chelsea thought as they crossed a courtyard with carefully manicured lawns, bright flower beds, and deep green hedges of Terran shrubs. Let's see what all the fuss is about.

The solarium was a high-ceilinged room of spacious proportions with tall multipaned windows and rich velvet drapes. It was done up in shades of blue, a cool and relaxing place even on this warm spring day. At first Chelsea thought the room was empty, it was so quiet and still; then a movement near one of the windows caught her eye, and she turned to see a pale slender figure clinging to the drapes.

Camilla. Dressed in robes of warm sky-blue, with her honey-blond hair swept up in soft curls on the crown of her head, she was the epitome of grace and elegance. One hand flitted nervously around her mouth, which was soft and full and painted a gentle rose. As one who had to work at beauty, Chelsea had always envied it in other women. But from the moment she saw Camilla again, Chelsea could not envy her nearly so much as she pitied her.

"Good morning, Camilla," Zachery greeted her softly, as though she were too fragile to bear the full impact of his resonant voice. "Do you remember me?"

The nervous hand flitted from Camilla's mouth to her delicate ear and back again, then came to rest on the blue velvet drape. Was she searching her memory behind those vacant blue eyes? "Zachery," she said finally, and her voice sounded oddly lost in the quietness of the room. "Zachery Zleboton. Your—your mother was on the *Homeward Bound.*"

"Yes, and I'm your lawyer," he reminded her.

But Camilla seemed not to notice that he had spoken again. "I'm sorry," Camilla apologized, as though the entire tragedy of the *Homeward Bound* had been her fault.

Zachery ushered Chelsea several steps closer. "Camilla, this is a friend of mine. I think you met her once. Her name is Chelsea Winthrop."

"Winthrop?" A little tremor ran through the ghostly Camilla, and her hand began to flit more rapidly. "There was a Captain Winthrop. And a doctor, ship's doctor, Jacqueline Winthrop. They had a son." She looked desperately at Chelsea. "Do you have a brother?"

Chelsea swallowed hard. She began to understand why Zachery had been so moved by this gentle lost soul. "Yes, Ms. Vanderhoff," she managed, "I have a brother, Cincinnati. You met him once."

"Oh, yes, Cincinnati." A smile broke unexpectedly across Camilla's face, and she stepped away from the drape toward them. "What a handsome boy! Like his father. Dark, wavy hair. I liked Cincinnati."

"He liked you, too," Chelsea said.

Then Camilla's features clouded again. "But he made me feel so sad," she said. "So sad. Poor boy. Poor boy."

At that Chelsea stiffened, too well acquainted with people's misplaced pity for Cincinnati. He lives a full life, she thought defensively. He laughs and he loves, and he hurts and he heals, just like the rest of us. We don't pity children, do we? Why pity Cincinnati?

But Zachery was more in tune with Camilla's thoughts. "Why did he make you feel sad, Camilla?" he asked.

"Because he didn't know that his parents were dead," she replied. "He didn't know, and I did. It made me feel sad to know."

Chelsea and Zachery exchanged a startled glance. "You knew?" Chelsea asked. No news of the disaster had been made public until after all family members were notified, nearly a full day after Cincinnati had spoken with Camilla in the Museum. "How did you know they were dead?"

"I tapped into the TRC reports as they came in," Camilla told them. "I had . . . passwords. Codes. Dillon needed information, all kinds of information. I got it for him."

Of course, Chelsea realized. You were his information specialist, and you had none of my scruples for how you came by it. So you have seen the original logs. You have seen what I would give my eyeteeth to lay eyes on. "Tell me," Chelsea said earnestly, drawing near the pale woman, "when you read the reports, did it seem—did it seem that there was something wrong? Something the TRC wasn't telling the public?''

Camilla gave her an odd, vacant stare. "Wrong?" Her mouth twisted into a wry smile. "Wrong for who? Wrong for Dillon? Or wrong for the crew?" Then her mind slipped sideways, and she began to chant, "Wrong, wrong, wrong for who? Wrong for Dillon? Wrong for the crew?"

Now Zachery stepped in and took hold of Camilla by her arms. It was a firm grip but gentle. "Camilla," he said sternly. "There were problems on the *Homeward Bound*. We know that. There was a navigational error and a probe that malfunctioned. Were those accidents, Camilla? Were they just accidents?"

But like an antique phonograph, Camilla's mind now jumped back into a well-worn groove. "He promised me no one would die," she said plaintively.

"Dillon promised," Chelsea prompted.

"I asked him, and he promised me. He said he paid his agent a great deal of money, and the man would surely come back to spend it."

Chelsea jumped, and Zachery nearly lost his grip on Camilla's arms. "His *agent*?" Zachery pressed. "What agent? Camilla, what was the man's name? Do you know?"

"He asked if I wanted to be Queen of Earth," Camilla whimpered. "Queen of Earth. I didn't want to be queen of anything. I just didn't want people to die. They were good people—did you know Captain Winthrop?" she asked suddenly, gazing up into Zachery's eyes.

"No, I never had the pleasure," Zachery managed.

Camilla's eyes drifted over to Chelsea. "You're his daughter, aren't you?" she asked.

"Yes."

"He was a good man, wasn't he?" Camilla said. "I mean, a truly, truly *good* man."

Chelsea's throat tightened. "One of the best."

"Camilla, what about the agent?" Zachery asked again.

"Dillon . . . wasn't a good man," Camilla said sadly. "I think I knew that all along. I should have known that. But he was so . . ." She waved a hand vaguely, unable to come up with the right word. Then, for just a moment, her eyes lost their vacant stare and there was a glitter of recognition in them. "I killed him, didn't I?" she asked.

Chelsea could see the pain that lanced through Zachery, pain that was more than just one soul grieving for another. "I wasn't there," he whispered.

"Camilla," Chelsea intruded softly. "The agent. Do you mean that Dillon had an agent onboard the *Homeward Bound*? Is that what you meant?"

But Camilla had slipped over the edge again. "He promised me no one would die," she said simply, and twining herself in the velvet drapes, she stared out the window with her soulless eyes and would say no more.

"We *have* to get those unedited log reports," Chelsea repeated. "Zachery, we *have* to. Camilla clearly stated—"

" 'Clearly' and 'Camilla' don't belong in the same sentence," Zachery interrupted. "And besides, she's been certified mentally incompetent. No judge is going to subpoena TRC's corporate records on the basis of a madwoman's testimony."

A madwoman, Chelsea thought. Oh, yes, she is mad as a hatter and lovely as a doe and so much more than a client to you. That was your despair when you asked me to come see her. Not despair for this unsolved mystery but for her, for the way you feel about her. Isn't that so?

They were back at Chelsea's apartment, pooling their information into a file Zachery had created under his professional ID and coded as client-confidential; they were not ready for their suspicions to leak out. So far the file contained a patched-up transcript of their conversation with Camilla, a copy of the edited *Homeward Bound* reports that had been released to the public, a synopsis of Chelsea's suspicions, and six personnel files.

Chelsea flung herself into a chair and brought up the personnel files again. "Zach, it has to be one of these six people. They were the ones who supposedly survived the plague, except that no one ever made it back. Zach, what if it was some kind of setup and those six actually *did* come back? Only at a time and place unrecorded, to be met by another ship, and—"

"Whoa! Slow down!" Zachery cautioned her. "What ifs can lead us in a thousand false directions." He had slipped his shoes off, as well as his outer robe, and draped himself along the length of her sofa in his tunic and fashionable pantaloons. It pleased Chelsea that he felt so comfortable with her.

"Let's start at the beginning if we're going to speculate," Zachery suggested. "First, we've jumped to the conclusion that Dillon wanted to sabotage the *Homeward Bound*, but why would he want to do that? Dillon was the largest collector and purveyor of Terran art and artifacts in the known universe. Why would he want a mission to Earth to fail?''

Chelsea blinked. ''Would the artifacts coming back be his?'' she asked.

Zachery took an audible breath. ''No,'' he admitted. ''But he could buy them.''

''And what if Earth were declared safe and open to commerce? What then?''

Zachery ran his tongue slowly across his upper lip. ''The value of Dillon's collection would go down,'' he answered. ''All right. That's a possible motive. How would he get an agent into the crew? A lot of people applied for berths on the *Homeward Bound*, and a lot of them were turned down. If you were Oswald Dillon, how would you ensure that your man got hired?''

''Bribery,'' Chelsea said simply.

''A large donation, perhaps,'' Zachery suggested.

''Or a private contribution to someone on the personnel committee.''

''This is Argo,'' Zachery replied. ''Private finances are open to scrutiny; corporate finances are not. Most likely Dillon made a hefty donation from his corporation to the TRC, with an understanding that so-and-so was to have a berth.''

''But we can't get at the TRC's financial records to verify that.''

''Exactly.''

Chelsea rose impatiently and crossed to the simulated window in her study/living room, where twilight was deepening into the glimmering lights of a city at sleep. Had it been a real window, she'd have seen only a hazy yellow glow over a forest of smudged-looking plascrete buildings. There was so much light pollution that it never really got dark here; the stars were faint glimmers in a steel-gray sky. ''Backward planet,'' Chelsea muttered, staring at the simulation with increasing antipathy. On her home planet of Juno simulated windows were unheard of, even in the largest cities. On that agrarian planet, the night was still velvet black and the stars glinted like jewels in the sky.

''Actually, Argo is considered a very modern planet,'' Zachery pointed out perversely. ''Unlike the early days of its colonization, when it had a distinct 'Wild West' flavor. I learned a great deal studying for the Argoan bar. You should see some of the laws that are still on the books from that time period.''

''Let's say Dillon bribed someone,'' Chelsea pursued, ignoring his attempt to bait her. ''Any understanding about a berth for his agent had to be reached with an individual, right? Someone with influence in the selection of personnel. My dad had a file on the TRC corporate structure, board of directors, et cetera, because they tried to get him to invest before the *Homeward Bound* embarked. I still have all his personal files. I'll bet I can dig up a list of suspects."

"And then what? Ask them if they took a bribe?"

Chelsea turned from the window. "I hope you don't do your own investigating, Counselor!" she laughed. "Never start with the suspect. Start with the janitor. Or a clerk, one of the little people. They see and hear a lot, and even if they don't understand what it is, they tend to be more talkative than executives. As long as you're not condescending," she added.

Zachery sat up. "Good. You start there," he said, "and I'll see what rumors are floating in professional circles. Then, before I leave town, we can compare notes."

"Leave town?" Suddenly Chelsea felt as though someone were squeezing her lungs, robbing her of breath. "You mean . . . back to Darius IV." It had to happen, of course, and soon. Zachery's firm would be wanting him back, generating revenue on other cases.

His eyes softened a little as he studied her. "It is my home," he said softly. "Although I find Argo . . . interesting. Quite literally 'a world different.' "

She forced a laugh. "You should see Juno sometime."

He smiled. "As long as I don't have to pass the bar there, too," he joked. Then he was serious again. "We'll have time to work on this; I won't be leaving right away. There are still some things I want to tend to in Camilla's case. Her treatment at Mountain Springs—I have to monitor it very closely for the family. For all its corporate focus, there are some pretty decent civil rights laws on this planet. I want to make sure they aren't overstepped in Camilla's case."

Ah, Zachery, she thought. And would you be so concerned if she were less beautiful and less fragile? Someone like me, for instance, with a long jaw and a quick temper . . .

"Do you think," Chelsea asked, "she may ever . . . get well?"

Slowly Zachery rose to his feet, slipped back into his shoes, and donned his robe. Chelsea watched, saw the ache in him, and regretted that she had brought up the subject. It wasn't his fault, after all, that he felt this way. *"You can't help what you feel,"* her mother had often told her. *"You can only help what you do about it."*

''If she does,'' Zachery answered finally, ''she'll have to stand trial for murder. And I don't think even I could get her off.''

With a sudden pang Chelsea understood the two-edged nature of his dilemma. Though he wanted nothing more than to see the lovely, ghostly Camilla recover her sanity and be a fully functioning human being, he knew that the moment she did, her life was forfeit. Poor Zachery! she thought. You've met a woman who has touched your soul, yet she herself has no soul to share with you.

Zachery crossed to take Chelsea's face in both his hands and, stooping low, kissed her forehead. Then, as though her understanding were a balm, he held her tightly to him.

Two wounded people, she thought, clinging to him with a candor she could never let anyone else see. Two wounded people who haven't resolved the loss of their parents, who can't accept the idea that God or fate or a freak of nature has taken these people out of our lives and there's no one to blame. It just can't be that simple; there has to be more to it. . . .

Please come home, Mom, she thought. Please come home, Dad. I miss you too much.

CHAPTER FIVE

The pain clutched at Hummingbird's stomach so that she gasped. "What is it?" Ironwood Blossom asked sharply.

Hummingbird forced a weak smile. "It's nothing," she lied. "The baby kicked me, that's all."

Ironwood Blossom watched her sister carefully as the girl took one or two cautious breaths, then returned to her work. They were in their mother's house on the cliff, making pica bread for the midwinter festival. They had carefully selected only the dried corn that was colored dark purple, and this Ironwood Blossom was grinding into a fine meal. Hummingbird mixed the meal into a thin lavender batter, which she baked on a flat rock in the cook fire and, being more clever with her hands than her older sister, folded it neatly into the unique pyramid shape of pica bread.

"Perhaps you should not sit so close to the fire," Ironwood Blossom worried. "I will cook for a while."

"No, I'm fine, really," Hummingbird insisted, deftly folding the next little cake. She set it aside to cool and reached for the bowl of batter.

Suddenly she cried and pitched sideways, spilling the batter onto the adobe floor.

Ironwood Blossom scrambled to her sister's side. "What is it?" she asked anxiously. "What is it, little one?"

Hummingbird clutched her stomach, panting. "Get Mother!" she whimpered piteously. "Get Mother, get Mother!" Tears spilled unchecked down her flushed cheeks.

Ironwood Blossom dashed to the door and pushed aside the hide covering that kept out the frosty December air. "Owl Woman!" she shouted down the pathway. "Owl Woman!" Then, remembering the cold air she was letting in, she stepped onto the path herself and let the hide fall back into place. She stood shivering in

67

her buckskin dress and leggings until several houses down a woman poked her head out the door of a stone house. "Owl Woman, call my mother! She is with Deer Foot. Something's wrong with Hummingbird!" Then she ducked quickly back into the warm house.

Outside, she could hear the message being passed quickly from house to house around the mountain. Soon Night Comes Quickly would be on her way home, along with Ten Toes the healer and probably one or two midwives. Then all would be well. They would tell Hummingbird what to do, and all would be well. Clinging to that belief, Ironwood Blossom knelt once more by her sister.

"You are having the pains again," she accused.

"Yes," Hummingbird squeaked. "But this one is worse, much, much worse." She trembled with stifled sobbing.

"When did they start?" Ironwood Blossom demanded.

"This morning."

"Why didn't you say something, you little fool?" Ironwood Blossom flared. "You should have been lying down resting, not hunched up over the fire!"

"I was afraid," Hummingbird gasped, "Mother wouldn't let me go to the midwinter festival."

"Ah, little one!" Ironwood Blossom lamented, cradling her sister's head in her lap. "There are more important things than midwinter festivals." Tears leaked down her cheeks as she watched the suffering on her sister's face. "You have the finest husband in all the village, you are loved by everyone who knows you, and soon you will be a mother. What is one midwinter festival compared to all that?"

"I'm sorry!" Hummingbird sobbed, burying her head against her sister's ample belly. "I'm sorry, I'm sorry, I'm sorry . . . ."

"Hsh, hsh," Ironwood Blossom crooned. She felt Hummingbird's hand tighten on her own as yet another contraction caught the girl. "It's all right; it's not your fault. This is a very ornery baby you are having; he seems to have his own mind about things already. No doubt he will be an old sourpuss like Wounded Hare, since he doesn't want his mother to have any fun at the festival."

Hummingbird tried to laugh through clenched teeth; then suddenly she shrieked.

"What?" Ironwood Blossom cried in alarm.

"I'm bleeding, I'm bleeding!" Hummingbird screamed in panic. "I can feel it, I'm bleeding, I'm bleeding to death!"

"No!" Ironwood Blossom cried sharply, as though she could forbid such a thing with her command. Heart pounding, she touched the fluid that darkened Hummingbird's clothing, but it was not sticky, nor did it stain her fingertips. "It is not blood," she told her sister. "I think it is just your water. Your water broke, that's all."

"But it's too soon!" Hummingbird wailed. "Only seven moons have passed."

"Hush, lie still," Ironwood Blossom soothed. "It doesn't mean your baby will be born right away. Thistledown's water broke early, and her baby was fine." She did not say that Thistledown's baby had come only two days after the water broke. "Just lie still. Lie still until Mother gets here."

The fire crackled and shot sparks into the room. Ironwood Blossom continued to cradle her terrified sister, waiting anxiously for their mother to arrive. At that moment she had no thought for the husband who hunted in the hills to the northeast.

Coconino stood still as a stone behind the pine tree, his breathing imperceptible. Any sound, any movement might give him away. Some forty feet ahead of him Red Snake crouched behind another tree, slowly waving a stick to which a bright red cloth was attached. Beyond the boy, in the shadowy half-light of the forest, a dark shape stirred.

Come, my brother, Coconino willed. Come, I know you are curious. So was Tala; he was a great friend of mine and very like you. Wise, cautious—but curious. So come see. See what it is that flutters on the stick.

Slowly, carefully, the Great Antelope advanced. It was a huge buck, man-high at its withers, with a splendid set of branched antlers. He sniffed the breeze nervously, but the hunters were downwind and he could detect nothing. One hoof stepped forward, piercing the thin layer of snow that coated the forest floor, then another hoof, and another. The creature stretched out its neck toward the fluttering cloth.

Behind him Coconino felt rather than saw Tree Toad lift his bow into position. With the slightest gesture of a finger Coconino bade him stop. Like so many young hunters, Tree Toad lacked patience. Red Snake was worse; that was why Coconino had set the boy to waving the stick. But they were quick to learn. He would ask them to help provide for his wives when he made his journey to the south.

The south. Each time he thought of it, his heart sang with joy. Now that he had decided to go, he was impatient to start. He was even impatient to find the Others, to get that part of the journey over with. If Lujan was indeed there, what was to say he would be vindictive? Nothing could change what had happened to them both. And perhaps facing his enemy would banish the dream that still haunted Coconino with its dry bones and watching eyes and bobbing lizard.

The snow was light under the thick canopy of the pine trees; they had crossed open areas where it lay knee-deep on the land. Coconino knew he should wait till spring to set out, when the Mother Earth would open the bounty of her bosom to a traveler, but that seemed so far away. With a small supply of dried meat and corn cakes he could set out after the midwinter festival and . . .

A branch rustled. Ah! There she was. A slow smile spread across Coconino's face as the doe stepped out of the foliage only twenty yards behind the buck. He had heard her dainty footsteps and known she was back there somewhere, hiding. Now she, too, came out to see what strange thing fluttered in her forest.

Now Coconino raised his bow with great deliberation and took aim. Behind him Tree Toad did the same. With a movement of his eyes Coconino indicated that the boy should take the closer buck; he himself would shoot for the doe.

Thwck! thwck! The doe dropped to her knees, Coconino's arrow deep in her heart. But the buck snorted and thrashed, pierced through the neck by Tree Toad's shaft. He lunged away through the undergrowth and up the sloping ground of the wooded mountain, fleeing in panic from his attackers.

Both man and boy broke cover and raced after the wounded animal. Coconino knew he could have loosed an arrow and brought the big beast down, but it was Tree Toad's kill. He ran only to keep his eye on the buck so the teenager could finish it off. It was what he would have done for Phoenix.

"Aiiee!" Tree Toad crowed as his second arrow struck the flank of the retreating buck, causing it to stumble. He ran two more steps, drawing another arrow from his quiver as he went and nocking it to the string. Pause, shoot—

The buck went down with a heavy thud. *"Aiiee!"* Tree Toad crowed again, and Coconino joined him. In a moment Red Snake pounded up, adding his victory whoop as though the kill had been his.

It was one thing the Witch Woman had never learned, Coconino thought with regret, this voicing of victory at the kill. Or did she? he wondered. What had she learned in all those years after he left her, before the Mother Earth finally called the stubborn woman to Her bosom? Twenty-five years, or so she had written on the hide scroll she left behind, a paper the People had kept for generations until his coming. Did she truly become Of the People? Mother Earth, did she ever learn to hear your voice?

At his feet, Tree Toad began the ritual, cutting the fallen animal's throat and pouring out its blood as a libation to the Mother Earth. Red Snake looked wistfully back at the doe; Coconino gave him a small nod and smiled as the eleven-year-old bounded gleefully to the smaller carcass and began the ritual there.

Soon I will have my own sons to take hunting, Coconino thought warmly and for the hundredth time. Or perhaps a daughter. I taught Phoenix to be a hunter; why should I not teach my daughter to be one? There is nothing in the Way of the People that forbids it. If a woman desires to be a hunter, then she may do so even if she is not a Witch Woman. No doubt my daughter will want to be like her father. She will grow up tall and strong, like Phoenix, and I will teach her all that I taught the Witch Woman.

Coconino glanced at the sun through the canopy of pine needles. It would be nearly dark before they hauled these fine animals back to the village. He sized up a nearby sapling and, taking a small hatchet from his belt, began to hew it down to make a travois. Perhaps, he thought, I will even name her for my Witch Woman.

Coconino lagged behind the boys as they approached the village from a side canyon. It was cold, and he was anxious to be back in his warm wickiup, drinking the hot tea he knew Hummingbird would have waiting. But he wanted the boys to go ahead with the travois to show off the fine buck Tree Toad had killed. It was the finest kill the fifteen-year-old had ever made, and on the strength of it he could begin to woo one of the village maidens.

Once Coconino would have swaggered into the village just behind them, basking in the admiration of those same maidens, flaunting his skill and his indifference. But that was another village, another time. Now he thought he would not go up to the village at all but would go straight to his wickiup on the canyon floor. He had had enough of adulation.

Even as he turned his steps in that direction, he saw a figure coming to meet him. Hummingbird! he thought. But no, it was the heavier, more deliberate form of Ironwood Blossom. That was curious, he thought. She did not usually watch for his return the way Hummingbird did.

Perhaps they are scheming again, he thought. Perhaps Hummingbird has decided Ironwood Blossom should be more bold toward me and has sent her older sister to do something that is not in her nature. That is like my Hummingbird.

Ironwood Blossom stopped about two paces away from him. Around them the twilight deepened, giving a silvery cast to the snow-covered landscape. "My husband," she said soberly.

"My wife," he replied. Trepidation filled him; she was always serious and reserved, but tonight there was a heaviness to her tone that made him uneasy. Not far away an owl hooted, impatient for night to come so it could begin its hunting. The rustling of pine needles told of a breeze higher up; it did not touch them here, and their breath puffed in frosty clouds around them. Coconino shivered.

"I have bad news," Ironwood Blossom told him quietly.

His heart lurched. Mother Earth, I don't need more bad news, he thought. Have I not had enough for one lifetime? He took a pace forward, trying to see his wife's face in the dim light, but the hood of her wrapping fur was drawn too far around it. "What is it?" he demanded hoarsely. "Has something happened to Hummingbird?"

She trembled then, just the slightest movement, but he saw it. "Hummingbird lives, by the grace of the Mother Earth," Ironwood Blossom said carefully, and there was deep pain in her voice that not even she could control. "But she lost the child."

For a moment Coconino stood dumbstruck. Lost . . . lost the child? His child? His daughter, whom he had wanted to become a hunter? Lost? His head became an echoing chamber where he grappled with the import of it.

Another life whisked away—this one before he had ever known it, ever touched it or held it in his arms— Another one! Another soul gone to the bosom of the Mother Earth— Cold seeped through his leather jacket, but Coconino did not feel it. He felt only the pain of the news, slicing through his shock now like an icy dagger to his heart.

My child!

My daughter!

My Witch Woman!

"*Aiieeeeeee!*" A cry of anguish tore loose from his lungs and echoed off the canyon walls, a thousand screams thundering through the night. All the pain he thought he had expunged in his Song of Grief resurfaced in that cry. Like a towering oak cut through with an ax, Coconino fell to his knees in the snow.

Instantly Ironwood Blossom was there, gripping his shoulders with both hands, tugging at him. "My husband, please," she pleaded, her reserve vanished with the intensity of her pain. But her pain was for Hummingbird, not for him. "She thinks you will be angry with her," Ironwood Blossom told him. "She thinks it is her fault."

In some distant corner of his mind Coconino thought that this might be the first time Ironwood Blossom had reached out to him voluntarily, without his initiating the contact. Why should he think of that now?

"Please go to her," Ironwood Blossom urged, weeping. "Please go and tell her it's all right. She is beside herself. Coconino, please."

He looked up into her face, the face of one who would ask nothing for herself but everything for her sister. And she was right; whatever pain he knew, however bitter this new death for him, he must not forget the devastation Hummingbird felt. Yes, she would blame herself, would Hummingbird, and she would be ashamed. . . . "Where is she?" he asked hoarsely.

"In our mother's house," Ironwood Blossom told him. "She was there when it happened, and we didn't dare move her back to the wickiup."

Coconino nodded, the shock having subsided into a knot in his chest. Slowly he dragged himself to his feet, leaning heavily on his stocky wife. "Take me there," he whispered, unwilling to make the journey through the village alone.

They found Hummingbird lying near the fire, wrapped in furs. She looked up as they entered and burst into tears. "I'm sorry, Coconino," she whimpered. "I'm sorry I didn't do it right."

But he had recovered himself now, banishing the ache to a lower level of consciousness, where it would not interfere with what he had to do. Brushing past Night Comes Quickly, he knelt beside the distraught girl and silenced her with a gentle finger on her lips. "Hush, little one," he soothed her. "What had you to do with it? Nothing. The Mother Earth gives and takes life, not you."

"But I should have—"

"Should have been Hummingbird, and that you were," he interrupted. "When have I asked you to be anything else? It was not your fault. Some children live, some children die; we do not understand why or why not. My own mother lost her first child."

"She did?" Hummingbird asked in surprise. Her tears subsided as she studied his face hopefully.

"So they tell me." He managed a smile. "I was not there."

It comforted Hummingbird that someone so illustrious had also known this calamity. She almost smiled back at him. Then suddenly her face clouded again. "But oh, Coconino, I wanted so much to give you a child!" she wailed, weeping anew.

At that his own tears started to flow, and he did not try to stop them, even in the presence of his mother-in-law. "And you will," he promised. "You will give me many children, and they will grow to be fine, strong men and women who will make the People proud."

"Listen to your husband," Night Comes Quickly urged. "You are young; you have a long life ahead. There will be other children for you, healthy ones."

"But not for a long time," Hummingbird sobbed, disconsolate. "Ten Toes said I must wait and heal before I—before we make another baby. By then it will be spring, and in the spring you are going away, Coconino. You are going away to the south. . . ."

"No."

The word sounded hollow and dead on his tongue. His heart trembled to speak it, but he said it again. "No, Hummingbird. I will not go away. I will stay here with you and Ironwood Blossom."

He looked across the dimly lit room to where his other wife sat, a look of genuine surprise on her face. Do you think I am such a monster, he wondered, that I would abandon her at a time like this? I never know what you think, my silent wife, behind that guarded face of yours. But I am not so unfeeling that I could leave now. Not now.

And not even in the spring.

His heart was heavy, but he forced the words out. "I will stay here, Hummingbird," he promised, "and you will have another child. And it will play with Ironwood Blossom's child. Then, when there are two together, two children of Coconino, one for each wife—then, perhaps, I will think once more of a journey to the south."

Inside him, Coconino felt a stretching of his soul as though it would break.

The rest of the village was silent when Coconino stepped out of his in-laws' adobe house and onto the ledge that fronted it. It was a narrow ledge; only a step or two in front of him the slope fell away sharply to the canyon floor. Manzanita, barberry, and other scrubby vegetation kept the slope from washing away both below and above the habitation, though it was much scarcer near the rounded top of the island.

Inside, Hummingbird was sleeping at last, a peaceful look on her childlike face. She had latched on to his promise like a child to a sweet and then drifted off to sleep clutching his hand. Only when he was sure she would not waken did he rise from his cramped position to seek the comfort of solitude in the night.

But even as he breathed in the cold and cleansing air, the door hide lifted and Ironwood Blossom stood beside him, a bundle in her arms. He looked down at it. "The child?" he asked.

"It was an early birth," she replied, "and so there will be no ceremony for it." That had been true in his day as well; a child miscarried or born very prematurely was returned to the Mother Earth without ritual. "I will take it to the far canyon wall," Ironwood Blossom told him, "and cover it with loose stones and gravel." She moved to go around him on the path.

"I will take it," he said, reaching for the bundle.

For a moment she hesitated. Is this some other oddity of mine? he wondered. Do the fathers of this time not lay their children in the bosom of the Mother Earth? But then Ironwood Blossom turned the bundle over to him—reluctantly, he thought. "It is my child," he explained. She only nodded and continued to look at the little bundle in his large hands.

"You can come with me," he offered. At that she raised grateful eyes to his and, unable to speak, simply nodded once more. Ah, so that is the way of it, Coconino thought. Fool, Coconino, to think that she suffers only for her sister. There is a closeness between them that you do not understand. The child was in some way hers, as well. He tucked his burden gently into the crook of one arm, took a deep breath, and set off down the path.

The moon was nearly full, making the snow-flecked landscape seem to glow in the night. They had no trouble picking their way down the trail toward the canyon floor. Soon they could hear the soft gurgling of the stream and see the dark, domed shape of their wickiup through the junipers and walnut trees that thrived at the water's edge. Coconino drew another deep, cold breath. "Tomorrow," he said, "we will tear down our wickiup and move into one of the houses on the cliff."

"Yes, my husband," Ironwood Blossom responded obediently. No joy, no distress, just acquiescence.

Frustration gnawed at Coconino. He wanted her to ask why so he could explain that he felt the trip up and down the steep slope might have been bad for Hummingbird. He wanted to tell her, tell someone, that he would take every precaution so that his wife should not suffer such a misfortune again, even at the sacrifice of his own sense of propriety. But Ironwood Blossom never questioned anything he did. As though she had no right to question, he thought, or did not care enough to do so.

The stream was a mere trickle at this time of year, and they crossed it on stepping-stones. His long stride bypassed some of the stones, while hers carefully found each one. On the other side he waited for her, looking down at the tiny bundle in his arm. It was the size of a jackrabbit, he thought. A very small jackrabbit. So tiny, so helpless . . .

Ironwood Blossom joined him, her foot crunching the shale that littered the bank. He fingered the soft leather of his bundle. My child, my child—"Was it a girl?" he asked abruptly.

She had pushed her hood back in deference to her exertion and the absence of a breeze here on the canyon floor. He saw the surprise on her moonlit face as she looked up at him. "Yes," she replied. "It was a little girl."

A knot formed in his throat again, and they trudged on. The daughter who would have been, could have been . . . He saw her with a bow in her hand, a child drawing a bead on her first moving target. He saw her hands, awkward with inexperience, smoothing the shaft of arrow. He saw her face white in death, being laid in a rock crevice, her bow and arrows close at hand. . . .

Mother Earth, why? he demanded silently.

Wind sighed through the vegetation far up the steep canyon slopes. *You never asked why before,* it chided him.

It was never my child before, he grieved. Never my daughter. A tear slid unheeded down his coppery cheek.

There will be other children for you. Another is in the making now. I will not take it from you, I promise.

He was aware of Ironwood Blossom then, walking silently, stoically beside him. The roundness of her belly had just begun to show through her bulky winter clothing. A boy child, he guessed.

Do you need to know?

At the foot of the western canyon wall they came to a gravelly area, the remains of a small rockfall. One or two stubborn manzanita bushes had taken root there, along with a thorny mustard plant. Ironwood Blossom knelt on the stony ground and began to scoop out a depression with her hands, but Coconino stopped her. Handing the small bundle to her, he himself began to dig the shallow grave.

The ache he had banished earlier rose up to choke him now. It tightened his chest, constricted his throat, rang in his head. Is it because I wanted her to imitate Phoenix? he asked silently. It was only a dream that she might be a hunter. I would not have forced the child into a path it did not choose.

A night bird called. *That is not what this is about.*

"Then what is it about?" he demanded aloud, fiercely. Ironwood Blossom looked up in alarm as his shout echoed off the canyon walls, sending birds flapping from their night perches and startling an owl into hooting its displeasure. Nearby a coyote began to bark, and the call was passed to another of its pack farther away, and another, and another, until it seemed the whole canyon was lined with the clamoring beasts. A cloud drifted briefly across the moon, throwing the cleft into deep shadow. Coconino waited.

But the howling died into the distance, the cloud slipped away from the moon, and there was no answer to Coconino's question.

Silvery light bathed them once more, but it seemed a cold light now. The moon, which Coconino had once felt was like a warm and close companion to him, was suddenly just an object in the sky. He no longer felt a kinship with nearby pines or the circling owl; he no longer felt a strength flowing to him from the gravel in which he knelt. He felt only a curious emptiness within. The radiant presence he had known all his life seemed to have seeped away like water into the pebbly soil of the rockfall. Slowly he turned his attention back to his digging.

It took only a moment to finish. Then he took the bundle from Ironwood Blossom's arms and placed it in the shallow trench. She began to sing quietly, a lullaby of the People. "Sleep, child, sleep in safety; no harm can touch you here." Coconino had heard the song often enough; his own mother had sung it to her children. "I will embrace you, as the Earth enfolds her own. . . ."

As the Earth enfolds this child, he thought bitterly. Enfolds her as she enfolded my friends, my Witch Woman. "I will give this child a name," he said.

He could feel Ironwood Blossom draw back and knew what was coming. "It is not usually done for an early birth," she ventured. "It was not yet a person."

"It was my child!" he grated through clenched teeth. "And I will give it a name."

She was silent then, and he drew a deep breath. It did nothing to relieve the ache in his chest. Once he had thought to give this child the Witch Woman's name, but then, how could he bury her? How could he draw the ground over her body, blocking her away from him forever, commending her to the bosom of the Mother Earth?

"I name her My Peace," he said softly. Then, with one powerful sweep of his arm, he pushed the loose soil over the tiny bundle and buried it.

CHAPTER SIX

Phoenix stole through the shadows of the offworlders' camp, silent and graceful as the clouds that drifted across the moon. The dome she sought lay just ahead, slightly east of the shuttle that dominated this central portion of the camp. She slipped from darkness to darkness as she skirted its perimeter, alert for any sound or motion that might indicate another human moving about.

The shuttle was white and silent where it squatted, a hulking form some sixty feet in length and half that in width. It rested on a myriad of tiny rods that hugged the ground and made a perfectly level foundation. In the filtered light it took on an eerie glow.

Suddenly there was a clang, and the two great doors of the cargo bay sprang out from the shuttle, then rolled to either side along their tracks. Phoenix flattened herself into the doorway of the nearest dome, which mercifully stood at right angles to the shuttle. Scarcely breathing, she riveted her eyes on the open bay.

It gaped like the maw of a dreadful monster, one that swallowed beings indiscriminately. A ramp shot out like a tongue, raising the hair on the nape of Phoenix's neck. It was this monster that had swallowed Coconino and refused to belch him up; she shuddered reflexively as she remembered. But as she peered inside, she saw that the rainbow tubes that had once converted it into a warp terminal had been removed. Now it was loaded with boxes, bags, and crates.

A man strode out of its benighted depths wheeling a hand truck loaded with boxes. He thumped and bumped it down the ramp to the hard-packed earth, an earth scourged of any vegetation by the constant pounding of human feet. For a moment he left the truck standing by itself while he returned to a control panel on the side of the shuttle to close up the vehicle turned warehouse. With a mechanical grinding that shattered the still night, the tongue ramp receded, the jaw doors rolled shut, and the monster sealed itself against intrusion.

Even after the man had disappeared into the darkness of the camp, Phoenix stood staring at the shuttle as though her very will could make it give up the prize it had stolen from her.

Karen thought she was going to make it out the commissary door without attracting Tony Hanson's attention, but her hand hadn't even reached the palm panel when he was there beside her. "Turning in for the evening?" he asked. "I'll walk you back. Don't want you to trip over anything in the dark, damage that precious cargo."

Karen shrank back a little and considered staying awhile longer in the noisy common room of what they had named "Camp Crusoe." But no matter when she decided to leave, Tony would be there, offering to light her way with one of only two working hand lights left. She sighed and palmed the door open.

"Tony!" Jacqueline Winthrop called from across the room. "Come here a minute."

Tony hesitated, his gaze shifting between the China-doll features of Karen and the strong, commanding face of Dr. Winthrop. The latter was seated with her friend Rita Zleboton, the chief engineer. Those two had a habit of putting their heads together and making decisions without consulting him. With obvious regret he opted to answer their summons. "Excuse me just a minute," he said to Karen, and swaggered to their table.

"Rita has been showing me this new plow the computer designed," Jacqueline began.

Karen slipped gratefully out the door and hurried off toward her dome house.

It was a mild winter evening with a thin cloud cover holding in some of the day's heat. Karen looked up at the moon as dark shapes drifted across it like so many restless ghosts seeking their peace. An owl hooted, sending a shiver through her; no wonder some primitive cultures had thought the owl was a harbinger of death. Is that what the People believe? she wondered. I wish they had not vanished; I wish we had not frightened them away.

A breeze eddied around the geodesic domes that constituted most of the camp. Karen drew her jacket tighter around her and hurried toward the sleeping quarters she shared with three other women. There had been talk of erecting some additional structures from native materials so that people could have more privacy, but Tony Hanson had snarled contemptuously about the waste of person-hours. They needed to be concerned about repairing the food synthesizer again, and finding a way to cure the hides of the animals they hunted, and scavenging the ruins of Earth for useful articles. He was right, she knew, but she longed for a little log cabin with a fireplace and a garden plot of her very own.

She was almost home now, if one could call it that. The domes were all identical, distinguished only by painted numbers and by location. The one she shared with Shel and Cyd and Monica was on the river side of the camp, near the Infirmary. They were reasonable roommates, courteous and not given to excessive moods. But Karen was not accustomed to sharing.

There, that was it just beyond this drying rack where someone's clean laundry lay forgotten. And none too soon, for the wind—

Suddenly a hand closed over Karen's mouth, and she was jerked back against a tall, bony body. "Don't make a sound," a woman's voice hissed. "I'm not going to hurt you; I just need to talk to you. Alone."

For a moment Karen stood paralyzed with fear. Then she did what she had learned to do long ago: she gave up and went limp.

At that her captor eased off a little. "I'm going to let you go. But if you make a peep, I'll gag you. Do you understand?" A pause. "Nod your head if you understand."

Slowly Karen nodded.

The woman let go of her waist first, then carefully uncovered her mouth. Karen trembled as the woman edged around and let her face be seen.

It was Phoenix.

"Good," the gritty woman grunted as she saw the look of recognition on Karen's face. "You remember me. Now, where can we go to talk?"

Glancing around, Karen saw the darkened Infirmary. Dr. Winthrop was still at the commissary. She indicated the building to Phoenix, who nodded and gestured to her to lead the way.

Once inside, Karen lowered herself weakly into a chair. Phoenix watched her a moment, repenting the fright she had given the younger woman, but she wasn't sure what kind of reception she'd have gotten if she'd simply walked up to Karen, and she couldn't afford to take the risk. She wanted to apologize, but the words died on her lips. If she was unduly cautious, it was the Others' fault, not her own.

Instead she continued to study her quarry. Karen shivered a bit, but it was only from the cold; emotionally, she had sunk into a calculated apathy. It was that place where nothing could surprise her, nothing could hurt her. Phoenix had seen it before, when Karen had been abandoned by Lujan as he tried to make his escape from Earth.

Karen shifted in her chair. The swelling of her abdomen showed through the loose cotton blouse and trousers she wore, pushed out the light jacket in an obvious way.

"Coconino's baby," Phoenix said matter-of-factly.

"Yes," Karen replied, "Coconino's baby."

They continued to stare at each other. Phoenix wondered how to proceed from here.

"Is it Rumpelstiltskin?" Karen asked suddenly.

Phoenix gave a start. "Is it what?"

"Rumpelstiltskin," Karen repeated. "It's an old fairy story; do you know it? A little gnome helps the miller's daughter spin straw into gold, and in return he wants her firstborn child. She can only get out of the bargain if she can guess his name. Rumpelstiltskin." Karen lifted vacant blue eyes to meet Phoenix's gaze. "You've come for Coconino's baby, haven't you?"

Suddenly Phoenix's stomach knotted. She had made careful plans for this abduction: arriving in the early evening, tracking Karen from the commissary, catching her alone. She had located a hiding place where they could stay tonight, perhaps lying low there for a day if Tony Hanson mounted a search in that direction. Nowhere in her plans was there a way to deal with Karen's accusation.

She rubbed her tired eyes with grimy hands, wondering what she could say that would sway the young mother to her side. "You might be better off with us," she suggested. "We know how to live here, how to harvest the land. We live at peace with the Mother Earth. Your people here . . ." She shook her head. "They're going to get into trouble."

"With the Mother Earth?"

It sounded too foolish to say. "With each other," Phoenix said instead. "Quarrels over how to do things, how to divide food and other necessities—we're five centuries past that. What happens when someone gets tired of taking orders from Tony Hanson? What happens when someone gets greedy and helps himself to community stores? What happens when those precious machines of yours run out of fuel?"

"They already have," Karen told her. "Chief Zleboton is working on a solar energy converter. It's not going very well."

"Leave it all behind," Phoenix urged. "Come up north with me. The People will take care of you. Coconino's mother, his sister—and there's a girl, like a prophetess, and she's having Coconino's baby, too. You won't be alone.''

Karen stared at her hands in her lap, at the swelling that was another life inside her. "I've always been alone," she said simply. "I guess I always will be."

The sentiment struck too close to home. Phoenix clenched her teeth with an anger whose source she refused to admit. "Do your friends know it's Coconino's baby?" she grated.

Karen shrugged. "Only the doctor."

"How do you think they're going to react when it comes out all dark-skinned with jet-black hair?"

Again Karen shrugged.

"I can tell you how the People will react," Phoenix persisted, kneeling beside Karen's chair. "They'll hold you in great honor as the Chosen Companion of Coconino. They'll respect you and your baby. The child will grow up like royalty."

Finally Karen's lip trembled just a little. But was that good or bad? She seemed to care about so little; did she care about the baby at all? Phoenix could not tell.

Suddenly the door slid open behind them. Phoenix jumped to her feet, her knife unsheathed.

Jacqueline Winthrop stood in the doorway, feet planted, a hard look on her face. "I heard voices," she said. "Karen, are you all right?"

Karen stirred as though from slumber. "Fine."

Phoenix eyed the woman in the doorway. She was slight, with white hair pulled back in a bun, a strong jaw, and a high forehead. Steely blue eyes bored into Phoenix. "Dr. Winthrop," Phoenix said gravely.

Recognition sparked in Jacqueline's eyes then. "Coconino's friend," she recalled, "from the Mountain. Phoenix, isn't it?"

Phoenix gave a small nod and sheathed her knife. "Please close the door."

Jacqueline considered a moment, then complied. With measured steps she brought herself almost within reach of the two other women. "I was sorry to hear you moved the People north," she said. "I looked forward to meeting them."

"Tony Hanson didn't," Phoenix replied.

That darkened Jacqueline's face. "I heard. In your place I'd have done the same thing, I suppose."

"I'm glad to see you alive," Phoenix said sincerely. "When you were overdue here, I was afraid Lujan had—"

"He tried," Jacqueline interrupted. "I wasn't on the aircraft. But Clayton was."

Even in the crisp, dispassionate tones of her voice, Phoenix could hear the pain. "I'm sorry."

"And I," Jacqueline responded, "about Coconino."

But Phoenix bridled. "He's not dead," she said quickly. "The warp terminal threw him into the future, that's all. He'll be along one of these days."

Jacqueline arched an eyebrow. "Is *that* what you believe?"

"It happens, doesn't it?" Phoenix demanded. "In the early days of warp travel, weren't there . . . accidents . . . in which time as well as space was warped?"

"And it still happens," Jacqueline said. "But even if that's the case with Coconino and Lujan, there's no telling that they'll come out of it *here*."

The idea licked at Phoenix's consciousness like a flame, threatening for a moment to sear her world. "They must," she whispered. "They have to." Then her eyes took on a coldly mocking character. "It has been foretold," she said with a slight sneer, as though daring the older woman to challenge what she knew she had no evidence with which to defend her belief.

But Jacqueline had had bitter experience in challenging what were clearly matters of faith and so she backed away from the topic. If Phoenix needed to believe her hero would return, Jacqueline would not play the infidel. At the moment, she was far more concerned with something else.

"What do you want with Karen?" Jacqueline asked.

"To take her back with me," Phoenix answered simply. They were two of a kind: straightforward, uncompromising.

"Not a chance," Jacqueline said.

"We'll take good care of her," Phoenix promised. "The baby will grow up among his own kind."

"Human beings? We have a few of those here, too."

"Among the People," Phoenix said deliberately. "I assure you, Dr. Winthrop, there is a very big difference."

"I don't care about the difference," Jacqueline said flatly. "I care about Karen. She has been pushed, shoved, ordered, raped, brutalized, used, and victimized for every one of the twenty-six years of her life, and I am *not* going to let anyone do that to her again."

"She will be *revered*," Phoenix said angrily, "and *protected* and treated with more respect than she has ever known."

"That's what they said to the bird as they locked it in its cage," Jacqueline snapped back.

"Is this cage so much better?" Phoenix demanded.

"This cage has adequate medical facilities!"

"And a grudge against the child's father!"

"We're not going to hold a baby responsible—"

"Stop," Karen said quietly, and utter silence fell across the room.

Slowly Karen rose from her chair. She faced Phoenix first. "If I go with you, what will the People expect of me?"

"They'll expect you to have a baby," Phoenix replied.

"Nothing more?"

Phoenix thought. What had it been like when she had first come to the People—dear God, only one year ago? One year ago, when she had not known the young man with the brooding face and the dazzling smile. Her voice choked as she tried to answer. "They'll offer to teach you," she said, "anything you want to know: preserving meat, grinding corn, working the fields. But they won't require you to participate." Then she added, "Except in the feasting and the celebration of life."

Now Karen turned to Jacqueline. "And what can I expect here?"

"Companionship," Jacqueline responded quickly.

"Tony Hanson's companionship?"

There was a pause. "I'll keep him off your back somehow. Karen, you're going to need help having that baby."

"I imagine the People have midwives." She turned to Phoenix. "Don't they?"

Phoenix gestured broadly. "Half a dozen children get born every year."

"And how many die?" Jacqueline asked. "How many mothers die?"

But Karen cut off Phoenix's rebuttal with a wave. "Don't answer that. It doesn't even matter to me."

Jacqueline stared at her, stricken.

Now the young woman seemed to have reached a decision. She looked Phoenix in the eye. "Give me your knife," she said.

Phoenix hesitated, then handed the young woman the flint-bladed tool. Karen eyed the edge. "Very sharp?"

"Sharp enough to skin animals."

"Sharp enough," Karen said. She swept both women with her gaze, a weary gaze for one so young. "I'm tired," she said simply. "I'm tired of all this, of everything. I just want life to go away for a while. Maybe forever. I'm going to keep this knife here," she told them, slipping it into the waistband of her trousers, "and if I get too tired, I'll use it on myself. Tell that to Tony Hanson," she instructed Jacqueline. "Tell him if he tries to come after us, I'll use it on myself. And you—" She turned to Phoenix. "Remember that if I get too frightened or too unhappy, the People will never have Coconino's baby."

Phoenix paled a little.

Karen gave the smallest flicker of a smile. "It's so easy to gamble when you have nothing to lose."

Krista could feel Clint Patrone's eyes on her as she crossed the campus of the Mountain installation toward the dining hall. She hated it when he watched her with that peculiar mix of contempt and jealousy. To her it made no sense that a man would take such personal offense that another man desired what he himself loathed; but then, Krista was only nineteen. She had much to learn about men.

Clint Patrone began to trail her—not with any intention of catching her, she was sure, but just to see where she was going. He spied on her constantly. *Just what does he think I'm going to do?* she wondered. *Corrupt an entire generation of schoolboys? Offer myself for lab experiments?*

Have a little fun?

Krista tossed her long blond hair. Fun! Ha. She snorted. *I haven't had any fun since—*

Since Coconino left.

Krista squeezed her eyes shut and tried to remember what it was like when Coconino first showed up on the Mountain with Debbie McKay. She had never encountered a stranger before, someone whom she had not known all her life. This one was magnetic: young, exotic, and very, very male. From the moment she had seen the moonlight glinting on his bronzed, well-muscled body, she had known what she wanted.

A tear escaped the corner of her eye, and Krista brushed it quickly away, for even in the midday sun the air was frosty, and the innocent moisture grew cold. It had been a glorious week playing Chosen Companion to Coconino. But he hadn't been playing. For him it was part of an ancient value system, one in which he gave her the most precious gift he knew: seeds.

Seeds. Abruptly Krista turned from the path that led her to the warm, crowded dining hall and headed instead for the Archives. To her left she saw Clint Patrone stop, waiting to see where her new course led. Make what you want of this, she thought. Lord knows the rest of the gossips here have.

As she hurried along, her coat snugged around her, she wondered again if old Ben Gonzales wasn't a little crazy. He'd come back from the Village of the People with some very strange tales. Coconino disabling a spaceship. A clash between the offworlders and the primitives. Coconino disappearing in the warp terminal. That dark, dramatic face and the dazzling smile, the strength and intensity that was Coconino, gone in an instant—

I cried for you, Coconino, she thought. I want you to know that I cried for you. I hardly knew you, you blew in and out of my life so fast, but when you had gone, I knew that I'd lost something unique. We all had. And that red fruit you gave me, so full of tiny black seeds? I kept it, Coconino. I kept your seeds. . . .

The heavy door of the Archives stuck, but Krista wrestled it open and slipped inside. Shelves of books and laser disks and other media stretched away to one side; she hurried past them toward the offices at the back. Maybe Mr. McKay had already gone to lunch. Maybe, like the other paranoiacs in this place, he had taken to locking his door.

But she saw with relief that the director of the Archives was still at his desk, immersed in something on his computer terminal. He was an unimposing man, thickening at the middle after forty years and graying at the temples. It made her smile to see him there: a calm, rational presence in a world that sometimes seemed to have gone mad. He knew more of the history of Earth than anyone else in the settlement, more of the people and the creatures and the things that had preceded them.

It was to him she had brought that red fruit late last summer to find out if they really were saguaro seeds that bristled inside the pulp. The giant saguaro cactus had been extinct for hundreds of years, after all. How could Coconino have given her saguaro seeds?

Dick McKay looked up from his work as she approached and broke into a smile. How nice to see someone smile when they saw her coming! It was a reception she seldom got anymore. "Krista!" he greeted. "Come in. How are you feeling?"

"Healthy as a horse and twice as hungry," she replied, unfastening her coat in the comfortable warmth of his office. "I was on my way to the dining hall, but I decided to check on Ralph."

Dick laughed, rolling his chair away from the desk and toward a windowsill. His wire-rimmed glasses caught the sunlight for a moment, and all Krista could see was his smile. She studied it, hoping to see some resemblance there to another smile she had loved, but he turned back, the evenness of his features and the fairness of his skin concealing any similarity. Someday she would ask him. Someday she would just flat out ask.

"Here he is," Dick said, bringing a clay pot back to his desk for her inspection. "Doesn't look any bigger, does he?"

Krista squinted at the tiny fleck of green in the grayish mulch of the pot. "I can't believe that little thing is going to grow forty feet tall," she said, shaking her head. "Not even in a hundred years."

"Well, if you take good care of him, he should," Dick replied. "Don't put him outside until he's at least, oh, twenty-five. By then he'll be about two feet tall."

"Poor little Ralphie," Krista cooed. "By the time you're big enough to get out of your crib, your mother will be an old woman." Her hands flew to her face in mock despair. "I may not even live to see you sprout arms!"

At that they both laughed, but in Dick McKay's face Krista saw something else flicker just below the surface, something unbearably sad. His eyes traveled for a moment to her abdomen, which swelled now with the other seed Coconino had entrusted to her. "You'll be there when it counts," he told her with a poor attempt at joviality. "The early years are the riskiest. That's when they need you most."

A movement caught Krista's eye; she looked up to see the front door open, and Clint Patrone stepped inside. "It's a hostile environment," she agreed.

Dick's eyebrows raised at her tone. Looking past her, he saw the muscular young man who pretended to peruse a shelf of disks. He frowned slightly. "Clint bothering you?" he asked.

Krista shrugged. "Not really. He just— He follows me sometimes. It gives me the creeps."

His frown changed to concern. With a hand on her arm, he looked up into her eyes. "If he gives you any trouble," he told her evenly, "if he says anything or—"

"I'll let you know," she promised, suppressing a shiver as she wondered just what the quiet scholar would do. She couldn't imagine him being violent, but there were many things about Mr. McKay she couldn't imagine. Like his ever being married to Debbie. Like the two of them engaged in earsplitting verbal battles. Like his taking a sudden interest in a pregnant teenager.

"I read those books you recommended," she told him. "On childbirth. They really were interesting. They don't teach that stuff to Level Four Health Techs."

"I recommend them to all expectant parents," he said.

But not personally, she thought. You don't go out of your way to personally put them in the hands of every expectant parent. Just me.

"Have *you* read them?" she asked impishly.

"Of course. When Tina was pregnant." He and his second wife had had their first child a little over a year before. "And once, long ago," he added. "When I was a young man and curious about such things." He grimaced. "Back in the Mesozoic Era."

But Krista ignored the wisecrack. "When you went to live with the People?" she asked.

The something flickered again, stronger this time. "Shortly thereafter," he replied.

"About twenty years ago?"

His smile died entirely. He looked away from her, spotted the plant. "Well, time to put little Ralph back on his windowsill," he said with forced brightness. "And you'd better get yourself some lunch. Keep that little monster well fed."

Krista sighed and turned toward the door. She'd been told Dick wouldn't talk about his time with the People. Rumor was that he'd been terribly in love with his Chosen Companion and that she had died in childbirth. It would explain a lot of things about Dick McKay. But it wouldn't explain why, when everyone Krista loved seemed disgusted with her decision to have Coconino's baby, the loner Dick McKay had gone out of his way to be supportive.

Suddenly she turned and faced him. "He was your son, wasn't he?" she blurted. "Coconino was your son."

For a moment the truth was written there, the truth she had read in a hundred looks, a hundred tiny gestures over the past six months. Then his face seemed to close.

"Jonathan is my son," he said tightly, and turned back to his keyboard.

But Krista was nineteen, and stubborn, and unwilling to let things go. "Why do you pretend?" she asked. "Why do you pretend he wasn't your son, that you never had any children before Jonathan?"

Dick's hands froze, poised as they were over his keyboard. For an aching moment he sat suspended, wrestling, Krista knew, with some inner demon. Then, slowly, his hands sank and his shoulders slumped and his body admitted defeat, even if his voice was still unable to do so. He dropped his head wearily into his hands, ran his fingers through his hair, then removed his glasses and wiped an arm across his weary eyes. "Because I was never a father to

him," he said finally. "Because I left him behind in the Village of
the People. And when he came here, I saw the man he'd become,
the kind of devotion he inspired in Debbie—in *Debbie*, of all people!"

Dick shook his head. "I've bungled so many things in my life,
Krista," he said sadly. "I have so many regrets. . . ." He heaved
a great sigh. "But I can't change any of it. I can't ever make it up
to Coconino. I can't ever have my son back."

A son lost not once but twice. A mistake regretted for twenty
years. Any hope of restoration denied.

"But you can have a grandson," Krista whispered.

At last he looked at her again, and the pain in his haunted eyes
made her want to weep. "If you will let me," he said, "I would
like that very much."

In her womb, the child stirred.

CHAPTER SEVEN

"Do you have a razor I can use?"

Janine Thornton gasped in fright, spilling the pan of biscuits she had just taken from the stove. The voice had come from the tall, bewhiskered man standing in the doorway of the cabin's bedroom, a man over six feet tall with light brown hair waving nearly to his shoulders, a man who had not spoken a word in nine months.

He seemed unconcerned now at the alarm he had caused. Janine scrambled after her biscuits. "I'm sorry, you startled me," she said, wondering how far from the house her husband was. "Are you hungry? I was just making some biscuits and eggs." She stood panting and clutching the still-hot pan with her pot holders. His eyes seemed to see right into her, those steely blue eyes that had gazed vacantly past everyone and everything for season upon season.

"Do you have a razor I can use?" he repeated.

"Well, you'll have to ask Casey when he comes in," she stalled. "He'll be along any minute; he's just tending to the animals. Won't you sit down? Have a cup of tea?"

He continued to stare at her a moment, then came into the room and sat on a bench at the plank table. His eyes continued to bore into her as she poured tea into a stoneware mug and brought it to the table. Her hands trembled, but she managed to put it down without spilling it.

Finally he shifted his eyes from her to the steaming cup. He sniffed it discreetly, then picked it up and sipped at it. "It's not tea," he said.

"Well, of course it's tea," she replied, then remembered their suspicion about his origin. "Well, it's what we call tea here. On Earth. At Camp Crusoe."

He grunted, sipped it again. "Do you have any coffee?" he asked.

"Coffee." Janine searched her brain but could not come up with a definition of the word. "No, I don't think so," she replied carefully, then asked, "Is there coffee where you come from?"

His gaze went unfocused, and for a moment she thought he was slipping away again. But his eyes fastened on the cup once more. "Lots of it," he replied. "They import it. From Darius IV."

Janine jumped in spite of herself. "Then you *are* from off-world," she breathed.

"Yes," he replied matter-of-factly.

Janine swallowed, took a slow, deep breath, and asked shakily, "How did you get here?"

"On the *Homeward Bound*," he responded.

The *Homeward*— Oh, but it must be another ship of the same name. "From what port?" she managed. That was the right phrase, wasn't it? From what port? Lunacy, to have this kind of conversation with a man from another planet.

"Argo," he said. "New Sydney."

Janine's heart thudded dangerously in her chest. "How curious," she said with remarkable calm. "The first *Homeward Bound* was from Argo, too. The one that brought our ancestors here."

"I know." He sipped mechanically at his tea. "That's the one I was on."

Janine sat down unexpectedly. "But—that was a hundred and seventy, hundred and eighty years ago," she stammered. It couldn't be; he was confused. All the original crew had lived and died in this place; their markers were in the cemetery on Winthrop Hill. The only people unaccounted for were the captain, whose aircraft was never found, and . . . Janine's head throbbed. "That would mean you're—"

"Derek Lujan," he said. "I am Derek Lujan, first officer of the TRC's *Homeward Bound*."

Tav Ryan glanced around to make sure they were not observed, then she slipped her durable plastic key into the aging lock of the command center dome. "In here," she murmured as the door retracted slowly. All the solar-powered doors worked slowly in the wintertime. Fortunately, their ancestors had had the foresight to bypass the old palm-code locks with plastic key units during the first generation, before there was no one left whose handprint could open them. Or who knew how to bypass them.

They slipped silently inside, five grown people sneaking around like a bunch of teenagers. Tav led the way, a big-boned farmer in her late twenties with short dark hair and work-hardened muscles. Behind her came Franz Johnson, a spare and scholarly mechanic; the new medic, Liza Hanson; and Casey Thornton. Last to enter the dome was her cousin, Mo, a hulking man of nearly forty years. He was also her closest crony and staunchest supporter in Crusoan politics; Tav didn't know what she'd do without him. She checked again to make sure they hadn't been seen, then closed the door.

"It's cold in here!" Liza exclaimed, stamping her feet on the hollow-sounding decking. "I thought all these old buildings had climate controls in them."

"They did, when the computer worked," Tav replied dryly, chafing her hands to warm them. "That's been a hundred years or so." Mountain dwellers had any number of misplaced notions about what level of technology the Crusoans maintained. Tav glanced around at the dust-covered equipment that had stood unused for at least a century. "I keep asking Exec to clear these antiques out and use the place for storage. But no, they want to hang on to them. As though someone were going to come along and reactivate something."

Liza nudged Casey. "Maybe your mysterious stranger could."

Casey threw a dark look at her. She was fresh off the Mountain, a young woman of twenty-four with dark curling hair and merry blue eyes, so unlike Doc Martin, who had passed away last winter. Casey missed Doc. They'd plowed a lot of miles together. This new medic seemed rather light of body and spirit for the hard job she had undertaken, but he supposed she might be tougher than she looked.

Franz leaned against a dusty console and crossed his ankles, a man of controlled gestures and precise grace. His skin was a warm brown, testimony to his Mideastern ancestry. "You've talked to him more than we have," he said to Casey. "What's your opinion? Is he really Derek Lujan?" Franz was the unofficial historian of Camp Crusoe.

"I don't know," Casey admitted. "Without a picture or a physical description of Lujan, how can we be sure?"

Franz frowned. When the settlement's computer had failed, all those records had been lost, along with massive amounts of other information that there hadn't been time to download. "The log reports that are extant," he told them, "indicate that Lujan disappeared in the warp terminal just before the *Homeward Bound* crashed. A time warp *was* given as one possible explanation. And the primitives, you know, have been saying for years that their Coconino is coming again.''

Tav waved a hand impatiently. "They only know what they were told," she scoffed, "and what they want to believe." The only daughter of farming parents, she had gone early into the fields and learned to handle an adult work load by the time she was fourteen. She had seen drought and disease and flood and fire take the fruit of her labor. Life had made a skeptic of Tavaria Ryan, though she was not yet thirty.

"Look at it this way," Casey said with the down-to-earth reasoning Tav valued. "If you were going to pick a false identity to assume, would you pick Derek Lujan?"

Their silence conceded his point.

Liza was not satisfied, however. "But the man is—pardon my clinical terminology—crazy," Liza put in. She had not yet found the rhythm of her new community and often seemed to be moving at a different speed than were those around her. It gave her the impression of being frivolous—an odd quality for a medic. But in fact, Tav had noticed, Liza was very astute. "Delusions of grandeur can mean assuming one is a genocidal dictator as well as a King Author or a Dr. Yuko," she pointed out. "Even if this man *thinks* he is Derek Lujan, that doesn't mean he is."

Mo shifted his considerable bulk. Because of his size, people tended to think he was slow-witted, but that was untrue. He was deliberate and very conservative, but Tav knew that when he spoke or acted, it was never a rash or unconsidered thing. "But if he's not Derek Lujan," Mo asked, "who is he?"

Again there was silence.

Tav ran her callused fingers through her short, dark hair. "Look," she said, "let's pretend for a minute he is who he says he is. Who *is* he? I mean, what do we really know about Derek Lujan? Bunch of legends handed down. And don't forget this guy has been catatonic for nine months; is he still the man today that he was, what, two hundred years ago?"

"Nine months ago, for him," Mo growled.

"Well, I can tell you what he *did*," Franz offered, "or rather, what he's suspected of doing—not much was ever proved conclusively. But that won't tell us what we really want to know."

"Which is?" Mo prompted.

Franz looked at his cohorts, four usually sane people who were meeting surreptitiously, without authority, and with one common fear. "What we really want to know," he said, "is, is he dangerous?"

* * *

Derek Lujan stared at his own reflection in the mirror. He was gaunt and pale but clean-shaven now except for his mustache, which was neatly trimmed; he felt better for it. Carefully he watched as the woman behind him combed out a lock of his waving hair and sheared it off with her scissors.

"Shorter," he directed.

She obliged by recutting the lock. When he said nothing, she took that as a sign of consent and continued cutting his hair to that length. She was a credible barber; she barbered most of the citizens of Camp Crusoe and had for fifteen years. They paid her in eggs, or vegetables, or ration checks as they were able. For this particular haircut she did not expect to be paid.

Lujan watched her work, her hands quick and deft. During the entire process his eyes never wavered, but his mind raced hither and yon like a newly caged animal.

Something's wrong! it shrieked. Something's wrong with me. This doesn't feel right. Nothing feels right! Time is out of joint, this camp is out of joint, *I* am out of joint. What's wrong with me? Why can't I snap out of this?

Zzzzzip, went the scissors, shiny metal scissors foraged from the ruins of a city downriver from here. The shorn hair curled around the woman's finger, soft, golden brown, glinting in the sunlight from her cabin window.

Nine months gone—no, a hundred years gone, two hundred. Dillon gone. Argo gone. Hope gone.

Zzzzip! went the scissors, shearing off his hair, shearing off time, shearing off his past.

Stuck here. Stuck here forever. No way out. Is there no way out? No ship, no contact with Argo, and they think we have plague. Yes, that's what they think. That's what I told them. *I* told them. But it wasn't me, no, it wasn't me that thought of it, it was Coconino's idea, yes, Coconino's idea. I see it now. He baited me, he lured me in, and then he destroyed my ship, my means of escape. . . .

"Longer on the top," he told the woman cutting his hair.

I was supposed to escape! I always escape. I am Houdini, I am Lujan, I was supposed to be the survivor, the one who got away without catching the plague, without being destroyed by Earth. But Coconino had other plans. He knew all along. He never intended to let me go. Never. Never, never, never. And he won, he *won*—

Zzzzzip! The hair curled, clutching at the finger that had shorn it. The woman dropped it onto the hard-packed earth floor, but a strand of it clung to her, refusing to let go. She shook her hand, and more dropped. The remainder she brushed away on her apron.

Not even my crew left to me. Not even the people I knew, the equipment I took for granted, a shared background. If I said, "Bring me a sonic calibrator," they knew what I meant. Tony Hanson, even Rita Zleboton—I could kiss Rita right now; if I saw her I would kiss her, she knows what a sonic calibrator is. These people don't even know what coffee is.

Coffee. Coffee for breakfast. No more coffee for breakfast—

How can I build a beacon? How can I get word back to Argo? Everything that might have worked for that was aboard the *Homeward Bound*—I saw to that, I did. And it all died with the ship, crash and burn, crash and burn—where? Where did it land? Maybe I can save something, something. . . .

Derek, Derek, Derek, do you honestly think anything survived the crash? If it had, wouldn't your crew have found it? Chief Zleboton, even Tony Hanson or the Johannesons— No, Coconino was very thorough. He and that woman, that angry woman, why was she so angry? What made her so bitter? It was a dangerous combination. I should have known it was too dangerous a combination. Should have known, should have, should have—

The fog began to drift back into his mind.

No! No more fog. Send the fog away. Banish the fog. Derek Lujan can't succumb to fog, and that's who I am. I am Derek Lujan. Derek Lujan. I can do this. I can handle this. Just relax, Derek. Relax. Focus. Breathe. That's right, breathe. In . . . out . . . in . . .

"Do you want it trimmed around your ears?" the woman asked.

He stared at her. What did she say? Did he need to answer? She was waiting, she was expecting an answer. He had to do something. He had to say something. Did he want—

"Yes," he answered abruptly. The woman hesitated, then went on with her clipping, bringing the point of the scissors close to his ears. He sat motionless, watching her in the mirror.

Yes, I am Derek Lujan. Derek Lujan—that means something. It implies something, something unshakable. What is it? *Where* is it? Where's the thing that is Derek Lujan? It is inside me, it is inside me somewhere. Push the fog away, find it. What is it that makes me *me*? Not my command, not my crew. Derek Lujan existed before all that, he must exist after. Not my career or my multiple degrees. Derek Lujan is . . . a kind of a man. A special kind of a man.

The image in the mirror began to look more familiar now. Is that Derek Lujan? he wondered. Is that who I am, that face, that expression? Yes. It is the me inside me. But it is not the me I show to others. What was that? What was that other face that I showed to Captain Winthrop, that I showed to Karen Reichert? A different face, a different expression . . .

He tested a smile, a mere twitching of the corners of his mouth. Yes, that looked familiar. He had smiled a lot before. Derek Lujan smiled a lot. The smile was a weapon, but other people didn't know that. It was a part of the look, like a mustache, like the dazzling white uniform—

Suddenly panic seized him. His uniform. Where was his uniform? The uniform was important; the uniform was part of the look—

I am not my uniform.

"Short at the nape?" the woman asked, standing behind him.

What was she doing back there? What was she doing with those scissors? Oh, yes. Cutting his hair. That was all. Cutting his hair. And waiting for an answer. What had she asked? The nape? Shorter?

"Yes."

But the tailored white uniform—it was important, wasn't it? There had been a reason, a specific reason, for the cut and the color. . . . To charm people. That's right. That's who Derek Lujan was: the man who charmed people, especially women. How was that done? How did I do that? The uniform, the smile . . . and the brain, oh, yes, that was important, too. Knowing all those things: warp physics, programming, Yuko's law, fifth-dimensional transportation— It dazzled them. I was . . . capable. Competent. I still am, the knowledge is all there. And another *c*, there was another *c* I used to describe myself. What was it? Capable, competent, and . . .

Charismatic, that was it. But—where is that part of me now? Is it still in here somewhere? Can I still charm people, can I still manipulate them? Can I make people do what I want? How do I try? Where does it start? What does it take?

"There you are," the woman announced as she brushed him off and whisked away the towel from his neck. "Is that better?"

She was smiling. Women used to smile at Derek Lujan, before. But this one . . . there was fear in her eyes. That wasn't the way it should be. He had never worked on fear. Greed, that was how he had worked. He used whatever it was people hungered for most: money, power, affection. What did this woman want most? To be loved? To be flattered? To be paid?

Derek smiled at her, a calculated smile. "Thank you," he said in a tone meant to convey his appreciation of her womanhood as well as her barbering skills.

But it didn't work. "You're welcome," she replied, and repressed a shudder. What this woman wanted most was for him to go away. Far away.

Abruptly Derek rose from the chair and walked out.

"I'm not a psychiatrist!" Liza Hanson was protesting. "I can't tell you if the man is potentially violent. I can't even tell you if he's *faking*. If you want a psychiatrist, go to the Mountain."

No one took that seriously. It was a long walk or a costly truck ride. The Executive Committee didn't authorize transportation lightly.

"We've got to watch him closely, then," Tav said. "Very closely."

"I want him out of my house," Casey avowed.

"We could watch him better if—"

"You keep him at your house!" Casey challenged.

"Well, if he's the ladies' man he's reported to be," Tav teased, "maybe I will." Tav had no excess of male company.

"I'll take him in," Franz offered. "My girls are away at school on the Mountain, and my boys are still at home. Makes sense for me to take him."

"I think we ought to boot him," Mo stated. "Give him a day's rations and point him into the sun."

"That's why you're known far and wide for your charity," Liza sneered.

"Listen, little girl!" Mo snarled, moving in on the medic. "Just because you studied—"

"Keep your voices down!" Tav hissed. "If Lazlo or Portia hears us making plans, we're in big trouble." Lazlo and Portia were other members of the Executive Committee. "You know the penalty for collusion to manipulate the Exec."

The Executive Committee was what served Camp Crusoe as a government. It settled disputes, made decisions, enforced policy. Tav was the youngest of the five members and the least conservative. On both counts she fought an uphill battle against the ponderous, lethargic remainder. She managed it by meeting with the people in this room to consolidate opinion and carefully plan strategy. It was a tactic widely used by all Exec members and highly illegal under the charter of Camp Crusoe. The Exec was supposed to be apolitical.

"You think Lazlo and Portia aren't meeting with their supporters right now," Casey asked, "deciding what we ought to do about this Lujan character?"

"No, I don't!" Tav snapped. "I don't think they'll get around to it for months. They'll let him go on living in your house, or Franz's house, or wherever he pleases until he's done something irreparable. Lazlo doesn't know the meaning of foresight, and Portia thinks the most heinous crime people are capable of is bad grammar. They won't wonder what to do about Derek Lujan until he's done something about them!"

"I'm the new kid on the block," Liza said, "but is that such a bad idea? Isn't a man innocent until proved guilty?"

"But if you see storm clouds brewing, you make sure you're within reach of shelter," Tav argued. "If this man is only unbalanced, he at least bears watching, don't you agree? And if he truly is Derek Lujan . . ." She let the implication hang in the air.

"We've got to have facts," Franz insisted. "The Exec won't listen without concrete evidence. We've got to document his behavior; we've got to—"

Suddenly the door began to slide open, and they all froze. Only members of the Executive Committee had keys to the old domes. Caught meeting in secrecy, they would have to do some fast talking to avoid the obvious charges of collusion. Tav could lose her seat on the Exec. The others risked censure and loss of privileges in the camp. They waited, hearts pounding.

One man stood framed in the doorway. He was tall and slender and had exquisite posture.

He was Derek Lujan.

No one spoke as the stranger stepped into the dome and looked around. He took in the cobwebs, the dusty equipment, the unattended consoles. The people he ignored.

Tav found her voice first. "How did you get in here?" she demanded.

Lujan made no reply, only held up his palm, wiggling his fingers. Jaws dropped as they realized his handprint had activated the ancient lock. Only the original crew of the *Homeward Bound* could do that.

Lujan strolled to one of the consoles, blew away a layer of dust, and inspected the instruments. "Computer went out," he surmised after a moment.

"Brilliant deduction," Mo muttered.

"Why does the door work?"

"It's a separate unit now," Tav explained. "All the dome doors have been detached from the other circuits and made to run off a solar energy unit."

Lujan nodded absently and crossed to a wall near the door. "Hey!" Tav objected as he raised his hands to a control panel, but before she could react further, he had popped off the cover and was studying the modifications. He grunted once, then moved to the next wall section and removed another panel.

This time Tav caught at his arm. She was a strong woman, her grip viselike. "You'd better leave those alone," she warned. Damage to the equipment in there might bring the wrath of the Exec down on them or go unnoticed for centuries. Behind her Mo moved into position to help her if she needed it.

But Lujan only stared at Tav with cold blue eyes. It sent a shiver through her tall, lanky body. "Do you have a probe?" he asked.

"Probe?"

"Yes. A long, narrow object. A pen. A nail. Something."

Slowly Tav's hand slipped from his arm. She fished inside her coat and pulled out a rattailed comb. Lujan took it from her and turned back to the panel. She saw him adjusting some switches, flicking tiny connections with the comb end. A soft humming began.

"What is it?" Mo demanded. "What's that, what have you done?"

"Hooked up climate control to the solar unit," Lujan replied. "It's cold in here."

Tav trudged away from the commissary dome, where fifty people had jammed into the confined space to hear the Exec's ruling. It should have been a victory that she had gotten them to deal with the issue at all, but it didn't feel like victory. It felt like defeat.

Her cousin Mo caught up to her, a reproachful look on his face. "Don't start with me, Mo," she snapped before he could say a thing. "I tried, swear to God I tried. But he fixed all the climate controls—every one of them, got them all working on the same solar units that run the doors. How could I fight that? Tell me how I could fight that."

Mo said nothing but scowled at the path that led away from the center of the settlement and to the bridge over the stream. He carried too much weight even for his large frame; it made his face jowly. "No Chin" her father used to call him, well outside his hearing. No Chin Ryan.

"They'll be sorry," Mo predicted as they walked along. "He's going to be trouble, count on it." Tav matched him stride for stride on the path, for while she did not have his bulk, she was nearly his height, and most of that was leg. Rangy; that was what they called her, she knew. Rangy Ryan. Hard worker, sharp-witted, but not the type you'd want to cozy up to in bed.

What did they know?

"At least he's out of Casey's house," Tav said. "Poor Janine. She's fussed over him for nine months, and now he turns out to be—" She didn't quite know where to go from there.

"Lujan," Mo finished for her. "He turns out to be Lujan."

For a while they walked in silence, past the last of the old white domes, through the yards of the earliest log cabins, around the knoll where the burned-out Mason house thrust ugly charred fingers to the sky. Eleven people had died in that fire; no one wanted to rebuild the place, although it was a choice homesite with good drainage and a view across the river to the common fields. Everyone knew Pop Mason, or one of the children, or Emmy Scinto, who had just married into the family. Emmy had been Tav's best friend.

"Kenny Johanneson's going to be sorry, though," Mo said finally. "Giving up his mother's place to Lujan."

"The Exec didn't exactly give him a choice," Tav commented dryly. " 'Kenny, is your boy going to want that cabin when he gets back from the Mountain?' 'Why, no, it's too small to start a family in.' 'Good! Then you don't mind letting Mr. Lujan use it for a while, do you?' What's he going to say with Lujan sitting right there, that manic look in his eye? Did you see that look in his eye?" Tav shuddered.

"I'll bet you a suckling pig old Ken went straight home and cut a crossbar for his door," Mo replied. Then, after a pause, he suggested awkwardly, "Maybe you'd better cut one for your door, too."

Tav barked a laugh. "What, and keep that handsome thing out of my bedroom?"

Mo seized her roughly by the shoulder. "Don't make jokes, Tav!" he snarled. "This guy's crazy. What if he finds out you tried to get him booted from Camp Crusoe?"

"Then we'll know someone on the Exec violated privilege."

"And what about you?"

She shrugged off his arm. "Did you ever wonder what happened to that sidearm Lujan was wearing when we found him wandering in the hills?'' she asked.

Mo recoiled. "I assumed—"

"Remember the first three letters in 'assume,' " she snapped. "And don't you worry about me. I sleep in safety."

Portia smiled sweetly at the time traveler. He certainly was a handsome man when he was cleaned up, resembling the Greek statues she had seen in books on the Mountain. He seemed rather young to be who he claimed, though. For some reason she had always pictured Derek Lujan as a just this side of middle age, maybe forty or forty-five. This man was in his midtwenties from the look of him. "How do you like your new home, Mr. Lujan?" she asked graciously.

They stood in the center of a rough wooden cabin. A metal stove stood to one side, a bed to the other. The table was folded flat against the far wall with a short bench pushed up against it. A small wardrobe with crooked doors was behind them, near the front door. "Where are the climate controls?" Lujan asked.

Portia gave a gentle laugh as though he were one of her grandchildren who had asked if there really were such things as dogs and ponies. "Why, Mr. Lujan, our cabins don't have climate controls. In the winter, you build a fire in the stove; in the summer, you sweat. Like everyone else," she assured him. "We get used to the smell."

"I want one of the domes," he said.

Her smile did not waver. "Excuse me?"

"I want one of the domes to live in," he repeated.

This time Portia's laugh was a little less indulgent. "Mr. Lujan, we don't use our domes for living space. They're community property, and they're needed to store our grain and vegetables and other supplies. We have a large population to support, you know, nearly a hundred families."

"I made the climate controls work in them," Lujan stated. "I want to live in one."

"I'm sorry, but that's just not possible."

Lujan turned on her with a stare that made Portia's blood run cold. Perhaps, she thought weakly, there was something to Tav's claim that he might be dangerous.

"I can fly the shuttle," he told her.

Portia forced a smile. "Can you? Isn't that nice! You know, when I was a little girl, we used to fly the shuttle to the Mountain once a year for the harvest festival, to trade with the settlements around there, and to take the older students to school. You should have seen it, loaded to the rafters with all kinds of things—oh, it was such an occasion! But then they were afraid that it would break down between here and there, and we couldn't risk that, so we stopped flying it. Now we send smaller trading parties, and the Mountain people come here sometimes, and the poor students—''

"I'll check it over," Lujan informed her, "and let you know if it's safe to fly. Those components shouldn't have deteriorated. If there's a problem, it's probably just dust." He reached out and wiped his finger through the layer of grit on top of the stove.

Portia watched him as he studied his dusty finger, just staring at it as though he had never seen anything like it. Poor, distracted man, she thought. I doubt if he'll ever recover. Pity. What knowledge he possesses. Just think what he could teach us, if he could teach. . . .

"Well, I'll leave you now," she announced, retreating toward the door. "No doubt you'll want to chop some wood and get a fire going. Tinderbox and matches are right there on the stove. If you need anything else, Mr. Johanneson's cabin is just over the rise." She paused. "Good-bye, then, Mr. Lujan," she called expectantly.

There was no response. She left Derek Lujan staring at the dust on his fingertip.

Ten-year-old Nathan Johanneson always referred to Derek Lujan as "the spooky man." He had been the subject of much childish speculation since his arrival the previous spring, and now that he had moved into Granny's old cabin, the temptation to visit was more than young Nathan could handle. Pa had already told him to give the spooky man a wide berth, and Ma had given a graphic description of all the horrible things that man might do to a boy of ten, but Nathan just couldn't resist. At the first opportunity he slipped out of the house and over the rise to the spooky man's cabin.

When he got there, however, he discovered his courage was in shorter supply than he had imagined. The cabin was dark and silent, with not even a puff of smoke from the chimney. Nathan crept cautiously forward and put his eye to a crack in the door. Granny had always hung her apron over the crack.

The spooky man huddled shivering on a bench inside the tiny cabin. Nathan knocked cautiously on the door. There was no answer. He knocked again. "Hey, mister," he called tentatively, "you okay?"

Still there was no answer. Nathan figured he had no choice but to go inside.

The spooky man didn't even look up. Nathan looked at him for a moment, just looked at him. He looked better than he had when he'd started talking last week but still a bit skinny. Even so, that didn't mean he wasn't plenty strong, and Nathan had reason to know. His older brother, Matt, was skinny as a rail, but Matt had carried a whole deer carcass home on his shoulders, and no one could take him at wrestling, no one. So Nathan chose prudently to keep his distance from the spooky man.

But it bothered him to see the man shivering like that. "Hey, mister," he asked, "aren't you going to light a fire?"

Steely blue eyes fixed on the boy and seemed to glint with the devil's own flame. Nathan wished his brother Matt hadn't gone to school on the Mountain but was somewhere Nathan could find him. Right now

"Don't know how," the spooky man said.

A grown man who didn't know how to light a fire? "Well, here, I'll show you," Nathan offered, having mastered the skill some three or four years ago himself. "You start with kindling—you got any kindling? No? Well, I'll find you some."

Twenty minutes later the boy had a bright blaze going in the stove and was stacking a few short logs nearby. He had borrowed them from his own house, having run over the hill to fetch them, along with a hatchet for splitting one into kindling. Lujan dragged his bench closer to the stove's warmth.

Matches, Lujan thought. Of course. Sulfur-tipped sticks. Sulfur had a low flash point, and friction generated enough heat to ignite it. Simple.

He did not notice the boy watching him until the lad blurted, "Did you really come in a time warp?"

Lujan's jaw clenched, his hands balled up, and he glared into the fire. "Yes," he gritted.

The firelight playing on the spooky man's face made him look even crazier than before. Nathan watched in horrified fascination. Finally he screwed up his courage for his next question. "Did that Indian come with you? Coconino?"

Lujan bolted to his feet. "What do you know about Coconino?" he roared.

"Nothing," Nathan squeaked, backing hastily toward the door. "Honest, nothing. Just my dad says he might have been in the time warp with you, and that's why his people say he's coming back someday. But he didn't show up with you.''

The fierceness of the spooky man's face grew to manic proportions. Nathan surrendered to his better judgment and fled headlong out of the cabin and over the rise for home.

In his cabin, Derek Lujan stood quivering with rage. Coconino! Coconino. Where have you gone, you devil? We came through the warp together—both of us materializing four feet off the ground and falling— I was dazed, I don't know how many seconds. Minutes, maybe. But I jumped up and you were still lying there.

Did you die? Was that it? Break your neck when we fell? No, no, you can't have died. Not yet. That would be too unfair, me trapped here and you dead. . . . So where are you? Where did you go?

Slowly Lujan turned and stared at the north wall of his cabin, as though he could see beyond it, beyond the intervening hills, past rivers and cliffs and fields of porous black lava, to a primitive village. They mentioned it casually, the Crusoans: the Village of the People. The Northern Village.

Your own found you, didn't they? he thought, his eyes glittering as he pictured the stocky men, the round women, the naked children. They found you and took you with them to their village. Not the one I visited; no, that one is deserted. They have another village, one hidden away somewhere in a canyon. And that's where you are now.

Hide while you can, Coconino, he thought. Hide while you can. Because I'm coming up there after you, and I'll find you, count on it. As soon as I can travel . . . as soon as I'm better . . . when the fog is gone, when it's truly gone and doesn't threaten to come back—

He started to shiver again, a shivering that had nothing to do with the temperature in the room. Indeed, sweat trickled down his face now, and his skin began to glow a faint pink. But slowly, carefully, Lujan brought the shivering under control, forced himself to be calm again, forced himself to be perfectly still.

I'll find you, Coconino, he vowed. Tomorrow, or next week, or next year, it doesn't matter; time is an illusion now. But I'll find you because we have a debt to settle, you and I, and I always collect on my debts.

Lujan picked up the hatchet young Nathan had left behind.
Count on it.

* * *

Coconino lurched awake, gasping, heart pounding like a drum in the Dance of Terror. He could still feel Lujan's hands on his throat, feel them cutting off his breath, choking the life from him while they watched, those eyes, expecting him to do something. And the lizard sat on its rock with its head bobbing anxiously. . . .

I need to escape this place, Coconino thought. I need to escape this Council and their repeated requests that I lead them. How can I lead, I who am so lost? No, I will go south and see what this Southern Village is and what kind of people live in it. For a time, just for a time.

He shivered as the sensation of bones crunching under his feet slipped back to him from his dream. If I could go there, he thought, if there were new sights to distract me, new animals to hunt, perhaps I would stop having the dream. I will see. But there must be a way to find that village without asking the Others, without risk of meeting Lujan.

On the mat beside him he heard Ironwood Blossom stirring restlessly, trying to find a comfortable position. There would be time, anyway, time to seek another solution. He would fulfill his promise to Hummingbird, and then he would go. Then he would escape into the blessed solitude of a journey, a chance to live with no eyes watching him, no one expecting him to be anything but a hunter and a storyteller.

Perhaps the People of the Southern Village had worn a trail to the camp of the Others, as the one he had traveled north on was well worn by generations of traders. That would be good, he thought. I could just follow the trail once I reached the camp of the Others. Then I would never have to meet with Derek Lujan, never have to look again upon the face of my enemy, and the dream would be only a dream and nothing more. Who is to say, after all, that this dream is of what is to come and not what has been? Has Lujan not robbed me already of what life I had?

But as Coconino sank back to his mat, the terror of his dream stole back over him and the mocking face of Derek Lujan would not leave his mind.

CHAPTER EIGHT

The idea had been gnawing at Chelsea for over a week, but she still hesitated to bring it up with Zachery. Let them exhaust every other option for information first; then, maybe in jest, she might bring it up. He wasn't going to like it. Not only was the information she sought illegal, but the method she wanted to use was border-line. No, Zachery was not going to like it at all.

But there were roadblocks everywhere else they turned. She had examined the public personnel files of the six crew members orig-inally thought to have survived the Terran plague, but she couldn't find anything to suggest that even one had been anything less than eminently qualified for his or her berth. She had requests out now for more detailed information on them all, searching for anything that might connect one or more with Oswald Dillon, but her hopes did not run high.

As for the idea of finding out who Dillon might have bought in the TRC, it was preposterous. Any member of the Board of Di-rectors, any major stockholder, any member of the personnel re-view committee could have made strong recommendations regarding the hiring of a particular individual. Had they? Only those involved knew, and they were not likely to talk. With the loss of the *Homeward Bound*, the TRC had plunged into financial ruin and was undergoing dissolution. People who had been asso-ciated with it were understandably skittish, wishing to be anony-mous and, barring that, not to say anything that might establish liability. When Chelsea tried to contact former employees with whom she had been acquainted, not one would respond. Everyone was scared.

"I have to see those unedited logs," Chelsea muttered, clearing screens on her console with a wave of her hand. "I have to know what the TRC knew. I have to—"

"Call coming in, Ms. Winthrop," said the well-modulated voice of her computer. "From your brother, Cincinnati."

Chelsea slumped back in her chair and felt a great relief wash over her. That was what she needed: the bright, sparkling face of Cincinnati to remind her of the joyous side of her life. "Wyatt: put it through," she commanded.

And there he was, grinning at her from a corner of her screen. She punched up the image to fill the whole frame and grinned back at him. "Hi, little sister!" he greeted, blue eyes sparkling with mischief.

"Hi, big brother," she replied, raking long fingers back through her blond tresses. His immaculate appearance always reminded her to straighten herself a bit. "What's new?"

"I got a raise today," he reported. Cincinnati worked at the Center for the Mentally Challenged, where he also lived and studied and found most of his recreation. He was a gardener and proud indeed of his shrubs and flower beds. Whether working with imported vegetation or with the scraggly native stuff, he had a determination and an eye for aesthetics that made his sector of the Center stand out.

His girlfriend, Susan, also worked at the Center, cleaning in one of the residence halls for those who, unlike her and Cin, were not able to maintain independent apartments. Susan seemed always to be cleaning; more than once Chelsea had had to ask her politely not to clean when she came to visit. "But I *like* cleaning," Susan had complained. "It's the one thing I can do really well."

They were both such dear, industrious people, but in the highly technical corporate society of Argo there was little chance they would ever be rewarded on a level equivalent to their effort. A raise, Chelsea thought now. From slave wages to indentured servant pay. "That's great, Cin!" she exclaimed. "I'm so proud of you!"

"I was pretty proud, too," he agreed. "Ask me what else is new."

Chelsea's heart skipped; Cin gave the distinct impression of having canary feathers around his mouth. What was her brother up to now? Please, God, no more murals on his living room wall. The Center hadn't been at all appreciative of Cin's "improvement" of one of their Independent Living apartments. "Okay, Cin," she said with forced joviality. "What else is new?"

His grin stretched from ear to ear. "Susan and I want to get married!"

* * *

"Married? That's great!" Zachery exclaimed when Chelsea told him over lunch. Then he noticed her expression. "Isn't it?"

Chelsea sank slightly in her chair and gave an exasperated growl. "Yes, it's great. Of course it's great," she agreed, and then grimaced. "But it would be a lot greater if Cin weren't such a blasted proud individual. And stubborn."

Zachery grunted. "Too bad he's nothing like you."

Chelsea was tempted to catapult a grikka nut at him with her fork, but she resisted. This was the fashionable Elliot's, after all, and she was a young professional woman. So despite the extreme pleasure that putting one right between Zachery's mocking eyes would have given her, she opted for dignity and decorum and only glared across the table at him.

"Seriously, what's the problem?" Zachery asked. "You are his legal guardian, aren't you? You can sign for him."

"Oh, yes, and Susan's parents are willing to sign for her," she replied. "The problem is, once they're married, they can't live at the Center anymore. They have to rent an apartment in the real world and pay real-world prices. Even with both of them working, that's going to be a stretch. I don't think Cin has any idea how devastating financial stress can be to a relationship. I want him to be married and happy, Zach, but the only way for him to be both is for me to augment their income."

Zachery chewed on a bread stick. "Let me guess. This is where his pride comes in."

Chelsea remembered all too well the day Cincinatti had gone to live at the Center. He was sixteen and scared but determined to learn the skills he needed to be on his own—not because it was his mother's idea, not because his dad thought it would be a good experience, but because *he* wanted to. He wanted to live like other people, to have a job, to date girls, to "be a man," he said. For Cincinnati, with the intellect of a nine-year-old, it had been no easy task, but over the past ten years he had achieved not only physical independence but financial independence as well. "You have to understand, Zach," Chelsea tried to explain, "that with the exception of tuition, which is handled through a trust fund, he's paid his own way for the last four years. It'll be a real blow to him to have to ask me for help now."

"Isn't there some kind of inheritance?" Zach asked.

Chelsea toyed with her salad. It was filled with leafy cabba and dark blue zillanberries, sprinkled with cheramik hearts. Of course there was an inheritance, and then there was Indigo Lawrence and her persistent offer. But the very thought of that option made Chelsea's blood boil. "It's all channeled through the trust fund," she hedged, not wanting to get into the business about Indigo, "and the guidelines for use of those monies are very specific. Living off campus and raising children aren't written in."

Zachery raised an inquiring eyebrow. "Children?"

"Oh, not yet," Chelsea hastened, seeing how he had misunderstood. "At least I don't think so. But it won't be long. I know my brother; that's where the 'stubborn' comes in. Other people get married and have families—Cincinnati will want the same thing. But with children there's not only the issue of cost, there's the issue of an emergency caretaker. He and Susan are both capable of providing routine care, but there are going to be situations in which their judgment is not adequate. They'll have to have someone right there, all the time."

"But surely Cincinnati will understand that," Zachery protested.

"Probably," she admitted. "But what can he do about it? He's going to expect *me* to come up with the answers to these dilemmas, and Zach, I just don't have them."

They fell into a brooding silence then, Zachery sipping his mineral water and Chelsea spearing the cheramik hearts in her salad. It's not fair, she thought. Why do I get stuck with this responsibility? Why did Mom and Dad have to die and leave me with a perpetual child? I love Cincinnati, but I'm not equipped to be his parent—

"Excuse me, miss."

Chelsea was startled to find a waiter hovering at her elbow. "Yes?" she asked, trying to cover her surprise.

He held out a portacom. "A call for you."

Chelsea hesitated; no one knew she was here with Zachery. They had been meeting for lunch nearly every day, but they skipped around town at random, sampling different cuisines and enjoying a variety of atmospheres. Elliot's had been a last-minute choice today, reached after Zachery had picked her up from work. "Who could have tracked me down here?" she wondered aloud, taking the tiny terminal.

"The command name is Alpha," the waiter told her, and vanished discreetly.

"Alpha: identify caller," Chelsea commanded.

"The caller is Morgan Loess," chimed the terminal.

She met Zachery's quizzical look with a shrug. "I don't know him, either. Alpha: request further identification."

In a moment the computer responded. "Mr. Loess has a business proposition he wishes to discuss with you."

"Salesman," Chelsea muttered through clenched teeth. "Alpha: tell Mr. Loess he has one last chance to identify himself before I disconnect."

Again there was a slight pause. Then the computer said, "Mr. Loess represents twenty-seven point five million universals."

With a snap of her hand Chelsea broke the connection. Then she signaled curtly for the waiter to remove the portacom from the table. When he had whisked it away, Zachery leaned back in his chair and studied her for a moment as she sat seething, chewing on the knuckle of her index finger.

"Well, you've a good deal more resolve than I have," he said finally, reaching for another bread stick. "I'm afraid I would have to know who was representing twenty-seven point five million redbacks."

"I know who he is," she snapped. "Or rather, I know who he's with: Indigo Lawrence. She owns a development company that wants to buy my parents' country estate on Juno."

Zachery dipped his bread stick casually into the merron dressing on her mangled salad. "That would be Terra Firma," he recalled. "On the northern continent, isn't it? Not far from Newamerica City."

"Zach, she must be having me followed," Chelsea realized suddenly. "How else could they have known I was here?"

"Well," he drawled, "Mr. Loess might have been lunching here himself when you happened to walk in. Such things do happen, you know."

"Then no doubt he'd have come to our table," she replied. "This company is getting downright obnoxious with its offer."

"If you can call twenty-seven point five million universals obnoxious."

"Zach, it's not for sale!" she snapped. "It's my home, it was my parents' refuge, my father's dream, and these people want to build an industrial complex in the middle of it with a spaceport and a waste disposal plant. If they offered me all of Oswald Dillon's money, I wouldn't sell!"

"I see," he observed dryly.

Just then the waiter appeared with a bottle of wine. From its distinctive label Chelsea recognized it as Icebe from the Junoan province of Icebe Lumoue. "Compliments of Mr. Loess," the waiter said as he put his hand to the stopper.

"Take it back," Chelsea growled.

The waiter was startled. "Pardon?"

"I said take it back!" she flared. "I don't want anything from Mr. Loess."

The waiter looked unhappily from one to the other of them, then retreated with the unopened bottle.

When he had gone, Zachery lifted his glass of mineral water once more. "It's a little outside my area," he said, "but I could file for a restraining order against this company."

Chelsea wilted a little and reached for her own glass of sennaran tea. "Well, maybe you could look into it," she agreed. "They don't seem to take any of my refusals seriously."

Zachery cocked an eyebrow. "Sending back Icebe is pretty serious," he remarked, reaching his fork across to sample one of her zillanberries. "What company is it, anyway?"

"Gator Star Development."

The fork slipped out of Zachery's hand and bounced off the table onto the floor. "Gator Star?" he repeated in astonishment.

Chelsea glanced up warily. "So?"

"Chelsea, they've developed half the light industry on this planet!"

"And I'm not going to give them a foothold on Juno."

He reached across the table and took her hand. "They're not known for their ethical business dealings," he cautioned.

"All the more reason to tell them to go—to refuse their offer," she amended. "Wouldn't you say?"

For a moment his hazel eyes searched her blazing blue ones with concern. Finally he withdrew his hand. "Just be prepared," he said, "for a lot worse than harassing calls and gifts of Icebe."

Chelsea closed her eyes and inhaled deeply. The warm musk of horses and the pungent aroma of hay filled her nostrils, crept into her blood, made her stomach flutter. John. John and horses. John and hay and experimental kisses. Sweet, erotic sensations flooded back to her—

"I told you I could find one," Zachery's voice interrupted her. "There *had* to be a riding stable. The planet was settled by Australians, after all."

With a sigh Chelsea opened her eyes to the plascrete walls of an immaculate riding stable. No creaky wooden walls, no dark, musty interior with chinks where daylight filtered through. And beyond the door no open prairies beckoning her to ride pell-mell through the grass: just carefully marked, artificially forested bridle paths. And no John.

But Zachery was there. She looked up at him, tall and athletic, looking as perfect in his blue jeans and riding tunic as he did in his business attire. I'd settle for Zachery, she thought. Right here, right now, in the hay—what would you say, Mr. Attorney? "Yes," I'll bet. But I won't ask; there's a guide waiting for us and three other riders who've paid their fee, and I'm far too proper to keep them waiting. And there are other reasons, though I can't think of them when you're so close and I'm so swept up in my memories. . . .

"You need a big silver belt buckle," she told him. "One with your name engraved in it. Cowboy Zach."

He laughed. "Well, now you know what to get me for Christmas."

Christmas. She led her saddled horse out of its stall and started for the door. "You'll be gone by Christmas," she said quietly.

"Maybe."

Chelsea looked up sharply as he joined her, leading his chestnut mare. "Keegan, Marshall and Ypsala have made an interesting proposal," he continued, "which I've passed along to my firm."

Her heart pounded as she recognized the name of the law firm that had had Camilla's case before Zachery had stepped in. "A proposal?" There was only one thing they could want from Zachery.

He slid the stable door open, and they stepped out into the dingy morning light. "The Vanderhoff case has called to their attention the lack of experienced criminal attorneys on Argo," he explained. "Here I am, a solid background in criminal law, I've already passed the Argoan bar—so they'd like to, in essence, contract with my firm for my services."

"Contract?" That part surprised her. "Not hire you outright?"

Zachery shook his head as he came around to the mare's left and put his foot to the stirrup. She was a docile old beast, immune to the maneuverings of novice riders; she would walk the trail from habit but was in no rush to get to the end of it. "Oh, they tried that first," Zachery admitted, "but I'm not sure there's enough work here to keep me busy—and challenged—for any great length of time. I don't want to give up my place and my seniority in *my* firm just to be put on waivers in a couple of years." He swung carefully into the saddle, trying not to look like the inexperienced rider he was. The mare waited patiently, with an unmistakable expression of boredom in her stance.

Chelsea mounted quickly and easily, though her horse was a world different from the long-suffering mare. He twisted and shied,

but with a deft tug of the reins Chelsea checked the spirited gelding's impulse to be off. No horse had gotten the best of her since
she was fourteen. "So they pay your firm, and your firm pays
you?" she asked.

"Something like that."

It seemed an unusual arrangement to Chelsea. "Will your firm
go for that?" she asked. Oh, please, let them go for it. I don't
want Zachery to go away, not now, not yet. He's the most interesting aggravation I've had in a long time.

"I don't know." Zachery stroked his horse's neck uneasily, but
the mare continued to ignore him. "I'd like to stay, though, I know
that. For a while, at least."

Chelsea watched his face as they set off along the trail with the
rest of their group. He had slipped off into thought—thinking about
the job offer? she wondered. Not likely. Thinking about me? No,
not with that faraway look in his eyes. Thinking about Camilla,
then. Of course.

Zach had been out to see Camilla twice in the past week, without Chelsea. Monitoring her treatment, he'd said. Sitting with her
in the solarium, coaxing her out for a stroll in the courtyard. Talking to her doctors, wanting her to improve, having to make sure
she didn't.

Chelsea tried to rouse him to another topic. "If you stay, it
would give us more time to work on the *Homeward Bound* case,"
she suggested as they fell behind the rest of the group.

He shrugged, drawn reluctantly from his reverie. "You're doing
all the work, really," he said. Then, "Anything interesting in the
personnel files yet?"

Chelsea snorted. "The most disgustingly squeaky-clean bunch
of people you've ever met," she groused, glad to see she had
distracted him. "Pure as the preachers of Peterpaul."

Zach laughed. "Not likely. Well, keep looking," he replied.
"Someone was corrupt enough to take a commission from Oswald
Dillon."

"Maybe I ought to broaden my search," Chelsea suggested.
"Check the whole crew. Maybe the agent reported himself dead
so that he could disappear on the return voyage."

But Zachery shook his head. "If he'd wanted to disappear along
with the *Homeward Bound*, why bother to report six people saved?
Six people survived because six people was what it would take to
bring the ship back."

"Only it never came back," she pointed out.

"Somebody goofed."

"Maybe." Chelsea hesitated, then broached her topic. Now was the time. "Zach, I need to see the original log reports from the *Homeward Bound*. We need to know exactly what happened, or at least how it was reported, if we're going to get anywhere. I know if I could see my dad's personal log—"

"Chels, I can't get them," he interrupted irritably.

"I know." She took a deep breath. "But Camilla can."

Zachery jumped so that Chelsea's horse shied, though his own plodded on unperturbed. She brought the gelding quickly under control, then forged on. "Zach, she said she had codes, passwords, that got her into TRC's files. That's how she knew about the plague before anyone else. Now, no doubt someone in Dillon's organization canceled all her passwords into *his* systems as soon as she was arrested, but chances are they didn't know about these illegal ones. And without a doubt the TRC didn't know. They may still be valid. All we have to do is get her to tell us what they are and I can use them to look at the files."

"Beside being illegal," he said tightly, "it's virtually impossible. Camilla talks about what she wants to talk about, without regard for what information we request. Believe me, I've tried to get more out of her. It can't be done."

The others were looking back at them from fifty yards ahead. Chelsea smiled and waved. "Don't worry about us," she called, "we're fine. This old mare could find her way in the dark." The guide looked satisfied at that and turned his attention once more to the trail ahead. Chelsea turned back to Zachery.

"What about psychotropic drugs?" she asked.

"Illegal," he responded. "No one on Argo wants their corporate executives subjected to therapy during which they might reveal company secrets. To tell the truth, I wouldn't want Camilla subjected to those drugs, anyway."

"As the daughter of a doctor," she remarked, "I think your concern is unnecessary. But that's beside the point, since we can't get the drugs and couldn't administer them if we had them." She wrapped the reins tighter around her left hand as the gelding tried to outpace the mare and catch up to the other horses. "So what about orphic somnolence?"

Zachery turned startled eyes in her direction. "What, that mystic mumbo jumbo?" he demanded.

"It's not mystic, and it's not mumbo jumbo," she insisted. "It's founded in hypnoscience. My mother used it on Cin when he had to have an injection, because he was terrified of needles. A combination of the proper harmonic tones can bring about a trancelike state—''

''And I suppose you know how to do this?'' he interrupted.

She hesitated. ''Well, as a matter of fact, with Mom away so much while we were in school, it was useful if Cin needed medical attention. . . .'' Her voice trailed off.

Unexpectedly a smile tugged at his lips. ''Orphic somnolence. Is *that* what you've done to me?''

She gave a low, throaty laugh. ''Listen to the beating of the drums and you won't turn down any more job offers on Argo.'' No, no, that wasn't what she'd meant to say; that was giving away too much. Quickly she reverted to her topic. ''No, seriously, Zachery. I've got the orphic recordings at home. I just used them last week when Cin needed a blood test for the marriage license.''

He pondered the idea as they continued along the path, her horse prancing impatiently, his plodding doggedly. She reached across and laid a hand on his arm. ''It won't hurt her, Zach,'' she assured him. ''I'm not sure it will help us get those codes—hell, I'm not even sure she'll go under in her condition. But it's something to try.''

''But using those codes would be illegal,'' he objected.

''Absolutely,'' she agreed. ''And if we used them for material gain or unfair advantage, I'd be dead set against it myself. But Zach, TRC is the one with the unfair advantage. They're withholding information, information about our parents. I don't care how many laws protect them; it's not right. It's just not right that we shouldn't know what happened to our parents.''

That struck an obvious chord. Zachery bit his lip. ''Let me think about it,'' he said finally. Then, ''Is the wedding on, then?''

Chelsea gave a wry smile. ''There was never really any doubt. When my brother gets an idea in his head, it's nearly impossible to dissuade him. But I did sit them both down and explain the financing to them. Showed them in black and white what it was going to cost.''

''And how did Cin respond to that?''

''He got this look in his eye,'' Chelsea grimaced, ''and said, 'I'll find a better job. One that pays more.' ''

Zachery chuckled. ''And will he?''

''I don't know where,'' she sighed. ''But God only knows—when Cincinnati puts his mind to something—''

Suddenly there were hoofbeats pounding frantically on the trail behind them. Chelsea's horse threw up his head and wheeled around, but she pulled him back tight. "Get off the trail!" she shouted at Zachery.

"What?"

"Just go!" She leaned over and gave the mare a vicious slap on the rump. Startled, the mare spurted forward along the path but from long habit would not veer to the side. Exasperated, Chelsea kneed the gelding forward, snatching up Zachery's reigns, and dragged the reluctant horse after her into the woods. A moment later three horses thundered around a bend in the trail and crashed past them. The gelding reared, and Chelsea leaned far forward along his neck to force him back to the ground. Then, with a powerful lunge, he bolted after the galloping horses while Chelsea dragged on the reins, forcing his head down, pulling him to the side, finally bringing him under control.

She was still dancing him in circles on the path when Zachery caught up, trying unsuccessfully to urge his mare to greater speed. "Are you all right?" he asked anxiously.

"Yes," she snapped, "no thanks to those idiots who tore past us. They must have run smack into the rest of our group. We'd better go see what happened."

Indeed, they found the three sweating horses and their riders milling with the more sedate group just up the trail. One of the women who had been with Chelsea's group was on the ground moaning, and another kept saying, "Oh, my goodness. Oh, my goodness." The guide, meanwhile, was berating the newcomers with great fervor.

One of the three, a gawky young man, was protesting. "It was an accident," he insisted. "My horse got away with me. I was hanging on for dear life. These two were just trying to save me."

Another of the newcomers, a trim woman of about fifty with artificially blond hair and fine crow's-feet around her eyes, turned her horse and trotted back to meet Chelsea and Zachery. "Are you two all right?" she asked.

"Fine," Chelsea replied icily. It hadn't seemed to her that any of the horses had been out of control. All three riders had appeared quite purposeful in their mad dash.

"Ms. Winthrop, isn't it?" the woman continued. "What a coincidence! At last we meet." The woman extended a gloved hand. "I'm Indigo Lawrence."

White-hot anger flushed Chelsea's face. A runaway horse, a skittish gelding—she didn't buy it for a minute. "Zachery," she said, "you're my lawyer. I want to press charges against this woman for reckless endangerment."

* * *

"Let it go, Chels," Zachery advised for the fourteenth time. "It won't hold up."

"I'm not letting her get away with this, Zach!" Chelsea fumed, pacing up and down her office. Like all the offices at Inverness Financial, it had a mock window that was an enhanced computer image of what the city outside would look like if only the sun were brighter, the vegetation more lush. Most days Chelsea just turned it off, finding it a tasteless reminder that the colors of this world were so muted that no one cared to look at them.

"Chelsea," Zachery persisted, "you'll spend a lot of money just to have a judge reprimand you for wasting his time. You can't prove intent on Indigo's part."

But Chelsea was in no mood to be reasonable. There was this business with Cin, and now new information about the *Homeward Bound* that had set a radical idea perking in her brain. "I was set up!" Chelsea snapped back. "They gave me the kind of horse lawsuits are made of, and then that woman charged me—she *charged* me with those three horses! She wasn't just trying to catch up; she was trying to spook my mount and cause me bodily harm!"

"Look at it from a judge's perspective," Zach told her. "Why would Ms. Lawrence want to do you harm?"

"Because she wants Terra Firma, and I won't sell it to her!"

"Look at it from an *Argoan* judge's perspective," Zach suggested. "Why shouldn't you sell it to her?"

Chelsea let loose with a string of words picked up in a childhood spent shipside. "That woman is not going to intimidate me!" she swore, kicking at her chair in frustration. The chair rolled back and smacked against a wall.

"Then take a piece of advice," Zachery said earnestly. "Don't aggravate her. Let this thing go."

Chelsea flung herself into the chair, knowing it was not just Indigo Lawrence's treachery that had her going today. "I will if she will," she groused.

"At least give me time to research the case," Zachery pleaded. "Let me find some deterrent, something stronger than a restraining order, something that I can use as a bargaining chip. Let's not fly off the handle with Ms. Lawrence; I guarantee that's not the way to deal with her."

With a deep sigh Chelsea resigned herself. "All right, I won't press charges. But I really don't need her complicating my life right now."

Zachery watched her a moment, read the brooding look on her brow. "Trouble with Cin?" he asked gently.

"Trouble with landlords who don't want to rent to Cin," she replied. "They want me to sign as guarantor; I don't mind, but Cin is determined to get a place that won't require that kind of assistance."

"How did you Winthrops ever get into space?" Zachery wondered. "You strike me as the kind who would insist that if you couldn't grow your own wings, you by-God weren't going to fly."

That roused a chuckle from Chelsea. "Wrong reaction," she told him. "If we couldn't grow our own wings, we were by-God going to invent them."

"Don't tell me you invented the spatial warp," he teased.

"No," she laughed. "We could never stay cooped up in laboratories that long. Hm." Her merriment faded as she slipped into another train of thought. "I wonder if that was Lujan's problem. . . ."

Zachery looked blank. "Who?"

"Derek Lujan," she elucidated. "First officer of the *Homeward Bound.*" Quickly she called up several documents on her office computer. "Look at this: three degrees in warp physics, a bona fide genius. Academic honors and job offers from a dozen research facilities, but he chucked them all to join the Merchant Fleet."

Zachery cocked an eyebrow. "Sounds like you might be right," he agreed. "Sick of theoretical studies, eager for a little adventure."

"But why the Merchant Fleet, then, and not the Service?" she puzzled. "The Service would make much better use of his skills."

Zachery shrugged. "Maybe he didn't care for military life. Maybe he was a pacifist."

"Not likely," Chelsea replied. "I just got some new information in from friends of my parents in the Merchant Fleet. Derek Lujan was the junior officer left in command of the *Aladdin.*"

At that Zachery drew back. He had just passed the bar on Darius IV when the *Aladdin* disaster made headlines throughout the galaxy. Its captain and two senior officers had been mortally injured in an explosion at an asteroidal mining installation. Racing against the clock to get the *Aladdin* away before a chain reaction blew up the entire asteroid, the young junior officer had jettisoned every shred of extra mass: cargo, supplies, equipment—and the three dying officers with their life-support beds.

"So that was Derek Lujan," Zachery murmured. A chill ran up his spine. True, Lujan's bold decision and quick response had saved the *Aladdin* and her twenty-eight remaining crew members from destruction, but the idea of jettisoning live human beings— even dying ones . . .

"Zach." Chelsea leaned across the desk toward him, hands clasped in front of her. From the moment she'd heard that story, a new thought had nagged at her. "Given the man's history, do you think it's possible he abandoned the crew of the *Homeward Bound* without waiting to see if they all died of the plague?"

There was a long pause as Zachery wrestled with the idea. "Now, that's a whole different approach than a saboteur onboard," he said at last.

Still he struggled. Chelsea watched him try to come to grips with the outrageous notion and all its implications. She herself still struggled with it. "Zachery," she said gently. "I know my father's dead. Even if the plague didn't get him, he had Tarusian fever, picked it up while he was in the Service. He had to be on medication for the rest of his life, and there was only a three-month supply on the *Homeward Bound*. I've come to accept that it was, as you said, almost appropriate that he died on the planet he so longed to see. But Zach, my mother die of an illness? Besides the fact that she was too good a doctor to expose herself, she was too plain ornery to die."

Zachery's face darkened, and Chelsea felt him teetering on the brink of rejecting the idea as foolish. "If he left them, Zach, if they were 'dying' and he just left them, I'll give you ten-to-one odds my mother is still alive. And yours, too."

Restless, Zach rose and began to pace. "We'll never get anyone to believe it," he said. "*I* don't believe it. It can't be."

"That would be much easier to determine," she said quietly, "if we could have a look at the reports filed from the *Homeward Bound*."

Zachery stopped, took a deep breath, and blew it out. "Get your orphic recordings," he said. "We'll go visit Camilla."

CHAPTER NINE

Phoenix was seething. She tackled the trail up to the village as though it were an offending obstacle, leaving her hunting companions far behind. Gone was the thrill of the hunt, the staggering beauty of the Red Rock Country, the excitement of chasing down bighorn sheep.

That little weasel Castle Rock was at it again.

This trip had done much to sooth Phoenix's overstretched nerves. Sheltered in Phoenix's house, Karen had not been a scintillating companion these past months. Phoenix had been only too glad to escape with Wounded Iguana and Hair Like a Rope. Flint had come, too, so to the sweet camaraderie with fellow hunters had been added the joy of helping flush the game for Flint's first major kill. But her high spirits had gone up in the smoke of their morning cook fire. As the four hunters roasted strips of fresh liver for breakfast, they gossiped about the women Flint should court now that he had proven himself a competent provider.

Inevitably Castle Rock's name came up. Phoenix cringed, for the little minx had once set her cap for Coconino, and when she met with a rebuff, she retaliated by embarrassing him in front of his friends, by setting him up for one of Phoenix's famous tongue-lashings. When she realized what had happened, Phoenix set out to rectify the situation, but her opinion of Castle Rock never rose very high. None of the coy, deceitful tricks she had seen the girl use since then had improved that opinion.

But although Castle Rock was older than Flint by two years, she was still considered a prize catch. Not only was she beautiful, her father had been one of the Men-on-the-Mountain, those teachers who had come to the People regularly in their old village to bring them new seeds or show them better ways of farming and making tools. Plus, Castle Rock had been the Chosen Companion of another such Teacher, perhaps the last of the Men-on-the-Mountain the People would ever know. And best of all, Castle Rock was pregnant by that Teacher.

"Well," drawled Hair Like a Rope, "at least she is pregnant. That much we know."

Indeed, Castle Rock was very pregnant. She had announced her pregnancy in September, which should have made her due only weeks after Nina, and Nina's delivery was imminent. Phoenix had run some calculations in her head and had her own suspicion about Castle Rock's due date, but the implication in Hair Like a Rope's remark had nothing to do with that. It had to do with a certain rumor Phoenix had heard whispered from time to time. Her eyes sparked dangerously.

Flint noticed none of that, crouched by the fire with the older hunters and trying not to shiver in the cool April morning. He was only beginning to have an interest in the maidens of the village, but he had a great deal of interest in gossip. "What do you mean?" he asked Hair Like a Rope.

Hair Like a Rope and Wounded Iguana exchanged sly glances. "The Teacher spent many evenings in the fields last summer," Wounded Iguana explained, "and Castle Rock was not often seen there."

Flint was naive but not totally ignorant. "She did not have to be there *often*," he pointed out.

Good boy, Phoenix thought, but she did not relax. She wondered if anyone would dare voice the rumor in her hearing—or Flint's.

"And we all know," Hair Like a Rope continued, "that it was not the Teacher who objected to her being a Chosen Companion for the Other when he visited our village."

At that Phoenix jerked to her feet, fists clenched. "The objection was made," she snarled, "because Castle Rock was already with child! It is not the Way of the People for a woman who is already with child to be a Chosen Companion."

They backed off then, seeing how angry she was. "Of course, Witch Woman," Hair Like a Rope demurred. "It was a legitimate objection and wisely made. If Coconino had not made it, no doubt someone else would have."

"If anyone else had known at the time," Wounded Iguana added pointedly, "that she was with child."

Phoenix turned burning eyes on the young man, who feigned great innocence with his open expression, popping a piece of liver into his mouth. The implication, of course, was that Castle Rock had had reason to tell Coconino before she told anyone else. Would a woman tell another man before she told the child's father?

It made Phoenix burn. But what to do? Rail at him? Tell him Coconino would never walk outside the Way of the People? That he would never sleep with a conniving little weasel like Castle Rock? Or simply threaten to dislodge Wounded Iguana's teeth from his jaw if he ever implied such a liaison again?

With great difficulty Phoenix chose not to do any of those things. Instead she forced herself to relax, to unclench her fists and her jaw, to sneer a benign sneer at them all. "Certainly *you* would not know," she taunted, knowing Wounded Iguana himself had brought gifts to Castle Rock's door, placing himself in competition for her hand. "Just because a woman fancies one man more than another doesn't mean she forgets her duty as a Chosen Companion." She gave a rather grim rendition of a wry smile. "Perhaps it only means she has good taste."

At that Hair Like a Rope hooted and poked Wounded Iguana, conceding the match to the Witch Woman. But there was an underlying tension to their eagerness as they packed up for the trip home.

Phoenix set a murderous pace, defying the younger men to keep up with her. In the end it was Flint they began to leave behind, so she slowed down and trudged doggedly through rolling hills that were bright with the morning sun and the myriad cactus flowers. Red and white, primrose and mauve, the delicate blossoms graced the land with their ephemeral beauty, reminding the hunters that winter had gone and the heat of summer would soon be upon them.

They took turns hauling the travois laden with meat, and Flint chattered on about wanting one of the horns from the ram he had killed to make a cup. But a dark mood had settled over Phoenix; she brooded on the rumor and wondered how many people actually believed that Coconino had fathered a child on Castle Rock.

How had the rumor started? That was not hard to guess. Castle Rock was a proud and vain creature, and Coconino's rebuff had piqued her. She was still striking back at him, claiming undue honor for herself, making people think he had cared for her. He had not! He had found her irksome and childish and—

And now, as Phoenix gained the pathway that encircled the village, she was furious with the conniving little wretch. She forestalled a visit to Nina's house, although she had been fidgety the whole trip wondering if Nina would deliver while she was gone. Nina had assured her this would not happen, and since it was convenient to rely on that prediction, Phoenix did so. As the trail forked, she turned her steps to the left instead of the right, which would have led her to Nina's house. She had another destination in mind.

"Castle Rock," Phoenix called out sharply as she saw her quarry kneeling in a common area near her house, scraping a hide with her mother and some other women.

Castle Rock looked up sharply at first, then modified her expression to a beneficent smile, though her eyes remained cold. "She Who Saves," the girl greeted politely. "The People rejoice that you have returned safely from your hunting trip."

But not you, Phoenix thought. You'd just as soon I'd died out there among the buttes; then there would be no one to contradict your malicious rumors. But I am still here, my pretty little wench, and I will not let you besmirch Coconino's name.

"How goes it with your child?" Phoenix asked in a tone that fairly reeked of sarcasm.

Castle Rock only smiled proudly and patted her belly. "He is very active," she replied. "I think he wants to come out soon."

He ought to, Phoenix thought, if you were truly pregnant when you told Coconino you were. But that was a lie, wasn't it, part of one of your schemes? One that backfired when he objected to your being Chosen by Derek Lujan. So you had to fix things up after the fact or look foolish in front of the entire village.

"A pity," Phoenix continued, "that his father is not here to see him born."

"Yes, a great pity," Castle Rock agreed coyly. "But that is often the way with Men-on-the-Mountain."

"Ah! Then the Teacher is truly the father of your child," Phoenix exclaimed.

The teenager's smile became smug now, and a wicked gleam lit her eye. "Of course the Teacher is its father," she said with an innocence in her voice that did not match her face. "Who has said otherwise?"

Phoenix flashed a cold smile. "Some foolish person," she replied. "Some foolish person who would give you more honor than you deserve."

In a flash, Castle Rock's smile faded and her eyes darkened.

"Some foolish person," Phoenix continued, "who would have us believe that Coconino left three children to the People and not two. But you and I know better, don't we? We know that despite your coy flirtation, Coconino rejected you. We know that in truth, Coconino couldn't stand you—that he avoided you, that he rebuked you and refused to consider you for a wife. We know that he sought his comfort with Nina in the Village of the Ancients, according to the custom of the People, and thus he conferred upon her an honor that you will never have: to be the mother of his child.''

Castle Rock's fists worked spasmodically in the face of this tirade. ''I never said,'' she gritted harshly, ''that he fathered my child.''

''Oh, no, you never said it,'' Phoenix agreed, ''but you let people think it. You never bothered to correct anyone, except with a smile and a sly wink. Well, I will give them something else to think, Castle Rock. If you were truly pregnant on the night the Other came to our village, then you should deliver your child before this moon wanes. But I don't think you were pregnant then. Because I saw you go to him that night, Castle Rock; I saw you go to Derek Lujan in his Machine, after his Choosing of you was refused, and I think that he is the father of your child. Not Coconino, not the Teacher—Derek Lujan. The Other.''

There was deathly silence. The other women working in the common area shifted uneasily, but Phoenix stood towering over the fifteen-year-old, waiting for her response. There was shock on that young, round face, shock that drained slowly away as Castle Rock's devious mind began to work. Phoenix could almost see it latching on to an idea with deadly intent. Finally Castle Rock smiled up at her persecutor, a smile of pure hatred in an otherwise beautiful face.

''I may have been hasty in proclaiming my joy,'' she told Phoenix evenly, ''but I was so eager to have the Teacher's child. And as it turns out, I was right; I am pregnant. But I assure you, Witch Woman—'' There was particular venom in that name. ''—I assure you, the Teacher is the father of my child. And who will ever know but me?''

Up and down the pathway people had poked their heads out of their houses, listening. Phoenix knew that she had gained nothing from the sly young woman except her undying hatred. The rumors would not stop; if anything, she had fueled them with her vindictive attack. People would still speculate on the parentage of Castle Rock's child; only now Derek Lujan would figure in their speculation.

''Witch Woman.''

Phoenix spun around to find Corn Hair standing on the path beside her. Corn Hair was unusual among the People; she was slender as a willow, with brown eyes and dusty blond hair that draped over one shoulder, long and unbraided. She carried her infant daughter in a sling against her breast, and two small boys trailed behind her.

"I heard your voice," Corn Hair continued in the same gentle, even tone with which she had accosted Phoenix. "I knew you would want to know. Nina has gone into labor."

Phoenix started, jerked from her blazing hostility to a concern for Coconino's true child. But she was not so taken aback that she did not recognize what Corn Hair had done. The gentle woman had interceded in the quarrel, separating the combatants before the battle became even uglier. Her soft brown eyes pleaded with Phoenix now: Come away. Let it go. There are more important things afoot.

Drawing a sharp breath, Phoenix left Castle Rock behind and started around the path toward Nina's house. Corn Hair followed more sedately, one son trailing her while the other ran off to greet the other returning hunters.

There was a knot of people outside Nina's door when Phoenix arrived. They were all women and young girls, for in the time-honored fashion all the strong, potent, brave men of the community had vacated the area. Occasionally one might find a husband staying with his wife through labor, but he would have to be a strong-minded husband indeed to fend off the midwives' snide remarks and constant attempts to shoo him out from underfoot.

Falling Star had complained of the practice. "It is my child," he insisted, "and no midwife is going to tell me I cannot stay and witness the miracle of new life ushering forth from the womb!"

The father of two, Juan had laughed. "You will be so rattle-brained and panic-stricken," he promised, "that when a midwife says 'boo,' you will shed your skin like a snake and slither away!"

Falling Star had fulfilled neither his own prophecy nor Juan's. On a distant riverbank his expectations had been obliterated by the fear and anger of the Others. Two days after his death his infant daughter was born far too early and expired within minutes. Falling Star's seed had vanished from the People.

But Coconino's will not, Phoenix vowed as she passed uncontested by the waiting women to Nina's door. There is this child, and there is Karen's, and both will live. Coconino's seed will go on.

Inside the adobe house it was still cool, and Nina lay covered with a blanket, a good absorbent cotton blanket, the kind that could not be replaced here where cotton would not grow. Her mother knelt at her head, ready to raise the young woman into the proper position for delivery when the time came. Branching River sat nearby, measuring time by tapping lightly on a drum.

As Phoenix entered, Nina began to puff and blow with the onset of a contraction, and Branching River increased the volume of her drumming. She marked the peak of the contraction with a sharp bang, then began to decrescendo, leading the laboring woman back into a more relaxed attitude. As her eyes adjusted to the dimness, Phoenix could see the sweat standing out on Nina's face, her hair clinging to her cheeks in damp strands.

Nina looked up then and saw the tall woman squatting in the doorway. "Witch Woman!" she panted. "Ah, it is time, then. I thought it must be soon." Then she lapsed back into a steady pattern of breathing, focusing her concentration on the drumbeats.

One or two other women pushed in past Phoenix, bringing water for Branching River and honey for Nina. Phoenix watched them at their ministrations, feeling as much an outsider as a husband might have felt. After a moment she crawled back outside and pushed past the waiters to squat on the path a few yards away.

Corn Hair was just arriving, with three-year-old Dreams of Hawks dancing to the drumbeats on the trail behind her. Phoenix could not help smiling at the little fellow, who was caught in the rhythm of the drum while being oblivious to its meaning.

"It won't be long now," Corn Hair told Phoenix, sitting beside her on the path with her feet extending over the edge, heels resting on the steep slope below. "The pains are very close together; soon Coconino's son will raise his voice to the skies."

There was sadness in Corn Hair's voice; it pricked Phoenix. "And perhaps the Mother Earth will hear it and take pity," she said, "and send Coconino back to us quickly."

"Yes, quickly," Corn Hair murmured.

"Perhaps he will be here for the birth of his other child," Phoenix suggested pointedly.

"Perhaps."

Corn Hair's quiet acknowledgment further irritated the Witch Woman. Did she really believe it, this unprotesting woman with a babe in her arms? Did it even really *matter* to her if Coconino returned? He gave everything for the People, Phoenix thought, and he deserves to be here and accept your accolades. He deserves to see his children. He deserves to live out his life in peace and prosperity with them—and with me.

"Coconino and I were good friends," Corn Hair said softly. Phoenix was startled; she hadn't been aware of any such relationship. "Growing up," Corn Hair clarified quickly; any friendship between a young man and a married woman would have been misunderstood. "Our wickiups were right across from each other, and our mothers were good friends. He would tease me about the color of my hair and that I must have had a Witch Woman for an ancestor. He was—" She hesitated. "He was special. I miss him."

Phoenix's throat constricted unexpectedly. "I miss him, too."

"Witch Woman, you are very jealous of his reputation, and I am glad of that," Corn Hair continued. "Many things can be said of a man when he is not there to contradict them. But—" She took a sharp breath. "Do not paint him a god, Witch Woman. From time to time he did walk outside the Way of the People."

Phoenix stiffened, staring at her companion.

"Not in any great way," Corn Hair hastened, "but as a child or a young man here and there slips from the path—he could err, Witch Woman, you know that he could."

"Are you saying," Phoenix asked harshly, "that he could have fathered Castle Rock's child?"

"Oh, no, Witch Woman!" Corn Hair cried. "I know that he detested her and that she is a sly and devious girl. But Witch Woman, when you defend him . . . you make it sound as though he could do no wrong. He could. He did. Now and again."

"He was the finest of the People," Phoenix hissed. "There has not been, nor will there be again, a man of his caliber among us. Until he returns."

"And on that day we will rejoice," Corn Hair agreed. "But let us rejoice to see a man, not a god."

Suddenly the drumming stopped. There was a moment of hushed anticipation, with only the wind breathing through the barberry. Then came the healthy wail of a newborn babe protesting loudly its abrupt change in station. Phoenix leapt to her feet and headed toward the door.

Before she could enter, another sound split the air, and she stopped short. It was a loud trumpeting, the like of which the People had not heard in nearly a year. "Tala!" Phoenix gasped, and whirled to face the far canyon wall.

There on its rim, silhouetted against foliage green with the spring rains, stood the mighty unicorn. He posed majestically with one forefoot raised, his proud head cocked toward the village. But he stood alone; no proud warrior sat astride to fly across the canyon and return to his People.

The child cried again. Again Tala trumpeted a loud response, like a cry of victory. *I hear you, child of Coconino,* he seemed to say. *And I salute you. Bear your father's seed nobly.* Then Tala snapped his huge leathern wings open, thundered across the hill toward the north, and flung himself into the sky.

Phoenix returned to her own house to find Karen huddled close to the cook fire. "Nina just had her baby," she informed the young woman. "A boy. She named him Nakha-a. It means something like 'harmony' or 'accord' or something. It seems like a good name." She hesitated. "I guess it's *'moh-ohnak.'* " Phoenix had never fully understood that concept of rightness that the People took for granted.

Karen did not respond. Phoenix looked closer and saw that the woman was trembling, her face pale and anxious in the firelight. "What is it?" Phoenix asked in consternation. "What's wrong?"

"It started this morning," Karen whispered. "The drums. They've been beating out her contractions since early this morning."

Phoenix drew back, puzzled. "You can't hear the drum from here," she said.

But Karen shook her head. "I was there. I wanted to know— what to expect." She gathered a fur closer around her shoulders, though on this side of the island butte the sun beat fiercely on the stone houses and its heat radiated in through the open door. "She was in pain. She never made a sound, but I could see it on her face. Each contraction . . ."

Phoenix moved to the trembling woman's side and put an arm gently around her shoulders. "I'm sorry I wasn't here," she apologized, frightened by Karen's shivering, uncertain how to deal with her. "I didn't stop to think you might—"

"Like a cramp," Karen went on. "Each one was like a cramp. But they got worse. I could see it."

"Well, it's all over now," Phoenix soothed.

"By noon I couldn't stand it," Karen told her. "I had to leave, I couldn't— God, what am I going to do?" Her voice rose to a wail.

"It's all right, it's all right," Phoenix hastened, hugging her awkwardly, trying to calm her down. "It's all over. Nina's—"

"They said she'd have an easy time of it, that she was a big girl, good hips—what's going to happen to *me*?" Karen asked hysterically. "Dr. Winthrop told me I might have a hard time because I'm so small. Harder than that? Is it going to be even harder than that?"

"Karen!" Phoenix snapped, giving the frightened woman a shake to get her attention. Her patience was gone, her nerves frazzled. "Listen to me! It's over. Nina's fine. And she has a baby now. A fine, healthy baby. So will you. Do you hear me?" Karen looked dazed, but her eyes were fixed on Phoenix's face. "So will you."

Suddenly Karen dissolved into weeping.

Panic welled up in Phoenix. She had no idea how to calm this hysterical woman. If only there were someone else who spoke Karen's language, someone else who could reason with her.

"Take me back," Karen said suddenly, seizing Phoenix's arm. "Take me back to Camp Crusoe. You promised you would any time I wanted to go. You promised. Take me back."

Phoenix's heart crashed against her ribs. She would not give up Coconino's child! She would not. "Karen," she stammered, and then slowly her wits returned. "Karen, you're eight, almost nine months pregnant. You can't make a trip like that now."

"You promised!" Karen begged.

"And I will take you back," Phoenix assured her. "But after the baby is born."

"Now!" Karen insisted. "Now, before it starts! Take me back where they have drugs for pain, where they can put me under."

"They won't do that," Phoenix told her, remembering the policy on the Mountain and guessing it might be the same at Camp Crusoe. "You have to be awake to help in labor. It's better for the child."

"But not for me!" Karen screamed. "It's not better for me!"

Her grip on Phoenix's arm was painful; Phoenix tried to pry her fingers loose. "Listen, Karen, listen to me. I can't take you back now. What if you went into labor on the trip? It's bound to happen if you exert yourself that way. Then what? No doctor, no midwives, just me and you, and neither of us has any idea what to do. You could die, Karen. The baby could die there on the trail. It's too late to start back. You have to wait till after you deliver."

Frantically Karen snatched at the knife she had carried in her belt all these months, but Phoenix was quicker, wresting the weapon away from the pregnant woman and tossing it far into the corner of the house. She heard the blade chip as it hit and winced inwardly, knowing how difficult it would be to reshape it, but for now she only wanted it out of reach of the desperate woman.

"And is that kind of pain any better?" she demanded, struggling to keep Karen's arms pinned at her side.

"At least it's quick," Karen sobbed.

"Is it?" Phoenix pursued. "Do you really know that? Have you ever watched anyone bleed to death?"

Karen's struggling diminished.

"The midwives have some medicines," Phoenix told her, "that they use for difficult labors. Nina didn't need them, but you can have them. I'll tell them to give you medicine, do you understand? I'll tell them to give you something."

Slowly Karen relaxed. After a moment she nodded weakly.

The crisis past, Phoenix studied her charge in the dim light. Outside the sun was setting; it cast its last beams through the open door and onto her face. Karen looked exhausted, an exhaustion that reached down into her bones. It wasn't just the baby, Phoenix knew. It was Lujan, too. And Coconino. And all the others before them, all the men who had used her and left her; they had worn her out almost beyond salvation. Almost.

Phoenix was moved. There must be something she could do to reassure the young woman, to give her some sense of self-worth, some reason to go on. "Come with me," Phoenix urged suddenly, pulling Karen to her feet and toward the door.

Karen went along limply, uncaringly, as she had gone along when Phoenix had led her back to the village from the camp of the Others. She had never complained, never questioned her decision, never shown any enthusiasm for the journey or what lay at its end. Her peace, it seemed, was in her passivity: there could be no conflict in her life if she refused to struggle.

It took only a few minutes to reach Nina's door, where the crowd of well-wishers had faded away. Phoenix pushed her way in without awaiting an invitation, dragging Karen along by the hand.

Inside only four people remained. Nina's mother stirred a pot of soup over the cook fire, a big-boned woman like her daughter. Her sister, Nina's aunt, was sorting through a basket of sotol buds, choosing the best-looking ones to steam for the evening meal. Nina herself was propped up against the low bench that was built into the room at the back, her hair freshly brushed, her infant son cradled in her arms. Seated nearby, gazing at the newborn, was Castle Rock.

Phoenix glared at the unwelcome guest. Looking up, Castle Rock returned the glare through narrowed eyes. But Nina, her face tired but glowing, was delighted to see them. "Kah-ren!" she greeted. "Come, see my son! Soon there will be a child in your arms as well."

Phoenix translated, but Karen only slumped to her knees, unmoving.

Nina looked at Phoenix in alarm. "Karen is frightened, Nina," the Witch Woman explained with an uneasy glance at Castle Rock. Did the scheming young woman have to witness this? "She is frightened about the labor. She is afraid of the pain."

"Oh, don't be, dear one!" Nina exclaimed. "It is not so bad. Once I ate wild onions that gave me a worse bellyache than this. And when I was done, I had nothing to show for it. See what I have today!" And she held out her son to Karen.

But Karen could do no more than raise her eyes to look at the securely wrapped bundle. Phoenix's translation of the speech did not prod her further.

"Nina is a prophetess," Phoenix reminded her. "If she says that soon there will be a child in your arms, then there will be. It means you're going to be fine and so is the child."

There was such compassion in Nina's eyes that Phoenix was ashamed her own response had been less charitable. Nina spoke slowly, knowing that Karen had picked up some of the language in the past two months. "You will have a daughter, Kah-ren. A beautiful daughter. And she will be a delight to the People and an honor to her father, Coconino." She leaned forward and stroked Karen's cheek lovingly as Phoenix translated. "What joy she will bring to those who love her! And what heartache. But that is the way of children, dear one. How dull life would be if we did not care enough for our hearts to ache once in a while!"

Slowly Karen lifted her hand and touched the bundled infant in Nina's arms with one finger.

"They will be great friends," Nina assured her, "your child and mine. Brother and sister, always. His wisdom will guide her, and her fire will spark their deeds."

Suddenly Nina's face darkened. "What is it?" Phoenix demanded.

But Nina shook her head. "I don't know. For a moment there was a thought, but it has gone, slipped away from me." Her face grew wistful. "It was a sad thought. But then, that is the way of children."

Now Castle Rock crowded in, never one to be left on the sidelines for long. "Tell me about my child," she begged prettily.

Before Nina could respond, Phoenix snorted contemptuously. "The get of that snake Derek Lujan?" she retorted. "Pray Mother Earth it dies before it causes us more harm."

"Witch Woman!" Nina hissed. Her eyes flashed, and her voice was like a slap. Phoenix drew back, smarting with her own guilt as much as from the uncharacteristic reprimand. "Do not even *think* such evil thoughts!"

And suddenly Phoenix was back in another stone house, on a distant cliff, with rain drizzling down outside. Her cheek stung from the physical blow Coconino had struck her, one justly deserved for another remark as caustic and hateful as this.

Karen stirred, and Phoenix knew that she had recognized Lujan's name. She hoped Karen had not understood any of the rest. "It's nothing," she whispered in Karen's language. "I was being stupid, that's all."

Hearing the regret in the Witch Woman's voice, Nina turned to Castle Rock and touched her belly gently. "It is only a child," she assured the pretty girl. "Its path is not yet chosen."

Castle Rock smiled weakly, blinking back genuine tears. "And it is *my* child," she added. "Surely I will have something to do with the path it chooses."

Surely you will, Phoenix thought. And that scares me as much as the idea that it's Lujan's child.

As though she had heard her thoughts, Castle Rock turned on Phoenix a look of utter contempt. We are not finished, Witch Woman, it seemed to say. I will not soon forget all that you have done to me this day.

CHAPTER TEN

Lujan watched as Tav stopped her tractor and climbed down from its seat. She was soaked with sweat, and as she lifted her hat and drew one arm across her brow, it left a trail of mud. She was tall, rangy, not the kind of woman he had ever found attractive, but a full two years after his arrival in this century, Derek was no longer fussy. Besides, she had something he wanted. Something he wanted very much.

Rising from the pile of stones where he had been lounging, he walked silently across the furrowed soil to stand behind her. The light color of his clothing had blended in with the gray and buff of the rocks, and he was sure she had not seen him, lying half-behind the pile as he had been. There was much to be learned from the native lizards. Lujan spent long hours studying them.

Tav stood on the shady side of her machine, of course, for even in March the sun beat down fiercely. This position was to Lujan's advantage as he came up behind her: his shadow did not give him away. She was reaching for her water bottle on the tractor when he spoke.

"Good morning, Tavaria."

Tav nearly jumped out of her skin, and Lujan smiled. She whirled around with fear written on her face, fear that the sight of him did not relieve. Good. Very good. He smiled at her.

"What do you want?" she demanded, her voice shaking slightly. Her eyes, he noticed, were looking past him and to the right and left, looking to see if anyone else was nearby, anyone who could rescue her. He controlled his urge to laugh and kept smiling at her, eyes fixed on her face.

"Why, I only wanted to see you," he told her. "Just to look at you." And as if to prove his point, he looked at her. He just stood there and looked at her.

For a moment Tav stood trembling; then she balled her hands into tight fists and tensed her body—for fight or flight? he wondered. "Go away," she told him harshly. "I have work to do." Then, with just the slightest hesitation, she turned her back on him and climbed up onto the tractor seat.

Lujan was mildly disappointed. She didn't have it with her, then. It must be hidden in her cabin somewhere.

"I made you a present," he called up to her. "A crystal-powered tiller for your garden. From some scrap material and the power unit on an old hand transmitter." Not as romantic as flowers, but to the Crusoans as amazing as magic. "I'll come to your house tonight."

"Don't do me any favors," she snapped, kicking the tractor into gear. Lujan stepped back as she trundled away on the clumsy machine, plow in tow, down the long, dusty length of the field. He kept watching her until she was nearly at the far end. Finally, still smiling, he turned and headed back toward the bridge.

It was a good five miles back to Camp Crusoe, and Lujan added that to his mental tally. It would make fifteen miles so far today; he intended to accumulate twenty-five by nightfall. By his best estimates, it was at least fifty miles to the Northern Village of the People, although no one could say for sure because no one knew exactly where it was. But he would find it. He would find it.

Striding swiftly along the dirt track, Lujan was blind to the splendor of spring all around him: a riot of wildflowers in yellow and orange, purple and blue; the ice green of new grass; the swelling buds on cacti and trees. Soon the paloverde trees would burst into bloom, becoming great balls of yellow on green trunks. From a nearby orchard the heady, sweet perfume of orange blossoms drifted on the breeze.

But Lujan was immune to it, fixed only on his purpose, his one purpose. Since the fog had lifted from his mind over a year ago, only one thing had consumed him: finding Coconino.

It had been too simple, really. Primitive traders from the Northern Village had been taciturn, as was their nature, but not suspicious. "Did you find a stranger north of here last time you came?" he'd asked.

"A stranger? No," they had replied. "We only found Coconino."

At that news Lujan had rushed to commandeer a landcrawler for the trip north, but the landcrawlers had all been disassembled and converted into other machines: tractors, harvesters, cargo vans.

He tried to take one of those, but they stopped him, those ignorant, thick-headed locals; they *stopped* him—

Easy, Derek, he cautioned himself. Easy. You don't want the fog to come back.

It had when he'd lost his temper over being denied a vehicle to carry out his mission of retribution. It had been weeks before it had begun to clear again, but he had learned his lesson. He had to keep calm. He had to keep the fog at bay. And he had to walk north.

No one in Camp Crusoe, however, knew the way. So he waited patiently until the following fall, when traders came again from the Northern Village. He asked about their route; they were evasive. He made several guesses and watched their faces; that worked better. After several conversations he discerned that he must follow the river north, through the Red Rock Country, then cut across to the east, past some lakes, and pick up another river there.

Unaccustomed to finding his way anywhere without grids and maps to guide him, Lujan turned his attention to obtaining an accurately scaled overview of the region he had to traverse. He had amazed the Crusoans by regenerating one of their computers, powered by crystals from the old warp terminal. With it he accessed maps the original crew had made of the vicinity and found what he thought to be the most likely location of the Northern Village. He would have to pass through rugged country to get there, and he might have to search a number of canyons and ravines, but he was sure he could find it—if he was properly prepared.

This past winter he had spent preparing. He studied wilderness survival from books, then turned to the locals for information specific to the area. He printed detailed maps from the computer, charted water sources along his route, calculated the size of the water container he would have to carry. He estimated the weight of the items he would need to pack, then filled a knapsack with an equivalent weight and began to walk. He walked around the camp, through the fields, into the wooded hills. He redesigned the knapsack. He refined his list of supplies.

And he worked on his Collection.

Lujan smiled now, striding through the fields toward the river and feeling light as air without his pack. He had worked on his Collection all winter long, and it was awesome. There were six knives of various sizes, all honed to razor sharpness. There was a cudgel with steel spikes and a bola made of two rounded stones and a sturdy length of rope. An old piece of rotor had been coaxed into the shape of a spear point and was affixed to a sturdy pole of pine. He had even begun work on a bow and arrows, although he did not have the primitives' skill with such a complex creation and was tempted to put it aside.

But he had things no primitive could have and even the Crusoans did not dream of. A few adjustments to a sonic wrench turned it into a painful instrument of torture, lethal at its highest setting. A surgical laser, collecting dust since its power pack expired, was pilfered and recalibrated to a wider field while retaining its pin-point accuracy. And the camp's garbage dump, just west of the settlement, gave up the cracked body of the original probe with its tiny augers and pinchers, most of which had now been made to drill and slice at Lujan's behest.

But what he wanted, what he sought discreetly and unflaggingly, was his disrupter, his "T-zer," as they were known in the fleet. He'd been wearing it when he tussled with Coconino in the shuttle; he was sure he'd been wearing it when he landed in the desert north of the camp. Then where was it now? One of the locals must have taken it from him. But who?

Since he had no recollection of being found by the Crusoans, he had to rely on their version of the story. According to Janine Thornton, Casey had been there—and if Casey, then most likely Franz Johnson; and if Johnson, perhaps his brother; and the four of them would have gone straight to Mo Ryan, and Mo to Tav. But which one had recognized the T-shaped piece of plastic as a weapon? Which one had disarmed him, and what had happened to the T-zer then?

Mo was the one who had tipped him off to its whereabouts. "Don't worry about Tav," Lujan had heard him assuring Franz Johnson. "If Lujan bothers her, she'll give him a dose of his own technology." That could mean several things, of course, but there was a look that passed between them; he was sure they meant the T-zer.

Well, if it truly was in Tav's possession, tonight he would have it. She knew he was coming; she was sure to have it close at hand. With the right pressure, she would bring it out of hiding. Then he would have it. And perhaps, just for spite, he would have the spunky Ms. Ryan as well.

"Oh, Coconino, is she not the most beautiful baby you have ever seen?" Hummingbird cried.

Coconino cradled the squalling infant in his large hands, marveling at the lightness of it, at the intricacy of tiny fingers and toes that twitched and waved in unaccustomed freedom. Beside him the midwife waited impatiently to rub the child clean, but she did not dare intrude on the great Coconino any more than she had dared do more than suggest that he get out of the way and leave birthing to women.

"Ah, she is a beauty like her mother," Coconino breathed, studying each feature, each limb, to make sure all was as it should be. "She is indeed the most beautiful—*girl* child—I have ever seen." The midwife made another reaching gesture toward the babe, and this time Coconino surrendered her reluctantly. Then he crawled the few paces to kneel by Hummingbird's head, gently caressing her sweating cheek. "You worked so hard, my little Hummingbird. I am so proud of you!"

"Rest now," said Night Comes Quickly, sponging her daughter's neck and face. "You have done well, little one."

"Oh, please let me hold her again!" Hummingbird begged, reaching toward her baby.

"In a moment," the midwife snapped, undone by so many exceptions to routine. "I must clean the child now and wrap it before it catches the coughing sickness."

Hummingbird recoiled, but Coconino hugged her gently. "Do not worry," he soothed. "Nothing will happen to your baby. Nothing will happen to our daughter."

The midwife threw him an apprehensive look, as though wondering whether he really had the power to guarantee that. It didn't matter; Hummingbird believed he did. "Oh, Coconino," she sighed happily. "I am the luckiest girl in the whole village. No, in the whole world."

Then she glanced over at the corner, where her sister sat nursing little Juan. "Well, one of the two luckiest," she amended. Ironwood Blossom grinned, a wide white splash in her dark face.

"Excuse me, Son-in-Law," ventured Night Comes Quickly. She was trying to finish bathing Hummingbird, and Coconino was in her way. He grinned at the older woman, an unrestrained, almost foolish sort of grin. Then he rolled to his feet.

"I need to stretch my legs," he announced, walking crouched over through the low-ceilinged house to the door. "And to tell all the world that my daughter is born!"

Hummingbird watched him go out, but as soon as the chorus of congratulations outside faded and she knew he was out of earshot, she turned urgently to her sister. "Ironwood Blossom! You know what this means."

The older girl's grin faded as she rocked her suckling babe. "He is a happy father, Hummingbird,'' she said. ''Perhaps he will stay.''

''You know that he won't,'' Hummingbird accused. ''He will leave now on his journey to the south.''

''He is Coconino,'' her sister replied petulantly. ''He will do what he will do.''

''But Ironwood Blossom, what if he doesn't come back?''

Ironwood Blossom looked up at her sister's distraught face. Dear little Hummingbird, always the worrier. As though any man would leave her. Ironwood Blossom sighed deeply. ''What if it is a hard winter?'' she asked gently, rhetorically. ''What if the rains do not fall and there is a bad harvest? There is nothing we can do, little one.''

''Rest, little mother,'' Night Comes Quickly admonished her daughter. ''This is not a time to speak of such things.''

''But how can I rest,'' the girl protested, ''knowing he may be gone when I awake and I may never see him again?''

''Coconino is not a man to abandon his children,'' her sister asserted. But her words lacked conviction.

''Ironwood Blossom,'' Hummingbird said. ''You must go with him.''

Ironwood Blossom looked up in amazement. ''What?''

''You must go along with him to the south,'' Hummingbird repeated, ''and see that he returns. He will not forget me if he has you there to remind him. Please.''

The older girl was stunned. ''But I—I have never traveled so far.''

''You are strong,'' the younger girl insisted. ''You have been climbing up and down this mountain to the river all winter and doing my share of the work while I had to lie abed with this child. I know you can make the journey. Please, Ironwood Blossom.'' Tears brimmed over in her dark eyes. ''Please, you must go with him.''

Juan had fallen asleep at his meal; with a deft finger Ironwood Blossom disengaged him and settled him in a basket at her side. ''He will not want me to come,'' she said in a low voice.

''Go anyway. Please,'' Hummingbird pleaded. ''For me.''

Ironwood Blossom rearranged her soft leather shirt. ''He is Coconino,'' she repeated. ''If he does not want me, there is little I can do. But I will go talk to him.''

As soon as Coconino had gotten clear of the many women clustered around his door, he had begun to jog along the path toward the trail that led off the island butte and up onto the western canyon wall. News of the birth had preceded him, and all along the way people looked out of their houses and called, "Blessings, Coconino! A daughter!" And he grinned back at each one.

Now he was halfway up the slope toward a group of crumbling stone chambers that faced his own mud house. He had given serious thought to repairing one of them and moving his family over here, when the children were a little older. Once he had, he was sure, others would follow and start a second community here on this cliff wall. It would give the People much-needed space on the island and go a long way toward solving a few family quarrels he knew of. But so far he had not come to a final decision.

A few minutes more and he was on the shelf that housed the broken houses. A banded lizard sat there, a fat, lazy fellow whose brown and green body blended with the dust and vines of this place so that Coconino nearly stepped on him before he scurried back out of the way. "Pardon, my brother," Coconino apologized lightheartedly. "I did not see you there. My mind was on my new child. A daughter."

For a moment he gazed out over the vast expanse of the canyon and felt that it had been formed for no other reason than to be the amphitheater for his joy. He gave a great, exultant cry and began to chant praises to the Mother Earth, thanks for the child safely born and the mother well and happy.

But when the first chorus of his song had died away in echoes on the far walls, a great emptiness settled over Coconino. Unfulfilled, he sat down where he was, gazing out over the wide canyon with its snaking river, down at the shaded areas where patches of snow could still be seen, down at the gravelly rockfall where his first child was buried. Not this year would he move his family to this new dwelling place. Now that his daughter was born, his second child living, he had fulfilled his obligation to his two wives.

Now he could go.

A cloud sailed across the sun, temporarily blocking its rays, and Coconino felt their absence as a coolness on his skin. It was a gentle reminder, that coolness, of the two-faced nature of his joy. He rejoiced in the birth, yes, but he rejoiced as well in his delivery from a responsibility, one that had weighed heavily on him since the winter before last. It had been a bitter thing to set aside his journey, and for a long time he had attributed the emptiness within him to this cause. Now the waiting was ended; he could turn his steps at last to the south.

The south! In his mind he had packed his gear a hundred times.

Jerky and tortillas so he would not have to stop to hunt, two canteens made from large gourds, his bone-handled knife, of course, his flint striker, a coil of strong yucca rope, and his bow and arrows. Everything else he could harvest from the land, or make as he needed it.

Yet something important was missing, and Coconino knew it. It had been missing for some time.

Mother Earth, may your hand be on me, he prayed silently, but the prayer felt awkward, hollow. It had been offered for the sake of form; it did not flow from his spirit.

Where have you gone? he demanded then, angry. That was from his spirit. He waited for an answer, but none came. There was only the faint impression of laughter from the breeze sliding over the lip of the canyon, from the birds trilling their mating calls. The lizard he had frightened earlier had not gone very far; it regarded him now with reproachful eyes. His despairing spirit grew angrier. Why won't you answer my questions?

Inside, a younger man answered him—the Coconino he used to be. *You are asking the wrong questions,* it said. *Do not ask where She has gone; rather, ask where* you *have gone!*

Very well, then, he conceded. Where have I gone? What has happened to me? Why do I feel so empty?

Because, the younger admonished, *you are not happy with what is given to you. You never were.*

It was true, Coconino knew. The Mother Earth had sent him a Witch Woman, and he had disdained her because she was tall and thin, because she did not have the golden hair and blue eyes that he dreamed of. Then, when he grew to love her anyway, she would not have him; it was his own fault. And finally, when she had promised she would spend her nights with him, Coconino had been swept away by the Magic Place That Bends Time. Now the Witch Woman was dead—bones, dry bones like the ones in his dream—

But she is not dead, his mind rebelled, and he clutched at the blue-green medallion around his neck. If only there were a Magic Place to bend Time back the other way, we could be together again. She lived another twenty-five years, the ancient letter said. She saw my children grown. She raised one as her own. A daughter.

And now he had this other daughter, one he had held in his hands, and all he could think of was the one Phoenix had raised, the one he had never seen. For two years he had lived with Hummingbird, had stayed by her side throughout the delivery, had cradled her and kissed her and meant every tender word he said to her, but when he walked out of his stone house and jogged down the path, it was Phoenix he wanted to see, Phoenix he wanted to tell of his joy in being a father. After two years, each time he turned a corner, he still expected to see her there.

Below him Coconino saw a sturdy figure start up the trail toward his resting place. She walked steadily, purposefully, with more agility than he would have thought possible. When finally she stood before him, she was breathing heavily, perspiration standing out on her forehead, but she was not spent. Far from it.

"Blessings, Husband."

"Thank you, Ironwood Blossom." He handed her his canteen, and she drank slowly, sparingly. "Won't you join me?" he invited when she seemed uninclined to initiate anything further.

Ironwood Blossom sat down beside him, her breathing returning to normal. Still she made no attempt to speak, gazing out over the canyon with him.

"Where is Juan?" he asked finally.

"With my mother," she replied. "He was sleeping, so I thought I would take advantage of it to get out of the village for a little while."

"And so you came here," he prodded.

"It seemed like a good place to come."

He gave up, then, leaving it for her to broach whatever topic she had come to discuss. Though he had lived with this woman as long as he had with Hummingbird, he still felt as though he hardly knew her. Quiet, self-effacing, she seemed to blend with her surroundings and attract no notice, possessing an uncanny instinct for when to keep silent. Or was it just that she was almost always silent?

"Has the Mother Earth suggested a name for the child yet?" she asked after several moments.

Coconino shifted uncomfortably. "She does not speak to me as clearly as She used to."

"Ah." Ironwood Blossom asked no further questions, neither did she imply that there was anything wrong with this condition. Coconino felt as though he had confessed a grievous sin, but Ironwood Blossom gave it no more notice than if he had told her he had shot at a quail and missed. Instead she sat and let the silence stretch on while the sun warmed their bodies and baked the dirt all around them.

"She should have a name of beauty, I think," Ironwood Blossom said after a while, as though she had been thinking of nothing else the whole time. "Something simple and beautiful."

"Yes," he agreed, "something clean and pure—like Snow."

He remembered his own amazement the first time he saw snow falling in the canyon. Until then he had only seen snow at a distance, high on the mountain peaks. All the lacy white flakes, drifting lazily down out of the clouds, had left him openmouthed in wonder. "Snow. Yes, I like this name," he decided.

But he missed the warmth, the glow inside that told him it was *moh-ohnak*.

Ironwood Blossom, however, nodded contentedly, as though it made perfect sense to her. "Snow," she repeated. "A fine name." Perhaps it was *moh-ohnak*, after all. "And now that she is born, you will start your journey soon."

Coconino drew a great breath, held it for a moment, and then expelled it in a huge sigh. "Yes," he replied, and found satisfaction in the answer. "Yes, soon I will start my journey to the south. Something there calls out to me; I must go and see what it is."

Again she nodded, as though this, too, were quite reasonable. She believes it, he thought. Why can't I?

"I will go with you," said Ironwood Blossom.

For a moment Coconino only stared dumbly, till the meaning of her words crept over him. Then he began to protest. "Ironwood Blossom, I do not even know where I am going," he sputtered, "where it is or how long it will take to reach there. Who can say how many miles I will walk? How many rivers I will cross? How many mountains I will climb?"

"I will cook for you," Ironwood Blossom replied, "and make a shelter against the rain."

"No cooking is needed," he replied. "I will carry travel provisions. And I can shelter under a tree or in a cave; the Mother Earth is bountiful."

"It is *moh-ohnak* that the son of Coconino should travel so before his first year has passed, don't you think?" she continued as though she had not heard him. "Juan will be a great adventurer, like his father."

The idea of Ironwood Blossom and her babe trudging along behind him depressed Coconino. The freedom of the trip appealed to him as much as anything else; what freedom would there be with a woman and child tagging along behind? "Ironwood Blossom, you will grow weary of it very soon, I fear."

"Husband," she said with a wry, sideways look, "I sit every day and grind corn from sun's first light to midday; then I tan hides from midday till sunset. The next day I rise and do the same thing again. Do not tell me what I will grow weary of."

At that point he almost surrendered, feeling pity for the monotony of her life and guilt that his presence had not enlivened it much. But he did not want her along. Finally there was nothing to do but say it bluntly: "Ironwood Blossom, I want to make this journey alone. I do not want you to come."

For the first time he could remember, she looked him levelly in the eyes, and there was no fear or flinching in her. "Husband, I will come," she replied.

Coconino knew a sinking feeling in his stomach. It appeared his second wife could be as unyielding as the tree of her name.

Coconino waited until he was sure Hummingbird was asleep. She had fed Snow and then put her back in her cradle basket and rolled over on her mat. Now he could hear his wife's deep regular breathing; it was time.

Silently he crept to the door, picking up the gear he had left there the night before. Slipping past the door hide, he stepped onto the path outside his house and stretched up to his full height. Dawn had not yet begun to lighten the eastern skies; he could be down in the canyon and out of sight beyond a bend before either of his wives woke and missed him.

Forgoing the path, he went straight down the steep side of the mountain toward the river. Ironwood Blossom would feel betrayed to rise in the morning and find he had gone without her. But he simply could not have the woman along. She would slow him down, get in his way—worse, what would he say to her on such a long journey? No, it was much better this way. When he came back and told her about the hardship of the trail, she would be glad she had not come.

At the bottom of the hill he stopped to relieve himself. Night birds were still calling—that was good. He wanted to be a tiny, distant shadow by the time the day birds began their rowdy chorus. Adjusting his loincloth, he turned and headed upstream.

"It is a good thing you have such a large bladder," came a voice out of the darkness. "I didn't know whether you would go upstream or downstream, and had you not paused so long, I wouldn't have caught up in time to see which way you went."

Coconino had stopped in his tracks at the first word; now he heaved a weary sigh and shook his head. "Ironwood Blossom, please don't do this."

"You do what you must, Husband," she said without rancor. "Allow me to do the same."

"Turn back now," he advised. "I won't stop and wait for you."

"Only leave me a trail, then," she replied. "I will follow at my own pace."

He threw up his hands in disgust and started off at a good hunter's jog. By the time he had reached the first bend in the river, he had left her far behind.

When he slowed to a walk some time later, however, he looked back and saw her rounding the bend, keeping a steady pace, the child slung across her back. His first thought was to leave the river and strike out across the rugged country to the southeast, where she could not track him, but his conscience would not let him lure her out into trackless terrain where she and the child might come to harm. So he stayed by the riverbed, hoping by midday he would be so far ahead that she would become discouraged and turn back.

The ground rose quickly, and by midmorning the canyon had flattened out and he was near the headwaters of the creek. It was time to veer off to the south in search of the lakes that would bridge the distance to the Red Rock Country. Coconino climbed a stunted pine and checked the trail behind him. Ironwood Blossom was still there. She carried the child in front now, nursing him, most likely, and she had cut a good walking stick at some point. On she came, relentless as time itself. Coconino scrambled back down and trotted on.

When he reached the first lake, he stopped, guilt-stricken. There was no mark to lead his wife to this place except the faint trace of his own passing. Was she tracker enough to follow it? Perhaps he should go back to see—but no, then she would have won. Then she would know that if she kept on, he would not suffer her to fall too far behind. That would never do. But he sat a long time concealed in the rushes by the lake, watching for her head to appear above the swell of ground that separated them. At last it did; Coconino rose quickly and crept away toward the next lake.

He had thought to reach the river that ran through the Red Rock Country by nightfall, but by midafternoon he knew that he would not. Worry for his wife's welfare had kept him too long at his rest stops, and now he found himself deliberately leaving a trail that she could not miss. At this rate he would be caught somewhere between the lakes and the river. And where would she be when night fell and the chill of the early spring evening settled on her and the child? Would there be shelter against the dew? Would there be biting insects or poisonous snakes? Had she brought a flint and striker to make a fire, or had she counted on the one in his pouch? Did she even have a blanket against the cold? It was too far now for her to get back to the safety of the island canyon by nightfall.

Frustrated, Coconino used several of the words he had learned from Phoenix. He was not quite sure what they meant, but they seemed designed to express his mood, so he used them. Thus vented, he sat down at the easternmost end of the narrow lake and waited.

It was still full daylight when Ironwood Blossom pushed her way out of the waist-high rushes and stopped, panting, in front of him. He had shot a duck while he waited and had it roasting now; she had seen the smoke from his fire.

For several minutes she said nothing but dropped gratefully to her knees and moistened her mouth from her gourd canteen. Then, "Will you camp here for the night?" she asked.

Scowling, he snapped a dry twig into pieces and fed them to the fire bit by bit. "Why should I be in a hurry to reach the Camp of the Others?" he groused. "It is a filthy place. If we camp here tonight and on the river tomorrow, then we can cut across and spend our third night in the Valley of the People. I long to see it again."

Tears of relief trickled down Ironwood Blossom's face as she unslung the child, who, Coconino could see now, was part of a larger bundle. When she spoke, her casual tone belied the tears that dried even now on her cheeks. "It is good," she remarked, "that Juan should see the place where his father was born."

"We can follow the creek from that valley down to the Camp of the Others," Coconino continued, "and perhaps find a trail to the Southern Village without actually entering the profanity of that place." And possibly, he thought grimly, before Derek Lujan knows I am there.

As Lujan expected, Tav Ryan was waiting for him. He saw her slamming shutters into place from the inside as he approached, could almost hear the metal bolt sliding from the door into the solid wooden jam. "Ta-*var*-i-a," he sang out as he approached with the awkward garden tiller.

"Go away."

But Lujan only laughed. "Open the *door*, Tavaria," he called in the same sweet singsong. "Open the door or I'll break it *do-*own."

"Go to hell."

His chuckle deepened, and his lip curled into a sneer. "Here's your garden tiller, Tavaria!" he shouted, and with a mighty heave he brought it up over his shoulder like an ax and smashed it into the door of her cottage.

The cabin was old, and the hinges weak; the door gave under the blow with a painful splintering and crashed onto the split-log floor. Inside, Tav stood braced against the far wall of the one-room structure, looking like a cornered fox.

The controlled panic in her eyes kindled a fire in Lujan. "Don't be shy," he leered. "Surely I'm not the first gentleman caller you've ever had."

Tav broke, diving toward the corner where her bed stood, reaching under the pillow—and there it was. The T-zer flashed in the light from the wounded doorway, an innocuous-looking device that exploded living cells, burning them up from the inside, leaving only charred ruin in the wake of its force. Tav held it awkwardly, unaccustomed to the horizontal grip, the careful balance of thumb on trigger button.

Lujan laughed at the sight. "Do you really think that's going to protect you?" he goaded. "You don't even know how to hold it, let alone fire it." Her hand trembled a little. "Go on, push that button," he challenged. "I dare you. Fire at me." He needed her to fire so that he could dodge and tackle her. It was all part of his plan. "Or is it that you really want me? Is that it, Tavaria? You want me, don't you? You want me to take you. Well, I'll be happy to—"

Suddenly Mo Ryan burst through the gaping doorway behind him, an animal roar on his lips. Startled, Lujan lost his balance and fell back before the big man. But Tav, too, was startled. She flinched—only flinched—and the T-zer fired.

Mo was reaching out for his cousin's assailant, reaching out, when suddenly his arm melted into a blackened lump. He howled in pain, thrashing against the wall of the cabin. Horrified, Tav stared down at the offending weapon in her hand. Lujan scrambled to his feet and lunged at her, but her reflex was quicker. Leaping aside, she sprang across the room to the stove, snatched open the grate, and cast the T-zer into its crackling flames.

Rage seized Derek Lujan. It was *his* T-zer, and he wanted it. He had plans for it. It was to be the deadliest weapon in his Collection. Flinging Tav aside, he reached for a poker to retrieve the weapon from the blaze. A tin of sausage drippings sat on top of the stove; as Lujan kicked the stove door back out of his way, the tin rocked, tipped, and began to drip down inside. Even as he bent over the open door, a great gout of fire leapt out into the room. Instinctively Lujan threw his hand in front of his face.

And then there were others there, brought by Mo's agonized roar, and they were pulling him back, dragging him out of the

cabin. They dragged Tav out, too, and Mo. Lujan watched helplessly as the entire building began to blaze. In minutes the wooden
structure was a sheet of solid flames. "Thieves!" he shouted at
the locals. "It was mine! It was mine!"

It took two of them to hold him back or he would have run once
more into the cabin after the T-zer. Finally they dragged him off
to his own cabin, out of sight of the disaster, and he began to quiet
down. The medic came and checked him. His hair was singed and
the skin of his face and hands was pink and tender, but that was
all. "Cool water," she prescribed, and stalked out. She had an
amputee to tend.

For a long time he sat on the edge of his bunk, staring at the
wall, seething inside. Like everything else that was his, the T-zer
was now gone. It would never grace his Collection, never be raised
against Coconino. Fog swirled into his mind, but Lujan caught
himself, clamped down hard on his anger, and willed himself to
be calm. He couldn't allow the fog to overcome him again. He
must be calm. He must control his rage.

So the T-zer was gone. He still had what was most important,
he thought, studying his reflection in the mirror. He had himself.
There were weapons enough in his Collection. And now that the
weather had turned fine, it was time to go.

As darkness settled over Camp Crusoe, Lujan finally rose and
crossed his tiny cabin to look out the window. It was as he thought;
they had posted a guard on him. He remembered someone grumbling about a meeting of the Executive Committee, and new laws
being needed, and perhaps locking him in one of the old domes.
They couldn't do that, of course—he could get out of a dome more
easily than he could get out of this cabin. And he could do that
well enough.

One dry run with all his equipment would have been a good
idea, to make sure it was packed efficiently, to make sure he had
not forgotten anything. But it seemed unwise now to expend energy on that. As it was, he would have to start off in a false direction in case they were foolish enough to follow him. Like the
primitives who came to trade, he would hike up the small tributary
creek that led northeast of Camp Crusoe, perhaps even losing his
footprints among the many that had traveled that path over the past
two centuries. Along the way he would stop and visit a site where
once he had been an honored guest.

He would go to the Valley of the People.

CHAPTER ELEVEN

The day Karen went into labor dawned hot and dry, even in that northern clime. The People were in their fields, cultivating the young corn, bean, and squash plants, while children gathered blueberries and currants, yucca stalks and prickly pear fruits. The stream in the canyon bottom had long since crested from the spring runoff, and now it would dwindle away until the torrential rains of late summer brought it roaring back to life.

Phoenix had gone out to hunt, but since the episode on the day of Nakha-a's birth she would not leave Karen alone. So it happened that Karen was with Two Moons when the first spasm tightened across her belly. They were sitting outside, enjoying the pleasant warmth before it became a burdensome heat. Two Moons was showing Karen how she decorated her clay pots with a black dye made from the sap of the mesquite tree. She saw the younger woman flinch and reach involuntarily toward her stomach.

"Is she kicking you again?" Two Moons asked smilingly. Then seeing that Karen did not understand, she simplified her comment. "Baby kick you?"

But Karen shook her head. "No. No kick."

Two Moons' eyes lit up. "Ah. More like a squeezing?" She pantomimed with her hands. "Squeeze?"

Karen stared at the old woman's hands, seeming reluctant to understand what she meant. "No," she said finally, shaking her head resolutely. "Gone now."

Half an hour later Karen gasped. "Ah," said Two Moons. "Good. Good." She took Karen's hands and showed her how to stroke her contracting abdomen gently to distract her attention from the sensation of tightening. "Do this. Do this."

Karen nodded tensely, stroked her abdomen for a few seconds, then stopped. "Gone," she said uncertainly. After a moment she tried to struggle to her feet. "Two Moons, I go house."

"No!" Two Moons forbade hastily, catching her arm and pulling her back down. "Stay. Too soon. Understand? Very early. Long time before you go to house."

Karen sank unhappily back to the ground, fear creeping into her eyes. Two Moons patted her gently. "Do not worry, child," she soothed, "do not worry. It will come, and it will go. Tomorrow will be a beautiful day. You will see."

But the next day was not beautiful for Karen. The mild contractions had continued until Phoenix returned in late afternoon, but they came no closer together. "Just often enough to keep me awake," Karen had whimpered. They kept her awake all night, too, and by the following morning they were fifteen minutes apart and a little stronger, but the midwives shook their heads.

"It will be a long time yet," they told Phoenix. "We will bring the drum this afternoon, but these are not pains to beat a drum for, not yet."

Phoenix relayed the message to Karen. "Medicine," Karen panted, sweating profusely even in the relative cool of early morning. "Tell them to bring medicine."

By afternoon the contractions were still a good ten minutes apart. Karen would moan now when they started, a piteous whining moan. Phoenix encouraged her to breathe as she had been taught, to stroke her abdomen, to focus on something other than the pain, but Karen seemed helpless to cooperate. She merely doubled over, hugging her stomach and whimpering until it was over.

When the midwives came to examine Karen again, they shook their heads over her behavior. "Why do you do this to yourself?" they asked, sponging the perspiration from her face. "Relax. Do some sewing. Weave a basket. When the pain starts, pant like a coyote. You wear yourself out unnecessarily."

"Medicine," was all Karen would say. "I want medicine."

But when Phoenix translated the request, Branching River shook her head. "The medicine will slow down the contractions, will slow down the baby's coming. It is not wise to give her medicine now. Later, when the labor is hard, maybe. But not now." She did agree, however, to start the drum, though she was afraid she would be drumming far into the night.

Women of the village stopped to see Karen, to offer what comfort they could, but if she understood what they said to her, she gave no sign of it. Nina came with Nakha-a, and Coconino's sister

Talia came, but Talia could not bear to stay long. Her own labor had been difficult, and the fruit of it lost. The other women, too, wandered away to tend to their families and houses. Soon it was only Two Moons, Nina, Phoenix, and Branching River.

About nightfall, as the temperature outside began to drop, the pains became sharper. Branching River looked satisfied now; this was the way labor should progress. But Karen began to scream. She pleaded with Phoenix for medicine; Phoenix in turn pleaded with Branching River. But the answer was still "It is too soon. She must pant and count the drumbeats."

By midnight even Nina had gone, sent away by Branching River. "You must get your rest," the old midwife admonished, "or you will lose your milk." The night wore on interminably; Phoenix's nerves were raw, her head pounded from lack of sleep, but she could not bring herself to abandon Karen. You got her into this, she told herself. If not for you, she'd be in Camp Crusoe—

Doing what? The same thing, most likely. But Doctor Winthrop would know something to do, something. . . .

Finally, what seemed like an eon later, the other midwives came, bringing an herbal brew with them. "Here it is," Phoenix told Karen eagerly. "Here's the medicine."

Karen gulped it down, heedless of the bitter taste. Immediately she relaxed, her terror seeping away like water into the desert sand. A peaceful look washed over her; she almost smiled.

But five minutes later another contraction gripped her, and she screamed. "It didn't help!" she sobbed. "It didn't help, it didn't help, it didn't help—"

"Hush," Branching River chided her, losing patience. "Even the youngest girls do not make such a fuss as you. Stop fighting the baby. It wants to come; you must let it come."

"Phoenix." Karen clutched at the Witch Woman's arm, digging her fingernails into her skin so that Phoenix winced and pried herself loose. But Karen latched on even harder. "Phoenix!" she cried wildly. "You take it."

Phoenix paused in her struggle against Karen's viselike grip. "Take what?" she asked, distracted and fatigued.

"The baby," Karen hissed. "You take it."

Slowly the sense of it seeped into Phoenix's benumbed brain. "You want me to have your baby?"

On the other side of Karen, Branching River lifted inquiring eyes.

"She wants me to take her baby," Phoenix repeated dumbly.

Branching River shook her head slightly, as though warning

Phoenix not to believe it. "It is the labor," she said softly. "Women often talk out of their heads when the labor is bad. She doesn't mean it. Later she will forget she even said it."

But a tiny hope flared inside Phoenix. It flickered there, fueled by dreams and old promises. Mother Earth, she prayed, let it be true. Let her mean it. I want this baby. I want to keep it. I want to have Coconino's child.

Karen screamed again, a wail that changed from pain to sheer terror as her water burst and flooded across the adobe floor. "Ah!" Branching River cried with a big smile. "Now things will hurry along. Perhaps the baby will arrive by morning."

As the sky over the eastern rim of the canyon began to lighten, Karen's contractions began coming rapidly while her voice faded to a hoarse whisper. Exhausted by fear and fatigue, she was unable to do anything but thrash convulsively with each one, and even her thrashing diminished as her strength wore away. She would not eat any of the proffered honey or drink any more of the herbal brew. In her delirium she called out names, none of which Phoenix recognized. She made rash promises for silence and good behavior, begged to be sent to a convent, pleaded for some kind of drug, and finally cursed a thousand curses known only to those who traveled the stars.

Then, as red and golden streaks of light shot up into the eastern sky, the infant made its appearance. A dark head slipped forth, covered with milky white vernix. "Push," Branching River instructed, but Karen was too spent to respond. So Two Moons pushed on the young woman's stomach while Phoenix held her propped up, and Branching River gently dragged the child out. Two other midwives had appeared unsummoned just after Karen's water burst. One cleaned the baby girl with soft furs while another took Phoenix's place, and they coaxed and prodded Karen until she put forth a last effort to expel the placenta.

"There. There, now," Branching River sighed as she sponged off the exhausted mother. "Now you can sleep. Have a look at your daughter, and then you can sleep."

But Karen turned her face away wearily. "Not mine," she murmured.

"Yes, yours," Branching River urged. "Your daughter and no one else's. She is a feisty little one; have a look."

Phoenix sat beside the other midwives, gazing in awe at the tiny girl. The child's arms and legs worked willfully, and her little red face wrinkled up as she screeched her disapproval of her new environment. Her head was misshapen from her trip through the birth canal, and a large birthmark covered most of one knee. Phoenix thought she was beautiful.

"Bring the child to its mother," Branching River called softly.

Eagerly Phoenix took the babe, bound now in a soft blanket, and crawled to where Karen lay. "Oh, look, Karen," she whispered, tears of joy trickling unnoticed down her cheeks. "Look what you've done."

But Karen would not look.

Branching River took the child and laid it on Karen's stomach. Still Karen would not open her eyes or make any move to cuddle it. Instead she muttered thickly, "Take it away."

Phoenix was appalled, yet the hope inside her flickered and flared. "Karen, just hold her," she encouraged, wanting Karen to love the child as much as she did; yet . . .

"Take it away," Karen repeated drowsily. "I don't want it." An instant later she was asleep.

"Perhaps," Branching River said doubtfully, "she will feel different when she is rested. You, Witch Woman—you must rest, too. You have labored nearly as long as she." Then the midwives went out, leaving only Two Moons, Karen, Phoenix, and the child.

The infant had settled down now, though it still wriggled inside its wrappings and complained softly from time to time. Phoenix cradled it gently, unable to stop gazing at the tiny miracle, the miracle she had helped deliver.

"It is a strong child," Two Moons commented, "to have endured such a journey."

"Yes, a strong child," Phoenix agreed. *Poor thing, you worked harder than any of us, didn't you? Don't worry, your mother will love you. I will love you.*

"It should have a strong name," Two Moons continued.

Phoenix fingered the silky black hair on the child's head. "And a beautiful one," she whispered.

"When Kah-ren awakes," Two Moons asserted, "we will ask her what fine, strong name the Mother Earth has suggested to her."

Phoenix's face darkened. For a moment her own mind had raced, seeking a name worthy of this miracle, of this daughter of Coconino. But the choice would not be hers. Not unless Karen persisted in her rejection of the infant.

Quiet ecstasy filled the Witch Woman, and she crawled to the door, stepping out into the brightening morning with the precious bundle. The sky was clear, deepening now from the pale gray of dawn into the rich blue of full day. *Can you hear me, Mother*

Earth? she wondered. Can you see this child I hold? She is yours,
a child of the People, a child of your son Coconino. *Is* there a
name worthy of her?

A curious lizard with two black bands around its neck crept out
of a crevice to stare at Phoenix, its eyes gleaming brightly in a
dusty brown head. Out over the canyon a hawk soared, circling
and bobbing on the air currents, dancing its own dance of joy
against the sky.

Sky Dancer, Phoenix thought suddenly, looking down at the
infant in her arms. That is what I would call you. If you were mine
to name, I would call you Sky Dancer.

The lizard nodded its head as though in approval. From the earth
beneath her feet and from the sun-baked adobe at her back, a peace
flowed into Phoenix such as she had not felt in a long time. It
drained all the bitterness from her and left her feeling warm, comforted, exalted.

"Sky Dancer," she whispered aloud.

It was *moh-ohnak*.

"I'm sorry," Dick McKay panted as he rushed into the ward,
sweat trickling down his neck. "The computer failed. I spent an
hour tracking down Pete Williams on foot just to have him tell me
it will take three weeks to design and manufacture a replacement
part—" He halted abruptly. "You don't need to hear this," he
said. "I just meant to be here. I'm sorry."

Krista looked up at him with a tired grin on her face. She wore
a crisp white gown, as white and crinkly as the sheets on her bed,
and her cheeks glowed rosy red in contrast. The smell of antisep-
tics was strong in the air. "That's okay," she told him. "You
missed the fireworks but not the parade. He's right here." She
reached down beside her bed and rocked the white wicker bassinet
on its stainless-steel frame. "Michael. Say hello to your—" She
stopped short, glancing at another patient across the way. *Grandfather*, she had almost said. But she couldn't say that, not where
anyone else could hear. Not unless Dick changed his mind. "Your
mom's friend, Mr. McKay," she finished.

Dick looked guilty as he pulled a chair up to her bed and sat
down. She could see his conscience warring with his stubbornness, trying to break through a wall set up long ago in pain and
fear. "He looks great," Dick told her sincerely. "Michael, you
call him?" He reached a finger into the bassinet. "Hello, Michael.
Welcome to the world."

Michael's hair was soft and fine and jet black. "No problems?"

Dick asked anxiously. "None of those heart-stopping emergencies we try not to think about?"

"Textbook delivery," Krista assured him. "And Michael's just fine. 'Ten fingers, ten toes, two eyes, and a nose,' as my mom would say." She smiled at Dick's worried expression. "Go ahead, pick him up."

Tenderly, almost reverently, Dick reached into the bassinet and lifted the tiny bundle out. Michael stirred a little but did not wake.

Across the way, the other patient peered in their direction. She was Clida Ivers, a middle-aged woman with a round face that seemed always puckered in disapproval, but perhaps it was only the discomfort she was in. Gallbladder, Krista had privately diagnosed, and was waiting to see if Dr. White confirmed that.

Clida fastened her bespectacled eyes on the baby. "Awfully red, isn't he?" she observed.

Krista flinched, then pasted a grim smile on her face. "Red as an Indian," she replied pointedly.

"Huh," the woman muttered. Then, "Oh!" as she realized what Krista meant.

Just then Nancy Aribeau bustled in. Nancy was a Level Three Health Tech and had been one of Krista's favorite instructors until Krista had decided not to terminate her pregnancy in its early stages. Then Nancy had become cold and aloof, radiating her disapproval in every word and look. After all, Health Techs were not supposed to start families until after they reached a higher grade level. And they were certainly not supposed to start families with primitives. Filthy primitives.

"Good afternoon, Mrs. Ivers," Nancy greeted Clida cheerily. "How are you doing today?" She ignored Krista and Dick altogether.

"Listen," Krista said quietly to Dick. "Dr. White said I could break jail tonight. Do you suppose you could commandeer a pedal car and deliver me to Lois Martin's house?"

"Lois Martin's?" Dick asked in surprise.

"Well, she offered," Krista replied, "and the way things are at home right now, I think I'd better take her up on it."

"I thought your mother had come around," he protested.

"She has, sort of. It's my dad. He was making remarks about babies wailing in the middle of the night and the house smelling like sour milk, and he thought he was through with all that. . . ." Her voice trailed off, and she shrugged.

"I'm sure it will sort itself out, Krista," Dick told her, "if you just go home."

"Mr. McKay, I haven't lived at home for four years," she replied. "I don't think this is a good time to start. And since I can't stay in the girls' dorm with a baby . . . ."

Dick hesitated. He wanted to offer her his own home, but he knew Tina would have fits. Absolute fits. Not to mention all the gossip it would give rise to.

"It's very generous of Mrs. Martin," he said. "I'll be glad to bring a car around for you."

Suddenly Nancy Aribeau was standing over them, eyes of ice and face of stone. "You need your rest, Krista," she said perfunctorily. "Lie back down. Dick, perhaps you could come back tomorrow."

Nancy could not see Dick's face, but Krista could. For just a moment his eyes glinted dangerously as he cradled Michael protectively in his arms. Then, "She won't be here tomorrow," Dick said softly.

"Don't breathe on the baby," Nancy instructed. "Heaven only knows what germs you're carrying."

"Do you care?" Krista retorted.

Nancy glared at her. "Of course I care. He's my patient, and so are you. Now you need rest, and so does he. Dick?"

Again his eyes darkened, and he hesitated, holding Michael a little closer to him. But his voice stayed low and calm. "Just a few more minutes," he said firmly. "Five minutes, I promise."

For a moment their two wills battled, and Michael began to whimper. "You're making him uneasy," Nancy accused.

"No, *you're* making him uneasy!" Dick flared. "Now, give me five minutes and there won't be a problem." He glared at her, and Krista glimpsed for the first time the fire that burned deep within Dick McKay, the one he kept carefully cloaked in social etiquette. Nancy saw it, too; perhaps that was why she finally gave ground and headed for the door. Dick relaxed a little and turned his attention back to Michael.

But Nancy couldn't quite leave it alone. She paused in the doorway, irked at being outfaced in her own domain. "This young woman made a choice to have a baby," she growled, "and if people keep fawning over her, and it—"

"One might almost think they respected her decision," Dick finished acidly.

Nancy drew back. "Honestly," she muttered, turning to leave, "I don't know why, when you have a lovely child of your own at home—"

"Lovely?" he mocked. "A lovely *pale-skinned* child? That's what you mean, isn't it?"

Nancy tried to protest. "I never said—"

"What makes a pale child lovelier than a dark one?" Dick demanded. "Does that make my son lovelier than Scooter Keegan's kids? They are a little on the dark side, aren't they?"

"No, of course not."

"Not skin color, then? Something else. Just the primitive bloodline, is that it?" he badgered.

Nancy was growing flushed and flustered, unable to stem Dick's tide of accusations. "There's nothing wrong with the primitives—"

"As long as they stay in their village and leave our women alone. Fine for us to go to their village, bless them with our knowledge and our progeny, but they'd best not try to return the favor."

"Favor!" she screeched. "Favor, to ruin one of my best Health Techs and burn down the Mayall Tower—"

"Ruin!" Dick roared, and in his arms Michael began to shriek. "Ruin, is that what you call it? Because she honored his custom of the Chosen Companion? Because finding herself pregnant, she chose to love his child? Because now that he is gone, she gives him the only immortality a human being knows on this earth?"

"Why would you want that—primitive—immortalized?" Nancy declared with all the hauteur at her command.

"Because he was my son!" Dick thundered. Then he seemed to crumple, clutching the squalling infant to his chest. "He was my son, and Michael is my grandson, and I will not abandon them again. I will not abandon either one of them again."

Nina sat on the path outside her house, humming to herself as she plaited yucca fibers into a strong cord. Nakha-a slept in his sling, held close against Nina's body. The sun was warm, and Nina's heart was overflowing.

Then a dark shadow fell across her; she looked up to see Phoenix with Karen's fussing baby in her arms. "Sky Dancer!" Nina exclaimed in delight. "Oh, let me see her!" Eagerly she took the little girl from Phoenix.

Phoenix knelt beside them, smiling in spite of herself. "It is a good name, isn't it?" she asked.

"It is *her* name," Nina replied simply. "What is the matter, Sky Dancer? Why do you cry so?"

The smile faded from Phoenix's face. "She's hungry," the Witch Woman said. "Karen won't feed her."

Nina looked up quickly, a sorrowful expression on her face. "Still?" she asked.

"It's been a day and a half," Phoenix replied. "Two Moons said we'd better find a wet nurse for her."

"Oh, let me!" Nina cried. "After all, she is Nakha-a's sister. It is only right they should share my milk." She moved the little boy's sling aside, and soon the girl child stopped squawking and was nursing hungrily.

"Nina?" Phoenix ventured after a moment. "Karen still wants to go back to the Camp of the Others. As soon as Branching River says she can travel safely, I will take her there."

Nina studied the thin, tough woman. "But you will keep Sky Dancer."

"Karen doesn't want her," Phoenix defended. "She told me to take her."

Nina sighed and settled herself more comfortably on the path, her back up against the wall of her adobe house. "She will come to regret that decision, I think."

"Sky Dancer belongs with the People," Phoenix declared. "She is Coconino's daughter."

"And you will raise her to honor him and the Mother Earth," Nina agreed. "I felt this the day Nakha-a was born and you brought Karen to me. But I couldn't say it then, and after a while the feeling went away, and I thought perhaps I was wrong. But I wasn't." She adjusted Nakha-a's sling and jiggled Sky Dancer comfortingly. "I will nurse her for you, Witch Woman. And you will teach Nakha-a to be a hunter, like his father."

The invitation startled Phoenix, but it sent a keen joy shooting through her breast. She had struggled with her relationship to Coconino's son; how far dared she intrude into Nina's domain? But the hunting was a perfect arrangement. Older hunters always took younger ones under their wing, made them toy bows, helped them craft their first arrows. This Coconino had done for Phoenix only one summer past; this she would do for his children.

Both his children, she thought, looking down at the baby girl claiming her first meal with more indignation than gratitude, pounding her little fist against Nina's breast. Yes, I will teach both his children to hunt, and when he comes back, he will be so proud of them both.

When he comes back.

As Jacqueline Winthrop stepped out of her climate-controlled Infirmary, the heat hit her like a palpable force. The sun had set fifteen minutes earlier and the temperature should be dropping soon, but in the murky twilight it was still hot and humid. Humid! Ha. Thirty percent humidity was hardly tropical, but with temperature readings of over one hundred degrees Fahrenheit, it was enough to make the castaways miserable.

She headed down the path toward the commissary thinking, I'm too old for this. Too old for these primitive conditions, too old to play survivalist even in a lush valley like this. The river flows year-round, thank goodness, but it's a long haul for bathing and drinking water. Now that they've built an irrigation system for the fields, maybe they'll see about piping water up here to the camp.

It hadn't occurred to anyone to use native water until their supply of purified water from Argo ran out in mid-March. By then the river was rushing with snowmelt, and it carried more than its share of silt, soot, and little beasties. Everyone took a turn falling victim to what they called "Coconino's revenge," but even before Jacqueline's medications had run out, they had begun to adjust to the local bacteria. After all, the primitives drank the water all the time; it was simply a matter of tolerance.

Jacqueline stopped on the path to get her bearings, for it was fully dark now. The suddenness of nightfall here still surprised her. Overhead the stars winked into being, and she paused to gaze upward for a moment. Let's see, that was Polaris there, in a constellation once known as Ursa Major, the Great Bear. On Juno, Polaris was part of a different formation: Bessie the Cow. On Argo, it was the forefoot of Tilda the Crocodile.

Slowly Jacqueline took in a deep breath, held it, blew it out again. She'd never see Bessie again or the Croc. Just as her children would never see the Great Bear. She thought of her children more and more these days, particularly of Cincinnati's birth. There had been complications . . . a tangled umbilical cord, oxygen cut off . . . . She knew it was Karen Reichert she ought to be thinking about, going through a difficult childbirth far beyond Jacqueline's reach, but somehow it was her own pain she kept coming back to. Cin. Willful, wonderful, precious Cin—

"Take care of him, Chelsea," she whispered softly, as she had so often in the past year. "He'll always need you. I'm sorry it had to be this way, but it's up to you now."

"Dr. Winthrop."

Jacqueline jumped, startled at the nearness of the soft voice. "Who's there?" she called irritably. "Don't you know better than to go sneaking up on an old woman like that? You'll give me a heart attack."

There was soft laughter in reply. "I doubt it, Doctor," said the voice, a woman's voice but strangely accented. "You and I are too stubborn to keel over like that." A slender form stepped out of the shadows, tall and straight, naked except for moccasins and a loincloth. Phoenix.

Karen. Why else should Phoenix show up here now? "Is Karen with you?" Jacqueline demanded.

Phoenix nodded. "I took her to her dome; it was what she asked. But I wanted to talk to you before I left."

Worry gnawed at Jacqueline's gut. "Is she all right? How is the baby?"

"The baby is fine," Phoenix replied proudly. "A healthy baby girl. We call her Sky Dancer."

As if in response, a night bird trilled boldly, its call a striking counterpoint to the symphony of crickets and tree lice. Jacqueline supressed a shiver. "And you've decided to keep her," Jacqueline guessed. She had suspected it when Phoenix had come to take Karen away. When they had first met on the Mountain, the tall woman had brought her X rays for Jacqueline's inspection, X rays that clearly showed blocked Fallopian tubes. She would never conceive, and that sorrow ate at her. Now Phoenix had decided to take what nature would not give her.

"Karen rejected the child," Phoenix replied with stately calm. There was none of the anger Jacqueline had seen during their last meeting, none of the desperation. "She had a difficult labor, and when it was through, she wanted nothing to do with Sky Dancer. She wouldn't feed her, wouldn't even look at her. It was her choice, not mine."

"And that's what you wanted to tell me."

"Yes." Phoenix took another step closer, and her features took shape in the starlight. There was no trace of the anguish Jacqueline remembered, though a sadness suffused her expression. "When you and I met on the Mountain," Phoenix began, "I liked you. I respected you. I don't want you to think . . . I want you to understand that we were as good to Karen as we could be. It was her choice to leave the child behind. I never asked it of her."

But you would have, Jacqueline thought. Wisely, she kept silent. Phoenix had satisfied her own sense of justice; there was no point harping on the might have beens.

"You'll need to examine Karen," Phoenix continued. "The midwives were afraid there might be some . . . internal damage. She bled more than they thought she should. I watched her very closely on the way here to make sure she didn't strain herself, and she seems to be all right. Tired but not sick. Still, you should examine her.''

"I'll do that," Jacqueline promised tartly.

They were silent for a moment. Phoenix shifted uneasily under Jacqueline's unforgiving stare, then said, "Doctor, I did what I had to do. For the People."

"For yourself," Jacqueline corrected.

Phoenix gave a painful half smile. "I am of the People," she whispered. Then silently she turned and melted into darkness.

"Phoenix!" Jacqueline called after her, and the tall woman returned, but not so close this time; her face was obscured in shadow. "Phoenix, what you did, taking Karen—it was wrong. I believe that sincerely. Wrong for Karen, maybe even wrong for you." Jacqueline would never back away from her stand on that. "But if your people ever want to come down out of the hills—" She took a measured breath. "I won't hold it against them. I want you to know that. What's done is done."

Phoenix gave a low, sarcastic chuckle. "And Coconino's part in stranding you here—will you hold that against us?"

"Me, personally? No," Jacqueline replied. "It's too late to change any of that. We have to go on from here."

Jacqueline could feel Phoenix's smirk in the darkness. "We will go on separately, thank you. I know the nature of my race too well: Tony Hanson and others like him would be glad of any excuse to take vengeance on the People. There would be 'incidents,' and though many would be saddened by them, it would always be too late." She shifted her weight and prepared to leave. "When Coconino returns, he may decide otherwise; until then, we stay in the north."

Again Phoenix melted into the shadows; again Jacqueline was reluctant to see her go. "Phoenix."

"Yes, Doctor." She stayed invisible this time.

"If you know the nature of your race, then you know that our curiosity is boundless. Coconino may return, but so will my people. Sooner or later someone will come looking for us."

Far away to the north a coyote barked, an eerie yapping bark. It was picked up by other coyotes nearer to the camp and passed on, closer and closer, until it rolled over them like a tide, dying away into the south. Phoenix waited until the last echo was gone before she spoke. "Let us hope," she said evenly, "that it is later. Much later."

CHAPTER TWELVE

Chelsea closed the drapes in Camilla's simple, elegant room at Mountain Springs Mental Hospital. They were white, lacy drapes with threads of gold and lavender spun through them—lovely, Chelsea thought. Just like everything about this woman. Delicate and graceful and a little old-fashioned. Was that the kind of woman Camilla was before the murder? Or was this simply the world into which she had retreated?

"Are you frightened, Camilla?" Zachery asked his pale client, who was seated in a white wicker fan chair in one corner. He had drawn up a stool close to her knee and was cradling her dainty hand between his powerful hands.

She looked up into his eyes as a child queen might look into the eyes of her most trusted adviser. "Will it hurt?" she asked in a small voice.

Chelsea turned from the window. "No, Camilla, it won't hurt at all," she assured the woman. "We're only going to listen to some music—very soothing music." She drew a recording globe and tiny earpiece from a pocket deep inside her robes. The globe was a dull bronze thing, looking old and worn, though its durability was such that it would last another hundred years without the slightest deterioration. Inside were a multitude of concentric globes, each encoded with complex musical tones and rhythms and the appropriate patterns in which to combine them. The whole globe was smaller than a walnut.

Chelsea wondered again if the procedure would work at all. Orphic somnolence required the willing participation of the patient; was Camilla capable of participating? It was highly successful with young children, but an undeveloped mind was not the same as an unstable one. Still, the technique had been successful for many victims of emotional or mental stress. If only she could capture Camilla's attention long enough to begin.

"May I start now?" Chelsea asked Camilla politely.

Camilla studied her with vacant blue eyes. "I like music," she said.

"Good." Chelsea smiled and slipped the globe into a player that nested in the computer console on Camilla's wall. Then she offered Camilla the earpiece. Hesitantly, Camilla held it near her ear.

From the tiny transmitter Chelsea could hear the beats and clicks of the music begin. They chimed pleasantly, and Camilla cocked her head to listen, then slipped the earpiece into place and began to move slightly with the music.

"Isn't it catchy music, Camilla?" Chelsea began, pulling up a chair near her, across from Zachery. "It feels like it's pulling you with it, pulling you into a dance, but I don't want you to dance. I want you to close your eyes and just feel the music. Let it become part of you. See the pulses as lights behind your eyes. Feel the harmonies flowing through your veins, washing through your body, washing away everything bad and leaving only sweetness."

Across from her, Zachery still looked unhappy. Earlier, in the flivver on the way out, he had grumbled, "I still say it's mumbo jumbo. Mystic gobbledygook that makes people feel like they've been in touch with the supernatural."

"Mystic, yes," Chelsea had agreed. "And it has been used in religious rites—as a matter of fact, that's how it got its name: orphic, for Orpheus. He was the Greek poet and musician who allegedly founded a cult that claimed to purify the soul and cleanse all evil from the body. But you may have noticed I'm making no such claims for orphic somnolence."

"Just another name for hypnotism," he had muttered.

"It is a hypnoscience, yes," she had said, "like videohypnosis and autocatatonia and other techniques that touch the subconscious mind. But it relies on certain harmonic increments and rhythmic patterns to fix the subject's consciousness rather than visual or mental images."

"But it's not predictable," Zach had responded bluntly. "It doesn't work every time."

Now, watching the blond woman sink into the music, Chelsea was greatly encouraged. There was still no telling if she would respond to their questions or if her responses would make any sense, but at least she was being drawn into the somnolence.

Soon there were the telltale flickering movements of Camilla's face as her body picked up the rhythms of the orphic music. Chelsea counted to twenty, making sure the trancelike state was deep enough, and then she spoke.

"Camilla, do you hear me?"

A long pause. "Yeeess." Camilla's voice was thick and slow.

"Good. Camilla, will you open your eyes, please."

With a slow fluttering Camilla opened her eyes.

"Do you know who I am, Camilla?" Chelsea asked.

Camilla opened her mouth carefully, her nervous system pulsing to one of the complex orphic rhythms. "Chelsea . . . Winthrop," she said, forming the words deliberately.

"And do you know who this is with me?"

Camilla turned her head slightly to look at Zachery. "You want to know about the murder," she said.

Chelsea and Zachery exchanged a look. "Yes, we are both curious," Chelsea said. "We think it was very unusual for you to do what you did. But then, Mr. Dillon was a very unusual man, wasn't he?"

"Unusual." The notion appealed to Camilla. "Yes, he was very unusual. It was—fascinating to work for him." Her voice, Chelsea noted, had dropped into a lower register, a calm and mellow voice unlike the high, light ethereal voice Chelsea knew. "He had such beautiful works of art everywhere. Captivating works. So full of emotion."

A change came over Zachery as Camilla spoke. Chelsea saw all the concern and reservation leave his face as he heard the effect the orphic somnolence had on her. She sounded rational, intelligent. He leaned forward in his chair.

"But Dillon had you doing some unusual work for him, didn't he?" Chelsea pursued, determined not to lose sight of her objective. "He had you tapping into other companies' computer systems. Like the TRC."

"He collected Terran art," Camilla responded. "So he was interested in the Earth expedition."

"And was he interested in seeing it succeed?" Chelsea could not resist asking.

There was a brief pause before Camilla replied. "That depends on your definition of success."

Now there was a flickering in Camilla's fingertips, and Chelsea recognized resistance that, if allowed to continue, would bring Camilla back out of the trance. "You don't have to answer that," she said quickly. "Let's talk about something else. How did you get into the TRC's computer system for Mr. Dillon?"

"I had passwords," Camilla told her. "Numeric passwords that I keyed in, so no voice recognition was required."

"And do you remember what they were?"

Again there was the slight hesitation. "Yes."

"Do you trust me, Camilla?" Chelsea asked. It was the key question in orphic somnolence. The subconscious would be revealed only if the subject trusted the guide.

"Yes," Camilla said finally. "I trust you."

Chelsea let out her breath, only then realizing she had been holding it. "Tell me what the passwords were," she continued.

A finger twitched. "Nine-nine-three-oh-seven-four-two," Camilla began. "Eight-six-nine-four-four-two-five; three-two-seven-eight."

Chelsea jotted them down quickly. "And was that all there was to it, Camilla?" she asked. "Just key in the numbers and you were on the system?"

"No." Camilla's fingers fluttered again. "Remember . . . wait for the number sign. Before the second password."

Chelsea made a note of that, too. But she knew she needed to back off and give her subject some reassurance, something to confirm her sympathy. "You didn't like using illegal passwords, did you?" she asked Camilla.

There was a long pause, but the fluttering in Camilla's fingers had stopped. "It was my job," she said. "I did my job. I was very good at it."

"I'm sure you were the best," Chelsea agreed, "or Oswald Dillon wouldn't have hired you."

"I killed him," Camilla said abruptly.

Zachery stiffened; Chelsea placed a discreet hand on his arm. "That's what people say," she said soothingly. "You must have been very angry."

"He promised me no one would die." It was the same plaintive remark, only this time there was a quality of desperation in it.

"But people did die, didn't they?" Chelsea encouraged.

"They must have." Camilla wet her lips, and her chin trembled just slightly. "I read the report from the first officer: thirty-one people died of some unknown disease. The captain and the ship's doctor—Cincinnati's parents. And when I told Oswald, he said, 'I know.' He knew."

"Did he know ahead of time they were going to die?" Chelsea probed.

But now Camilla hesitated again. "I don't know. Maybe. He wasn't surprised. But he said—"

Abruptly, Camilla stopped.

"What did he say?" Chelsea prompted.

Camilla's fingers flickered. "He said, 'You realize, of course, that this is probably a ruse.' "

Chelsea jumped. "A ruse? He thought the deaths were a ruse?"

"I don't know." Camilla's hands were trembling now, but Chelsea forged on.

"What did he say exactly, Camilla?" Chelsea fought to keep her voice calm. "What exactly were his words?"

The trembling spread to Camilla's arms. "He said, 'My guess is that Earth holds some secret we wouldn't want bandied about, and that is why only a few will return. Undoubtedly there are treasures to be had, and my agent will bring us a few samples. Excellent ploy, this plague.' " There Camilla's voice broke off and returned to its high, childish timbre. "But they did die, didn't they?" she asked, almost pleaded. "Didn't they? That's why I killed him. Because they all died, and he promised me—"

Suddenly tears spilled down her cheeks, and the last vestiges of the orphic somnolence slipped away.

Chelsea sat alone in her apartment, staring at the blank computer screen in front of her. She had left Camilla trembling in Zachery's arms like a child who'd had a nightmare but couldn't remember what it was. It was unlikely they would ever induce her to undergo the orphic somnolence again, not after the trauma this episode had produced. It was unlikely Zachery would ever consent.

But they had more information now than even Chelsea could deal with emotionally. Camilla had confirmed the presence of Dillon's agent in the crew of the *Homeward Bound* and his desire to have Earth's treasures for himself even at the expense of thirty-one lives. That, along with the passwords, would have driven sleep from Chelsea's grasp for days.

But the unexpected news that the plague not only might have been survived but might have been fictitious— Each time she thought of it, Chelsea's heart began to pound. Her mother might still be alive. Her mother might still be alive.

Of course this was going to warp her judgment when she looked at the TRC files. She would read conspiracy everywhere, would know that behind each recorded action there was a malevolent force at work. Or perhaps the reports were a lie. Who had filed that final report, the one about plague? Never mind; they all had to be in on it, those who expected to return. At that point, if there really was no plague, they all had to be in on the secret and they were all covering up for having murdered—or marooned—thirty-one people.

And none of it was evidence that they could take into court. Illegal documents, illegal testimony—how would they ever get anyone to mount a rescue expedition? Because that was clearly called for now, a return trip to search for survivors.

Chelsea was still staring at the blank screen when Zachery arrived just after dark. He said nothing but knelt beside her chair and put his arms around her. For moments they stayed that way, their heads nestled together, drawing strength from each other's touch.

Finally Zachery spoke. "What do the reports say?" he asked.

"I haven't looked at them yet," she admitted. "I downloaded them into our files and got out of the system as fast as I could, but I haven't had the courage to look at them."

"A Winthrop without the courage for something?" he mocked gently. "Come, pull them up. We'll look at them together. Perhaps Zleboton fortitude can seal the chinks in your armor."

So together they read through the daily dispatches from the *Homeward Bound*'s ill-fated journey. They read the captain's log, the officers' logs, the medical log, the personal logs. To Chelsea it was obvious: someone had sought to abort the mission from the moment they had shipped out. In the log entries that followed her father and mother's descent to the planet's surface, nothing rang true. Lujan's reports of a desolate, burnt-out planet were, in her mind, blatant fabrications. Why, then, would so many people have warped down to the surface? It made no sense. And a virulent plague on a dead world? How convenient. How utterly convenient.

Then she spotted it. "Zachery, look at this!" she exclaimed.

It was nearly dawn, and he rubbed his tired eyes, trying to improve their focus. "What?" he asked.

"This entry here," she said, pointing it out on the screen. "The one in my mother's medical log. 'Clay and the others are showing signs of respiratory distress.' Zach, Clay was her familiar name for Dad, at home, off duty. She never used it in front of the crew; she would never put it in a report."

He was slow in following her line of thought. "Then you think her report was falsified?"

"I *know* it," she avowed. "My mother did not write this log entry."

Still he seemed sluggish in catching the import of her statement. "Then there really was some kind of cover-up going on," he responded finally. "But by whom? Dillon's agent, the TRC, or some third party we haven't even dreamed of?"

Groggily, Chelsea turned to stare at him and saw that he was as weary and punchy as she was herself. That was why he seemed so slow in perceiving what was obvious to her. For a moment she thought of getting a bottle of stimulants from her medicine chest, but a rumbling in her stomach changed her mind. "I think," she said, "we need some breakfast."

"My eyes could use a break, I know that," he admitted as she stumbled into the kitchen and rummaged through the cupboards. In five minutes she had produced unimaginative but fairly edible breakfast fare. They spoke little as they ate. Afterward they continued to sit at the dining table and stare blearily at each other.

"What do we do now?" she asked. "Now that *we* know, how do we prove all this to someone or at least cast enough doubt to interest people in a rescue mission?"

But Zachery shook his head. "No one's going to spring for a rescue mission," he said dully. "They could hardly raise enough money and interest for the first one."

The thought was unbearable to Chelsea. They had proof now, illegal proof but something concrete. There had to be a next step. "Relatives of the crew?" she suggested.

He snorted. "If you combined the assets of all the relatives for the next twenty years, you might hire a six-passenger in-system ship. Chels, only corporations have the kind of money it takes to launch a rescue mission."

"Then we go to the Interplanetary Museum," she decided, thinking of the richest corporation she knew. "Even with Dillon dead, they have a vested interest in Terran artifacts."

"All Dillon's holdings are being run by the government," he reminded her. "*They* have a vested interest in keeping Argoan corporations solvent and staving off competition from the Troaxian Cartel and very little else."

"*Someone* must care!" she flared. "Somewhere in the universe, someone must care that there may be thirty-one people stranded on a hostile planet!"

"We care," he said simply. "You and I care. And unless Dillon had—"

Suddenly Zachery broke off.

"What?" Chelsea prompted.

Abruptly he rose and began to pace, deep in thought. "There's something—when I studied for the bar, there was something—" But he shook his head. "I'll have to go back and research it. I'm too tired, and it's only tickling at a corner of my brain.'' He picked up his outer robe from the sofa where he'd tossed it hours before.

Chelsea felt a sudden emptiness as she realized he was leaving. It didn't feel right, his leaving. She wanted him to be close to her; she *needed* him now, now that they had found the falsified log report, now that they knew . . .

As though he felt it, too, Zachery paused and put his arms around her, holding her tight against him for a moment. Then he let go, and the emptiness rushed back at her like a cool draft. She trailed him to the front door. ''Call in sick,'' he advised her. ''Get some sleep. I'll call you later, when I've sorted it out.'' Then he palmed the door open and was gone.

Chelsea stood looking after him, too weary to move or even to think. After the adrenaline rush of having found what she was searching for, she felt drained and inexplicably depressed. Finally she dropped onto the sofa and before she knew it had slipped into exhausted slumber.

''Cincinnati, not now,'' Chelsea was saying as Zachery let himself into her apartment the next night. Cincinnati's shining visage lit up the screen. He was obviously excited about something and not at all willing to be put off.

''But don't you think it's a good idea?'' he persisted.

Her voice was oddly impatient. ''Cin, I have to think about it. I can't think about it right now. Zachery just came in.''

''You two sure do spend a lot of time together,'' Cincinnati snickered.

''We're working, Cin,'' she snapped.

''Well, you better cut that out and find something more fun to do,'' he advised her.

''Cincinnati.'' Chelsea took a deep breath. ''Cin, let me think about this. I need to think about this. I'll call you tomorrow, okay? Bye.'' And with very little ceremony she cut the connection.

''A little testy, aren't we?'' Zachery teased, pulling up a chair. He took her hands and drew her around to face him. ''Well, put all that aside because I have the most interesting news. Remember I told you there was something in the Argoan criminal statutes I had to research, something that might solve our problem in financing a rescue mission?'' She nodded almost imperceptibly. ''Well, I found it. Under Argoan law, if one individual is shown to be criminally at fault in the death of another, the spouse and children of the deceased are entitled to the perpetrator's property and holdings.''

Chelsea only stared at him in noncomprehension.

"It's an old, old law, left over from the early frontier days of the planet," he explained. "But what it means is that if we can prove Dillon was responsible for the deaths of the *Homeward Bound* crew—including our parents—then his entire fortune comes to us. Not to parents or siblings or other relatives of crew members, just spouses and children. There were no surviving spouses, so there's only you, me, and Cin." He smiled broadly. "What do you think of that?"

Still she only stared at him numbly. Then suddenly tears welled in her eyes. "I lost my job," she said simply.

Now it was his turn to stare dumbly. "What? How?"

"I don't know; they wouldn't tell me," she gritted, masking the hurt with anger. "Just that my services were no longer needed. Oh, they're giving me the whole severance package: three months pay, letter of recommendation—but there's no *reason* for it!" She was on her feet now, pacing, her voice trembling. "I was the best techno-investigator they had; the chief investigator promised to recommend me to replace him when he transferred to the Capidocian office. It's not an economic measure. No one else is being laid off; it's just *me* they've singled out."

Suddenly her path was blocked by an immovable object six feet five inches high. "Chels," he interrupted her.

"What?"

But there was nothing to say, so he just enfolded her in his arms and held her for a long moment.

"Well, you can't do anything about it tonight," he said finally. "Tomorrow you can update your résumé and start making contacts, but tonight—tonight you need to go dancing."

"Dancing!" she exclaimed.

"Yes, dancing," he insisted, drawing her toward the door. "You do dance, don't you? If not, I'll teach you. Come on."

"But Zach, I'm still in my work robes," she protested, "I feel grimy and—"

"Doesn't matter," he replied. "I'll take you to a place where everyone throws their outer robes in a corner, along with their shoes, and they dance till the sun comes up. That's what we're going to do—we're going to dance till the sun comes up."

A small giggle slipped out of Chelsea. "Well, Cin told us to find something fun to do," she said.

Zachery palmed the door, and it swished open. "Smart man that Cincinnati; I like him. What was he bugging you about, anyway?"

Chelsea waved a hand as Zachery towed her down the hall toward the lift. "He has this idea," she told him, "for a better job."

"He's going to replace you at Inverness Financial?" Zach guessed.

"No!" Chelsea made a face at him. "He wants to raise dogs."

"Raise dogs!" Zachery exclaimed. "On Argo?"

"That's the problem," Chelsea growled. "He wants to go back to Juno and live at Terra Firma. I can't let him and Susan go back there and set up a business on their own; it just isn't going to work. But how do I make him understand that?"

"Tomorrow," Zach said firmly as he propelled her into the waiting lift. "You make him understand tomorrow. Tonight—we dance."

"You're a bad influence, Zachery," Chelsea accused as they stumbled back to her apartment in the faint light of early morning. She was giddy and muddled from lack of sleep and a champagne breakfast at the New Sydney Hilton. "But I have to admit, it beat the hell out of moping around the house."

"Dr. Zachery cures all," he proclaimed, more than a little giddy himself. "Slay dragons tomorrow; slay sorrow tonight."

"Did you make that up?" she asked.

"I must have. No one else will claim it."

Chelsea giggled as she palmed open the door and stepped into the living room. Zachery followed her. "Well, I guess I don't have to worry about calling in sick," she said. "How about you, Mr. Attorney? Need to call your office?"

"My office is on Darius IV," he replied. "and I'm still waiting to hear from them on the lend-a-lawyer deal. Should have a decision next week."

"Hm. Think you'll need a good investigator if you stay?" she asked.

"I'll need one helluva good investigator," he told her, "if I'm going to prove Oswald Dillon had an agent sabotage the *Homeward Bound*."

"Oh, that." Chelsea flopped down in an easy chair. "Doesn't it strike you that there's something wrong with that scheme to get Dillon's money?"

"You mean besides the fact that I have no evidence?"

"I mean," she said, "that we're going to prove Dillon killed our parents in order to get his money to mount a rescue mission to prove that he didn't really kill our parents."

Zachery threw her a sideways glance. "Let's see them take away the money after I've spent it," he challenged.

"You're in a very peculiar mood," she remarked. "I think you're drunk."

"Worse than that," he replied, sprawling out on the sofa. "I'm tired. I'm getting too old to pull two all-nighters in the same week."

For a few moments they lounged in companionable silence. Then Chelsea spoke up. "Hey, Zachery?"

"Hmm?" he grunted sleepily.

"You never talk about your father. Who was he?"

"Some officer who talked smooth, dressed well, and deposited a few chromosomes before he moved on."

"Oh." She nestled more comfortably into the chair. "Was it hard growing up without a father?"

"It was hard growing up without money."

"I guess I was pretty lucky," she commented drowsily. "I had two parents, and a brother who was special, and a horse, and three dogs. Can you believe I tried to run away from home once? I guess all kids do. But Cin caught me, and he was just frantic. He literally *dragged* me back. I was six, and I was already looking out for him instead of the other way around," she remembered. "I thought that was the way life went, that it was just my turn to be older, and eventually my parents would be the kids and I'd be the parent. Zach, how am I going to help Cin and Susan financially if I don't have a job? They won't even let me stay on this planet if I can't show a means of support."

But Zachery was asleep, snoring softly.

I'll get another job, Chelsea promised as she drifted off to sleep herself. In a matter of weeks. I've got experience, after all, and great references. I'll get another job. And I'll talk Cincinnati out of raising dogs.

Judge Richard Melhew was a slight man with an oval face and fastidious hair that was growing prematurely white. Even in his judicial robes, seated behind an enormous wooden desk that after centuries was still the obligatory bench, he was less than imposing. Yet he had a reputation for meting out justice with the precision of a surgeon, leaving the deal makers gasping from his legal scalpel and the forthright stunned by the deftness of his decisions. The attorney facing him knew that reputation, and it made the man uncomfortable. Judge Melhew frowned down at him and at the woman with him. "Do you call this evidence, Mr. Zleboton?"

Zachery took a deep breath. "No, your Honor, I call it an allegation."

Melhew drummed his fingers on the edge of his keyboard and looked from the screen of his computer to the lawyer and back again. He liked the stealthy silence of using a keyboard, hidden away behind the facade of the bench, to call up information he needed without the people before him knowing what he was looking at. No doubt Mr. Zleboton and Ms. Winthrop thought he was looking at a copy of the claim they were filing against Oswald Dillon's estate. In truth, Melhew was studying a complex chart of Dillon's holdings. The man had been into everything, absolutely everything! Except, it seemed, the *Homeward Bound*.

"And do you have any evidence to *support* this allegation?" Melhew asked tartly.

"No, sir," Zachery replied honestly. "Not at the moment. But we're in pursuit of such evidence. Our claim is simply to forestall distribution of the assets before we have the opportunity to produce evidence."

Melhew snorted. "You're a bit premature," he observed. "Considering the question of the legality of the will and the normal machinations of the probate court, I'd say there's no danger of a distribution inside three years."

"We're aware of that, your Honor," Zachery replied quietly. "It may take us—longer—to find what we need."

You are clutching at straws, Melhew thought. You are wasting the court's time with unsubstantiated accusations. There is nothing to connect Dillon with this ill-fated mission to Earth; even if your claim were correct, he was far too clever a man to leave any trace of that. I knew him—and disliked him—enough to be sure of that.

But I have checked into your background, too, Mr. Zleboton, and you are no fool. Neither is that woman who sits there watching us, biting her tongue to keep from blurting out her passionate belief in this claim. Why are you doing this? Are you hoping for an out-of-court settlement, some little piece of the Dillon estate offered to you by the legitimate heirs so you'll go away and not gum up the works for them? No. I might believe that of you, Zleboton, cool attorney that you are, but not her. That is not a lust for money written on her face. I have sat on this bench long enough to know the difference between passion and lust.

The simple truth, then, is that you believe what you say. You believe that Oswald Dillon in some way caused the loss of the *Homeward Bound* and the deaths of your parents. But believing it and proving it are two different things. In my courtroom, you must prove it.

"Did you know Oswald Dillon?" Melhew asked sharply.

"No, sir, I hadn't the pleasure."

"It was no pleasure," Melhew replied curtly. "My daughter interned at his Museum one summer; even she had the good taste to detest his manipulative nature. What makes you believe you can prove a connection between him and the *Homeward Bound*?"

Melhew watched the cool lawyer's inward struggle. Zleboton wanted to protest, to proclaim the righteousness of his cause, to cry out for justice, but he had no evidence, and he could not. He wanted to list all those rumors and inconsistencies, the threads and flecks of information from which he had leapt to his conclusion, but the lawyer in him would not allow it. You are wasted on that side of the bench, Melhew thought. With your conscience and your regard for the law, you should be in my place.

"There is no such thing as the perfect crime," Zachery said finally. "Somewhere Oswald Dillon made a mistake. I will find it."

"Not likely," Melhew grunted. But he turned back to his computer and tapped the silent keys, bringing up another file. It was a message from the presiding judge advising him that it was in the best interest of the Argoan government for this claim to be accepted for "further investigation." That directive made Melhew want to reject the claim. What did it matter if the Argoan government made money off the Dillon estate all the while it sat in limbo? That was not a criterion on which to base his ruling.

But how had these people come up with Dillon as a suspect in a case of what they believed to be sabotage? The idea was so intriguing. . . . How could there be no connection between the czar of Terran artifacts and the expedition to Earth? Yet the facts pointed to that conclusion.

The facts were incomplete.

Melhew turned back to face the claimants. "I will take this matter under advisement. I'll give you my answer next Thursday at two o'clock. Until then we're adjourned."

"Well, I have good news and I have bad news," Zachery greeted Chelsea as she opened her apartment door a week later.

"Good," she groused. "Because I have bad news and I have bad news."

She was slouched on the sofa, flipping through an electronic directory on the coffee table. Her blond curls looked wilted, and her face showed the strain of the past week. "Job search not going well?" he asked.

She snorted. "I've had more doors slammed in my face this week than the Ptolemy nebula has stars," she avowed. "Zachery, I contacted three companies that are competitors of Inverness, and I swear they were falling all over themselves to get me in for an interview, but by the time I got there, everything was cold and formal and they were just going through the motions."

"Better check your references," he advised.

"I did, and do you know what?" She turned off the directory with an angry wave of her hand. "Half of them said they praised me from here to Antares, and the other half were never contacted. I don't understand what's going on, Zach."

He loosened his outer robe and joined her on the sofa. "Lot of companies are skittish right now," he told her, trying to buoy her spirits. "The Troaxian Cartel just made a hostile takeover of Rausma on Lepvaas, and people are afraid the entire colony is going to come under Troaxian control. It's made the whole Argoan market a little shaky." He put a comforting arm around her shoulder. "Don't worry, Chels, it'll bounce back. Give it a couple of weeks before you get discouraged."

"I guess I am expecting too much too soon," she admitted, leaning back and closing her eyes momentarily. "So what's your good news?" she asked with forced brightness.

Zachery grinned, a broad splash of white in his dark face. "My firm went for the deal," he told her. "I'll be on Argo for another year, at least. And . . . ." He paused dramatically. "Judge Melhew accepted our claim against Dillon's estate. God only knows why; I thought we were dead when he got the case. He isn't known for giving in to political pressure. But for whatever reason our claim is on the books, and with any luck we'll get a different judge next time. If it's someone who plays politics, I'm sure if we can give them something that resembles evidence or even a new allegation from time to time, they'll be content to let our claim ride until we can prove it solidly."

"Aye, there's the rub," she commented dryly.

"Maybe not." He settled an arm confidentially around her shoulders. "While I was making nice with the people at my new office, I discovered something that got me thinking. It seems one of their clients was a member of TRC's Board of Directors."

"Really?" Chelsea pricked up a little, then slumped again. "But even if you learned something from him, we couldn't use it in court—client confidentiality."

"So there's no point in *me* learning anything," he agreed. "But what I *can* do is cozy up to him, then introduce him to you—at a social function, for instance. Anything *you* learn is fair game."

Chelsea hesitated. "It's a long way around," she hedged, "but I guess it's a place to start. That and those personnel files. I want to trace this character Lujan's every move; maybe I can link him to Dillon somehow and—"

The mellow voice of the computer interrupted her. "Message coming in, Ms. Winthrop."

"Wyatt: identify," she called.

"The caller is Indigo Lawrence of Gator Star Development Corporation."

Chelsea was about to utter a sharp refusal, when Zachery gripped her arm. "Play a hunch," he said, eyes glittering. "Take the call."

For a moment Chelsea balked. Then, "Wyatt: put it through," she commanded.

Across the room, the well-manicured image of Indigo Lawrence sprang up on the computer screen. "Hello, Ms. Winthrop," she called.

Slowly Chelsea crossed into range of the camera in her own unit. In those few steps she transformed herself from a worn and wilted woman into a brusque, purposeful one. "I'm here," she called out sharply.

Indigo's face settled into a cold attitude. Her gray eyes had struck Chelsea as calculating even at their first meeting on the bridle path, but tonight there was a smugness to them. Chelsea waited for the older woman to speak.

"I saw your name on the employables list in public information," Indigo began. "Have you fallen on hard times?"

"I'm currently in the job market," Chelsea said coolly. "I haven't fallen on anything yet."

"I'm glad to hear that," Indigo lied. "Well, a bright young woman like you, so well qualified, shouldn't have any trouble. No doubt you'll be snatched up by someone before the week is out."

"No doubt."

"But if your fortunes don't change shortly," Indigo went on, "I want you to know my offer still stands. At twenty-seven million."

"Twenty-seven?" Chelsea echoed, wondering why the woman had lopped half a million dollars off her bid. Unless the property had suddenly become less attractive, a lower bid meant either Indigo felt she had a better bargaining position or Chelsea had a worse one.

A worse one? Did she think unemployment had softened Chelsea? Did she think it *could* . . .

Suddenly the pieces fit together, and a sea of red swam before Chelsea's eyes. "You vicious piranha," she breathed. "You motherless—*you* did this to me, didn't you? You forced Inverness to dump me, and now you've gotten to all the places I sent my file."

"Whatever are you raving about?" Indigo asked calmly—too calmly.

"Is this just punitive, or do you really think you can force me to sell?" Chelsea demanded.

"You're a Winthrop, dear. No one can force you to do anything." Indigo laughed.

"You're damned right!" Chelsea snapped. "And you can take that smug look off your face right now, because Terra Firma is not for sale, not now, not ever. And it doesn't matter how many job opportunities you ruin for me; I don't need them. I don't need any of them."

"Really?" Indigo mocked. "Are you planning to live on fresh air and sunshine?"

"On this planet a person would starve," Chelsea retorted. Fresh air and sunshine! Oh, how appealing! "But I'm not planning to stay here in your grubby sphere of influence." Oh, it was so clear now, so perfectly clear. Cin had the answer. Cin had the perfect answer. "I'm going home, Ms. Lawrence," she told her tormentor. "I'm going to take a very wise young man's advice: I'm going to go home and raise dogs." And with a defiant slap Chelsea cut the connection.

Then she turned to see the stricken look on Zachery's face. Oh, dear God, Chelsea realized suddenly. He's just rearranged his life to stay here on Argo, and now I've gone and—

Slowly Zach crossed the room and took her hands. I'm sorry, Chelsea thought. I know you wanted us to work together on tracking down Dillon's agent, on making a case against them. . . . I'm sorry. I couldn't give in to that woman. I couldn't. Please understand, Zachery. Please.

With eyes full of hurt and disappointment he looked down at her. "Take a piece of advice from another young man?" he asked. "Raise horses, too. For yourself, Chelsea. Raise horses."

CHAPTER THIRTEEN

The Well.

At the sight of it, Coconino's chest tightened as though a hundred rawhide bands had enwrapped his heart and begun to dry, to shrivel and shrink and squeeze the very life from him. Ah, Mother Earth, must I pass this place again? This is her final resting place. This is the Well of She Who Saves.

It should not have surprised Coconino that the trail forged by generations of traders had brought him to this spot. This was, after all, where Climbing Hawk and the others had found him two years before as they made their way back after trading with the Others. It was not the most direct route to the camp of the Others, but She Who Saves was a great heroine of the People, and they always stopped here to pay homage. It was said she descended into the Well and never returned, but Coconino could not believe it. It had to be another exaggeration, as so many tales of him were exaggerated. His Witch Woman take her own life? Never. It could not be.

Slowly he approached the rocky rim, reaching out to touch the large stone on which he had found her pendant—his pendant. It had been set here to mark the place where her body lay; now it hung around his neck to mark the place where her soul lived on. You are not dead! his mind shrieked. You cannot be dead. I feel you with every breath. How can you be gone from me? How can your life be spent while mine wears on and on?

Behind him Ironwood Blossom waited silently, respectfully. Her husband's emotions were a billowing storm that anyone could feel; she did not try to intrude.

It had taken them an extra day to reach this place. He had awakened the first night to find Ironwood Blossom sobbing silently from the painful cramps in her legs. It angered him that she would not wake him for help, and as he gently massaged her stricken muscles, he meditated long and bitterly on her unwanted subservience.

But then, it only represented the opposite response that her father had to the same underlying belief: the divinity of Coconino. Pine Pitch came running with every trouble and complaint, petitioning the great god Coconino to do something. Ironwood Blossom, on the other hand, would suffer in silence rather than trouble the great one with her little aches and pains. "I am your husband," he chided her. "Do me the favor of treating me as such. If you have pain, if you have trouble, I want to know about it."

"Yes, my husband," she gasped obediently.

He growled and fell back to brooding, drawing her toes up to force the knotted leg muscle straight. After a few moments he spoke again. "If I were another man and not Coconino, would you have let me sleep undisturbed while you suffered so?"

"You are not another man," she replied pragmatically.

He grunted in disgust and began to work on her other leg.

After a while she said, "If you were another man who had bidden me not to follow him and I had done so anyway, yes—I would have let you sleep. You did not ask to have this trouble."

That was true, he thought. "But whatever made you so stubborn that you would do this thing?" he demanded.

"I am very stubborn," she apologized. "It is one of my worst faults." Then, after a brief silence, she added, "I made a promise to my sister."

Aha! Now the truth would come. "What kind of promise?" he asked.

"To bring you back to her."

Oh, yes, he could hear Hummingbird in her childish panic extracting that very vow from her sister. "I told you I would return," he grumbled. "Do you not take the word of the great Coconino?"

"I know you mean to return," she replied. "But no doubt you meant to return to your Witch Woman, too."

No, he thought now, gazing down at the pool of water that lay at the bottom of this broad, deep hole, this lake-in-a-hill. I did not believe that I would return to her. I took for myself the words of an Ancient, of Black Elk: it is a good day to die. So armed, I went into the camp of the Others, expecting never to leave it, expecting never to lie in her arms and know the sweetness of her body twined with mine.

But ah, Mother Earth! I never expected I would have to go on living without her!

Ironwood Blossom felt the storm in him crest; she shuffled to his side and peered over the edge at the considerable drop to the lake below. The walls of the pit were jagged rock. "Must I go down there to fill my canteen?" she asked innocently.

Unexpectedly, Coconino laughed. "No," he told her with a sad shake of his head. "The river is just over there, out of sight. There is no need to climb down into the Well." Of course, he had not told Phoenix that on their first visit to this place. It had seemed to him a great joke when she insisted on going down so she could refresh her tired, sweaty body in the cool water.

Is that what you did at the end? he wondered. Had your life made you so tired and sweaty that you only wanted to slide into the cool water, to let all your troubles wash away? Or did you come here because it was your starting place? Here, in this place, we laughed together for the first time, and the walls of bitterness you had built around yourself began to crumble. Here, in this place, I learned to respect your tenacity. Here, in this place, I gave you your name: Phoenix.

Ironwood Blossom studied her husband as he gazed into the dark waters. How he must have loved her! she thought. See the grief even now on his face. He seldom wakes in the night anymore, but he has not forgotten. He will never forget.

There was no jealousy in the young woman as she watched him. It had never occurred to her to want his love, for it had never occurred to her that she might be worthy of it. She wondered from time to time if he might ever love Hummingbird the way he loved his Witch Woman, but in her pragmatic way she decided it was probably better if he didn't. This passion for Phoenix seemed so consuming, she did not think it was possible for a man to love that way twice.

Watching him now, she felt what she had felt so many times before when confronted with his love for Phoenix: pity. He seemed so tormented. As he gazed down into the water, his hand went impulsively to the thong around his neck, to the blue-green stone in the shape of a bird.

Suddenly she gasped. Coconino tore the pendant from his neck and drew back his arm to cast it into the depths of the lake, but he stopped, poised. The storm raged again across his features: anger, pain, despair, bereavement. He fought a battle mightier than his battle against the Sky Ship, an eon of conflict waged while Ironwood Blossom held her breath.

Finally his face softened, the tension slipped away, and his hand dropped to his side. It was a battle he could never win. Slowly he pulled the thong back over his head and pressed the pendant against his chest.

You cannot discard her, can you? Ironwood Blossom thought. You have tried: wailing your grief on the island when you first came to us, burying your first child in the rockfall in the canyon. Each time you tried to lay your Witch Woman to rest with the other dead, but you can't let go. To you she will never be dead. Perhaps it is because you didn't see her die.

"Come, my husband," she urged gently, hoping to draw him from this place and its painful memories. "Let us go down to the river now and quench our thirst. Is it much farther to the Valley of the People?"

Coconino took a deep breath and turned away. "It is a good distance," he said. "How are your legs?"

"Much better," she lied. "I am sure I can make it."

"If not," he said, "we will stop along the creek. I would as soon see that valley in the daylight."

They took time to eat, shaded from the strong sun by the trees that grew along the steep cleft of the river's bank. Ironwood let Juan nurse as she partook of the dry corn bread seasoned with spices she had brought. From upstream she could hear water splashing where a tunnellike outlet from the Well spilled into the creek, keeping the spring-fed pool from overflowing.

It was so pleasant there by the water's edge that Ironwood Blossom wondered how she could delay her single-minded husband and give her tired, aching legs a longer respite. Coconino was a great storyteller when he could be coaxed to render one of the legends of the People. Perhaps if she could draw a story from him now . . . "May I ask you something, my husband?" she ventured, hoping to satisfy a point of curiosity as well as stall for a little more time.

"Of course."

"When Climbing Hawk found you here, they say there were two men who fell from the sky. Who was the other one? Was he another of the heroes of the People?"

Dark anger flashed in Coconino's eyes, and Ironwood Blossom winced, regretting her attempt. "I did not see who it was," he told her coldly, "but I do not think it was a hero."

She did not even try to make sense of that, only searched desperately for something else to say to change the course of his thoughts and stem his anger. But no ideas came, and so Ironwood Blossom opted for silence as she packed up their meager provisions to continue the painful journey.

With a graceful unfolding of his limbs, Coconino rose to his feet. He had discarded his leather tunic and leggings the day before, bundling them into a pack that he slung behind him, and now he stood before her in only a loincloth, his well-conditioned muscles rippling as he moved. But there was agitation in his face, in his stance. It was as though she had started a rock slide with her innocent question and there was no stopping it until it had run its destructive course.

No hero! Coconino thought. No, no hero but an enemy, and a deadly one. Does he wait for me there, in the camp of the Others? What will he do if he sees me again? Was my dream a prophecy or only a bitter memory of what has already been? Suddenly fearful, Coconino looked around him, but there was no rock shelf, no dry bones, and no lizard bobbing its head in anticipation.

Should he tell Ironwood Blossom about his dream, warn her of the danger into which they might be walking? One look at his second wife gave him the answer to that. She had shrunk into herself, avoiding his eyes like a frightened child. His dark reply to her simple question had brought her to the brink of tears, as though she bore some guilt for it. He could not tell her the dream. It would frighten her too badly to think that such a monster walked the Mother Earth so near to them now.

And she would blame herself, he thought. This wife of mine would find some way to bear the burden of it on her own shoulders. She would see herself as the watching eyes, as one of those depending on me, expecting me to save them. He shivered.

She might be right.

Ken Johanneson rapped once on Casey's door and flung it open. "He's gone."

Casey looked up from the table, startled. Ken was carrying a projectile rifle, the kind some of the Crusoans used for hunting. "What do you mean, gone?"

"I mean he's gone," Ken repeated. "I found the guard out cold—one of Lucy Rikov's boys. Said Lujan came out of his house to use the latrine, and the next thing young Rikov knew was when I threw some water in his face to bring him around."

Casey was on his feet, headed for the door. "Any idea where he went?" he asked, reaching for his broad-brimmed hat. It was only March, but the midafternoon sun could burn a man's face and neck in no time.

"Up into the hills, headed north, I think," Ken replied. "I sent my boy Nathan to fetch Beeza—she's about the best tracker we've got. We'll find him.''

From the table Janine sent an imploring look her husband's way. "Can't you just let him go?" she pleaded.

But Casey shook his head. "After what Tav told us, I'd never feel safe with him out there loose, never knowing when he might show up again. No, the Exec may drag their heels deciding what to do with him, but one thing I know: We can't let him go off and hide.''

A heavy walking stick was propped against the wall by the door. Casey owned no gun, but the stout ironwood staff would turn any kind of blade. He snatched it up and, with grim determination, followed Ken out the door.

Coconino kept them close to the sheltering bank as they walked on toward the Valley of the People. It was rough, hilly country, speckled with creosote, mesquite, and a variety of cacti. Here by the water's edge grew riparian trees: sycamores and willows and white-barked eucalyptus. Coconino was glad of their shade, but gladder of the cover they provided.

The agitation that had begun as they rested near the Well continued to grow as they traveled closer to the camp of the Others. "Are you tired?" he asked Ironwood Blossom anxiously. "We can stop here for the night.''

"No, let us go on," she said. "I am sure I can make it to the Valley of the People.''

So they went on, and with each step the terrain became more familiar. Here, just around the bend in the stream, the banks would flatten out into a fairly level place. Once the People had kept their fields in that place. They could save time and steps if they climbed the steep bank and found the ancient causeway that cut across between the loops of the creek and led to the eastern edge of the village site.

But Coconino was loath to do it. Not only was it a steep climb for Ironwood Blossom and the babe, but there would be little to screen them from watching eyes once they gained the ancient roadbed. Coconino was not sure why that bothered him; surely the Others would not travel this far from their camp. Theirs was a pleasant place where two streams converged: this one and the one he and Ironwood Blossom had followed through the Red Rock Country. It had good soil for fields and plenty of water for irrigation. Why should they come five or more miles northeast to the Valley of the People? And as for Lujan—how could he know Co-

conino was coming? He couldn't, of course. There was nothing to
fear.

Still the thought of reaching the Village of the Ancients, perched
high on a cliff wall just ahead, kept Coconino driving onward. It
had been a place of sanctuary for the Survivors during the Year
That the Rains Would Not Stop; it represented the Mother Earth's
protection to generations who followed. If only they could reach
that adobe fortress before dark, it would be a safe place to spend
the night.

Lujan gazed up at the awesome cliff dwelling plastered against
the soaring rock wall like a fortress. Here and there openings were
visible, small squares and T shapes that were windows and doors
in the five-story complex. It hung in a huge, shallow limestone
cave on the southeastern face above a small stream, baking in the
golden spring sunlight.

The ladders were gone. He had hoped to climb up to it, to
challenge his nagging discomfort with high places, to struggle
against it and win. But without the rough wooden ladders the People had used to climb from one rock shelf to another up the face
of the cliff, he did not think it could be done.

Still, he approached the rock wall across the rolling ground that
swelled up from the stream. Here and there could be seen the
remnants of a cook fire, a broken pot or a stone tool cast aside in
haste as the People had torn down their wickiups and traveled north
some 180 years earlier. Franz Johnson would know the exact time
span; Lujan did not much care.

As he drew nearer, he noticed a couple of small openings much
farther down the cliff, to the right of the man-made dwellings. The
openings were rough, eroded or hewn in the natural rock. Tombs?
he wondered. Or perhaps storage caves? He climbed across the
rubble of a small rockfall toward them.

They turned out to be small caves. Inside one was a large clay
pot, cracked in two. A lizard shot out from under it and stopped
squarely in front of him, as though issuing a challenge; Lujan
recoiled, remembering an encounter with a deadly snake near this
village. But the lizard was only one of the collared variety, which
he knew to be harmless. Taking up his club, he swung at it, but
the lizard skittered quickly out of the way and escaped into the
sunlight outside.

Withdrawing from the first cave, Lujan turned to the second. A
musty smell wafted out of it, and he hesitated. Was that a sound?

He strained his ears. Yes, it sounded like mewing, a faint mewing as though a cat were trapped inside.

Slowly, carefully, Lujan approached the cave entrance. He cursed himself for not having brought a hand light, but then, it was extra weight, and he hadn't expected to be exploring caves. Trading his club for a knife of reasonable size, he dropped to his knees a safe distance back and let the sun stream into the cave over his shoulder as he peered inside.

Huddled together in a ball were three mountain lion kittens.

Only when he came across the tracks of a great cat at the water's edge did Coconino stop and search seriously for a suitable place to ascend to the high ground above the stream. The cat, if it was hungry, was a more likely threat than Derek Lujan in this place. After a few moments he spotted an old trail angling up the slope toward a stand of mesquite. Coconino took his wife's pack from her, babe and all, as he had on the second day of their travels when she could hardly walk; then up the trail they went. At the top they paused for her to catch her breath.

"We are very near now," he told her, and knew from her smile how tired she was. "This is the way my friends and I would take when we had been hunting so we wouldn't have to go past the fields. We were afraid that some farmer would see us and ask us to help him pull weeds or clean out an irrigation ditch."

"You did not like working in the fields?" Ironwood Blossom asked, surprised to think of her illustrious husband shirking odious chores like any other teenage boy.

Coconino laughed, a hearty laugh but soft. "I *hated* the fields," he confessed, and some of his anxiety drained away with the memories. "I would skin a hundred rabbits and dress out a thousand quail rather than spend one afternoon digging in the dirt!"

Encouraged by his improved mood, Ironwood Blossom laughed, too. Coconino thought it was the first time he had ever heard her do so. It was a rich, low sound, not like Hummingbird's bubbling giggle. It pleased him.

"During harvest, of course," he continued, "we had no choice. Everyone went to the fields. But we would carry our throwing clubs and pray for some unfortunate rabbit to venture near. Then off we would go after it, leaving our harvest baskets behind." He grinned. "I do not like having the People treat me as a god, for I am not, but I do not mind getting out of fieldwork because of it."

That made her laugh even more and clap her hands in glee. Coconino thought of a dozen other stories he could tell her to make her laugh: the time he and Juan had been cornered in a rock crevice by a surly rattlesnake until fat little Chubby Hands, who was several years younger, came along and removed the snake with a stick. Or the time Falling Star had rigged a snare to catch his arrogant friend and Coconino had found himself dangling upside down in a tree with Juan and Falling Star on the other end of the rope. How those stories would make her laugh!

Her eyes sparkled so and her grin was so honest that he reached out to touch her cheek, to brush back the long dark hair from her face. Immediately she flushed and cast her eyes down. He had never shown her such attentions in the daylight.

Carefully he lowered her pack and leaned it against a tree. Juan slept blissfully, secure in his wood and leather cradle. We should go on, he thought. On to the safety of the Valley of the People, where we can hide in the Village of the Ancients if we must. Time enough to encourage her smile then.

In the dark, when he could not see her face. In the dark, when she expected his touch.

Coconino took his wife's face in both his hands. "Let us rest here awhile," he suggested. "From here I can find my way in the dark if I must." And as he bent to kiss her, a feeling washed over him that he had not known in a long time.

It was *moh-ohnak*.

Lujan never heard the mother cat's approach until, with a snarl of rage, she sprang. Twisting around, he saw only a blur of motion, a tawny flash blotting out the sun. Instinctively he threw his left arm up across his face. Then the two-hundred-pound animal crashed into him.

Pain slashed through Lujan, searing white-hot pain as the cat bore him to the ground. Claws raked across his chest and his neck, but his right hand still clutched a knife. Lujan stabbed at the animal, felt the sickening resistance of living flesh as the blade sank home, and heard the puma's cry of pain and rage.

Pain!

Fangs tore at Lujan's arm, claws slashed across his abdomen, his groin, his face. Screaming, Lujan tried to curl himself into a ball, but the cat had him pinned. His knife twisted out of his hand—he was helpless before the animal's fury.

From somewhere he heard a shot, the sharp *crack* of a projectile rifle that crashed against the cliff wall and echoed back from the hills across the creek. The cat's body sagged, convulsed once more, then became a dead weight on top of him. The last assault on his senses before he blacked out was an overpowering smell of blood.

Casey reached him first and hauled on the mountain lion's body, but it was too heavy for him to move alone. Then Ken was there beside him, and together they tugged the carcass of the dead cat off to one side. Beeza knelt beside Lujan and gave a low moan. "Oh, God," whispered the veteran tracker. "Oh, God. Oh, God."

Heart pounding, Casey stood and looked down at the mangled body of the man he had nurtured in his home for nine months. Flesh hung in tatters, and blood covered almost every inch of his torso.

"Your shirts," Beeza said suddenly. "For God's sake, give me your shirts. We've got to stop this bleeding somehow. We've got to get him back to Camp Crusoe . . ."

Casey's hands moved independently of his numbed brain. They stripped off his shirt, tore away the sleeves Janine had so carefully sewed onto it, and handed it over to Beeza. But his mind protested, Dear God—what can Liza Hanson do with a mess like this?

Coconino stirred, thinking the ground so near his home was softer than any other ground he had slept upon, and warmer, and more comforting. Ironwood Blossom's voice filtered through to him: "Husband, will we stay here tonight?"

The chittering of birds mingled with the gentle scratching of the leaves overhead, and the shade was pleasant, and the brook gurgled nearby. "Yes, we will stay here," he murmured, wonderfully relaxed and spent after their lovemaking.

"Shall I build us a shelter?" she asked.

A shelter . . . a shelter. If he thought about it, he would know how wise that was, but . . . "No, the Mother Earth will shelter us," he replied thickly, and rolled over to retreat once more into slumber. He had been dreaming . . . a marvelous dream. Where was he? Oh, yes. He was down inside the Well, walking the rock shore of the lake at its bottom. . . .

From the murky waters his Witch Woman rose, swimming strongly toward him through the floating plants and algae. She was a strong swimmer, and soon she climbed up on the bank and walked dripping toward him. Her feet were bare, and she wore only her hunter's loincloth. Little bits of algae clung to her long hair and shoulders.

"You're taking your sweet time," she accused him.

He smiled fondly at her. "It is not my choice," he pointed out.

"And you—what is this I hear of you? Are you truly She Who Saves?"

Phoenix shrugged her bony shoulders, beautiful shoulders to him. "When I have to be," she admitted. "I don't like it much, but it keeps people in line."

He wondered what line it kept them in, but wisely he said nothing. Instead he studied her to see if she had learned anything while he was gone. "There is gray in your hair," he observed.

"That is not *my* choice," she came back. "Time passes, and which of us can stop it?"

"But time has been bent," he reminded her. "Can it not be bent again?"

For a moment she studied him, and he saw the familiar mask slip into place, the mask she wore when she wanted no one to know her pain. "There is no one here who can bend it," she whispered finally. "Only those who live beyond the stars can do that."

That was the price. Resolutely he pushed the thought from his mind, for it did no good to dwell on it. He did enough of that when he was awake; he did not want to waste this precious dream so foolishly. In this dream he wanted only to look at Phoenix, to drink her in, to know what had happened to her after he left. "You have not fared so badly," he observed.

A wry smile twisted her lips. "Nor have you. *Two* wives, Coconino? Greedy man."

His smile was warm and wistful. "Together they do not make one Witch Woman." Then, "How is my daughter?" he asked.

Joy broke across her face like dawn across the eastern sky. "She grows like a desert broom," Phoenix replied proudly. "Strong and agile like her father, but with her mother's beauty. Not mine, fortunately," she joked with a deprecating gesture toward her own tall, thin form.

"Yet you are more beautiful than any meadow," he told her. "Yours is a fierce and challenging beauty, like that of the rugged cliffs."

"It is a challenge to *find* it," she replied, and he thought, She *has* grown. When I knew her, she would never make such jokes about herself without bitterness in her voice. There is no bitterness now. But then, how many years had passed since together they had torn the Sky Ship from its place and were torn, unwillingly, from each other's arms?

"This bending of time is very strange," he said, shaking his head. "I do not understand it. Only two summers have passed for me, but for you . . ."

"Time is not a river," she told him, "that bends back on itself. It is more like a coil of rope whose loops touch and twist through each other."

Desperation tinged his voice. "And how do I move from one to the other?" he asked.

Darkness had overtaken the sky, and faint stars began to glimmer in the circle of night over their heads. Phoenix stretched a long arm toward the tiny lights. "Only they know."

Longing filled Coconino, and he wanted to take her in his arms, to hold her close and never be parted from her. But she was becoming a shadow in the darkness. "They will come again, I suppose," he whispered.

"It took them five hundred years last time."

Now it was his turn to smile wryly. "I am closer to them than you, then."

"Perhaps if I hurry," she suggested as she began to fade.

Something rustled near Coconino, but it was not a sound to be feared. Branches. Despite his sleepy remark, Ironwood Blossom had cut a few small branches and was spreading them over her sleeping husband like a blanket. She had built a small fire as well and placed Juan's carrier near its warm glow. The March air was growing crisp, as though the day's heat had followed the sun to the other side of the world.

"Ironwood Blossom," he called drowsily.

"Yes, my husband."

Phoenix had gone, but the longing within him had stayed. "Come keep me warm," he invited.

There was a brief hesitation. Then she was kneeling beside him, warm and solid and no vanishing dream. Watching her struggle out of her leather tunic, he thought how much better soft cotton was for a woman to wear. Then he drew her to him and thought of nothing else for a time.

CHAPTER FOURTEEN

Phoenix crouched in the underbrush on a mesa east of the canyon, her leathery skin long since grown immune to the prickles and scratches of the vegetation. Fine lines creased her forehead and ringed her eyes, and streaks of gray filtered through her long black braids. But the arm that held her bow was as strong and resilient as the ironwood tree, and her eye as sharp as a hawk's.

She was watching two youngsters stalking a small doe through the grass and brambles. Both were sinewy adolescents, shy of muscle yet, but the boy showed signs of inheriting his father's broad shoulders and stature. The girl, as she crept noiselessly along, was slimmer and fairer, and she would soon lag behind in height. Both wore loincloths and had their jet-black hair caught in headbands of woven yucca fiber.

They worked as a team, Nakha-a circling right and Sky Dancer left, creeping ever closer to their quarry. Once the doe jerked her head up and both young hunters froze, but after a moment she went back to browsing and the youngsters resumed their inexorable approach.

They drew within ten yards of the deer. Now! Phoenix thought. You're close enough, and she's getting skittish.

As one, the two young hunters sprang upright, bows drawn, muscles taut. Now! Phoenix thought again. Don't hesitate, don't give her a chance, quick, while she's frozen—

"No," Nakha-a said suddenly, lowering his bow. Sky Dancer hesitated; then she, too, eased off the tension on her bowstring and watched the frightened doe bound away.

Slowly Phoenix rose from her own hiding place, jaw set. No doubt the boy had a reason; Nakha-a was never without a reason that made sense to him, even if it eluded others. He turned back to her now, picking his way through the foliage with none of the purposeful grace he'd shown in stalking.

"She had fawns," the lad said simply. "Twins. They would have died without her."

Phoenix gave a great sigh and forced a smile. She had long since given up asking the boy how he knew such things. Like Nina, he simply knew. "You are a wise boy, Nakha-a," she told him. "You are your father's son."

At that he smiled, a guileless, unpretentious smile that left no doubt whose son he was. The more he grew like his father, the more it made Phoenix's heart ache. Thank Mother Earth, she thought, that there is as much of Nina in his visage as of Coconino or I wonder if I could bear it.

As it was, watching him made her wonder about the boy Coconino had been. Had he, like Nakha-a, been quiet and reflective? Had Coconino possessed this quality of detachment, of having his mind somewhere else as he wandered through the village or beside the stream?

"We will hunt rabbits instead," Nakha-a announced. "If you don't mind, Witch Woman." It seemed to Phoenix that his voice had a slightly lower timbre than it had had yesterday.

"But I didn't bring my throwing club," Sky Dancer complained, knitting her dark eyebrows. "I can't hit a rabbit with my bow. I just keep losing arrows."

"Here," Phoenix said, untying her own throwing club from a thong at her waist. "You may use mine." It was a highly polished piece of white oak with stick figures of hunters etched into it. The etchings were darkened with charcoal, and a tuft of red hawk feathers adorned one end to signify the blood of the animals that had to be spilled for the People to eat.

Sky Dancer's dark eyes widened in amazement. "Mind you, don't lose it," Phoenix cautioned gruffly.

"I won't, Mother," the child promised; then she seized up the club without hesitation. That is more like Coconino, Phoenix thought. He never hesitated to grasp a challenge, a responsibility. Though he had great respect for many things, nothing overawed him. Not Tala, not the Men-on-the-Mountain—not the Others.

"Will you look for more deer, then?" Nakha-a asked.

"Yes," Phoenix replied. "They should be coming up from their lowland pastures, seeking better graze now that spring has come to the high country, too."

Nakha-a simply nodded and trotted off to the northwest, with Sky Dancer close behind him.

Watching them go, Phoenix's heart swelled with immeasurable pride and an acute sense of longing. Ah, Coconino, if you could only see them! she thought. How proud you would be! They learn the Way of the People eagerly, wanting only to serve the Mother Earth. And they bear with honor the name of their father, knowing the value of your sacrifice—and mine.

Phoenix sighed deeply. Thirteen years had passed while she clung to the hope that Coconino's travel through time had been but a brief one. Now the pain of his absence had lessened, and at times she could even permit herself to think, If he does not come this year . . . or in ten years . . .

If he does not come at all, some whispered, and Phoenix would glare at them. "He comes again," she stated flatly. "Nina has said so."

Nina has said so.

A pain stabbed at Phoenix as she thought guiltily that she ought to ask Nina about what was happening. But somehow she could not bring herself to. Once Nina's eyes had been quiet and confident, knowing that the Mother Earth had blessed her above all other women of the People by giving her Coconino's son; the gift of prophecy was so much icing on the cake—"seasoning on the meat," as the People would say.

And those People came daily to ask Nina's advice on matters: everything from where to go hunting to which suitor to accept. In the beginning Nina had realized the danger of such soothsaying and had been careful to give general prophecies rather than simple answers. Sometimes it was all she knew, but mostly, Phoenix knew, it was that Nina was wise beyond her gift and knew when to withhold information as well as when to give it.

But nowadays when people asked her opinion, Nina's eyes wore a haunted expression. Her answers were less gentle, and she had been known to snap at people and refuse to give any kind of answer. Maybe, Phoenix thought as she trotted through the chaparral, she's just getting tired of it all. Maybe she's grown disgusted with people who don't want to think and reason for themselves but want everything laid out neatly for them. Maybe that's all it is.

So Phoenix did not question the younger woman on this change in her. Perhaps, she thought wryly, it is only that she spends too much time with me. But deep inside Phoenix knew that this was not the reason. Slowly, relentlessly, Nina was losing her gift.

Looking back, it was all too easy for Phoenix to see the pattern. The gift of prophecy had come when Nina had become pregnant, and as long as her son was an infant, nursing at her breast, cuddling close during the cold winters, Nina's gift had been constant and trustworthy. But as the boy grew older and became more independent, Nina began to hesitate in her prophesying. There were times when even her general guidance was faulty. As the child began to show signs of his own gift, Nina came less and less to the common area to grind corn with the other women, preferring the solitude of her own house.

It grieved Phoenix that this should happen. After twelve years with the distinction of having borne Coconino's son, Nina remained husbandless. Her gift of prophecy had seemed to Phoenix a sort of compensation for the fact that despite her great honor, no man was inclined to take her for a wife. Now was even that gift being taken away?

Yet why should that be unfair? Phoenix demanded of herself. At least for a time she had it. I have served the Mother Earth since that day on the Mountain when I turned my back on my own kind and declared that I was Her Daughter, and in all these years since I have never again heard Her voice.

Perhaps you didn't hear it then, a part of her taunted. You had been without sleep a long time, you were injured, and Coconino had fled the Mountain in pain at the arrival of the first Others. Perhaps it was only that you *wanted* to hear Her, and so you thought you did.

But I want to hear Her now, another part of her protested. I want so much to hear her as Nakha-a does: casually, certainly. I want the peace of knowing that thus and such is right and thus and such is wrong.

Ah, but that is the province of the young, her cynical soul replied. As Nakha-a is young. As Coconino was young. When they are older, they, too, will struggle as you have struggled these many years.

But even as she came within sight of the hills where the Great Antelope sometimes came to browse, Phoenix did not believe that Nakha-a would ever struggle to hear the voice of the Mother Earth.

With a soft thud the polished throwing club scored only a pitiful dent in the hard ground while the jackrabbit scampered away. Sky Dancer used one of her mother's favorite words that was not of the People and trudged to retrieve the club.

"It's all right, Sky Dancer," Nakha-a comforted as he trotted past her. "I missed, too; only I have to go farther to retrieve my arrow."

Sky Dancer watched with envy as her brother bounded through

the clumps of sage and thistle and unerringly located a shaft that had missed its target cleanly. Nakha-a had never, as long as she could remember, ever lost an arrow. But then, not only was he Coconino's son, his mother was a prophetess. He had more blood of the People in him than she did.

With a sigh Sky Dancer picked up the beautiful club and dusted it off. Although she idolized her mother Phoenix, who was such a strong and clever hunter, she knew that somewhere to the south in a forbidden village lived the woman who had actually given birth to her. A woman of the Others, Kah-ren. And because Phoenix had not been born of the People yet was counted one of the greatest among them, Sky Dancer knew that she herself could be as good as, and even better than, her foster mother. But she would have to work at it because she was not born to it in the way that Nakha-a was.

A pitiful squealing caught her attention, and she froze. It was the sound of a wounded rabbit. Nearby, Nakha-a heard it, too, and looked around in confusion. Sky Dancer raised her club slowly, searching with her eyes for the source of the bleating.

Laughter cut through the air. Sky Dancer flushed angrily as she spotted Coral Snake and three of his friends lounging in the shade of a mesquite tree. Coral Snake cupped his hands over his mouth and made the wounded rabbit noise again. It was maddeningly accurate.

The boys had piled their bows and quivers against the tree, along with a young gray fox and a mangled-looking hare—more likely the fox's trophy than their own. Coral Snake was the youngest of the four, being only days older than Sky Dancer, but he was the obvious leader of the group.

Nakha-a glanced over at them, smiled absently, and trotted back to his sister. "I'm hungry," he said. "Let's go back and see if Grandmother has any beans cooking."

"Oh, great son of Coconino," Coral Snake called out. "Where is your kill? Has it vanished in a Magic Place, like your father?"

"Oh, great son of the traitor Lujan," Sky Dancer called back, "where are your dark eyes?"

At that Coral Snake sprang to his feet and came toward them, flanked by the three older boys. They were no taller than he, but they were broader of shoulder and their faces were beginning to drop the smoothness of boyhood for the more prominent noses and brows of adults of the People.

"My father was a Man-on-the-Mountain," Coral Snake said evenly as he drew up in front of Sky Dancer. "I bear the last

offering of *linaje nuevo* the People will have from the Teachers.''
And his eyes glittered a pale, piercing blue.

"Perhaps I should talk to Grandmother," Nakha-a said, turning
back toward the village. "It might be good to ask Teachers to come
to us again."

" 'Perhaps I should talk to Grandmother,' " Coral Snake mim-
icked. "And what makes you think Two Moons will listen to a
child like you?''

Again Nakha-a flashed the boy an absent smile and turned away.
"Come," he said to Sky Dancer. "Let's find some sotol to take
back to my mother."

Coral Snake reached out and gave the retreating Nakha-a a vicious shove. "I asked you a question, *bobo*!" he snapped. "Are
you too stupid to answer?''

Nakha-a stumbled forward, then spun to glare back at Coral
Snake. But he made no move toward his tormentor, only straightened himself and started away again.

This time Coral Snake stooped to pick up a rock. "Watch out!"
Sky Dancer cried, and flung herself at the bully, knocking him to
the ground.

Immediately his three friends joined in the fracas. One jerked
Sky Dancer back by her hair, while another kicked at her. The
third threw a rock at Nakha-a that did not miss.

"Sky Dancer, stop!" Nakha-a called, wading in to defend his
sister. "Coral Snake, let her go. Jumping Squirrel—''

But Coral Snake had little interest in fighting Sky Dancer. He
twisted to his feet as his friends pulled her away and launched
himself at Nakha-a. They tumbled around and around on the
ground while his friends stood jeering and urging him on. Two of
them held Sky Dancer back, while the third aimed well-placed
kicks at Nakha-a any time he threatened to pin his adversary.

The girl writhed furiously, trying to kick or bite her captors, but
they only twisted her arms around so that she screeched in fury
more than pain. Still she would not surrender but shouted depre-
cations at the four boys, impugning their sport, their parentage,
and their future wives.

With the help of the second boy, Coral Snake had Nakha-a
facedown in the dirt. "Pay homage to the Mother Earth," Coral
Snake taunted. "Taste of Her bounty. Suck at your mother's
breast." Blood flowed from Nakha-a's nose where the other boy
had smashed it against the hard ground.

"Serpent!" Sky Dancer screamed at the bully. "Sneaking,

twisting coward! You hide under rocks! You crawl in coyote dung! Your father was a serpent, and your mother is a—''

Suddenly a tall shadow fell across the struggling boys, and young, strong arms hauled Coral Snake back. In a moment the newcomer had him in a viselike grip with his arm twisted painfully up behind his back.

Dreams of Hawks was fifteen, the second son of Corn Hair and Lame Rabbit. ''Is this the valor of the People?'' he asked gravely, letting his eyes nail each of Coral Snake's cohorts in turn. ''Four against two? Is this something a man can brag about at the Elvira and tell to dazzle the maidens of the People? For shame, *compadres*. Show me you are men and not boys. Go home now, and we will say no more about it.''

Sheepishly the three backed away, retrieving their weapons and their kill. Then, with a last glance at the still-captive Coral Snake, they faded over a hill and back toward the village.

Now Dreams of Hawks loosed his grip on the instigator. ''Is this your doing, Coral Snake?'' he asked, turning the bully to look him in the eye.

Coral Snake smiled smugly. ''Ask the son of Coconino how he likes the taste of dirt,'' he gloated.

But Dreams of Hawks was neither ruffled nor deterred. ''I am asking the son of Castle Rock if he started this fight.''

''*She* started it,'' Coral Snake sneered, pointing at Sky Dancer, who was helping Nakha-a to his feet.

''You were going to throw a rock at Nakha-a when his back was turned!'' she retorted.

''If she started it,'' Dreams of Hawks continued, ''why is it Nakha-a who bleeds?''

''It is nothing,'' Nakha-a protested, wiping at his bloody nose with a tuft of grass. ''I will be all right.''

''I was going to get to her next,'' Coral Snake bragged.

''Ah! What a bead that would be on your string of pride!'' Dreams of Hawks remarked. ''To have beaten a girl while your friends held her arms.''

''If she is going to hunt like a boy,'' Coral Snake retorted, ''she should learn to take a beating like a boy.''

''I would take no beating from you,'' Sky Dancer vowed, ''if you were not such a coward as to strike from behind, and with three friends to hold your victim for you!''

''Prove that!'' Coral Snake challenged. ''Come. Right now. We will let these two be witnesses.''

Sky Dancer dropped the weapons she had just collected and

advanced on him threateningly. Coral Snake poised himself to meet her charge.

But Dreams of Hawks stepped between them. "Enough of this," he barked. "There is work enough to spend your energies on without squandering them on senseless fighting. Nakha-a, take your sister home. Coral Snake, you will help me carry my kill back to the village."

Reluctantly Sky Dancer gave ground, letting Nakha-a tug her away to retrieve their bows, quivers, and clubs. A last backward glance showed her Coral Snake was sneering after them as Dreams of Hawks handed him a deer's stomach filled with the animal's tender organs. Dreams of Hawks himself shouldered the carcass of a small white-tailed buck and set his face toward the village.

"Now, there is a fine young hunter and one whose company you should keep," Castle Rock advised her oldest son when Dreams of Hawks had gone on his way. She had grown plump and prosperous in the past years, and her round face was as fair and beautiful as ever. Her husband, Walks in Silence, was the envy of many men.

"He is an old woman," Coral Snake muttered, casting aside the kidneys that Dreams of Hawks had offered him for his help in carrying the meat back to the village. "All he does is moon around after his brother's wife and avoid the other young men of the village so they won't tease him."

But Castle Rock waved such talk aside. "That was a year ago," she said, "and in my opinion the girl regrets having chosen the older brother—he's lazy and shiftless like his father. But this second son—they say he is a good friend of the sons of Juan, who was second in skill only to Coconino."

"Coconino, Coconino!" the boy said. "All people talk about in this village is Coconino."

"Well, Coconino was something to talk about," Castle Rock admitted. "But you, my son—" She pinched his cheeks, and he winced and pulled away. "You are something they will all talk about, and very soon. You are more handsome than Coconino ever was, and if you stay with the right hunters, their skill and their reputation will rub off on you."

And as she beamed at her son, Castle Rock spoke with absolute sincerity. The boy was handsome in a way few other village children were. His features were strong but even, his teeth straight, his hair slightly rippling beneath his yucca headband. Already he was growing strong and tall, and the village women grinding corn in the shade would often speculate on which girl would be a match for him.

But most striking were Coral Snake's eyes. Their clear blue color in his coppery face caught and held one like the glittering colors of his namesake. Among the People, blue eyes were thought to indicate a powerful Magic.

Suddenly there was a commotion on the ledge outside Castle Rock's door. "Castle Rock!" came the strident voice of the Witch Woman. "Where is this son of yours who disgraces the People by picking a fight of four against two?"

Castle Rock shot her son a startled glance. "That old man-woman whines like a coyote," he whispered, "because her girl hit me and I hit back."

In her own mind Castle Rock was sure that was not the whole story, but she ducked through the low doorway out onto the path. Though she was a full head shorter than the Witch Woman, she drew herself up in an imposing stance. "Who bellows at my door like a wounded buck?" she asked imperiously.

Phoenix ignored the remark. "Is he hiding inside, your cowardly whelp?" she demanded, her bony wrists resting on her hips as she bent slightly at the waist to meet Castle Rock's challenging eyes. "Does he let his mother come out and fight his battles for him?"

"And where is your daughter," Castle Rock shot back, "who struck at my son but did not want to take what she served up?"

Indeed, Sky Dancer lingered farther down the path, embarrassed by her mother's intervention and looking as though she wished to melt into the adobe of the houses.

But Phoenix took no notice of her daughter's plight. "Your son is aptly named," she spit at the squat woman before her, "for he slithers away from the truth if that is the story he told you. He and three others set upon Nakha-a; if Sky Dancer struck him first, it was to protect her brother."

"No doubt he needs protecting," Castle Rock sneered. "He is too weak and spiritless to stand up for himself. I think sometimes the Mother Earth confused the two of them in the womb, making the boy soft and womanish while the girl swaggers like a rooster jay."

This only fanned the fire of Phoenix's anger. "The children of Coconino are not weak," she retorted, eyes blazing. "They do not need three other bullies to help them attack other children and break their noses."

"Is the son of Coconino a mewling puma kitten," Castle Rock

returned, "that he cries to you over a beating?" Her eyes glittered with dark pleasure as she goaded the older woman.

"No ill-gotten son of a stinking liar like Derek Lujan could ever beat Coconino's son in a fair fight!" Phoenix snarled.

Now Castle Rock's face twisted into a cold smile. "Ah, but my son is the son of a Man-on-the-Mountain," she said. "Coconino's son was gotten on an ugly girl with no hope of a husband, and you, Witch Woman—you had to steal a child because the Mother Earth would not give you one of your own!"

Phoenix's vision blurred, and her fists clenched. With teeth gritted she took one menacing step forward.

"Enough!"

The voice brought her back from the edge of madness. Phoenix looked up to see Nina approaching along the narrow path, followed closely by Nakha-a.

"Enough, I say," Nina continued, stepping around Castle Rock to stand between the two combatants. "Will you disgrace yourselves before the whole village with this foolish quarrel? Witch Woman, is this the example you set for the People? And you, Castle Rock, do you sow seeds of harmony with such words? From ages past the People have survived only because we struggled together, not against one another. Angry words like these are not in the best interest of the People."

At that Phoenix drew back, and Castle Rock, too, seemed to retreat from her stance. Cooperation was the hallmark of the Way of the People. Yet the quarrel between them was old and bitter; it was not easy for either one to back away from it. They continued to glare at one another in undisguised hatred.

"I beg of you, put aside your complaints against one another," Nina pleaded, "regardless of what they are or how justified. Think first of the People. Let there be an end to this dispute."

For a moment longer Phoenix glared at Castle Rock. Then at last she drew herself up to her full height, turned on her heel, and stalked back down the path.

Castle Rock smiled smugly and withdrew into her house. Someday the Witch Woman would go too far with her verbal scourging, and the People would withdraw their favor from her. Someday she would offend the wrong person, and the license that was granted her because of her close relationship with Coconino would be revoked.

She watched from the shadows as the skinny little girl with the light brown skin straggled along behind her adoptive mother, clad only in a hunter's loincloth and headband. And someday, Castle

Rock thought, my Coral Snake will take the daughter of Coconino for his bride, and I will live to displace this Witch Woman in the Council of Two Moons.

Phoenix found her daughter sitting on the bank of the stream, throwing pebbles into the water. It was running deep this year, and the usual stepping-stones were well underwater even though it was already the Moon of the Cactus Flowers. Shadows from the canyon walls were growing deep as the sun sank away beyond the western rim.

Wordlessly Phoenix sat on the bank beside Sky Dancer, scooped up a handful of pebbles, and began to toss them in as well. "Your father used to do this," she remembered, "when something troubled him. There must be something soothing in the act of throwing small rocks."

Sky Dancer only shrugged.

"The Healer has set your brother's nose straight again," Phoenix tried after a minute. "She smeared clay across it and told him not to wash it off until the new moon appears. Nakha-a said now his mother can't scold him for having such a dirty face."

That got a little smile out of the girl, but she quickly forced her lips back into a frown. Ah, Phoenix thought, the world is being punished for treating Sky Dancer so cruelly.

So she just waited.

"Why does he pick on Nakha-a all the time?" the girl demanded finally. "Why can't he just leave us alone?"

"Because he's jealous," Phoenix answered. "He is not a child of Coconino."

"I wish he were," Sky Dancer said bitterly, "if that would mean he'd leave us alone. I don't mind sharing the honor; I just don't want him to pick on us anymore."

Phoenix gave a great sigh. "I wish all the world could be children of Coconino," she agreed. "Then they would all be good and honest, and they would put the good of the People before their own personal gain. For your father—" Phoenix's voice tightened, and she took a deep breath before continuing. "For your father, serving the Mother Earth *was* gain. It was not *all* he cared about, but it was what he valued most, even above his own life."

Dusk settled quickly on the canyon floor. Already one or two stars were twinkling overhead. An owl raised its voice, and in the distance a lone coyote cried mournfully.

"When is he coming back, Mother?" Sky Dancer asked, her

face slowly vanishing in the fading light. "When will he come back and make people like Coral Snake walk with more respect?"

The cry echoed her own heart, but Phoenix did not know who to ask. Slowly she turned back to the stream and tossed another pebble into the swiftly flowing water. It hurried past them with no regard for their question or the bits of stone that passed through it. "I wish I knew, little one," Phoenix sighed. "I wish I knew."

CHAPTER FIFTEEN

Coconino's brow furrowed as he looked down from the knoll to which they had climbed and over the vast Sea of Grass to the south. There was no water in sight. He hefted his gourd canteen and tried to discern some feature in the featureless land that would indicate that a stream ran down out of the mountains, but there was none. Only miles and miles of gently rolling prairie, covered with grass and dotted by yucca.

Beside him, Ironwood Blossom shifted her backpack and checked her own canteen. "Enough," she said encouragingly. But still Coconino frowned.

When, on the fourth day of their journey, they had arrived at the Valley of the People, there were puma tracks everywhere and the strong smell of blood. Although he longed to wander through the ruins of his village, to find the place where once his mother's wickiup had stood, fear for his family's safety had driven Coconino to move on quickly. There were many tracks along the creek going southeast toward the camp of the Others, and that had made him even more skittish. As they drew within sight of that place, he crossed to the far side of the stream and made Ironwood Blossom and Juan wait while he scouted ahead.

He found the lush river valley filled with large fields, such as the Men-on-the-Mountain kept, and the Others were hard at work in them, using their Machines. Wooden houses now dotted the landscape, but the ugly white domes were still there, with the hulking form of the Magic Place That Bends Space still squatting in their midst. But it was dead now, so the People said, and in truth, it looked like a gigantic carcass lying wasted and useless in a village full of other offensive sights. Taking his family, he detoured far up into the hills to avoid the place.

Ironwood Blossom had looked unhappy at that. But true to form, she had said nothing, only followed him as he looped his way back to the stream again. As he had suspected, a traders' trail ran to the south, as clearly marked as the one they had followed down from the north. Glad to be past this dreaded obstacle, Coconino had been all too eager to continue downstream along the trail.

For weeks now they had followed it from one watercourse to another through the mountainous country southeast of the camp of the Others. It was obvious that people had passed this way only a few weeks before. There was evidence of their camp fires, of their shelters against the night chill, of the birds and small animals they had roasted for their meals.

As they drew farther from the Others and closer to the mysterious Southern Village, Coconino's heart had begun to lighten. Ironwood Blossom proved to be a fair traveler once her legs had grown accustomed to the continuous walking. And when they stopped in the evenings and she took little Juan out of his restraints, his eager curiosity delighted Coconino. At one year he was just beginning to toddle about, so it took watchful eyes to keep him from investigating the fire or the cactus too closely.

The nights were sweeter, too, for Ironwood Blossom's company. Awkward and self-conscious by nature, she seemed embarrassed at first by Coconino's undivided attention. But as they traveled through unpopulated country with no one to answer to for their behavior, she began to respond more readily to his advances. It became a game for him to tease her at unexpected moments, to playfully unfasten her garments as they hiked by the river's edge. She, too, became playful, and often during their midday rest they wound up splashing each other with creek water, tugging and tripping in the icy runoff while Juan watched unperturbed from his pack on the shore.

Comforted by the knowledge that he was going in the right direction and lulled by the carefree existence of the trail, Coconino ceased to hurry. If he wanted to play with his son, or make love to his wife, or stop to stalk an animal whose tracks he came across, what did it matter? Eventually he would follow this trail to its conclusion, and eventually he would find what he had come in search of. In the meantime he told tales to a woman with worshipful eyes and thus begin his son's instruction in the stories of the People.

In the second week of their journey they entered a region that was forested with giant saguaro cacti. Ironwood Blossom had never seen those towering plants, though legends had described their forty-foot bulk and the waxy white blossoms that gave birth to red fruits bristling with seeds. "You planted them *everywhere*," she breathed, awestruck.

"I planted none of them," Coconino replied frankly. "I only brought seeds back to the People. I do not know who planted them. Perhaps my mother, Two Moons. Or perhaps those who came this way to establish the Southern Village."

"Did you plant the ones in the west?" she asked innocently.

He was surprised. "Are there more?"

"So the hunters say," she told him. "They tell of traveling straight south of the camp of the Others, not east as we have come, to the place where Coconino planted the giant saguaro."

It was another foolish exaggeration of the kind Coconino wanted to forget. He tugged at Ironwood Blossom's belt. "I have planted many seeds," he said suggestively, "but none to make such giants as these."

She giggled. "It will do you no good to plant seeds now," she reminded him. "As long as Juan is nursing, no other seeds are likely to ripen in *this* field."

But Coconino tried anyway.

His joy had been undiminished until the trail took a sudden turn. It left the river it had been following and headed west through a dry pass between two mountain ranges. Now it bent sharply to the south again, leading into a large stretch of prairie. There were mountains on his left, to be sure, and another small range could be seen far to his right, but there was no river to follow and no promise of a lake ahead. Coconino had climbed this knoll hoping to put his fears to rest.

But nothing he saw relieved him. Logic told him that since it was spring, there ought to be any number of small streams running down out of the closer mountains. Logic also told him that the People of the Southern Village would not make a trail that did not lead to a water source. But Coconino had a nursing woman with him who needed extra water, and those who had made the trail undoubtedly had not.

Coconino considered the options and found there were none. To leave the trail would be foolhardy. To go back without reaching his objective was unthinkable. There was nothing to do but go on.

So Coconino set off down the hill with Ironwood Blossom following and entered the Sea of Grass.

They were not a stone's throw into the empty prairie when Coconino began to feel a prickling at his back. With no protecting trees or shrubs, with the comforting hills growing ever distant behind them, he felt inexplicably vulnerable. Increasingly, he felt a desire to turn and look behind them.

What is it? he wondered. What is back there? Is it Lujan? Has he somehow learned of my journey and followed me here from the camp of the Others?

Just once Coconino turned and looked behind him. There was nothing.

Onward they went, but the feeling only grew worse. The grass on either side of the trail grew nearly thigh-high, and even where it was trodden down they had to step carefully, for they could not see what lurked in that carpet of vegetation. More than once he stumbled over a tiny yucca plant obscured from view, and all around him he could hear the soft rustle of lizards and insects scurrying away from their passing.

"What is it, my husband?" Ironwood Blossom asked as he threw yet another furtive glance over his shoulder.

"I don't know," he replied honestly. "It is very strange. I feel as though some great animal creeps up on us from behind, sending its hot breath down my spine. But there is nothing there."

"Is it the Lu-jan?" she asked fearfully, for he had told her after they had left the vicinity of the Others just who it was he had feared to find there.

"No, I do not think so," he said slowly, but he looked around to make sure there were no dry bones and no lizard perched on a rock. "I did not feel it until we entered this Sea of Grass."

Then it came to him, and Coconino felt ashamed. Once before he had known this sensation. Once before he and Phoenix had come to a vast prairie east of the Black Lands, a place where the bosom of the Mother Earth was unbroken by tree or mountain for as far as the eye could see. Without a second thought they had run into it, but before long their hearts had begun to beat unnaturally and they had felt a great looming presence, like some beast of gigantic proportions waiting to devour them. For Coconino, who had spent all his life in rugged desert country littered with cacti and shrubs and hills and scrubby trees, the featureless prairie had been an emptiness he could not bear.

Now it was happening again. He, who loved the Mother Earth and sang the praises of her great beauty, had found a portion of her that he feared and disliked. It was foolishness to feel so about any area that had not been fouled by careless humans, about the smooth, unsoiled skin of the Mother Earth. Yet he felt it, and the feeling would not go away.

"It's all right," he said gruffly to Ironwood Blossom, trying to hide his chagrin with himself. "It is only that there are no trees."

That seemed to satisfy her. Trees meant water, of course, and a lack of trees in this prairie meant they did not know where their next source of water would be. The early spring days were quite warm so far south. For days now they had traveled with the barest of clothing: he in the cotton loincloth he'd worn from the Times That Were and she in a simple apron of woven yucca fibers. They could not travel far without more water. No wonder, she thought, Coconino is uneasy.

But though he pressed on doggedly and made no more furtive checks of the country behind them, he had not conquered his fear by recognizing it. I will never reach the Southern Village, he thought despairingly. The Father Sky will weigh down on me and crush me before I emerge from this sea. I will drown here, sucked in by the grass and swallowed up off the bosom of the Mother Earth. I will be lost in that empty place through which I passed from the Times That Are to the Times That Are to Come—I will forever be falling, falling, falling—

> "Hear, O Wind,
> Child of my Mother . . ."

Startled, Coconino missed his step and lurched forward awkwardly.

"Are you all right, my husband?" Ironwood Blossom asked anxiously.

"Yes, yes," he muttered gruffly. "I only stepped in a rabbit hole." In truth, he had done no such thing. It was only the sound of her voice penetrating his terror that had tripped him up, the sound of singing. He had not heard her sing since they had buried his first child together. Why is that? he wondered. He strode on a few steps before he glanced back at his wife. "I so seldom hear you sing," he said.

"I'm sorry; I will stop," she apologized quickly.

"No! No, do not stop," he said quickly. "I like to hear singing." Even now, after these carefree weeks on the trail, these weeks of learning to be at ease with each other, did she imagine her singing offended him? Is that why he had never heard her in their house in the island canyon? Or had she never felt enough joy in his presence before to sing? "Please go on," he encouraged.

She swallowed once, and he could see her self-consciousness.

But Coconino had bade her sing, and so she sang. It was a high, clear voice, as light and haunting as the wind of which she sang.

> "Hear, O Wind,
> Child of my Mother,
> Hear my song of courage;
> Hear my song of endurance.
> I am of the People,
> A grandchild of the Survivors.
> Even as Alfonso
> Lowered himself on a rope through the rain,
> So I have lowered myself
> Into an unknown void. . . ."

Coconino drew a deep breath as the words of the song recalled the courage of his ancestors, who had survived a great flood to establish their village in the Valley of the People. It is no accident, he thought, that she sings this song of courage and hope. She has read my heart and seen the fear in it.

> "You, O Wind, are my only witness;
> You alone see my courage. . . ."

The notes floated in the air above the Sea of Grass and were swept away by the wind, swallowed up, so it seemed, by the vast emptiness around them. Coconino felt a chill despite the increasing warmth of the day.

> "Yet I ask no other witness,
> Save the Mother Earth Herself.
> It is to Her I must be true. . . ."

Ah, Mother Earth, Coconino thought, are you truly in this place, in this Sea of Grass? Once I could feel your presence with every step I took, but since I came to this time . . . No, he realized. Since I knelt on that rock slide and buried my child. Since that time you have been so removed from me.

Yet I know you are here. Only once have I been where you were not: on the Sky Ship of the Others. That was a cold place, devoid of your presence. This is a warm sea, rich with the smell of you. So why can't I feel you here? Why don't I ever feel you the way I used to?

> "Blow, wind!
> Blow to my Mother.
> Tell Her I never lost faith."

As Ironwood Blossom's words died away, Coconino felt the emptiness rush back in on him. Only then did he realize that while Ironwood Blossom sang, the sensation of a monster at his back had been held at bay. "Do you know this song?" he asked her, and began to sing.

> "The sun rises to reveal the beauty of Mother Earth;
> It sets to cloak Her joining with Father Sky.
> The moon casts its glow on their marriage bed,
> To dress the Mother Earth in mystery."

Ironwood Blossom picked up the melody, one of the most ancient of the People, and they sang together.

> "Many are the children of the Mother Earth;
> Two-leggeds and four-leggeds and winged creatures.
> The snake that slithers on the ground is Her son.
> The fish that swims through the lake is Her daughter.
> I will never forget that I am kin
> To all the creatures of the Mother Earth."

Coconino felt a distinct lightening of the pressure weighing him down. It brought home a lesson he'd thought he'd learned long ago: that when there was the least joy, that was when one most needed to sing the praises of the Mother Earth. "Do you sing to our son?" he asked Ironwood Blossom.

"Sometimes," she replied. "When we are alone."

"You must sing to him often," Coconino instructed, "so that he learns all the songs of the People." Songs that were always in my ears, he thought, when I grew up. Why have I neglected this duty to my son?

So he added, "I will sing to him, too, I think."

As if he knew they were speaking of him, Juan stirred in his pack. Coconino dropped back to look at the child. "Do you hear that, my son?" he asked. "If you are to be a true son of the Mother Earth, you must learn to sing Her praises." The child looked up at him with bright dark eyes that were hardly more than slits in the strong sunlight. "Come, let us sing more songs for him."

They sang two more, one about the Earth's bounty in providing for her children and a sadder one about the dangers of invoking her wrath. Then Ironwood Blossom sang one Coconino did not know, about an owl that witnessed the birth of a fawn. In his turn, Coconino sang about the Grandfather, that great saguaro cactus he had found on the side of a hill during his journey to the Mountain, the one whose seeds must have spawned the forest of saguaro through which they had passed earlier.

"Such a fine, fat boy we have," Coconino observed. "And heavy. Let me take him for a little while." Ironwood Blossom gave a grunt of relief as he lifted the pack from her back.

Instead of slinging the child on his own back, however, Coconino tucked the pack into the crook of one arm. He still felt the emptiness pressing up behind him, and the idea of leaving the child exposed to that was disquieting. But even as the mountains on their right tapered away to low hills, up ahead the trail seemed to angle toward a larger range just beyond. Perhaps that is the end of the trail, Coconino thought. Perhaps there we will leave this Sea of Grass and find a cool mountain brook.

Juan continued to watch his father with curious eyes. "What wonders you will see with those eyes," Coconino assured the boy. "You have only passed through one winter, but before another arrives, you will see the Southern Village of the People."

"I think he will be a great adventurer," Ironwood Blossom put in. "Like his father."

"His father has seen too many wonders," Coconino replied tightly. "I would not wish for my son or anyone else to see the bending of time that I have beheld."

"No, no," Ironwood Blossom agreed quickly. "But to have seen the Mountain, and the camp of the Others—and, oh, to have ridden on Tala!"

An invisible fist squeezed Coconino's heart at the mention of the great beast. "Now, that," he said, "is something I would wish for my son." He looked down at the boy, who was winking and blinking as sleep threatened to overtake him again. "Have you heard yet, my son, of the great kachina they call Tala? The one-horned antelope with wings like an eagle?"

The child blinked and continued to watched Coconino's face.

"Ah, I see you have not," Coconino continued. "I have been remiss, indeed, in my duty as a father. Listen, then, and I will tell you how it was."

Drawing a deep breath, Coconino began his tale. "Long ago, during the Before Times, one of the Sisters of the Mother Earth sent a present to Her. It was a strange and wondrous creature, an antelope of great size, larger even than the Great Antelope of the Black Lands. The name of this creature was Tala, 'And,' said the Sister of the Mother Earth, 'it has three secrets.' 'What are they?' asked Mother Earth, but Her Sister said only, 'When they are needed, you will see them.'

"Soon afterward the Mother Earth grew angry with Her children for being so careless and greedy, and so she withheld Her bounty from them. Many people tried to hunt Tala, thinking to eat him, but Tala could never be found. It was then that Mother Earth saw the first of his secrets, that he could change his color to look like the rock or the tree trunks. She was delighted with this clever animal and gave him Her special blessing so that he survived the Before Times.

"When those who defiled the Mother Earth had fled and Her wrath had passed, only the People and the Men-on-the-Mountain were left as two-leggeds upon the land. Yet Tala hid from them, for he did not know if they still sought his life. Many generations passed, and Tala was remembered only in the legends of the People.

"But the time came when the Others decided to return to Mother Earth and She had need of a servant to send them away. 'Coconino,' She called to me. 'Go to the Red Rock Country and see what is there.' So I went, and it was in that place that I first saw Tala. He called to me that we were brothers and that I should follow him. Then he leapt from the top of a butte, and I beheld his second secret: Tala had wings and could fly like the ancient eagle."

Juan was blinking hard now, and he gave a great yawn. Ignoring that, Coconino went on.

"I could not fly like Tala, and so I lost him there in the Red Rock Country. I had to travel a long time with—" Here he glanced at Ironwood Blossom and decided to amend his story slightly. "—a long time into the Black Lands, beyond where our village stands now, until I was ready to give up and return to the Valley of the People without him. But just when I was most discouraged, the Mother Earth took pity on me and whispered in Tala's ear that he must follow me, and not the other way around. So when I came upon him cropping thistles near the river, I leapt onto his back and he carried me with him into the skies."

Ahead of him the mountains grew larger, a beacon to the travelers, drawing them onward. The menace at Coconino's back seemed to have fallen behind, caught in the center of the Sea of Grass while he and his family crawled slowly out of it.

"So we flew to the Mountain, we two," Coconino said, "and there we discovered that the Men-on-the-Mountain had built a great tower that spoke to the sky and called the Others back to Mother Earth. This was a great abomination, and so the Mother Earth commanded us to tear it down. 'How?' I asked. 'How can one man and one beast tear down a tower that speaks to the sky?'

" 'Ah, but Tala is no ordinary beast,' She replied. 'He is a kachina, a spirit animal, and his hidden gifts are three. Only two has he shown us so far; let us ask him what the third one is.' So we asked, and Tala stomped his forefoot and shook his head, and suddenly he spouted lightning from his horn. 'O ho!' I cried. 'That is how we shall defeat the tower. We shall call down thunder and lightning and burn it to the ground.' "

Was that a line of trees on the horizon? A line of trees surely meant a stream flowing down out of the mountains. Coconino caught his breath and quickened his pace.

"And did you?" Ironwood Blossom prompted.

"Hm?" Coconino stared blankly at her for a moment before he remembered that he had not finished the story. "Oh, yes. When the sky had grown dark so that no one could see us approach, Tala and I flew to the tower and struck at the Machine That Spoke to the Sky. I carried a great stick of metal, and he called forth the lightning from his horn, and we set fire to that place as a lesson to the Men-on-the-Mountain. It is not for us to decide who may and may not walk upon the bosom of the Mother Earth. She will decide, and She alone."

Suddenly movement on the horizon caught Coconino's eye. The line of trees was plain now, marking a wash that surely had to have water at that time of year. And stretching toward them, the intervening land had been cleared. Green plants grew up in contrast to the dried yellow-brown of the grass, plants whose nature was familiar to Coconino. Corn and beans and squash grew in carefully cultivated fields at the edge of the stream.

"Look!" he cried suddenly, pointing to three figures who ladled water out of that creek and into irrigation ditches by means of hide buckets attached to poles. It was this movement that had caught his eye. "Look there, Ironwood Blossom! Men and women are tending fields here. We have found the Southern Village of the People."

It was not the first time another hunter had accompanied Phoenix and the children, but it was the first time Sky Dancer had issued the invitation. Nakha-a was prone to invite his uncle Flint or Aunt

Talia's second husband, Raven's Wing; that was to be expected, since he was a pensive child and more at ease with older men than with boys his own age. But Sky Dancer had never before shown an interest in sharing these times together with anyone else. She was fond of her other relatives, especially her grandmother Two Moons, but Nina, Phoenix, and Nakha-a were her world.

Until now. Sky Dancer was twelve, and the first traces of approaching womanhood were creeping through her. Phoenix watched her now as they crept silently through the hills east of the canyon, hoping to flush some quail or perhaps a hare. She still looked all arms and legs, but high cheekbones accented her fine-boned features, and the long black hair she had carefully braided today was thick and glossy. You will be a beauty, Sky Dancer, Phoenix predicted. Like your birth mother.

Just then a fox leapt out of the brush and bounded away. Of the four arrows that zinged after it, Sky Dancer's was one of two that struck the mark squarely.

But you will be a hunter, like me, Phoenix thought with pride. She gave you that delicate nose and a body that will be better proportioned than mine, but I have given you the confidence to do what you desire in life. Even though that desire may not always be to hunt.

"Aiee! A fine, fat fox!" Dreams of Hawks crowed. He was older by three years and taller by a head, and his longer legs had allowed him to reach their fallen prey first. His was the other arrow that had buried itself in the rust-red pelt. He grinned back at Sky Dancer, his lean face made more handsome by that smile, and she blushed happily.

"Good shooting!" Nakha-a called, striking off to the right to search for his arrow, which had gone astray.

"A clean hit," Dreams of Hawks observed as he inspected Sky Dancer's arrow. "You have considerable strength for your age."

Thank God he didn't say "for a girl," Phoenix thought. Sky Dancer might have tackled him on the spot. But the older boy was being tactful, and complimentary as well: Sky Dancer did not have as much strength with the bow as Nakha-a did.

Sky Dancer squatted down beside him in the prickly desert weeds. "Will you offer its blood?" Dreams of Hawks asked her.

Eagerly she took her knife and cut cleanly across the fox's throat. As its blood spilled forth onto the earth, she chanted in a high, sweet voice, offering a prayer to the Mother Earth from whom came all nourishment and comfort.

Then she drew out her arrow, and Dreams of Hawks', too. "It

is not a good hide," she remarked, running her hand across the patchy red pelt and drawing it away covered with loose hair. "But the tail is nice. Do you want it?" And there was such an earnest expression on her face as she offered it to Dreams of Hawks that Phoenix had to cough and cover her mouth to ward off laughter.

Dreams of Hawks smiled indulgently, as he might humor one of his younger sisters. "Yes, I would like the tail," he said. "I will add it to the trophy pole in my mother's house."

"Clean the fox well," Phoenix called to them. "The season is warm, and it is a long way back to the village. I will help Nakha-a find his arrow."

A small smile twisted her lips as she turned away from them. Though he treated Sky Dancer like a younger sister now, in two years she would come of age. It might be quite a different story then. The idea appealed to Phoenix; not only had his mother, Corn Hair, been a friend of Coconino's, she was known in the village for her patience and quiet wisdom. Two Moons had once invited her to sit on the Council, but Corn Hair had declined.

"It is too great an honor for me," she had said simply. "And too great a burden. I have burdens enough to bear." With six children and a worthless husband, she was not argued with.

Dreams of Hawks seemed much like his mother, quiet and unassuming. Oh, there was gossip, to be sure: his older brother had courted a young maiden last summer, and just when it seemed a betrothal announcement was due, young Dreams of Hawks— fourteen at the time—had shown up at the girl's door with three fat ducks. The girl's mother had tried to be tactful about the gift, but when all was said and done, it had to be refused.

Poor boy, Phoenix thought. He must have been crushed. But he seems to have weathered it well. And he is a striking boy, with strong, well-proportioned features, and he's a fair hunter by all accounts. Ah . . . time alone will tell. Sky Dancer is her father's daughter; she will make her own judgment, and her meddling foster mother would do well to keep her mouth shut.

"Ho! Witch Woman!" Nakha-a cried out suddenly. "Look at this!"

The urgency in his voice brought her running. He had stopped short on the far side of a low paloverde tree and was gesturing excitedly at the dirt. Sky Dancer and Dreams of Hawks also trotted over to see.

A jumble of bones littered the ground for several yards around the tree. They were large bones, larger than any deer or antelope bones Phoenix had ever seen and much thicker. She picked up a broken one to examine it and found it was hollow and therefore very strong and light.

Suddenly a cold fear clutched Phoenix. She began to search through the bones. "What is it?" Sky Dancer asked, but Phoenix waved her to silence. She knew what it was even before Nakha-a picked up the single braided horn.

"Tala," Sky Dancer whispered in awe.

Wordlessly Phoenix took the horn from the boy. Her eyes brimmed as she remembered the noble beast that had been Coconino's companion on their adventures, oh! so many years ago. She had not seen Tala since the day Nakha-a was born. From time to time his trumpeting call had been heard in the village, but always from far away, and even that had not been heard in several years. The strength seeped from Phoenix's knees, and she sank slowly to her haunches.

"Is it truly Tala?" Dreams of Hawks asked wonderingly. His brother remembered, though he himself did not, having seen the great beast on the day Coconino and Phoenix flew into the Valley of the People on its back.

"It is Tala," Phoenix whispered tightly. Memories flooded over her: a proud beast with a look of disdain in his telescoped eye. He had had a special disdain for her, taking fiendish pleasure in unseating her when she rode behind Coconino. But how loyal the beast had been to his true friend! How right they had looked together, Coconino seated on the back of the majestic unicorn. How she longed to see them both again.

Nakha-a laid a hand on her shoulder in a childish attempt at comfort. "He was an old beast," the boy said softly. "Old beyond imagining, even when my father knew him."

Phoenix looked down at the horn clutched in her hands. "Was he, Nakha-a?" It was clearly two horns twisted together as one straight shaft. The base was jagged where it had been broken off from the skull, and the interiors were hollow. "Tell me what else you know," she pleaded softly. "Tell me about Tala."

The boy shrugged. "He was a proud beast. And a stubborn one."

Phoenix gave a half laugh, half cry. "Like your father." Then, "What else?"

Again he shrugged, a little helplessly. "I do not know what you want me to say, Witch Woman."

She looked around at the bones scattered on the ground, bones that had been bleaching there for several years. Scavengers had tugged at the noble beast's carcass; there were teeth marks on some of the bones. "Tell me he didn't die alone," she whispered.

Nakha-a shifted uneasily. "But he did," the boy told her uncomfortably. "He was . . . old. The younger bucks took away his does. They forced him out."

"Younger bucks?" Sky Dancer asked eagerly. For some time she had nourished a secret hope that one day she, too, would see Tala. Perhaps she would even ride him as her father had done. It was hard now that the old unicorn was gone. But her brother's words gave her hope. "Younger bucks like him?"

But Nakha-a shook his head. "There were no other bucks like him. Even his children were not exactly like him. He was . . . what is the word?"

"Unique," Phoenix replied sadly. "He was unique." Slowly she reached out and picked up a rib bone, a flat shaft nearly the size of Sky Dancer's bow. "Did one of them defeat him here?"

Nakha-a knelt beside her and picked up another rib bone, cradling it in his arm like firewood. He paused to stroke its smooth surface, then picked up another and added it to the first. "No, they did not follow him here," he said, studying a femur as though the story were written in its length. "He wandered here in search of . . . someone. I don't know who. My father, perhaps. But he didn't find him. Finally he lay down in the shade of this tree, but he disturbed a rock as he did so. There was a rattlesnake under it. It bit him, and he died."

Phoenix wagged her head dully. "A snake? No, it can't be. It can't be that he succumbed to a snake. He who carried Coconino to his attack of the Mountain tower, he whose lightning brought down the great Sky Ship from its place—"

"Nevertheless," Nakha-a said sadly, adding to his stack of bones, "that is how it came to pass."

Dazedly Phoenix looked around at the scattered remains. "We can't leave him here," she muttered. "We can't just leave him here to bleach in the sun like this."

"Should we take his bones back to the village with us?" Dreams of Hawks asked. "Surely they have great magic in them."

But Phoenix shook her head. "No," she said firmly. "No, I will not have his bones carted back to be ground into powder or waved over sick children. He was a creature beloved of the Mother Earth, and he deserves . . . something else."

"Perhaps," Nakha-a suggested, "we can find a more hallowed place to lay his bones, where they will not be disturbed."

"Yes," Phoenix agreed. "Let us find a resting place for Tala."

So they constructed a travois and put the bones on it. With Nakha-a in the lead, they set off over the rough country back toward the river. Here and there the land heaved itself up in small outcroppings, and shallow caves and rock shelves dotted the landscape, but although Nakha-a would pause from time to time, he passed them all by, saying, "This is not the place."

Still gripped by a profound sense of loss, Phoenix trudged behind the boy, uncomplaining. In her mind she tried to picture the unicorn humbled, defeated, lying down to die. "It's not right," she said finally. "We cannot tell the People that Tala died in such disgrace."

"It is no disgrace to be old," Dreams of Hawks offered. Though his face and tone were respectful of her grief, it was clear that he did not understand the nature of it.

"But to be thrust out of his place—no." Phoenix shook her head again. It was patently unacceptable. Tala must be remembered as a strong and vigorous animal, a worthy companion for Coconino.

"Then what shall we tell them?" Sky Dancer asked innocently.

Tell them? Phoenix's mind began to turn. Of course. She could tell them some other story, a better story, about Tala's end. The People were forever embellishing their stories, adding things, changing them to make a better story. Why shouldn't she do that for Tala?

"We will tell them," she said after a moment, "that Tala wandered here with his wives, choosing to be near the place where Coconino once found him. We will tell them that a pack of coyotes tried to run down one of his fawns, but Tala fought them off with his sharp hooves and scorched the ground behind them with the lightning from his horn. And when the coyotes were gone, a puma came and crouched on a ledge above the herd, waiting to pounce on an unsuspecting doe. But Tala picked up his scent and charged just as the puma leapt from its place, so that it was impaled on Tala's horn and died. Then, exhausted, Tala lay down in the shade of a tree to rest. And while he rested, a snake crept up upon him— a coral snake."

"But a coral snake's mouth is too small," Dreams of Hawks interrupted. "It could not bite such a large animal as Tala."

"It found him," Phoenix gritted, "lying down and bit the tendon that bulged out on his foreleg. It was a coral snake."

Behind her Nakha-a shook his head. "No, Witch Woman," he protested softly. "Let it be a rattlesnake."

"I will say it was a coral snake," Phoenix insisted. "It makes a better story."

Nakha-a looked unhappy but said no more.

"While he rested, the coral snake crept stealthily," Phoenix continued, "and struck. Tala squealed and bit the snake, and that is how we found him: with the head of the spiteful serpent crushed between his teeth."

There was a moment of silence. "It is a good story," Dreams of Hawks ventured.

"A good story," Sky Dancer echoed.

"It is no farther from the truth," Nakha-a admitted, "than many stories about my father."

"It is *mostly* the truth," Sky Dancer said. "No doubt Tala defended his children and his wives many times. And he did die of a snakebite. They were just on different days."

"Here," Nakha-a said suddenly, stopping on a rock-strewn shelf before a shallow cave. "This is where we should place Tala's bones." He indicated a crevice in the shelf where a stubborn paloverde had forced the rock to crack. Dirt and twigs had collected in the chasm, which was a foot wide and proved to be several feet deep. Nakha-a began to clear it out.

Following her brother's example, Sky Dancer knelt and began to excavate the debris. Dreams of Hawks joined them, and in moments the cleft was cleared. Then carefully, reverently, they unloaded the travois and placed the bones in the long crack, filling it up and mounding it over with the dirt they had removed.

Phoenix watched them as in a dream. Gone, gone, hidden from sight, she thought. Like Coconino. But Coconino is coming back; it is Tala who is gone forever. Tala, and Juan, and Falling Star—

"Witch Woman?" Nakha-a tugged gently at her elbow. "Witch Woman, the horn."

Phoenix blinked and looked down to discover she was still clutching the braided horn in both hands. Slowly she approached the mound of debris that covered the bones and knelt before it. "Good-bye, my reluctant comrade," she whispered, and twisted the base of the horn deep into the pile, a singular marker for a singular beast.

A voice came to her out of the past—her own voice: *Coconino? He appeared to just me, by myself. Does that mean anything?*

Without question.

What?

I do not know.

What does it mean now, Phoenix wondered, that we have found the dried-up bones of this legendary kachina?

CHAPTER SIXTEEN

"The bag, ma'am?" the security guard requested curtly.

Exasperated, Chelsea tossed her satchel up onto the counter and watched the guard go through it. Each hologlobe, each registration portfolio, each pallet of cosmetics was meticulously examined with a variety of instruments. "What does that one do?" she asked as the guard fed her hand-held recording unit into a boxlike device.

"Checks to see if there are any underlying patterns in the data," he replied crisply.

Good grief, she thought, they're checking to see if I'm smuggling coded messages in my account books. Has the whole universe gone mad?

It had, of course. As Chelsea headed out of the Newamerica City spaceport and toward the garage where her flivver was waiting, she knew she faced yet another ordeal before the vehicle would be let out of the port's tight security. Ah, well, she sighed inwardly. If it's this bad here on Juno, I'm glad I chose to leave Argo when I did.

It hadn't been bad in the early years, which was something to be thankful for. For the last twelve years, as she had warped from planet to planet choosing prime breeding stock, there had been few such security checks in the spaceports, no restrictions on her travel. Though Cin began winning prizes for his show dogs in the first year, it was not until she'd sold her first filly eighteen months later that they'd begun to make headway on their loans. Two years after that they had shown their first profit, and now . . .

Chelsea sighed a great sigh of contentment as she slipped into the worn seat of the flivver. Now Winthrop dogs went for premium prices on Argo and Darius IV, and the sale of one Winthrop yearling could sustain a family of four for six months. That was in addition to stud fees, show prizes, and board and pasturage revenue. Now, thank God, buyers came to *her*, so that the only time she had to leave the planet was to check out new stock or show one of the horses. I wonder what Indigo Lawrence thinks, Chelsea mused, knowing that by trying to force me out she forced me into such a successful enterprise?

It took her twenty minutes to clear security and be allowed out of the spaceport. Damned Troaxians, she thought. This is all their fault. I thought Argoans were bad, but at least they stick by their legal system. For the Troaxians, anything is legal if you can accomplish it successfully, and the only crime deserving punishment is failure.

It began with the Troaxian Cartel moving into asteroids and moons in different star systems with hostile corporate takeovers. Once the single-company installations were under Troaxian private control, the government of Troax moved in. Soon they had a sphere of influence that included eight moons, twenty-one asteroids, and a large share of three planets, in addition to their homeworld. Eight years ago the Argoan government had begun regarding Troaxian nationals as hostiles, and six months later Argo and all its allies—including Juno—had "closed their borders" to Troax entirely. There was no commerce between members of the two alliances, no tourism, no exchange of information. Espionage was reported to be rampant in both directions.

For Chelsea's ranching operation, it had been both bane and blessing. Troaxians loved horses, and she had just begun to cultivate a market there for Winthrop stock. But with the loss of Troax as a source of fine equines, people within the Argoan sphere of influence had to look elsewhere; many of them looked to Juno and the high-quality animals Chelsea and Cincinnati were raising.

The rolling prairies slipped away under her flivver now, and Chelsea felt more relaxed. The best thing about traveling was coming home. She'd put on no makeup when she had left the hotel that morning, had only slipped into a faded denim jumpsuit and brushed through her long blond tresses. They were straight now; spending her day with the animals and the wind, she had lost her ambition to fuss with artful curls. A simple leather and wood clasp held her hair in place at the nape of her neck.

Below her the prairie grass was golden brown with the heat of late summer. Good fodder, she thought, to put up for the winter. Not like three years ago, when I had to buy hay. And the corkberries were beginning to turn from gaudy red to a deep purple-black. Soon Cin and Susan and the two children would be pestering her to let them go berry picking in the thickets along DuMonte Creek.

On impulse, Chelsea swerved to the west and flew low over the winding stream that crashed down out of the high Lobo Mountains, wandered crazily across tableland colored rust with ripka bushes and scrubby blazons, and trickled slowly through the vast prairie to eventually water the northwest quarter of the Winthrop holdings. It was always muddy with the rich black soil no matter how slowly it wandered through its shallow channel, but it always ran. Always. In the early days of the planet's colonization farmers had drained it almost dry for irrigation, but the discovery of a huge underground lake and the passage of strict laws concerning water harvesting had saved the DuMonte. Now, as in the days before the coming of humankind, the lazy stream meandered through an otherwise dry country and provided refreshment for wild turkles, sealots, morphs, and pirarras as well as the llamas, cattle, and sheep that were raised here.

It was the pirarras Chelsea was worried about. Like Cincinnati, those birdlike creatures were fond of corkberries, and also like Cincinnati, the colorful yellow and red pirarras were quite charming—that is, until they were annoyed. Then their vicious claws and beaks could tear a full-grown dog to pieces in a matter of seconds; humans lasted only slightly longer. For most of the year the pirarra flocks avoided the pungent odors of humans and horses, hopping and flopping through the tall prairie grass in search of small mammals such as leppas and morphs. But when the corkberries ripened, the pirarras ventured close to inhabited areas, seeking their favorite treat.

Sonic sticks are effective, Chelsea told herself. I could just give Cin two or three of them and have him plant them in the ground around where they're picking; that should do it.

But "should" didn't satisfy Chelsea. She knew she wouldn't be comfortable unless she were standing there watching over them, a wide-angle stunner in hand.

There were no pirarras visible along the creek now, though. Chelsea lifted the nose of the flivver as she crossed at last into Terra Firma, and opening the throttle all the way, she took the most direct route home.

Home. As she set the flivver down in a whirl of dust, the yard around the ranch house was bustling with activity. Susan was grooming the golden retrievers, her very favorite of the four breeds of dogs the Winthrops now raised. Her eight-year-old daughter, Verde, was playing with a litter of weimeraner puppies, and ten-year-old Arizona Clayton Winthrop was in the paddock riding a chestnut yearling bareback, while their watchful chief wrangler, Marsha, guided the horse in careful circles.

"Verde?" Zachery had echoed when Chelsea called him to announce the arrival of her niece. "I can understand Arizona—that was the location of the mountain installation where the *Homeward Bound* was supposed to search for life. But Verde—doesn't that mean 'green'?" "For the Verde Valley," Chelsea had explained. "From what I can tell from the logs, that was where the shuttle made Earthfall. Cin has this thing about place-names."

Cincinnati himself came running up as Chelsea popped the seals on her door and stepped out of the flivver. "Chelsea, look, it works!" he cried, holding up a headset composed of preposterous-looking fibers and dials. "Watch! Watch what Domino does when I think pictures at him."

Chelsea leaned against the open hatch and smiled indulgently as her brother fitted the headgear on himself and turned to face his Dalmation sire, Domino. The dog was also wearing a contraption strapped to its head, and were it not such a long-suffering old creature, it would no doubt have been scratching furiously to rid itself of the troublesome device. But dear old Domino wagged his tail hopefully, hesitated, then turned and lumbered over to where Verde played inside a run with the weimeraner pups.

"See?" Cincinnati declared triumphantly. "I thought a picture of Verde to him, and he went to her!"

Chelsea shook her head. Oh, the implications were far-reaching for such a device; using dogs to assist physically challenged people had a long history, dating back to seeing eye dogs and before. But to communicate with a dog by direct brain wave transmission still seemed a bit creepy to Chelsea. However, Cincinnati seemed delighted to play with the new technology, and the Bendichi Manufacturing Company was delighted to have him testing their prototype.

"Very good, Cin," she told him. "But I don't think you'll get many dogs to put up with that headpiece."

"Oh, they're going to do—whatdoyoucall—in their brains."

"Implants," Chelsea supplied.

"Yeah. But I told them, not on *my* dogs. I don't care *what* you can get them to do, you're not going to cut into my dogs' brains."

Chelsea looked past him at the kennels. "Yeah? How about your children's?"

Cincinnati looked puzzled. Chelsea waved a hand toward the runs. "Verde just tried to let Domino in and managed to let all the puppies out."

"What?" Cincinnati spun around. "Verde!"

"I'm sorry, Papa!" the little girl called. "I'll catch them again."

Chelsea laughed and headed for the house, leaving father and daughter and overprotective Domino scrambling around the yard after the puppies.

"Chelsea!" Cin called after her. "Zachery called. He says call back; he wants to talk to you about business."

"Right." Suppressing a smile, Chelsea thumbed the latch and strode into the spacious house. It was a sprawling single-story structure with numerous windows and light, airy furnishings: simple, practical, and elegant—Jacqueline's touch still, after all those years. Susan was a fanatic housekeeper but not a decorator, and Chelsea had ceded the house to her, so very little had changed over the past twelve years.

Turning right into the kitchen, Chelsea slung her satchel carelessly into one corner and flopped into a chair before the full-wall screen. "Mazie: call Zachery," she instructed, and waited while the computer made the appropriate interplanetary connections.

So Zachery wanted to talk to her about business. Monkey business, most likely, and Chelsea's smile bubbled into a laugh. Zachery was a partner in the ranch, of course; he had fronted her a good deal of money in the early years, and she was proud of the fact that his stock in Terra Firma was now worth five times what he'd paid for it. But Zachery's frequent trips to Juno over the past twelve years had had little to do with checking on his investment.

She had never intended for them to become lovers, but it was almost inevitable that they had. They had watched one too many sunsets together. Their mutual regard and mutual need had made it comfortable. He had been out to see her not six weeks before, so no doubt this "business" would involve her coming to Argo to visit him. As much as she hated leaving Terra Firma again so soon, the prospect of a romantic weekend with Zachery was tempting.

Of course, it would mean turning down another one of his proposals of marriage. Every time they were together, from their first passion-filled encounter on the knoll behind the stable, he had ended by cradling her in his arms and pleading, "Marry me, Chelsea." At first it had been painful to refuse him; during those first hard years when the business was struggling and Susan seemed always to be pregnant, Chelsea would have loved to fall back on someone else's strength. But Zachery's legal practice on Argo had caught fire, and he could not leave it, and she would never again leave the comfort and contentment of Terra Firma. So firmly, patiently, she always told him no.

"Besides," she would inevitably quip, "you're in love with Camilla."

He didn't like that comment. Perhaps that was why she always made it. Over the years, while Chelsea had worked at cracking the mystery of the *Homeward Bound* by examining files and records and countless histories, Zachery had continued to visit Camilla. He was convinced that trapped inside her mind somewhere was the name of the agent or the TRC contact or some other useful information. Chelsea had gone with him the handful of times she had been back on Argo, but the ghostly beauty had never given them anything but the bittersweet pleasure of her company.

Suddenly the screen filled with Zachery's image. He had put on a little weight since Chelsea had first met him, but he was still a striking figure in his emerald-green robes and the latest fashion that he wore so well, a turban. At forty-two he was beginning to show the signs of overwork around his eyes, but that was all. "Chelsea!" he said with some relief in his eyes.

"Zach, that hat was made for you," she told him, putting her boots up on the kitchen table, an act for which Susan scolded her repeatedly. "So," she drawled, giving a throaty chuckle, "what kind of wicked debauchery do you have in mind this time?"

But Zachery did not laugh. "I wish that was why I'd called," he told her. "Chelsea, please come right away. Camilla is dying."

Sleep had not rid Phoenix of her terrible depression. Because they had wandered so far from the village, the four hunters had decided to camp overnight near the place where they had laid Tala's bones. But they had all slept poorly and risen before dawn, so that now they approached the village through the winding canyon as the sun was only halfway to its zenith.

Something was wrong on the island cliff, and Phoenix sensed it even before she could see that activity in the village was not bustling as usual. No women clustered in the shade to grind corn; no children ran up and down the path or played their games by the stream. No young men sat on the hillside, shaping their arrows or polishing their throwing clubs or sharpening hoes for the field. No maidens gossiped as they carried water jars up the path to the village.

"Grandmother," Nakha-a whispered suddenly as they reached the base of the hill.

Phoenix turned sharply to him, searching his face. His eyes brimmed with sorrow. "Can't you feel it?" he asked her. "Can't you feel it in the wind? Can't you hear it in the call of the doves?

She's gone, Witch Woman. She has gone to the bosom of the Mother Earth.''

For a moment Phoenix only stared at him dimly. Then she bolted for the village above, ignoring the path and climbing straight up the steep, heavily vegetated incline.

Sky Dancer would have gone after her, but Dreams of Hawks caught her arm. ''Let her go,'' he said softly. ''She is a Witch Woman, and her grief is different from ours. That is what my mother says.''

''But I am her daughter!'' Sky Dancer cried. ''And it is my grandmother who is gone. I grieve for her, too!''

''All the People grieve for her,'' Dreams of Hawks replied. ''Who will lead us now?''

It had not occurred to Sky Dancer before. ''Who will lead us now?'' she echoed, turning to her brother.

But Nakha-a's stoicism had dissolved in the wash of his own grief. ''What do I know of these things?'' he sobbed. ''Let the Council settle such matters. Only let me mourn my grandmother.''

''Go ahead,'' Dreams of Hawks instructed them, pushing them gently toward the foot of the path. ''Go into the village together, the grandchildren of Two Moons, the children of Coconino. Go as hunters.'' He handed Nakha-a the dressed fox. ''I will come behind. I will help Fire Keeper build up the Elvira to dance the Dance of Grief for a great woman of the People.''

The women of the People had already gathered at Two Moons' chamber when Phoenix arrived. They were keening softly as she entered, a subdued weeping that pervaded the air and slithered under her skin to raise her hair on end. Talia knelt beside her mother's body, dressing her in her shawl of office and her ceremonial moccasins. Flint knelt nearby, weeping openly, holding one of the irreplaceable cotton blankets to receive the beloved leader. And Nina was there, clutching a leather pouch that had been Two Moons', trembling and keening with tears flowing freely down her face.

They all looked up as Phoenix entered. ''What happened?'' she asked in anguish, but no one answered.

Phoenix crawled across the stone floor to gaze on the peaceful, withered face of Two Moons. ''Was she sick?'' Phoenix asked desperately. ''Did she have a fever? Did her heart give out?''

They only looked at her and were silent.

''The Mother Earth has taken her,'' Nina said finally, seeing that some explanation was wanted. "She sang sweetly to Two Moons in the night, and this morning we found her spirit gone from her flesh."

"But she wasn't even sick," Phoenix protested, her voice choking and tears smarting in her eyes. "She wasn't even—she wasn't—"

"Blessed is the Mother Earth," Flint chanted, "and blessed are the children she calls unto herself. They sleep in her bosom and are comforted in the arms of their Mother."

Now the others took up the chant, the Song of Death. Soon they would carry her out of the stone house and away into one of the side canyons overlooking the fields of the People. There she would be laid to rest in a cleft of rock, covered with stones, to be cradled for eternity near the People she had served. Then the mourners would return to the village, where the ceremonial fire Elvira would roar at the foot of the island butte and the People would dance out their sorrow in the light of its flames. For Two Moons they would dance the rest of the day and most of the night. Then they would go back to their lives and their labors, waiting for the Dance of Birth, which was sure to follow in the course of time.

But Phoenix sat trembling in a corner of the house, watching the preparations, unable to join in the keening. Dear God, what will we do now? she wondered. When the Mother died, Two Moons was there to carry on. But who has Two Moons groomed for the task? Nina? She is not forceful enough to lead. Me? Not me. I can't—they don't like me. They fear me, they respect me, but they don't really *like* me. How can I lead?

The answer crept up to her from the floor of the adobe house, seeping up through the soles of her feet, into her legs and spine, trickling gently upward to touch her grieving, frightened mind.

Together, it said. Nina and Phoenix together. One's patience, the other's strength. So it should be.

But Phoenix rocked herself in the corner, stubbornly denying the voice in her head.

"I have been thinking," Nina said quietly.

It had been a week since they had danced for Two Moons, and the Council was gathered in the chamber that had been hers, that was by default the Council chamber as well.

"So have I," Phoenix said quickly, "and I do not think we should choose a leader. I think the Council should lead."

They looked at her with what she had learned was a look of

patience for the Witch Woman who did not really understand the Way of the People.

Nina sat across the circle from Phoenix, still young-looking for a woman of the People but still hawk-nosed and gap-toothed. Her hair had begun to gray though she was only thirty, but having only one child, she was not as weathered or stooped as others in the room who were near her age. "I have been thinking," Nina continued, unmindful of the interruption, "that perhaps we should go back south."

"Back to the Valley of the People?" Phoenix erupted. "Back within striking distance of the hatred of the Others? Never!"

"No, not back there," Nina answered calmly, "but to another place. When we found Two Moons, she held this pouch in her hands," she explained, showing a small leather bag. "It is filled with seeds of the Grandfather, which Coconino brought to us before he departed." She opened the bag and showed the tiny black saguaro seeds inside. "We know that these seeds will not grow here in the north; we have tried, but it must be that the season is too short for them, as it is for the cotton plants."

Carefully Nina retied the thongs of the pouch and fixed it at her waist. "I think that Two Moons brought these seeds out for a reason," she continued. "I think she meant for us to take them south, where they will grow, where the cotton will grow, but not near the camp of the Others. I think that we should go beyond that place. Far beyond it." She gathered her ceremonial shawl closer around her and stared at the small fire in the center of the room, whose smoke told the people outside that the Council was in session.

It sounded like a prophecy, but Phoenix was not fooled by it. This was a plan of Nina's devising, not the word of the Mother Earth. "Don't be foolish," she retorted. "Here we have houses, and our fields are planted, and there is game in the hills—"

"And snow in the winter," Nina added, "and more of the coughing sickness."

"Not in recent years," Phoenix said. "I know there is only one harvest here instead of two, and no cotton, but there is enough. We have learned to adapt to this place, and we have made it livable. Ask the children. Are they unhappy here?"

Around the fire, the other Council members sat somber and brooding. It was something to consider carefully, and they would not speak in haste.

"The crops are in the ground already," Gray Fox conceded.

"I did not mean to move the village now," Nina said. "I meant in the fall, when the harvest is in and we can carry with us enough food to last the winter. By spring we can have found new fields to plant and new places to hunt. And we have not forgotten how to build wickiups.''

Still the Council was silent, considering. Phoenix looked anxiously from the face of one to another. ''We can't leave here,'' she insisted. ''This is where Coconino will know to look for us. You said he told you of this place, Nina, that he said it would be a good place to live. You heard him say it.''

''Yes, I did,'' she admitted. ''But Witch Woman, that was long ago.''

The hair rose on the back of Phoenix's neck. ''And what if it is? He is coming again. You told us that, too.''

''No doubt he will come,'' Nina agreed. ''But we do not know when. And in the meantime . . . He will find us, Witch Woman. He is a good hunter, and he will find us. Never fear.''

But Phoenix was adamant. ''We will wait for him here. I will not have him think we forgot him or care nothing for his words to us. Coconino said to move the tribe to the island canyon, and in this canyon we will stay until he returns.''

''Nina meant no disrespect,'' Many Waters spoke up. ''Coconino was a brave and wise young man, and his sacrifice—''

''He's not dead!'' Phoenix snapped. ''Don't speak of his sacrifice when he's not dead!''

''I meant the cost of his deeds,'' Many Waters soothed. ''Having to go through the Magic Place to the Sky Ship, wandering lost between times, losing his friends and now his mother.''

Phoenix shook her head; they could never grasp the concept of time travel, that Coconino was not in limbo somewhere, lost or sleeping. She had given up trying to explain.

''We will never forget,'' Nina assured her. ''But we can remember in another place.''

''Yet She Who Saves has a point,'' Gray Fox said. ''Coconino told us to wait here. We do not want to offend him when he returns.''

''Offend him?'' Nina echoed.

''He is the favorite son of the Mother Earth,'' Laughing Jay agreed. He was the youngest member of the Council, a young man of Flint's generation. ''If one so favored spoke of this place, then we should stay. It must be what the Mother Earth wills.''

In the dim light of the Council chamber Nina's eyes narrowed. ''The Mother Earth uses many tools,'' she said carefully, ''and has different messages at different times. Thirteen years ago She used Coconino as Her tool and gave us a message through him and through She Who Saves about moving to the north. But She did not say we were prisoners here.''

''Has She told you we should move?'' Phoenix challenged.

Nina's usually impassive face went hard in the firelight. It was the first time anyone had spoken openly of the loss of her gift. The Council drew a collective breath as it waited to see how she would respond to this direct confrontation.

''She does not speak to me as She once did,'' Nina said finally in a low voice. ''But that does not mean that I cannot discern Her voice in other ways.''

''Many of us hear the voice of the Mother Earth,'' Ernestina put in, ''by thinking long and carefully about things. This was the way of the Mother when She led us. This was the way of Two Moons. Do you say, Witch Woman, that we do not hear Her voice as well as you?''

Now it was Phoenix who drew back, wounded. How could she admit that she never heard the voice of the Mother Earth? ''I say only that the words of Coconino were clear,'' she replied. ''I need no other voice to guide me.''

''This quarreling gets us nowhere,'' Many Waters interceded. ''Let us think about this thing until the moon grows full. Then we shall meet and talk about it again.''

''Done,'' Nina intoned quickly.

''Done,'' Phoenix agreed. Then Fire Keeper put out the Council fire, and they all rose to make their way outside.

But Nina put a hand on Phoenix's arm. Reluctantly, Phoenix stayed behind as the others filed out.

''Witch Woman,'' Nina said softly, ''we must be of one mind in this matter.''

''Then prepare to stay,'' Phoenix said coldly, ''for I will not leave.''

The hardness had gone from Nina's face, and she was once again the quiet, patient woman Phoenix had known for over a decade. Sadly Nina shook her head. ''Do you not see what you are doing, Witch Woman?''

''I see that I am staying where Coconino can find us,'' Phoenix replied.

''You are telling them,'' Nina said pointedly, ''that Coconino's words must be obeyed as the will of the Mother Earth.''

Phoenix caught her breath. ''I'm only telling them what I think,'' she dodged.

''No, Witch Woman, you are telling them *what* to think,'' Nina persisted. "Coconino was a great man, without question, but he was a *man*. Do not make him otherwise."

It was the same complaint Corn Hair had voiced years before, and Phoenix liked it no better now. "When have I ever said he was anything else?" Phoenix demanded.

Nina sighed. "When did he become not 'a favored son' but 'the favorite son' of the Mother Earth?" she asked wearily. "When did it become as important to wait for him as to listen for the voice of the Mother Earth? When did it become necessary to obey without question the words of a hunter and a storyteller? Witch Woman." Again Nina grasped Phoenix's arm, and though Phoenix drew back, Nina's grip stayed firm. "Do not make him into a god."

"I do no such thing!" Phoenix protested. "I only give him the praise and the honor he is due, for he has saved not only the People but the Mother Earth as well. Should we now run and hide from him?"

"He will find us," Nina repeated. "Only let him find us whole and healthy, in a better place than this."

"Let the Council decide these matters," Phoenix said, pulling away at last. "Or let them choose a leader who will decide. But I will stay here."

Nina shook her head. "You do not understand, Witch Woman," she said. "It is you and I who lead now. There was no choice to be made. It is you and I, because that is the Way Things Are. You cannot think only of yourself any longer. I know you loved him; I know you serve the People for his sake. But serve them by thinking more of their welfare than of Coconino's memory. Help me lead them south."

"Never!" Phoenix said, and strode out of the Council chamber.

Jacqueline Winthrop eased her tired bones into the wicker chair on her crude sun porch. Mike Thornton had built the porch for her, attaching it more or less to the side of her domed quarters. The roof was a latticework of thorny ocotillo stalks thatched with yucca leaves, and the low sidewalls were pieces of cholla wood, hollow and by nature riddled with holes.

In her arms Jacqueline cradled a small bundle, a red-faced infant wrapped snugly in a thin cotton blanket. For the moment it seemed content to sleep, and Jacqueline was content to grin foolishly at it, clucking and cooing like a mother hen.

Soon Rita Zleboton came out from inside and joined Jacqueline on the porch. Originally each woman had had her own dome, but as the younger castaways began to marry and wish for more privacy than the four-to-a-hut domes allowed, it became obvious that there needed to be changes in the hierarchy of the settlement. So Rita and Jacqueline, good friends anyway, had moved in together to help the housing crunch.

Rita stooped over and looked down at the tiny visitor. "Stealing babies again?" she asked. "Or is there something you forgot to tell me?"

"Found it under a cabbage leaf," Jacqueline quipped.

"I thought as much." Rita squinted at the child once more. "Hrmph," she grunted. "Skinny little thing. Must be that new Johanneson baby. Yeah, no hair, just like his daddy."

"It's a girl," Jacqueline grumped back. "Angelica."

Rita plopped down in her own wicker chair, a larger and sturdier one than her friend occupied, meant for the kind of abuse she was prone to give furniture. "Now, my Zachery—there was a baby. Nine pounds ten and a half ounces when he was born. Shook the doctor's hand, cut his own umbilical cord, and headed for the door."

Jacqueline chuckled. "Independent, eh?" She jiggled the little one in her arms. "Chelsea was like that. Couldn't be a doctor like her mother, you know—had to pick something that took less schooling so she could be out in the thick of it as soon as possible."

A round laugh shook Rita's large frame. "They just can't wait, can they?" she observed. "Can't wait to have all the responsibilities, all the headaches, make all those stupid mistakes for themselves." She pointed across the settlement to where a rough-hewn log house was going up. "Like Cyd and Torpi there, moving out of a climate-controlled dome and into an unheated, uncooled wood house, trying to accommodate their growing family." Her eyes twinkled. "Of course, you and I were never like that, were we?"

"Never," Jacqueline scoffed.

They sat in the dwindling daylight, watching the sun splash red and gold fire across the western sky.

"Do you suppose they ever met?" Rita asked after a moment.

"Who?"

"Your kids and mine."

"Undoubtedly," Jacqueline replied.

"What makes you say that?" her friend asked.

"Because your son is lobbying every government in the colonized universe to send a ship after us, and my daughter is turning

Argo upside down to find the financial backing for it." Jacqueline looked over at Rita slyly. "Don't you think?"

Rita gave a great sigh. "I wouldn't be surprised," she admitted. "Zachery always was one for hopeless causes. But to tell the truth, Jackie, I'd rather they just built a little log cabin like that one over there and settled down to enjoy life."

Gazing out to the north of them, Jacqueline saw the first star wink to life in the darkening sky. "Not a chance," she whispered.

The hospital room was clean and light and airy, and the smell of it made Chelsea gag. Zachery was already there; she doubted he had left it in the last two days. His face was stubbled, something unheard of for the immaculate attorney, and his eyes were ringed with a weariness she had never seen before.

Camilla lay on the white sheets, a gaunt, pale creature lost even in that small bed. Her eyes wandered in Chelsea's direction as the younger woman entered quickly and crossed toward them. "Angelica?" she asked in a soft, high voice.

"No, Camilla, it's Chelsea," Zachery told her. "You remember Chelsea. Chelsea Winthrop."

"I saw your mother last night," Camilla said.

Chelsea and Zachery exchanged glances. "How is Mom?" Chelsea asked Camilla.

"Tired," Camilla replied. "She works too hard."

"But other than that she's well?"

"As well as can be expected." Camilla shifted, a small rustling motion in the crisp hospital linens. She looked hollow and emaciated. "I'm tired. I'm going to rest now," she announced, and promptly fell asleep.

Chelsea drew Zachery aside. "What happened?" she demanded.

"She stopped eating three weeks ago," he replied. "They've got her on nutrients, but she's given up, Chelsea. She's just given up."

"What's this about my mother?" Chelsea asked. "Is she hearing voices now?"

Zachery waved her off. "She probably doesn't even know who you are. Half the time she doesn't know who I am. The other half . . ."

"What?"

He rubbed a hand across his stubbly jaw. "Damn, I need a shave," he muttered. "Stay with her, Chels, because sometimes . . ."

"She's lucid," Chelsea guessed.

"Almost. It seems like it. I don't know," he admitted. "Maybe I just want her to be." He crossed to the door. "Give me ten minutes. I need to get out of here."

"Take twenty," she called after him. Then she settled herself in his chair beside Camilla's bed. "Now, don't go away," she whispered to the sleeping woman. "Don't you dare go away till he gets back, because he'd never forgive himself, and I don't want him to have to live with that. Okay?"

Camilla's eyes opened slightly, and she glanced up at Chelsea. "Are you the angel of death?" she asked, and her voice was foreign, neither the high sweet voice of madness nor the low rich voice of reason.

"No," Chelsea said simply, waiting to see where Camilla's mind would wander next.

But it seemed fixed there temporarily. "I'm waiting," Camilla said gravely, "for the angel of death. I want to explain to him. Or her."

"Explain what?" Chelsea prompted.

"No, no, you're not her," Camilla protested. "Or him." And she drifted off again.

Almost lucid, eh? Chelsea thought. Poor Zachery. He wants so much to believe that Camilla can come back from that dark place in her mind where she's been hiding for thirteen years. He wants so much for the fairy princess to be rescued from her prison.

"Ms. Winthrop?"

Chelsea looked up, startled. The room was empty. It took her a moment to realize it was Camilla who had spoken. "You are Chelsea Winthrop, aren't you?" Camilla continued, and Chelsea recognized the quality of her voice now. It was the one she had heard when they'd had Camilla in orphic somnolence years earlier. It was a sane voice.

"Yes, I'm Chelsea Winthrop," Chelsea stammered.

"You don't know me," Camilla said, offering her hand, "but I'm—acquainted—with your parents. By reputation. I'm Camilla Vanderhoff."

Chelsea shook the extended hand, at a loss for a reply. "Pleased to meet you," she managed finally.

"Have you had any news from them?" Camilla asked. "Is the mission going well?"

For a moment Chelsea's jaw worked soundlessly. Then, "They've had a few problems," she said.

Oh, Zachery, please come back, she thought. Please come back and see her while she's almost well. Please come back, because I never know what to say to this woman, this woman who murdered the man who murdered the *Homeward Bound*.

"Problems?" Camilla's face looked bleak, almost guilty. "I'm—sorry to hear that. I'm . . . truly sorry. . . ." Then a look of horror crept over her perfect features. "They're . . . dead, aren't they?" she asked. "Oh, my God, they're . . . they're all dead."

"No."

The voice from the doorway was so sharp and resolute that Chelsea jumped. Zachery stood framed in the opening, and it occurred to Chelsea that had she not known him, she might have thought he was Camilla's angel of death.

"Zachery?" Camilla turned in his direction. "Zachery, they're all dead, thirty-one people, they all died, and I helped him—I *helped* him—"

"No, Camilla," he repeated, stepping into the room. "It was a ruse, just as you told us. We sent a rescue mission, and we found them on Earth, still alive."

"But—" she sputtered, "but—the reports—"

"Were false," Chelsea chimed in. "You helped us prove Dillon's involvement, so we used his money to send a rescue mission, and they're all right. They're all fine. No one died."

The lie was bitter on Chelsea's tongue, the more so because she wanted it to be true. Are we as daft as Camilla, she wondered, clinging to this futile hope after thirteen years?

Zachery was beside her now, kneeling by Camilla's bed, taking her thin hand in his. "Because of you," he whispered. "They're all safe now, because of you."

"I . . . was afraid . . . I'd killed them," Camilla said, her voice fading. She closed her eyes and gave a soft sigh.

Zachery clenched her hand, as though by sheer force he could keep her there. An intensity burned in him that Chelsea had never seen before, not in their most intimate moments, and like a flame the old jealousy flared to life in her. But the creature in the bed was so pitiful, so helpless that Chelsea could not sustain her bitterness. Soon she would be gone, leaving Zachery and his grief for Chelsea to deal with. Soon.

Then Camilla's eyelids fluttered, and she looked up once more into Zachery's eyes. "Was it the letter?" she asked.

Zachery seemed unable to speak. "What letter?" Chelsea prompted.

"The letter Dillon was looking for," Camilla said. "The one that connected him to everything. He found one and burned it, but he knew there was another. At least one more. Did you find it? Is that how you proved his complicity?''

"Yes," Chelsea whispered. Then, with a glance at Zachery, "*You* helped us find it. You saved them all."

A smile spread across Camilla's face, and the wrinkles faded from her brow. "Thank God," she breathed, and slipped away.

Tears collected in the corners of Sky Dancer's eyes and a crisp fall breeze chilled them, but she disdained to call attention to them by wiping them away. She faced her half brother on the narrow path outside her mother's house, hating the situation, knowing it was far beyond the control of two twelve-year-old children. Even if they were the children of Coconino.

"It will be a great adventure," Nakha-a blustered, though his bravado did not fool her for an instant. "None of the People has been as far south as the camp of the Others for thirteen summers. I shall be able to put to the test now my knowledge of the language of the Men-on-the-Mountain that the Witch Woman taught us. I shall be the one to speak to the Others."

"I wish you would not," she told him gruffly. "I wish you would avoid their village and simply go south without stopping there."

"But we must stop there," he replied pragmatically. "Because those who come with us are so closely related, we must have *linaje nuevo* before we move on."

The village had split along family lines, with most of the farming families joining Nina in the quest for a better climate, while the family of Two Moons and those who had known Coconino best stayed behind with Phoenix. Many had tried to heal the rift, including Flint and Corn Hair, but both women were resolute, each sure that what she did was right.

"What do you think?" Sky Dancer had asked Nakha-a privately, knowing her brother's heightened mystic powers.

But he had only smiled sadly, enigmatically. "I think I won't have to worry about Coral Snake picking fights with me anymore."

I'm glad that bully is staying in the north, Sky Dancer thought now. I will give him his comeuppance one day, and my brother will be free of him forever. If that is the only good in all of this, perhaps it is worth it.

"I will see your birth mother," Nakha-a pointed out. "Would you like me to give her a greeting from you?"

But Sky Dancer only shrugged, convinced that as her world was torn apart here, nothing could go right. "She probably does not want a greeting from me," she said bitterly. "If she asks, say that I am of the People and that I follow in the footsteps of my true mother, She Who Saves."

Nakha-a regarded her a moment. "It would be truth, anyway," he said. "But perhaps it would be better if I said nothing."

"Do as you think best," Sky Dancer grumbled. "You were always smarter than me."

"Not smarter," he demurred. "I only listen better." Then a sly look crossed his face, and he cuffed her gently. "At least I leave you with a good hunting companion," he teased.

Despite herself, Sky Dancer blushed furiously. "My mother is the best hunting companion," she insisted.

"Ah, but not so interesting as Dreams of Hawks."

"He's already of age," she protested. "He will not wait for me."

"We narrow his choice," Nakha-a pointed out, "by our leaving." Then, because it hurt too much to talk about, he said, "Besides, our father waited until his twentieth summer to take a maiden."

"But our father was Coconino."

"And a man, my sister," he countered. "Just because he did many amazing things does not mean they were easy for him. In truth, that is what made him so great: that it was no easier for him than it would be for you or me or some other one of the People."

Sky Dancer toed the ground with her bare foot. Nakha-a seemed to know so much more about the father they had never met than she did. Was that part of his gift? she wondered. Or was he one of those, like Two Moons or Corn Hair, who just understood people?

"Will he come back, Nakha-a?" she asked finally. "Will he truly come back to us?"

"To the People, yes," Nakha-a answered certainly. "He has only skipped over the years as a pebble skips over a pond. But how many years? That I do not know, my sister. That I do not know."

CHAPTER SEVENTEEN

Coconino paused at the edge of the field, watching the five men and women who had stopped their hoeing when they saw him approach out of the Sea of Grass. They leaned on their tools and stared at him with curious eyes, but there was no hostility or fear in them. Coconino nerved himself to speak.

"Good day, my brothers and sisters."

Smiles broke across their faces. "Good day, friend," they greeted him. "Welcome. Have you traveled far?"

"Very far," he replied, relaxing somewhat. With a gesture he called Ironwood Blossom out of the tall grass, where he had instructed her to wait with the child. Even now she came timidly and lingered behind her husband, peering out at the strangers.

"Have you come from the northern village, then?" asked one of the men. He had a triangular face and a mouth that seemed accustomed to smiling. Like the other men, he wore a cotton loincloth, while the women had knotted short cotton skirts about their waists. One of the women had constructed a large-brimmed straw hat for herself.

"Yes," Coconino replied. "From the Northern Village." The familiar cotton clothing was a welcome sight. For two years he had seen only leather and yucca fiber garments. Perhaps he could trade one of his finely made arrows for a loincloth of soft cotton.

"Then you must be tired," the speaker guessed. "Come and refresh yourself at the stream. Then we will take you back to our village. It is some distance; we have just moved to our summer camp higher in the mountains, where it is cooler."

Coconino was anxious to go on, but he could see that Ironwood Blossom was weary, so they crossed the field and settled in a mesquite bosquet at the edge of the stream. The day was warm, and Coconino doused himself thoroughly in the cold water; then he took Juan from Ironwood Blossom and brought him to play in the water, too. With the comforting presence of trees and mountains, he was soon at ease again.

Ironwood Blossom was not. She crouched in the shade, throwing furtive glances back in the direction of the farmers. After a few moments she did lay aside her pack and splash cool water on her sweaty torso, but her attention never strayed long from the workers in the field.

Sitting on the bank of the stream, dandling his son in and out of the water, Coconino noticed her abiding concern. "What is it?" he asked. "They seem very friendly."

"My husband," Ironwood Blossom ventured, her voice tinged with fear, "I have never before in my life met people whose names I did not know!" Earnestly she searched his face. "What do I call them?"

Coconino shrugged. "No doubt they will tell us," he said with all the nonchalance of a veteran traveler. "That was the way of the Men-on-the-Mountain when I visited them, and even the Others. They would offer their hands, like this—" He demonstrated a handshake for her. "And they would tell me their names."

"And did you have to tell them yours?"

"Of course!" he laughed. "How would they know it if I did not tell them?"

At that a thought occurred to Coconino. These people did not know who he was, did not know he was the great Coconino. If he were to tell them some other name and make Ironwood Blossom call him by it, too . . .

"Will you tell them my name?" she pleaded. "I am afraid to speak to them."

"Afraid?" Again he laughed. "Why should you be afraid? They are of the People, just as we are. They are children of the Mother Earth."

Yes, he told himself. They are children of the Mother Earth. Why should I be reluctant to tell them my true name?

Just then one of the women from the field approached them. She was a young woman, perhaps twenty, but heavily built in the manner of the People. "If you have rested," she said, "I will take you to the fields farther south, where the rest of our people are working. One of the children will guide you up to our village."

They struck off through lush fields of cotton toward the telltale line of trees that marked another stream tumbling down out of the mountains. As they walked, they came to plantings of squash and beans, and close to the second river they found corn. It was here that several dozen adults were at work, aided by older children. A girl of eight was dispatched to lead the travelers upstream into the leafy refuge of the mountains.

She was a bashful girl, and Coconino did not intrude on her silence. Instead he watched the changing terrain, taking note of landmarks so that he could find his way up and down this trail again. As the land rose higher, the trees grew tall and he could seldom see through their canopy, but now and again there would be a clearing and the bright blue sky would shine through.

Whenever the trees gave way, he could see to both north and south the walls of the canyon through which this stream ran. There were rugged cliff faces and odd spires of rock decorated with pale green moss and lichens. Unlike the buttes of the Red Rock Country or the Black Lands, these spires looked like spindles or stacks of oblong beads strung from earth to sky. Red and russet, buff and brown, some looked so precarious, he wondered that they did not fall from their high perches and take half their neighbors with them.

The climb was a steep one, but the cool shade made it infinitely more comfortable than the long hike across the level fields had been. They stopped once or twice to let Ironwood Blossom rest, and young Juan fussed and fretted to be out of his confining pack. Their young guide seemed quite charmed with the little boy. "Do you have younger brothers and sisters?" Coconino asked.

She lowered her eyes shyly, and he thought she was not going to answer. But, "Two," she chirped finally. "And another one soon, Mother says."

The barrier broken, she chattered the rest of the way up the mountain. Her father and mother were both working in the fields, and she and her older brother had gone along to help while her grandmother kept the little one. Her grandmother wove blankets, the most beautiful blankets in the whole village; everyone said so. Her grandmother was descended directly from Father Nakha-a, so that meant that she was, too, although her father was not.

The child did not notice how Coconino started at hearing the name of his son in this place. *Father* Nakha-a? Could it be that his son was an honored ancestor here? Or was there another with that same name?

But they were all Father Nakha-a's children, the girl went on, his adopted children; that was what her grandmother said. She thought, though, that her grandmother said it so that her father wouldn't feel bad. Her cousin Digs in the Dirt was not descended from Father Nakha-a, although his sister White Fawn was, though the little girl did not pretend to know how that was. She meant to ask her mother soon, though, for her mother had promised she could stay for the birthing of this baby because she was nearly a maiden herself, and everyone knew that the women talked about many woman things at a birthing, such as which maidens ought to marry which young men, and how many wives a rich man could have, and whether a woman could have two husbands if they promised not to argue over whose children were whose.

Coconino was relieved when the sounds of breaking wood and the laughter of children reached them above the rushing of the stream. In a moment the trees gave way to an alpine meadow where there were fifty or more sturdy wickiups, newly thatched and hung round with the trappings of family life. Old women sat sewing and cutting up tender plants for the cook pots, while old men shaped implements of wood or bone. Some younger women were spreading strips of meat on drying racks near a smoky fire, while a number of young men worked on green wood for bows. Everywhere there was laughter and the buzzing of voices gossiping, telling ribald jokes, teaching the children the stories of the People.

But the sight that warmed Coconino's heart more than any other was that of several great looms scattered throughout the village. Gaudy red yarns, striking black, mellow mustard, and pale off white dangled on shuttles or flew back and forth in the hands of skillful women as blankets and bunting and thin shirting material grew strand by strand, thread by thread.

"What are they doing?" Ironwood Blossom gasped. "Is it magic?"

"It is the magic of the People from generations ago," Coconino answered gaily. "They are weaving!"

The sight of strangers in their village brought activity virtually to a standstill. Their tiny guide dashed away and came back tugging an old woman by the hand. "Grandmother, Grandmother, these are strangers; they have come to us from the northern village!"

At the sight of her, Coconino gasped. She was a stately elder with gray hair clasped at the nape of her neck. As tall and as broad-shouldered as Ironwood Blossom, she was somehow rounder and softer of build than the younger woman. But it was the cut of her features that startled him, the familiarity of her face, so that for a moment he could not speak.

"We bid you welcome, travelers," the dignified woman said

gravely and with just a trace of nervousness. "Are things well with you in the north?"

No, Coconino wanted to shout. No, in the north the People are few in number, and the Council whines for my intervention in everything, and no one remembers how to build a loom. We mistrust everyone we meet, and no one encourages the young to go on great adventures.

"We are well, honored one," Coconino replied politely. "But it seems to me our southern kin are better."

The woman smiled, a gap-toothed smile such as Coconino expected from an honored grandmother, yet the absence of those teeth seemed out of place in this face. "Tell me," Coconino continued. "The child spoke of Father Nakha-a. You are his child, are you not?" And mine, Coconino thought. For your face is so like the face of she who bore me: my mother, Two Moons.

Pride flushed across the woman's face. "I have that honor. Do you know of Father Nakha-a even in the Northern Village?"

"*I* know of him," Coconino answered softly. I know of him from a letter, one kept by the People for generations until my coming. It told me the names of my children in that time: Sky Dancer, Michael—and Nakha-a."

"We are pleased that you have come to our village," the woman said. "Father Nakha-a said that one day our northern kin would come and that we must wait for that time and not seek them out ourselves. I am glad the Mother Earth has blessed these old eyes by allowing them to see this day. Come! Sit in the shade and refresh yourselves. Empty Basket, bring food for our guests. Chipmunk, run up the trail and see if your father is coming back yet from the Thinking Place."

"I am here," called a deep male voice, and a strapping man with a rounded belly sagging over his loincloth came out of the forest to the southeast. "I was on my way down from the Thinking Place when I saw our guests arrive in the fields below. Welcome, travelers. I am One-Eyed Fox, child of Father Nakha-a and nephew to this illustrious woman, Dancing Knife." He stopped before Coconino, his bearing kingly, his confidence supreme. "And by what names are you called, travelers?"

Coconino hesitated. "My wife is Ironwood Blossom," he began, "and my son is Juan." What would they do if he gave them his true name? He had had a bellyful of admiration in the north. It would be so simple to pick another name. . . . But it would be a lie. Coconino drew himself up to his full height, some inches greater than One-Eyed Fox's. "And I am Coconino."

"Coconino!" One-Eyed Fox barked, and around them the People tittered. "No, you cannot be Coconino. No one is named for Coconino, for the legends say that he will come again. Therefore, we do not use his name for our children."

The hair on Coconino's neck prickled slightly. "You misunderstand me," he said carefully. "I did not say I was named for Coconino. I *am* Coconino." Now he would have to prove again who he was, as he had to the People of the Northern Village when he had first arrived there.

Around him there was a spattering of gasps, and One-Eyed Fox looked puzzled. "But you cannot be Coconino," he said. "I only just saw him today, from the Thinking Place."

Now it was Coconino's turn to be confused. "You *saw* me?"

"I saw Coconino," One-Eyed Fox corrected. "He sleeps in the hills northeast of us."

Coconino shook his head. "I do not know what you saw," he replied, "but I am Coconino. I have come from the Times That Were, from the great battle with the Sky Ship, and I have been living in the Northern Village for three summers."

The two men stood regarding each other, younger and elder, neither hostile but neither willing to give ground. Finally a smile tugged at One-Eyed Fox's lips. "Indeed, you are bold enough to be Coconino," he allowed, and the people clustered around them murmured their amusement.

For a moment Coconino teetered on the brink of annoyance; then he decided congeniality was a better course. After all, these people had not seen him fall from the sky; why should they take him at his word when they knew nothing about him? So he smiled, too. "It grows dark," he observed. "If you will allow us to stay the night, perhaps tomorrow I can show you I have Coconino's skill with the bow, as well."

"And I will take you to the Thinking Place," One-Eyed Fox agreed. "There we shall see Coconino."

The aroma of roasting meat filled the air, and mounds of tortillas, bean cakes, and spicy corn bread surrounded the Elvira. Mushrooms that grew rampant in the forests of the southern mountains flavored everything, and a tart drink made of crushed berries mixed with honey flowed in quantities that rivaled the nearby stream.

Coconino was hard pressed to understand his southern relatives. They questioned his identity, yet they made a feast for him such as the People of the north had never done.

Ironwood Blossom huddled near him, overwhelmed by the strangeness of everything, but One-Eyed Fox's oldest daughter, Eyes Like a Deer, seemed to have made it her business to ease the older girl's discomfort. She chatted easily with Ironwood Blossom, fussed over Juan, and asked her questions about the village in the north. It was a great relief to Coconino, who had been afraid that his reticent wife would burst into tears at this great commotion in their honor.

Coconino was surprised to learn that One-Eyed Fox was not the leader of the southern village. That honor fell to an aging farmer named Corn Grows Tall, who was also descended from Father Nakha-a. In fact, half the families in the village claimed to be descended from that great leader, and the other half were trying to marry into them.

When the People had sated their hunger and settled back comfortably in the lush green grass outside their wickiups, the storytelling began. There were stories aplenty about Father Nakha-a and his wisdom: how Father Nakha-a found the Thinking Place high on a mountain peak; how Father Nakha-a settled the marriage dispute between two cousins who had eloped with one girl; the conversation Father Nakha-a had had with a black bear, the first such creature the People had ever seen. The tale of this monster fascinated Coconino, and he resolved to ask One-Eyed Fox more about it later.

Then Dancing Knife spoke up. "Who knows a story about Coconino?" she asked, and a murmur went around the fire.

"I know a story," a hunter named Swift Thinker piped up. "When Coconino was a boy, he went out to hunt a badger. His stepfather had forbidden him to do so, for the badger is a vicious animal and Coconino had only his second bow, being then in his ninth summer.

"But Coconino was Coconino, and out he went to hunt the badger. When he arrived at its den, though, he found the badger waiting for him. Before he could even nock an arrow, the badger charged after Coconino, and the little boy jumped up the nearest tree, leaving his bow on the ground below him. There he sat until, late in the day, his stepfather came looking for the missing boy. His stepfather was so angry with the boy that he would not kill the badger but let Coconino stay in the tree until the badger went into its den for the night. Then Coconino sneaked out of the tree and slunk back into the village. He never again went against his stepfather's wishes."

The People chuckled merrily at this story, and Coconino's

cheeks burned. Beside him, Ironwood Blossom sat slack-jawed in amazement. "Who told you this story?" Coconino demanded.

"Why, Three-Legged Coyote told it first, of course," Swift Thinker replied. "Although it was told to me by Gilded Finch."

"Three-Legged Coyote?" Coconino gulped.

Ironwood Blossom tugged at his sleeve. "Do you know this Three-Legged Coyote?" she asked in a whisper.

"He was my mother's uncle," Coconino hissed. "I did not think anyone but my stepfather knew that story."

"Then it is true?" she asked in astonishment.

"I was a boy," he defended in covered tones. "What did you expect, that I was perfect as a child?"

"Yes," she replied frankly, and then uncharacteristically she giggled and hid her face in her hands.

"I know another story of Coconino," said Dancing Knife, settling herself more comfortably with a shawl around her shoulders to ward off the night chill and the forest insects. "When he was a young man, he dreamed of paying court to a Witch Woman from the Mountain."

Coconino gasped.

"He dreamed of a fair-skinned beauty with hair like sunlight and eyes the color of Father Sky. So much did he desire this Witch Woman that he declined to take a wife of the maidens of the People. Then, in his twentieth spring, while Coconino was out hunting, a Witch Woman arrived at his village."

Like a man who had fallen from a cliff and knew he had to land on the rocks below, Coconino saw where the story was headed but could do nothing about it.

Dancing Knife told the story with relish and with no few looks in Coconino's direction. "When Coconino returned, the Witch Woman had disappeared into the Council Chamber high in the Village of the Ancients, in the old Valley of the People. Impatient to see his love, Coconino climbed to that high place and perched himself on a rooftop, waiting for her to come out.

"Waiting in the courtyard below him, however, were several of the maidens of the People. Now, Coconino had declined to take a wife, but being a young man, he was fond of gazing upon the maidens anyway. As he sat there in the sun, watching their lovely faces, admiring their shimmering black hair, he began to think the thoughts that young men think." There was a titter from the maidens present, and the unmarried men jabbed each other in the ribs with great smirks.

"As he was lost in his thoughts, the Witch Woman came out of the Council Chamber and started down the ladders toward the courtyard. Coconino rushed to the edge of the roof to catch a glimpse of her, but his head was still spinning and he lost his balance, tumbling off the roof of the house and into the courtyard at her feet.''

That brought a general laugh from the crowd, and Coconino grumbled to his wife, ''I did not fall from the roof. I jumped down through the ladder holes and came through the door, but a small child tripped me up.''

''And at this sight of the would-be lover flopping in the dust, the Witch Woman threw back her head and laughed like a coyote,'' Dancing Knife concluded, and several of the young men set up a yapping in imitation of a pack of coyotes.

For a moment Coconino waited in excruciating anticipation for the rest of the story, for the news that the Witch Woman was not fair and lovely but tall and thin with skin and hair as dark as any of the People. But that did not seem part of Dancing Knife's tale. She took up a bowl of the berry juice and looked around for the next storyteller.

As troubled by this reprieve as he was by the embarrassing story that had been told, Coconino growled, ''And does no one know any stories of the great deeds of Coconino? How he tore the Sky Ship from its place and flung it to the ground? How he defeated the Others by not allowing them to return to their homes on the distant Sisters of the Mother Earth?''

Dancing Knife settled her knowing eyes upon him, and they were the eyes of Two Moons hauling her son up short. ''Yes, we know those stories, too,'' she agreed. ''And we tell them often. But Father Nakha-a bade us also tell the stories of Three-Legged Coyote to teach our children that the most foolish of men can be a great hero and the most heroic of men can be very foolish.''

Smarting from the truth of his own son's assessment, Coconino rose and turned from the fire. But he was arrested by a small voice piping up from near his feet. ''I would tell a story.''

Coconino turned back to gaze in amazement at Ironwood Blossom. She was trembling like a leaf, a fine sweat standing out on her forehead, and she could not raise her eyes from the ground. But she took a deep breath and continued. ''This is not a story of the People,'' she prefaced, ''but a story of what happened two springs ago, when some of our men were coming back from the camp of the Others.''

Slowly Coconino dropped to his knees beside his timid wife and listened in shocked silence as she forced herself to go on speaking. "They came near to the Sacred Well of She Who Saves, and a boy named Tree Toad who was scouting ahead saw two men drop from the sky. He ran to get the others, and when they came back to the place, they found only one man, dazed and struggling to his feet."

Her voice was shaking, and she paused to swallow. "He was a young man of perhaps twenty summers," she went on, "and he said his name was Coconino. He said that a Magic Place had torn him from the Time of the Coming of the Others and that he awoke only as our men found him. That man is my husband." Now she raised her eyes to the silent throng and thrust out her chin. "He wears the token of She Who Saves," Ironwood Blossom concluded, "and none of my village will challenge his right to do so."

Tears formed in Coconino's eyes as he watched his wife sink back into a huddled ball, clutching their sleeping son to her breast. He did not even look up as Corn Grows Tall approached him and knelt to examine the medallion around his neck.

Then the old man reached across and touched Ironwood Blossom's trembling arm. "We will not challenge it, either," he said gently.

"Come," said One-Eyed Fox, crossing around the fire toward them. "It grows late, and you have had a long day of traveling. Come share my wickiup tonight, and tomorrow we will help you build one of your own for as long as you wish to stay among us."

Coconino rose and helped Ironwood Blossom to her feet. The courtesy was extended, he knew, not in honor of the great Coconino but in honor of the courage shown by his timid wife.

The pleasant sounds of the forest were a delight to Coconino. He awoke early and lay on his mat listening to the chirping of birds and insects, the whisper of the branches high overhead, and the steady drone of the stream. He and Phoenix had often camped in wooded areas, and waking to these sounds brought back a flood of memories: toiling through the pine forests of the Red Rock Country in search of Tala, camping near the Fire Mountain in the Black Lands, teaching her to stalk and to use the bow . . .

Inside the wickiup a form rose and picked its way carefully toward the door. Coconino raised himself and squinted until he could make out One-Eyed Fox's eldest daughter, Eyes Like a Deer. She paused in the doorway and looked back at him. "Pardon, Coconino," she whispered, and slipped out.

Across the way another form stirred. Soon the whole village would be waking. Coconino's bladder urged him to abandon his mat and his memories and get on with the business of the day. With a glance at his sleeping wife and child, he slipped quietly to his feet and stole from the wickiup.

The scent of moisture was heavy in the air, and dew covered the entire camp. How different this place was from the Northern Village or even from the Valley of the People where he had grown up. There was something in the earthy smell of the forest that roused him, and he wished for his own wickiup and the privacy it would afford him and Ironwood Blossom.

By the time he returned from relieving himself in the forest, Eyes Like a Deer was stirring up the cook fire in front of the family's wickiup and setting water to boil in a skin bucket. She smiled at him. "I hope I did not wake you," she said softly in deference to the number of people still sleeping in the camp.

"No, I was awake," he assured her. "I was listening to the sounds of this place. They put me in mind of . . . many things."

"My mother says it is a good sign that I am forced from my bed so early in the morning," Eyes Like a Deer continued, shouldering a large clay pot. "It has been nearly two moons now since we visited the Camp of the Others." She looked up as One-Eyed Fox came back from the forest, where he, too, had answered the call of nature. "Good morning, Father," she greeted, and headed for the stream with her jar.

Coconino turned to his host. "You took your daughter to the Camp of the Others?" he asked in surprise, trying to imagine why one would take a maiden of such tender years on so long and arduous a journey.

One-Eyed Fox broke into a smile. "Yes, we took ten maidens this time," he told Coconino. "An auspicious number, don't you think? We have great hopes for Eyes Like a Deer, too. Her mother has been watching closely for the signs."

"Ten maidens?" Coconino echoed. This was even harder to grasp. "Why would you take ten maidens on such a journey?"

One-Eyed Fox seemed mildly surprised. "Why, to be Chosen, of course. It was the tenth spring."

"Chosen!" Coconino went rigid with shock. "You allow your maidens to be Chosen by Others?"

One-Eyed Fox was puzzled by his guest's consternation. "Of course. How else are we to have *linaje nuevo*, new blood? Do not the northern People do the same?"

"No!" Coconino snapped. "We would not—" But he stopped short, realizing that his sharp reply was bound to offend the older man. "We do not seek *linaje neuvo*," he amended.

Now it was One-Eyed Fox's turn to be shocked. "Oh, this is bad," he said gravely. "The blood of the People will grow thin and weak if it is not refreshed from time to time. Father Nakha-a decreed that every tenth spring those maidens who wish to be so honored should be escorted to the camp of the Others, that they may be the Chosen Companions of the men there. Sometimes only one or two children are gotten in this way, but with ten maidens making the journey this spring, we hope for at least five."

Coconino suppressed a shudder. That the blood of the People should be polluted with the blood of the Others . . . perhaps, now, by the blood of Derek Lujan himself . . . "Are you not afraid," he asked carefully, "that the evil of the Others will taint the People?"

One-Eyed Fox laughed heartily. "You northerners have strange notions indeed! The Others are not evil. They are different, I will admit; their clothing is strange, and their speech is stranger still. And they are ugly; that much I grant you. But they are much as the Men-on-the-Mountain must have been when our ancestors lived in the Valley of the People and Teachers came to them there." One-Eyed Fox fished in a pouch that hung from the outside of his wickiup, brought out a handful of crushed leaves, and threw them into the skin of boiling water. "Of course, I have never seen a Man-on-the-Mountain myself. But I imagine they were much like the Others."

Coconino squatted by the fire and kept silent. For so long he had nursed his fear and hatred of the Others as the defilers of the Mother Earth. But what was it Phoenix had said to him when the Others had first arrived? "People are people, Coconino, some good and some bad." Perhaps it was true. Of the Others he had met, only one had been truly evil. . . .

"Tell me," Coconino said to his host. "When you were in the Camp of the Others this spring, was there among them one called Lujan?"

"Lujan?" One-Eyed Fox cocked an eyebrow. "You mean the evil one who brought the Sky Ship and threatened the peace of the Mother Earth? Lujan is always present among strangers, and we must always be on guard for his manifestation."

It took Coconino a moment to realize that One-Eyed Fox had spoken of a spirit, like an evil kachina, who lived from age to age and might seize the body of a person or an animal to wreak havoc. He shook his head, "No, I mean a man," he explained. "A man like me, who passed through the Magic Place as I did, a man with light-colored hair and blue eyes, a man with dazzling speech and the heart of a serpent."

"A man." One-Eyed Fox rubbed his chin, taking in the import of Coconino's allegation. "There was a man," he admitted, "who was possessed of a strange spirit, and they called that spirit Lujan. I remember because it surprised me. This man did not appear evil but only a harmless *bobo*, a fool, a crazy person. He would walk through the village with a pack on his back, talking to himself, and he constructed machines. Is this the man you mean?"

"Did his hair lie in ripples?" Coconino asked. "The color of polished oak?"

One-Eyed Fox could only shrug. "I can hardly tell one Other from the next; I do not remember. I remember only that his mind was as jumbled as a den of rattlesnakes."

Crazy. *Sze-sze-moh*, having an upside-down spirit. Coconino considered the implications of that. One-Eyed Fox seemed to think it made the man harmless. But if indeed it was Derek Lujan, might that harmlessness, even the craziness, be a pretense? Lujan was one who could spin a lie like a spider spun a web and catch as many unsuspecting victims in it.

Or even if his mind had gone soft, could he ever truly be harmless? When one plotted and schemed as naturally as one breathed the air or digested food, could even madness change that? A river forced from its channel only found a new course and sometimes a more treacherous one.

A chill came over Coconino. Perhaps he and Ironwood Blossom would stay with the southern People for a long time.

The members of the Executive Committee looked up uneasily as Liza Hanson walked in. Slowly she looked from one face to the next, meeting each pair of eyes with a hard stare that was far removed from the genial, gentle blue eyes they were accustomed to seeing in Camp Crusoe's doctor.

"He'll live," she said finally.

Murmurs and released breaths whispered around the room. But was it relief or disappointment? Liza looked across at Tav Ryan, a haggard caricature of her former self. Would she ever learn to forgive herself for maiming her cousin Mo? Not likely. Not for a long time at least. And was she disappointed now that the perpetrator of the entire incident was going to live?

I should have let him die, Liza thought, reading their faces. A little less care in my stitching, holding back on the antibiotics—it would have been easy, and you would have looked the other way, wouldn't you? Thanked me for it, probably. But I couldn't do it. He's a human being and my patient, and I couldn't do it.

Portia cleared her throat delicately. "How long," she asked carefully, "do you think it will be before he—that is, until he can—"

"Till he's mobile?" Liza filled in, her voice hard and cold. "Till he can walk around and open doors and sneak up behind people and go looking for more weapons?" She nailed Portia with a look. 'Weeks, I'd say. Months, most likely. But it will happen, ladies and gentlemen. Believe me, it will happen."

Portia straightened her already straight shoulders and patted her perfectly styled hair. "Then we have some time," she said.

"Time?" Weariness caught up with Liza, the fatigue not only of repeated surgeries but of the mental war she had waged, the battle between her instincts and her ethics. "The time has come and gone, Portia. The time was before he ever developed an arsenal of—things. The time was before he started a fire, and gave his guard a concussion, and nearly got himself killed. Time ran out on you long ago, Portia, and I am sick to my stomach from trying to mop up after you."

There was a moment of shocked silence. Then one of the men present bristled and huffed, "If you think this job is easy—"

"Easy?" Liza echoed. "Hell, no, the job's not easy. What you did was easy. What you did was nothing, was stand back and see what happened, and you did it *because* it was easy. I couldn't do that. I had to decide whether to let that bastard die or try to save him. I had to make a choice, and I made it—right or wrong, good or bad, I had to *do* something. Now it's your turn."

Another man cleared his throat. "Just what would you have us do, Dr. Hanson?" he asked coldly.

"Make a decision," Liza snapped. "Just make a goddamned decision."

CHAPTER EIGHTEEN

"So if you were Derek Lujan," Chelsea asked Zachery's image on the screen in her kitchen, "trying to keep a letter out of Oswald Dillon's hands, where would you hide it?" The image was confined to a small square just left of center. Around it were arrayed a dozen files of various types: a speculative grid of Lujan's movements and contacts in the months prior to his application to TRC, a collection of statements from survivors of the *Aladdin* disaster, an independent interpretation of Lujan's routine psychological tests, Jacqueline Winthrop's medical log from the *Homeward Bound*. They represented the gleanings of fifteen years of research.

There was a few seconds' lag as the transmission from Juno was warped through space to its destination, received, and responded to. "Honestly, Chelsea," Zach complained from his office on Argo, "you jump to more conclusions than anyone else I know."

"That's because you hang around with Argoan lawyers," she said dryly. "They have no imagination, Zach."

Again the lag. Then, "Well, yours is working overtime!" he accused her. "First of all, what makes you think the letter Camilla referred to was left by Dillon's agent from the *Homeward Bound*? And second, why are you so convinced Derek Lujan was the man?"

Laughing, she brushed aside the spec graph and set her standard "current awareness" searches to running in its place. Then she concentrated on his face. Even with the annoying time lags, it was good to be able to talk to him—expensive but good. She'd seen so little of him in the three years since Camilla's death; she'd begged him to take some time off and come stay at Terra Firma for a while, but he'd declined. Work, he'd said. Guilt, she thought. It was the worst kind of grief and knew no comfort.

"Use your head, Zach," she insisted now. "Lujan had to be

251

the agent. Besides being highly placed and the only ranking officer to survive the 'plague,' he was the only one with both the brains and the balls to pull it off.''

The time lag was a little longer this time. ''Well,'' he conceded, ''you're probably right. You've been investigating the man for the past fifteen years; you probably know him better than his mother.''

''Or his stepmother,'' she added, remembering the stories she had heard from one of Lujan's classmates. ''Now, *there* was an interesting relationship.'' She waited for the disgusted look she knew was headed toward her via the fifth dimension. ''But be that as it may,'' she went on, ''the man was no one's fool. If he took Dillon's commission to sabotage the *Homeward Bound*, you can be damned sure he purchased some kind of insurance for his safe return. I don't know why we didn't think of it before; maybe because we're not criminals.''

''Well, one of us isn't,'' Zachery muttered.

She ignored the remark; she took his best shots without comment, out of habit, just as he took hers. ''Zach, you work with the criminal element,'' she said, tapping on the tabletop in front of her with a light pen. ''Put yourself in Lujan's shoes. What kind of letter or document would you construct to ensure that your employer didn't arrange your untimely demise?''

''Chelsea, the criminals I work with got caught, remember?'' he pointed out. ''They're the stupid ones.''

''Pretend,'' she urged him. ''What kind of information would Dillon be afraid of?''

''Anything that would link him with a crime,'' Zachery supplied.

''Which is what Camilla intimated. And where would you hide such information?''

He paused, drummed his fingers on his desk. ''Good question,'' he said. ''Dillon seems to have had access to all kinds of protected records.''

''Remote access,'' Chelsea said with a secretive smile.

''Remote access?'' he echoed.

''That is, access through a computer system from an outside point,'' she explained. She'd been pondering her new theory for several months, and now she felt ready to share it with Zach. ''It's an archaic term, from the days before the Evacuation, when they first invented telecommunications and people were able to link stand-alone computers to other distinct computer systems. But I think the term sheds some light here.''

"Perhaps it sheds light on Juno," he retorted. "Here on Argo I'm still in the dark."

Chelsea stifled a smile, knowing it would only irritate him more. How strange that after all these years his dour humors should amuse her as much as his jesting ones! "Look, Zach," she explained patiently. "The computer system doesn't exist that can't be tampered with if you have proper access. What kind of document do you have to physically have in your hands to alter or destroy?"

He blinked. "A paper document." Finally it registered with him. "You mean when Camilla said Dillon destroyed the letter he found, she meant an actual ink-on-paper kind of letter?"

"And probably a handwritten one at that," Chelsea agreed. "They're harder to alter, and it's easier to detect forgery. Now, where would you keep a paper document?"

"Beats the hell out of me," Zachery responded. "It's not an issue I deal with on a daily basis."

"Me, either," she admitted. "Particularly with my background in information investigation. But Zachery, I'm sure we're looking for a paper document, and I'm sure it's in the hands of a person who was told to reveal its contents if certain specifications were met."

"Such as Lujan not coming back from Earth," Zachery guessed. "But then, where is it? It should have been revealed long ago."

"There must have been more to the trigger," Chelsea mused. "Some condition beyond his nonreturn."

"Or the document's already been found," Zachery suggested. "And destroyed, like the first one."

"That's possible," she had to admit, "but I doubt it. Dillon died before the news of Lujan's death was released; he couldn't have intercepted the information as it was revealed, which would be the most vulnerable point. And Camilla seemed certain he hadn't found it before that time." She sat up. "Zach, I'm going to start sending messages to everyone Lujan ever knew or had contact with. Someone's got to have that letter."

He sighed, recognizing the determination in her voice. "Just don't send any messages behind Troaxian lines, will you?" he chided gently. "These days the government is as jumpy as a kid in a haunted house. I'd have a devil of a time proving you aren't a spy."

His image disappeared, and even as it faded, Chelsea felt a tug of regret. It seemed, suddenly, such a long time since Zachery had last proposed to her. He had stopped quite suddenly when

Camilla died. At the time she'd thought it was part of his grieving, but in three years he still had not returned to his old pattern. Had he given up on her finally? Or was it that with Camilla gone, it was too scary?

With a sigh Chelsea turned back to the wall screen and set up a program to begin selecting individuals to whom she would send her message. Before she could set the parameters, however, a block of light began flashing from the section of her screen where her current awareness searches were running. "Mazie: quadrant D, section two—what triggered that light?"

"Mention of *Homeward Bound* in a news report from Xerbus," the computer intoned. "A historical preservation society that maintains an Earthward radio receiver reports that it believes it has intercepted radio transmissions from an exploration team to the *Homeward Bound* nearly sixteen years ago."

Chelsea's jaw dropped. "What?"

"Please make your question more specific," Mazie responded.

In the background Chelsea could hear the entryway door being flung open as Cincinnati clumped into the house.

"Mazie: show full text of referenced article," Chelsea instructed, shunting aside the other program she'd begun. Of course—radio signals sent from Earth toward the *Homeward Bound* not only would have reached the ship but would have kept on going in space indefinitely. Depending on the latitude of the exploration team and the point of rotation of Earth on its axis, those signals might just now be reaching the nearest populated planets. It was just such a message—picked up hundreds of light-years distant from Xerbus, on the far fringe of the galaxy—that had sparked the Terran Research Coalition decades before.

But the radio signals aimed at *Homeward Bound* would not have been log reports, edited or otherwise. They would have been the unaltered transmission of the exploration team. Chelsea's mind raced. The *Homeward Bound*'s daily dispatches, warped through space from Earth to Argo, had arrived with only a few hours delay; would those radio signals, nearly sixteen years on their journey, confirm or deny what was in those reports? Would they speak of a plague or of treachery?

"Hi, Sis, what's up?" Cincinnati chirped from her elbow.

Chelsea silenced him with a wave of her arm. "Mazie," she snapped. "Get me an address on the organization that claims to have picked up those signals. I want a copy of everything they can get that might be connected with the *Homeward Bound*."

"The *Homeward Bound*!" Cincinnati exclaimed. "What is it? What signals? What's going on?"

With a sigh Chelsea turned and looked up at her brother. He looked more like their father every day, his hair beginning to gray at the temples, his face acquiring character lines. I know Dad's dead, she thought to herself. But what about Mom? Is there any chance, after sixteen years, she could still be out there, waiting for us? And even if she is, how can I get anyone to go after her? Or how can I get my hands on Dillon's money and go myself?

"Cincinnati, sit down," Chelsea invited him soberly. "There's something I think I should tell you about."

Drums echoed throughout the canyon from the tiny enclave nested in the many rock niches of the island butte. After a long winter, spring had broken onto the Village of the People with a riot of bright flowers and edible plants. Now the crops were in, the first fruits of cactus and trees were filling the baskets of the gatherers, and the People were eager for this time of rejoicing. This celebration would renew their spirits, filling them with hope for their future.

In an open area where the women usually gathered to grind corn, the flames of Elvira leapt high into the night sky. Clustered around her, above and below the ledge and strewn the path in both directions, the People jigged and bobbed in the rhythmic dance of celebration. Seated in places of honor were a young couple dressed in ceremonial ribbon shirts. The shirts were made of leather, of course, and not cotton, but the long fringes that fell from sleeve and yoke were painted in colorful blues and reds, and polished wooden beads were knotted artfully among them.

Leaning against an adobe wall, out of the way of the dancers, Phoenix fought back a swelling in her throat. She sipped now and again at the sugary sweet *tay-ayoh* in her horn cup, but her mind was not on its flavor. It was on the glowing face of Sky Dancer, lit orange-red by the flickering flames as she beamed up at the boy beside her.

Not boy, Phoenix thought. Man. Only I still see him as a child, and her even more so. But it has been over a year since her womanhood ceremony; that makes her fifteen, and according to the customs of the People, this is a prime age for a maiden to marry.

For the past year Phoenix had lived in dread of the day when Dreams of Hawks would arrive at her door with a bighorn sheep slung across his shoulders or dragging a fat javelina sow, ready to pay court to Sky Dancer. Each time he climbed up to the village with game she would pray, Please, Mother Earth, not today, not yet. Let me keep her a little while longer.

But privation had delayed the young man. After Nina had led her band of followers south, winter had howled down out of the north with a vengeance. Like a wild kachina intent on destroying those who stayed, it blew snow through the canyon with savage fury, keeping everyone indoors for days at a time. Even when the wind had gone, the cold hung on with the viselike grip of a Gila monster, and it seemed nothing would shake it.

Finally, a reluctant spring arrived, but of those remaining in the north, there were hardly enough farmers left to tend the communal fields properly. Hunters who should have used their sharp eyes and quick reflexes bringing in game manned the irrigation ditches. Women far gone with child toiled long hours hoeing the tender plants, and children who could barely walk toddled behind them pulling at thorny weeds. The old and the infirm sat for long hours in the merciless sun, driving off rabbits and other vermin that threatened their crop. Phoenix herself had spent many sixteen-hour days in the fields, fighting back her own despair and trying to encourage the People.

Their hard work had yielded only a fair harvest, but it was enough. The following winter was less harsh, so that for most of the village that second summer was less intense, with people bringing wiser hands to the task.

For Dreams of Hawks' family, however, it was a year of tragedy. His mother, Corn Hair, had collapsed in the fields, seized with an early labor. The child—her seventh—was born dead, and Corn Hair herself was too weak and ill to work for many months. Her oldest daughter, then fifteen, had recently married and was caring for the children of a dead sister-in-law, so Dreams of Hawks had taken it upon himself to shepherd his younger siblings to the fields each day to join in the labor.

That left him no time to hunt, of course, and he could not achieve a prize worthy of laying at Sky Dancer's door. Even when his mother recovered and he had more time to spend with his bow, every piece of game was needed to fill the mouths of his family. His hunter father, Lame Rabbit, provided little to the cause, and in rage Phoenix threatened to order him into the fields, where at least he would not be wasting his time, but Sky Dancer pleaded with her not to.

"Think of Lame Rabbit's shame," the young girl had begged. "And that shame will fall upon Dreams of Hawks, too. Please,

Mother, leave well enough alone. Dreams of Hawks and his mother will manage. They always have.''

It was at that moment that Phoenix realized how perceptive her foster daughter had become. In Nina's absence, Sky Dancer had come to be a tempering force for Phoenix's often rash reactions.

The next winter Lame Rabbit had gone out to collect wood and had not returned. Dreams of Hawks spent three days searching for his father, with nothing to show for it but severe frostbite and two blackened toes that the Healer had to cut away. Were it not for the boy's physical pain, Phoenix would have thought him and his family better off for the loss of Lame Rabbit. At least there would be no more nearly fatal pregnancies for Corn Hair.

Finally, in late spring, Dreams of Hawks had arrived with a mule deer buck to lay at Phoenix's door. For a moment she just looked at the youth, looked at the lean, athletic body, grown strong with hard labor, looked at the narrow face with the somber eyes that had already seen most of a man's responsibilities, looked at the quiet hope written there.

What would you think of him, Coconino? she had wondered. What would you think of this youth who courts your daughter? Would you call him unworthy? Undoubtedly, for who could be worthy of the daughter of Coconino? But I like him, this sober young man. And more important, Sky Dancer likes him.

Behind her Sky Dancer had sat motionless, holding her breath. Finally a smile had tugged at Phoenix's mouth, and Dreams of Hawks broke into a relieved grin. Enough of sorrow and want, Phoenix thought. Let there be joy.

There was joy on their faces now, as they drank *tay-ayoh* from a single cup. Phoenix's eyes misted as she watched, and she knew how lonely her stone house would be without the innocent, pragmatic presence of Sky Dancer to fill it.

''You look proud, She Who Saves,'' came a deep voice from near her elbow. Phoenix glanced over to see Flint standing there, his bare chest slick with sweat from dancing. One could hardly see in him the scrawny adolescent who had begged his half brother to let him participate in the raid on the Camp of the Others, oh, so many years ago. He was no taller than Phoenix but was at least twice her girth with a barrel chest and strong, stocky legs—the image, said those who remembered, of his father, Made of Stone.

''I am proud,'' she replied. ''He is a good boy—man—and will make a fine husband. And she—''

''She,'' Flint finished, ''is the most beautiful maiden in the village.''

Is she? Phoenix wondered. To me she is: slender and graceful, with shining hair and bright black eyes and a face whose features are dainty but sharp. That is not the beauty of the People, who are round in body and broad in face, yet they always remark on it, this exotic beauty of hers.

Beside her, Flint cleared his throat. Something was on his mind. "I have been thinking," he began after a moment. "I have accumulated several hides this winter that my family does not need. So have Raven's Wing and Hair Like a Rope. We thought perhaps, if you would come with us, we would journey to the camp of the Others and see if they have need of these things."

Phoenix looked up sharply. "I do not care what they have need of," she said harshly. "We will not go to their camp."

"It is only that we are curious," Flint persisted, "if they raise cotton and corn as we do or if—"

"They raise their hands in anger!" she snapped. "Flint, you of all people must remember how it was, how they burned Juan and Falling Star at the river's edge, how—"

"I remember," he cut in harshly. "Believe me, Witch Woman, it is not something one can forget. But I also remember the feel of cotton against my skin and a full belly through every winter. I remember that you have been to their camp twice—once to bring Kah-ren to us and once again to take her back—and that you suffered no harm there."

"That was different," she blustered. "They don't see me as a threat; they see me as a spokesperson, as a peacemaker."

"Which is why we need you with us," he explained. "That, and to speak to them in their own language. Tell them we wish only to trade some furs for—"

But Phoenix shook her head, turning from the crowd and lowering her voice. "It doesn't matter who I am; if I showed up with three or four men of the People at my back, armed with bows, they would be filled with fear. Fearful people are dangerous people, Flint. It is not worth the risk."

He was silent, and Phoenix thought she had made her point. But just as she was about to turn back to the festivities, he touched her arm. "It is not just the cotton," he said softly, "and the food. We need *linaje nuevo*."

For a moment Phoenix only stared at him in shock. Then, "Have you eaten locoweed?" she demanded.

"She Who Saves, we are small in numbers," he pleaded, "and this past winter claimed four more lives. The Men-on-the-Mountain taught us long ago that marrying close relatives will make the babies sick, perhaps even mad. So they gave us their *linaje nuevo* through their Chosen Companions. But the Men-on-the-Mountain come to us no more. Where are we to get the *linaje nuevo* to keep the People strong and healthy?''

Eyes blazing, Phoenix snapped her long arm out and pointed at Sky Dancer. "There, Flint," she barked. "There is your *linaje nuevo*. There are no cousins marrying cousins yet; she is enough for now."

With that Phoenix turned on her heel and stalked away.

Inside the house on whose wall Phoenix had been leaning, Coral Snake skulked in the shadows. His arm was splinted between two sturdy sticks and wrapped around with leather thongs. So you would not have us go to the Others, eh? he thought. Perhaps that is what I will do: I will go to the camp of the Others and bring back a wife. Then I will be like the great Coconino. What would you say to that, old man-woman? You and that man-woman daughter of yours . . .

Idly he tugged at the lacings of his splint. It did not hurt him much now, but at the time the pain of it had been awful. He'd been hunting in the forest when he had come across Sky Dancer, also hunting alone. Her long hair was caught in braids, and she wore a simple loincloth and a soft strip of leather tied around her breasts for greater comfort when she ran. It left most of her slim, attractive body exposed. When he had suggested that they hunt together, she had refused him rudely. So he had made an alternative suggestion, which she liked even less, and when he had laid a hand on her to enforce his suggestion, she had taken up her throwing club and cracked it across his bow arm.

Abruptly the drums changed rhythm, and Coral Snake slipped to the door to peer out at the activities. Fearing the ribbing he would get about his broken arm, he had not deigned to attend the wedding, but he watched, smoldering, as Dreams of Hawks led his new bride down the path into the canyon, toward a ceremonial wickiup constructed at the creek's edge. Their friends followed them to the foot of the butte but stopped there as the couple went on alone, with only one torch to light their way. That torch would be planted outside the wickiup to burn until morning.

What a pity, Coral Snake thought, if that torch should accidentally fall against the wickiup and both of you burn alive. But no—that would not be satisfaction enough. When I take my revenge, Sky Dancer, I want you to know who it is that takes it. And I want you to know that when you are gone, I will go after your precious brother Nakha-a next.

I must plan it carefully, he thought. These two moons, while my bow arm is healing, I will make careful plans for how I will bring down the children of Coconino.

It will be a long summer.

Krista saw Michael coming and turned away from the window of her office, shaking her head. It was going to be a long summer.

Sitting back at her desk, Krista ran her fingers through hair that was still thick and glossy and sun-bleached. She'd picked up a few pounds over the years, what with bearing three more children, but nothing that a couple of months of dieting and some exercise wouldn't get rid of. If, she sighed, she could ever find the time to exercise. Along with her Level Four Health Tech classification had come a number of administrative duties, and with the youngest of the girls not yet in school . . . Thank heaven for Michael, who was so good about looking after his younger half sisters. The boy was such a blessing . . . and such a curse.

She heard his footsteps in the hall then, the careless, athletic stride of a teenage boy. She had seen him swinging up the walk to the infirmary: shirtless and tousled, fresh from a game of racquets with his grandfather, Dick McKay. Does he know, she wondered, how the girls are beginning to look at him? Is that why he persists in walking the compound bare-chested and windblown? Or is he, like his father, entirely unconscious of the effect his dark skin and eyes have on the women of the Mountain?

The other boys were beginning to notice, she knew. It would get him in trouble, this casual, seductive behavior. The pale and ordinary-looking boys up here couldn't compete with Michael's exotic appeal, and it was only a matter of time until that began to rankle.

Please, God, just don't let there be any more fights, Krista pleaded silently. I don't think I could go through that again. Knowing that not a week would go by without some bully picking a fight with Michael, knowing that sooner or later it would be more than just a bloody nose and a black eye, and knowing there wasn't a thing I could do about it.

From the time he had started school Michael had faced the harassment. "Savage boy," they called him, and "redskin," and "half-breed." If he tried to withdraw, they hounded him; if he tried to strike out, they ganged up on him. Krista had spoken to parents, who were remarkably unsympathetic, and Dick McKay had been beside himself, finding his own sons at the head of the pack.

Well, they were all a little older and a little wiser; they had found other diversions more interesting than pounding on Michael. Maybe they were growing up finally. Maybe they realized you couldn't hold a son responsible for the sins of his father. Maybe in time he would be just another inhabitant of the mountain installation, working at a job, settling down to raise a family—

And then Michael was there, pivoting into her office with a hand on the doorjamb, pausing to chin himself on the lintel, dark, dazzling, fifteen. *"Chee-eeya, Madre,"* he greeted her cheerily.

Different. Flaunting his difference. "Michael, you know I don't speak a word of that language," she snapped irritably. And for just a moment his eyes reproached her: Maybe you should.

Then he flung himself into a chair, hooked his elbows over the arms, and folded his hands across his flat, bare stomach. "Well, how's this, then?" he said. "What's up, Doc?"

In spite of herself, Krista found the corners of her lips twitching upward. Michael saw it and grinned, an unfettered contagious grin that ended any hope of being cross with him. "Aunt Jenny's blood pressure," Krista quipped, pointing to a chart on her desk. "I'm going to make that woman give up teaching if she doesn't learn to relax."

Michael only laughed and found a new way of slouching in the chair. "Hey, Ralph's looking pretty good," he commented, eyeing the potted saguaro that had outgrown its place on the windowsill and now had a table of its own. It was still only twelve inches tall, but it was plump and healthy.

So are you, Krista thought. But she kept that to herself. Instead she asked, "How was work?" Michael was spending the summer working for his grandfather in the Archives. Dick was working frantically to make hard copies of innumerable files stored on optical media. The equipment that could access the data was dangerously near failure, and there was no hope of constructing replacements. The computer age on the Mountain was nearing its close.

"Pretty good, I guess," Michael conceded. "We're making progress. Ababba has me sorting through all the old records, seeing which ones are most critical so we can save those first."

Ababba—grandfather. It was the only name by which he had ever called Dick McKay. It was Dick, of course, who had undertaken to teach the boy his father's native tongue, aided and abetted by Lois Martin. It became a secret code between them, a bonding that left even Krista out and played no small part in the anger and jealousy Michael received from Dick's sons. She had known it would not be easy for the boy, being the son of the man who had destroyed their hopes of contact with distant planets. But she couldn't help thinking that he kept doing things to aggravate the situation.

"Well, I'm ready for a swim," he announced, heaving himself out of the chair and coming around the desk. "I think I'll see if Janice and Hilary want to come down to the catch basin with me." He bent to kiss her on the cheek. "See you later, Mom."

But she caught his arm before he could escape. "Swimming?" she asked sternly, and pointed to an incriminating red mark on his neck.

Michael blushed fiercely through his dark coloring. "Ah, Mom," he mumbled in embarrassment. "I can't help it if she gets carried away."

"Michael, I don't want any angry parents pounding on my door," she warned.

He tried to shrug off her arm and her comment. "Jesus, Mom, don't worry about it, okay? I'm not stupid."

No, she thought, but you're fifteen.

And how old were you, a voice inside her asked, when you began?

Fifteen.

But fifteen was so much *older* then than it is now. . . .

"Will you watch the kids tomorrow night," she asked, "if Tim and I go over to the Cordobas' after supper?"

"Sure," he agreed. "Have a good time." Once again he tried for the door, but she caught his wrist.

"Michael—"

"What?"

She took a breath. "You know, I think Tim would be just thrilled if sometime you would ask *him* to play racquets with you."

"You married him, not me," Michael grumbled, then saw her flinch and recanted quickly. "Look, Mom, Tim and I get along just fine. Let's leave it that way, okay?"

Krista sighed and dropped his wrist. "Okay. Don't stay down at the catch basin after sundown, all right?" she cautioned. "I don't want anyone breaking a leg picking their way back up the mountain in the dark."

"Right, Mom. See you later."

And he was out the door with an almost audible rush of air, leaving a trace of male musk in the air.

No use making a big fuss about it, Krista thought as she turned back to her work. Michael would do what he wanted to do, whether it was learning the language of the People or becoming the best racquets player on the mountain or leading some girl down the garden path. Dear God, don't let my girls be this hard to raise, she prayed. With increasing responsibilities here at the Infirmary, I just haven't got the energy to spend.

"Aunt Chelsea?"

Chelsea looked up at her nephew Arizona and recognized the unhappy look on his face. At thirteen he was caught between loving his father desperately and being embarrassed by him. Chelsea remembered that age distinctly.

"What is it, Ari?" she asked.

"I think you better go talk to Dad," the boy mumbled. "He's down at that marker again, and it's time to feed the dogs, and Mom's in town with Chayna and Verde and—"

"It's all right," Chelsea assured him, rising quickly. "I know what he's brooding about. I'll go talk to him, then we'll both come and help you with the dogs, okay?"

"I don't mind feeding them all," Arizona protested belatedly, "but they get awful excited if it takes too long."

She gave his shoulders a quick squeeze, the most she could get away with these days without embarrassing him. Then she slipped out of the house and trotted over the hill toward the north, where a single spreading butterleaf tree crowned a small knoll.

Cincinnati was seated on the ground gazing at a stone slab some three feet high and four feet broad. It had been his idea, and he'd bought it with his commission from the prize money won by his first interplanetary champion show dog, Tsarina. It was Junoan marble and bore an inscription in plain block letters: THERE IS ONLY ONE ROAD WORTH TRAVELING: THAT WHICH VENTURES FORTH. —CLAYTON WINTHROP.

He didn't look up even when Chelsea's shadow fell across him. For a moment she regretted her decision to tell him about the radio signals, about what she hoped to learn from them. All these years she and Zach had only said that they thought Mr. Dillon might have been responsible for the loss of the *Homeward Bound*; they had never mentioned their suspicion that the plague had been a ruse and that some of the crew might have survived. They hadn't wanted to get his hopes up only to have them crushed.

And I shouldn't have told him now, she thought. See what I've done? He's only a child, after all, with a child's mind—

—and a man's responsibilities. A man's feelings. A man's rights.

"We have to go get them," he said suddenly.

Chelsea shook her head helplessly. "Cincinnati, we can't. It takes lots and lots of money to buy a ship, and we just don't have it."

"Not even with our partners?" he asked earnestly.

"Not even with our partners." She knelt on the ground beside him. "Besides, we don't know for sure that anyone survived."

"We don't know for sure they didn't!" he shouted, his volume rising with his agitation. "What if she's out there, Chelsea? What if Mom's out there, without Dad, without us; what if she is?"

"Then she's taking good care of the people with her," Chelsea replied.

But Cincinnati would not be distracted. Rising, he began to pace fretfully in front of the stone marker. "Why do we have to have a ship, anyway?" he whined. "Why can't we just get in a warp terminal and go there?"

"Because it doesn't work that way," she told him in a voice edged with exasperation. "You have to have a warp terminal at the other end to receive you, and even then there's a limit to how far something can be warped and arrive on target."

"But ships do it," he insisted.

"And they frequently arrive thousands of miles off their mark," she responded. "Cin, we just don't have the technology yet."

"Then let's get it," he pouted. "If they can invent something that lets me think pictures at my dogs, why can't they invent a warp terminal that will get us to Earth?"

"First, they have to want to go," Chelsea pointed out, "as badly as you and I do."

Cincinnati chewed on that for a moment; then he snorted contemptuously. "Yeah, the only place they'd want to go," he said, "is to Troax and blow up the cartel's headquarters." His agitation melted somewhat in his disgust for the galactic tension that seemed to escalate daily. Finally he dropped back down to sit facing the marker. "Ouch," he grunted. "I fall a lot harder than I used to."

Chelsea was relieved to see his mood lifting. "You're getting old, big brother," she teased him. "Forty years under the bridge— your bones are going to start creaking like Tsarina's pretty soon." The Airedale dam was eleven years old and suffered from arthritis. "Come on," she said, giving him a play cuff on the shoulder, "let's go help that son of yours feed the dogs."

Grunting, Cincinnati clambered back to his feet. "I don't want to think about Tsarina getting old," he grumbled. "I want her to be young and live forever."

Chelsea slipped an arm around her brother's waist, and they started back toward the house. But there was a weariness in both their steps, and Chelsea thought: seventy-nine. If my mother is still alive, she is seventy-nine years old, on a hostile planet with none of the medical services we take for granted.

The sky was darkening, and here and there faint stars were winking into existence. Soon the sky would be filled with them, an explosion of cold fire in Juno's unpolluted sky. They had blazed their icy light on the first settlers of this planet; they would glint and gleam long after Oswald Dillon and Indigo Lawrence and the Troaxian Cartel were vague memories.

I've got to get there somehow, Chelsea vowed. I've got to get to Earth and find Mom before it's too late. . . .

The wind blew harsh and merciless out of the northwest, howling through the island canyon, driving snow through the smoke holes and even under the heavy fur door covers, into the adobe houses of the People. The Howl of Death, they called it, and they clutched their tokens and their talismans, hoping to keep any evil kachinas out.

Phoenix sat hunched near her fire, a deerhide wrapped around her, sipping at a tea made from leaves that Sky Dancer had collected last fall. She and Dreams of Hawks had brought it back from a hunting trip that had netted nothing else; she was too wise a girl to come back empty-handed. The brew was bitter but warming; yet there remained a cold knot in Phoenix's stomach that nothing could reach.

It's my fault, she reproached herself. I should have listened to Nina, I should have gone, it's my fault, it's my fault, it's my fault. . . .

The winter had set in early and hard. Wild potatoes and other roots that were usually collectible farther into the fall were suddenly frozen in the ground. Deer and antelope, sensing a protracted cold season, had headed south early, and burrowing animals were snugged away a full moon sooner than usual. The People were left with only a modest harvest and half the amount of dried meat they usually put up.

By the time the winter solstice approached, something had to be done. Phoenix led a band of hunters to the Red Rock Country to seek out animals in its more temperate clime. Flint had come, and Dreams of Hawks, and several others; Sky Dancer, in the early stages of pregnancy, had elected to stay behind, much to the relief of her mother and husband.

It had been a disastrous expedition. They had searched for days without finding anything to shoot at. Then Smooth Pebbles had fallen and broken his leg. Phoenix was able to set it, a feat that gained her no little respect in the eyes of the other hunters, but they were faced with transporting the injured man up out of the Red Rock canyon and across miles of rugged terrain on a travois. His sharp cries of pain punctuated their journey.

Then, half a day away from the village, Dreams of Hawks had broken out in a fever. By the time they reached the island butte, his breathing was labored and he was wracked by a deep cough. He collapsed inside his house, trembling and sweating.

For days he had lain there, wrapped in furs, delirious at times, and coughing up blood. The Healer applied poultices and brewed medicines while the elders chanted prayers to the Mother Earth, but the fever failed to break. Sky Dancer tended him doggedly, as though her determination could make the medicine work, but to no avail. Two nights before, Dreams of Hawks had drawn one last, rattling breath and yielded up his spirit to the Mother Earth.

My fault, my fault, Phoenix lamented bitterly. This wouldn't have happened if we hadn't split the tribe. I should have made Nina stay, or I should have gone with them.

Why didn't you come, Coconino? her distraught mind raged. Why didn't you come so there wouldn't have been a problem? If only you had come this summer, come to see their wedding. Then we could all have gone south, and found Nakha-a, and been whole again. . . .

Not his fault, the stone floor seemed to whisper up to her. Not his choice.

No. But my choice. My choice to stay. I have to wait for Coconino. "Mother Earth!" she cried aloud. "I have to wait for Coconino!"

Peace, came the answer. *Peace. Wait.*

But in her bitter self-castigation, Phoenix did not hear.

Sky Dancer's shriek had echoed through the canyon. She had wept and raged so that Talia wanted to bind her arms for fear she might hurt herself. "Calm yourself," the girl's aunt had pleaded. "Think of your child." But Sky Dancer had been beyond rational thought, so great was her despair; like her aunt so many years before, she miscarried her child.

"It was not even a child yet," old Cactus Flower had said, as though that were some comfort to the bereaved girl.

In her grief Sky Dancer had turned on her mother. "Why didn't you listen to Nina?" she had demanded. "Why didn't you take us to the south, where the corn grows better, where the winters are not so cold? What good to wait for my father in this place if we all die?"

She's right, Phoenix thought bitterly, staring into the flames that flickered and faltered in the erratic draft. I should have let them go. I should have let them all go and only stayed here myself. I should have turned over leadership to Nina and let them all march away.

But not Sky Dancer. Mother Earth, I could never let them take Sky Dancer with them! She is mine, she is all I have, she is my life—and I have condemned her. I have condemned her to this harsh climate and my tedious vigil. Had I known this would happen, could I have sent her away, sent them both, and stayed on by myself? Had I known the lives my choice would cost, would I have gone, too?

But how could I know? she demanded. How do I know even now that they found anything better? Were they greeted with hostility at the Camp of the Others? Did they find a place to spend the winter, a place with water and plenty of game? Or did it go hard for them? Did they find good fields in which to plant their corn in the spring, or are they huddled now in some desolate land, wishing they had stayed here with us? Are they too proud to come back?

Am I too proud to leave?

Maybe Flint was right, she thought. Maybe we should have sent a trading expedition to the Others with furs, with pottery and jewelry. Lujan was fascinated by the handcrafted goods; they might be, too. Maybe we could have traded for some grain, some vegetables. . . .

Maybe our children would have been dazzled by their Magic. Maybe our maidens would have been dazzled by their men. . . .

It was too risky. That had been her decision last summer, and the more she thought about it, the more reasons she found not to go. It was not just the danger of fireshooters and old grudges, she reasoned, it was what the People might learn in that place. How to lie. How to seek after worthless goods. How to desecrate the Mother Earth.

We must wait here, she told herself. We must wait here so that when Coconino returns, he finds that we have kept the Way of the People, that we honor the Mother Earth. He must see that the sacrifice he made was not in vain, even if it means other sacrifices. Like Dreams of Hawks.

"She Who Saves." The voice outside her door was muffled, scarcely audible above the constant whistling of the wind.

Phoenix bolted to the door and pushed back its hide cover, wondering what new tragedy had brought someone out in the storm. Two figures ducked quickly inside, followed by a flurry of snowflakes and a blast of cold air. Wrapped in furs, Phoenix could not even tell who they were.

"You are foolish to go out in this weather," she protested. "The path is slippery with snow, and the wind is strong enough to blow you off your feet."

The larger bundle unwrapped itself, revealing Talia. "It was necessary," the woman said simply. At thirty-one, Talia was old. Her face was lined, and her hair grew gray in streaks. Each day she looked more and more like her mother, Two Moons, with the same gentle, round face and portly figure, the same touch of wisdom in her eyes and voice.

Now she helped the other figure push back covering furs, and Phoenix's heart pounded erratically as she saw Sky Dancer. Crouched close to the fire, the girl was pale and drawn, her eyes red, her face too thin. "What are you doing out of bed?" Phoenix chided, throwing another log on the blaze and kneeling beside her daughter. "You should be resting; you shouldn't be out walking around."

"I wanted to come home," Sky Dancer said flatly. She did not look up from the flames. "I want to live here with you again. I can't stay in that house by myself."

Phoenix's throat tightened, and her arms flew out to embrace the girl.

"I'm sorry for what I said, Mother," Sky Dancer whispered. "You did not make the winter come early or the animals leave. It is easy to look back and say what should have been done; it is not so easy to look forward, as you have had to do, and see what ought to be."

Tears spilled from Phoenix's eyes as she stroked her daughter's hair, rocking her gently as though she were a babe again. "Hush, little one," she crooned. "The Mother Earth will not abandon us even if we make bad choices. She has rescued the People from worse straits than this; somehow she will bring us through again. And here we will be when Coconino comes again."

"Yes," Sky Dancer echoed dully. "When Coconino comes again."

CHAPTER NINETEEN

"You are deep in thought, Coconino."

Coconino glanced over to see the bulky form of One-Eyed Fox in the firelight. "I was pondering the stars," he responded, gesturing for the older man to join him.

"That is good." One-Eyed Fox lowered himself to the ground with a grunt. "You are a thinking man, then, like Father Nakha-a. He said it is good for a person to sit and think upon things greater than himself."

"Like son, like father," Coconino commented wryly.

One-Eyed Fox laughed softly. Coconino liked him; he was an even-tempered man, patient and perceptive. "Tomorrow," One-Eyed Fox said, "I will take you to Father Nakha-a's Thinking Place. It is a long journey, and we will spend the night there, where you can ponder very many stars."

Coconino hesitated. "I was going to hunt tomorrow," he hedged. "The People have given me a great feast; I want to give something back to them. A deer, maybe, or perhaps this monster bear you speak of."

At that One-Eyed Fox laughed roundly. "Oh, no, Coconino, you do not want to hunt the bear," he assured the younger man. "Your little arrows would only make him angry, and that we do not want. No, we do not hunt the bear unless he becomes troublesome, and then we send six men, knowing only five are apt to return. We dig a pit with sharp stakes at the bottom and try to lure the bear into it. It is not a joyous thing at all when we hunt the bear."

Coconino grunted, embarrassed at his error. He had not imagined that anything lived that he could not kill with his bow. Even Tala, the great kachina, could have been brought down by a well-placed arrow. The bear must be an even greater kachina than that.

"On our way back from Father Nakha-a's Thinking Place,"

One-Eyed Fox offered, "we can hunt. At this time of year many
animals come to the stream to drink, for the snowmelt has gone
from the pools higher up and the summer rains will not replenish
them for some time. Soon even this stream that runs through our
village will shrink, and we will dig pits in it where the water can
ooze up from Mother Earth."

"So it was in my village," Coconino told him, "if the rains
were late. My stepfather—" Yes, that is who it was! One-Eyed
Fox reminded Coconino of his stepfather, Made of Stone. Not in
looks but in manner; Made of Stone was patient and slow in judgment, though Coconino remembered taxing that patience on more
than one occasion.

Two Moons' face in Dancing Knife, Made of Stone's tempera-
ment in One-Eyed Fox—had he reached a place where spirits are
reborn—

—or was he haunted by those he had lost along the way?

And who will I see next? Coconino wondered. Will I find the
viperous Castle Rock here among these People? Will Corn Hair
glide through this village with her quiet pain? Will Juan's laughter
come to me from one of these wickiups?

"We will leave early," One-Eyed Fox told him. "Bring two
canteens, for we will leave the stream by midday and climb the
rest of the way where there is no water. I know you are tired of
travel food, but you must bear with it for two more days. It will
be worthwhile; you will see."

Coconino nodded graciously, seeing that there would be no
avoiding this trip without offending One-Eyed Fox. But he did not
relish the prospect, and it had nothing to do with eating travel food
for another two days. He told himself that he simply had no curiosity about this Thinking Place that bore his son's name; obviously
the People here made too much of the boy, and his Thinking Place
would only be a disappointment to Coconino.

Yet there was more to it that he was loath to admit even to
himself. From the Thinking Place, the People claimed to see Coconino. It was not possible, of course; it was someone else, some
impostor, perhaps only a grave or a marker.

But they do not say that they have seen Coconino's place, he
reminded himself. They say they have seen Coconino. Is it a vision, a dream? They do not call it that, either.

Coconino looked up once more at the stars gliding silently overhead. What will *I* see, he wondered, when I reach this Thinking
Place? Will I truly see myself?

And if I do, will I like what I see?

* * *

Zachery trembled as Chelsea brought her files up on the kitchen wall screen. She had called him out from Argo, insisting this could not be done over the telecom, but she had not insisted that he drop everything to do it. "Wrap up your case," she had told him. "Plan to stay for a while, make your trip worthwhile. The Troaxian trouble is making travel difficult, so allow yourself plenty of time."

Was it just that she, like so many others, was afraid war would break out soon and wanted the comfort of his presence? Perhaps she hoped he would be trapped there if the Centrallies, as Argo and its allies were known, grounded all space travel.

Or had she really found something of grave consequence in those radio messages?

It had taken him several weeks to rearrange his schedule, and when he had, it gave him a strange feeling of bereavement. He had lived and worked on Argo for fifteen years. What if there really was a war and he couldn't get back? What if he never got to finish these cases he'd taken on? What if all his personal possessions had to be abandoned?

Life would go on, he thought. Differently, but it would go on. What if I were caught on Argo and couldn't see Chelsea and Cin and his family for years?

You have been caught, a voice inside him said. Caught in your work, caught in your world, caught in your ways. Tear loose, Zachery. Prepare for the worst or the best. Pretend you are going to Juno and never coming back.

So he had taken the things he didn't want to lose: his grandfather's ring, his collection of Draconian crystal miniatures, and a holo of his mother. The holo of Chelsea he left behind; it was much better to have the real thing.

They were seated now at the kitchen table of the Winthrop ranch house, the wall beginning to fill with blocks of text. Chelsea was in her favorite worn denim jumpsuit, a diminutive package of precision playing the controls of the computer like a rare musical instrument. "The message was terribly fragmented," she told him, "and it took me a while to reconstruct it. But I've documented my extrapolation techniques; I've had them tested and verified by experts in the field—that's why I told you not to rush out here; I was waiting for their response. I'm confident now, though, that they'll hold up in any court of law. We've got him, Zachery. We've got Lujan in a bald-faced lie, in an obvious attempt to defraud. All that's left is to prove his connection to Dillon."

Zachery wet his lips and studied her calm, intent face. "Was the radio message sent after the *Homeward Bound* gave her death report?"

Chelsea heaved a great sigh. "No. Unfortunately, it's not so clear-cut as that or I wouldn't need to rely on these extrapolation techniques. This message was sent after first Earthfall, only sixteen days into the mission. Here, look at this." She used a light pen to point out a fragmented paragraph on the left of the screen. "There was a good deal of interference that caused the transmission to break up in spots, but these are the pieces that came through clearly."

Chelsea wielded her light pen like a scalpel, isolating the phrases as she spoke. "This is the phrase that made the Xerbus station believe they were picking up *Homeward Bound*'s exploration team. 'Earthfall at the base of—' then static, then 'cherries.' That was my father's pet phrase for a smooth landing: it went down like cherries. I asked Xerbus to do a voicegraph on the message to verify it, and there's no doubt—it's my dad's print. He sent this message."

Her voice was so calm, so controlled, that it made Zachery wonder. How fiery she had been in the beginning! How quick to jump to conclusions. And he—he had been eager, inspired, pouncing on clues, scrutinizing each one to see how the puzzle pieced together, to see if it would all hold up in a court of law. Now that solid proof of malfeasance seemed to be in their hands, it seemed totally unreal. Where was his energy, his excitement? He felt only dread.

Is that what she feels? he wondered. Is that why she's so calm? It's not that I don't care anymore—far from it. It's just that I'm tired. After fifteen years, I'm so tired.

"Now look at this." Chelsea's face glowed as she practiced what had become for her an art—explaining how various phrases in her documents supported her point. You should have been a lawyer, he thought. Why couldn't you have been a lawyer? We could have set up a practice together somewhere instead of being light-years away from each other.

" 'Jack' . . ."—Chelsea's light pen picked out the words— " 'headed up with jet packs,' and here, unmistakably, 'send Lujan with the shuttle.' Zach, there was no one on board named Jack; I think this is the first syllable of Jacqueline, with the rest having been garbled in the journey through space. It means my mother went with Dad when he made Earthfall. The synopsized reports

TRC put out say that she warped down to the planet's surface *after* my father and others were stricken with a plague.''

The intensity in her voice grew, became edged with excitement as she warmed to her task. Zachery felt its pull, felt his tired psyche being pulled into the hunt, lifted and lightened by the growing enthusiasm in her voice.

''Now look at this,'' she continued. The pen flashed again, made the words twice the size of the remainder of the text. '' 'Send Lujan with the shuttle.' If my dad didn't have the shuttle, he had the mini-shuttle. Those were the only two methods of transport to the surface until the warp terminal was set up, and the warp terminal would have been in the shuttle's cargo bay. Now, the log reports that we have from the *Homeward Bound* indicate that Lujan escaped the plague because he was never on the planet's surface. Zach, either he disobeyed a direct order from the captain or his claim not to have been planetside is a bald-faced lie.''

Zachery considered that carefully. ''Unless there were extenuating circumstances,'' he pointed out. ''Lujan may have been *unable* to carry out your father's order.'' Was it just habit that made him question everything? Or had he been at this so long, he just couldn't believe solid evidence when he saw it?

''Could be,'' she conceded. ''But I believe Lujan was already on the planet's surface when this message was sent; that's where the extrapolation comes in.'' She brought up a series of program parameters and let them ripple across the screen, knowing they would mean nothing to him but wanting to show how detailed and extensive they were. ''I took samples of my dad's speech patterns—not his writing but his speech—and constructed a linguistics program that I ran against the radio fragment. The object was to extrapolate the full content of the message. This is what I got.''

A new piece of text leapt into being on the giant screen. It read

Captain Winthrop to *Homeward Bound*. Reichert, do you read me? [pause for reply] We've made Earthfall at the base of the mountain; no problem, it went down like cherries. As soon as we secure the mini-shuttle, Jacqueline and I are headed up with jet packs [phrase missing]. Don't wait for my report; send Lujan with the shuttle as soon as he can be reached. Captain out.

Zachery whistled. ''You got all that from the original fragment?''

''Based on a word here and a phrase there and an analysis of my father's speech patterns.'' Chelsea hitched her chair up closer to his. `` 'As soon as he can be reached.' Zach, Lujan wasn't on the ship. There's really only one other place he could have been.''

Their eyes met. She was so certain, so dead certain, and in his heart he agreed with her. After all, he was the one who had started all this by going after Camilla Vanderhoff's case. Camilla . . .

Zachery rose and paced the kitchen, rubbing the back of his neck. It still left them with no way to reach the stranded crew, if indeed they had been marooned and not murdered. For that they needed to connect the culprit with Oswald Dillon. But the claims he kept filing against the Dillon estate were getting weaker and weaker, and soon even the government of Argo would have to concede that there was no longer a reason to delay disbursement. However, if suspicions of foul play could be aroused . . . ''Chelsea, how do we know that Lujan claimed he was never on the planet's surface?'' he asked.

Chelsea snorted. ''It says so in his report! The last one filed from the *Homeward Bound*!''

''Does it say that in the public reports?''

At that Chelsea stopped short. Her face darkened, and for a moment Zachery thought she would cry, but she only lowered her eyes. ''No. No, the public reports only say that six of the crew escaped the plague. It doesn't say why.''

He almost wished she would cry. It would give him an excuse to hold her.

''And it is generally assumed that those six died anyway,'' he went on, ''so they might have been exposed to the disease. They might have been planetside.'' Why did he need an excuse to hold her?

Chelsea shook her head and insisted, ''But Lujan's report—''

''Was obtained illegally.'' He drew her to her feet, intending to wrap her in his arms. ''Chels, you can't use it as evidence.''

But unexpectedly she resisted, and he saw her jaw take on its stubborn set. She was not through discussing this snarl. ''All right, maybe that part won't hold water, but TRC's official statement said my mother warped down *after* my father, to tend the ailing crew members.''

''Does it say she hadn't already been down?''

Again disappointment crashed across her face. Cry, Chelsea, he thought. You used to cry in my arms. How long has it been? Why is it so hard this time? ''No. No, I guess it doesn't say that,'' she had to admit.

''And what more logical explanation,'' Zachery went on, ''than that in going back up to the ship she unknowingly brought the plague with her. Between her and Lujan, the remaining six crew members were infected.''

Chelsea's eyes slid to the side, down to the surface of the table, where all the controls for the wall screen were arrayed. She had spent three days setting up the elaborate linguistics program, making it interpret the ragged radio transmission. The technical aspects of it were unimpeachable; one of the experts who'd reviewed it urged her to write a paper on her methods. It couldn't be that she was thwarted again, and by the same roadblock.

The last message from her father indicated that he was waiting for Derek Lujan. What had happened when the man had arrived? Or had he simply never shown up, leaving Clayton and Jacqueline Winthrop stranded on a mountaintop? How long could they have survived, just the two of them?

Or were there more?

''Zachery,'' she began, ''you know that the log shows they had picked up signals of some kind from that mountain.''

''The illegally obtained log shows that, yes.''

''Damn it, Zach!'' she said, pulling away. ''That illegally obtained log catches Derek Lujan in a blatant lie! And then there's that log entry attributed to my mother, the one where she calls Dad 'Clay.' It's an obvious forgery.''

Suddenly she came back to him, reaching her tiny, work-worn hands up to grasp his broad shoulders. ''There are so many things out of sync in these reports, Zach, especially when compared to this radio transmission. We have to get legal copies of the reports. We have to be able to bring them into evidence. TRC went bankrupt—who wound up with their corporate records? The government?''

At that Zachery drew back uncomfortably and could not hold her eyes. ''Chelsea, we can't get to their records.''

''Why not?'' she demanded. ''The organization is defunct; those records have to be in someone else's control by now.''

It was something he'd learned three years earlier, just after Camilla's death, but had avoided telling her. ''They are,'' he admitted, ''but not ours, and they won't ever be.'' Why had he waited, waited until the news could only be more crushing? ''Someone bought up the remaining assets of the Terran Research Coalition, which included their headquarters, their equipment, and the corporate records. It was a package deal; the bankruptcy court insisted.''

''Someone?'' Chelsea felt a tightening in her chest. ''Who?''

"Chelsea . . ."

"Who!"

Zachery sighed deeply and wiped a hand across his brow. "An old friend of yours," he said at last. "Indigo Lawrence."

For a stunned moment Chelsea only stared at him. Then suddenly she turned and kicked her chair halfway across the kitchen, barking obscenities through clenched teeth.

Zachery waited until the flood had crested and Chelsea leaned angrily against a refrigeration unit, arms braced, head drooping. Then, "Chelsea," he suggested gently, "it's been fifteen years. Maybe it's . . . maybe it's time to—"

"It's time to grab that gray-eyed bitch by the hair and shake her till her eyes fall out of their sockets!" Chelsea raged anew. "She's got no reason to sit on those records, nothing to hide, nothing to be gained by holding on to them."

"But she has a memory several light-years in length," he reminded her. "And you denied her something she wanted very badly: a foothold on this planet. She's going to deny you what you want just from spite."

Chelsea stopped and sagged against the counter this time, staring sullenly out the kitchen window into the yard. Arizona and Verde were helping their dad clean the dog runs. Both were dark-haired and slender, both well beyond their parents' mental abilities already. Soon, Chelsea thought sadly, Cincinnati will be helping *them* with chores. And me—how am I going to raise two teenagers when I have all this going on? How can I run the ranch, keep on searching for Lujan's letter, raise the kids, *and* take on Indigo Lawrence—again?

Chelsea took in a deep breath, blew it out rapidly. "Does she still have an office in New Sydney?" she asked Zachery.

"Indigo? Yes, I believe so."

"Good." Chelsea straightened up, though she felt somehow older than her thirty-eight years. She was tired, Zach was tired, and her mother's eightieth birthday was only months away. "I'm going into town tomorrow and buy the trendiest robes I can find," she told him. "I'm going to my hairdresser, I'm going to get a manicure—" She looked down at her rough, callused hands. "—or maybe a good pair of gloves. And I'm going to set up a holoconference with the illustrious Ms. Lawrence."

"Chelsea," Zach cautioned, knowing better than to try to dissuade her, "she won't give you something for nothing, and there's only one thing she wants from you."

"I know," Chelsea said softly. "We'll . . . negotiate."

* * *

Coral Snake swaggered to She Who Saves's door and tossed a fat raccoon on the ground in front of it. "A gift for you," he called out in mocking tones. "For a mother of such good fortune."

There was a shuffling sound inside, and the Witch Woman poked her head out. She looked at the raccoon, then at the smirking youth, and her face glowered dangerously. "Do not play games, boy," she warned. "I have no patience for them." Then she disappeared back inside.

"What games?" he protested loudly. "I have brought a gift to your door. You have a daughter, do you not?"

Phoenix's head popped back out. "My daughter is in mourning," she hissed, "and your cruelty is despicable."

"Mourning? Still?" he echoed in feigned surprise. "But that was last winter, and here it is midsummer. Ah, well. Tell me, then, when I may return with my gift."

"When snow burns like tinder!" she snapped.

Coral Snake looked very sober. "I'm afraid the raccoon will smell bad by then."

Phoenix ducked out of the house and stood eye to eye with the obnoxious boy on the path. When had he gotten so tall? Soon he would pass her in height, something few men of the People ever did. But then, his father had been tall.

"Get out of my sight," she hissed, "before I throw you down the mountain and laugh as I hear your bones breaking every time you bounce!"

At that Coral Snake threw back his head and laughed. He picked up his raccoon and walked laughing back toward his mother's house. How easily you are goaded, old man-woman, he thought. And your daughter, too; I know she sat just inside the door seething with rage. But I have only begun my sport, old man-woman. My quiver is full of a thousand tiny arrows.

And every one will be aimed at the two of you.

Zachery's heart leapt as Chelsea stepped into the holoconference room she had rented in Newamerica City. She hadn't lost her style, that was certain. The elegant white robes were wrapped tightly around her slender body in the latest fashion, with as much of her right shoulder and back showing as propriety allowed in professional circles. A froth of white lace was woven artfully into her upswept hair and bloomed in a pasqua flower behind her left ear.

Magnificent, he thought as she crossed the room to greet him.

It was the same confident flare, the same rippling grace that had so struck him when he'd first seen her at the memorial service for the *Homeward Bound*. Not a place to have your heart stolen, but from the moment he'd laid eyes on her, Zachery had been unable to think seriously of another woman. The moment he'd gotten back to Darius IV, he launched himself in pursuit of the Vanderhoff case just to get back to Argo, just to see this dazzling creature again.

What irony that she never believed him! Surely the woman knew how sensuous she was—knew it now; it was painfully evident in the way she carried herself in those robes. Why wouldn't she believe that she had captured him body and soul long ago? Why did she persist with this notion that he loved Camilla and, now that Camilla was gone, Camilla's ghost?

There was something special about Camilla, no denying that, and maybe what he had felt for her could be called love. But it was the kind of love one felt upon meeting a child with a terminal illness or a doctor dying of an illness contracted from her patients. It was the kind of love that embraced tragedy rather than fulfillment. It was not the kind of love that thought dirty socks commingling in the laundry was a pleasant notion and breakfast at the same table the ultimate in contentment.

"I hope you weren't waiting long," Chelsea said as she approached. "I got caught in a taxi during the general alert. What was that, anyway?" There were fine lines visible now around her eyes and just at the corners of her mouth, but she was still stunning by anyone's standards.

"Unidentified freighter approaching the planet," he told her. "Turned out to be a drone whose ID signal went on a couple of minutes late. *That* company's in for a major fine."

"Damn Troaxians," Chelsea muttered. "They'd better not attack during my holocon."

"You'd have less trouble with them than with Indigo Lawrence," he observed with a touch of whimsy. "Although for a backwater farm girl, you are devastating."

"Flattery," she accused. "Tell the truth. You're afraid I'll say something uncalled for and botch this whole affair."

He smiled tenderly. "I *know* you'll say something uncalled for," he told her. "That's why I want to be there, when the connection melts."

Chelsea laughed and led the way to two elegant chairs, which were the only furniture in the room. "Well, I'm glad you're here," she told him. "Maybe you can at least keep me from saying something I could be sued for.'' Then she called out, ''Demosthenes, put my call through.''

All around them an office materialized—an opulent office dripping with art and acquisition. This was Indigo's office, then, and not just another holoconference room. Leave it to Indigo to have holographic capabilities right in her office.

From a desk just in front of them Indigo Lawrence rose to her feet, a delayed response due to the brief delay in warping the images back and forth across light-years. Indigo looked even younger than she had when they had first encountered her at the riding stable fifteen years before. Cosmetic alterations, Chelsea thought privately. The blond hair was always a bleach job, and now the smooth skin is just as phony. She's sixty-five if she's a day.

But as she came around the desk, Indigo's step was still spritely, and her voice as she greeted them was robust. ''Ms. Winthrop, Mr. Zleboton! Welcome.'' She extended her hand, and in the custom of holographic conferences, Chelsea passed her own hand through its image.

''Well,'' Indigo began when they were all seated and had exchanged the customary artificial pleasantries. ''To what do I owe the pleasure of this conference?''

It's no pleasure, Chelsea thought, but she smiled and launched into her carefully prepared explanation. ''Ms. Lawrence, I know that we've had our differences in the past.'' Was Zachery wincing? ''But something has come up that I think warrants us putting aside those differences.''

Chelsea waited for the message to be received on Argo and a response to appear in the holograph, but Indigo only smiled and waited, leaning back in her chair with her fingers steepled in front of her chest.

''I understand,'' Chelsea proceeded, ''that when you bought the property belonging to the defunct Terran Research Coalition, you also came into possession of the original reports transmitted back from the *Homeward Bound*.'' After considerable thought, Chelsea had decided to try a direct approach. Indigo was the master of deceit; there was no hope of beating her at her own game. Chelsea hoped honesty would be a better weapon. ''I also understand, from another source, that there is information of a startling nature in those reports.''

''And if there is?'' Indigo asked after the transmission delay.

''There could be a great deal of favorable publicity,'' Chelsea pointed out, ''attached to bringing that information to light.''

"Favorable publicity." Skepticism tinged Indigo's voice.

Chelsea leaned forward in her chair, trying to convey an air of confidentiality. "I have reason to believe," she said, "that the so-called plague that swept the crew was a fraud. I have reason to believe that if those records are made public, they will show that the officers and crew of the *Homeward Bound* were victims of either sabotage or mutiny."

Indigo gave a dry chuckle. "And you think bringing that to light will gain favorable publicity."

Chelsea felt her hackles rising, but she forced herself to remain calm. "You could be the person who uncovered a scandal. A folk hero. Your name would go into history books."

Now Indigo leaned forward and rested her arms on the huge desk, gray eyes cold and flinty in contrast to the smile still on her lips. "Ms. Winthrop, I'm already a folk hero, and not for uncovering scandals. If I go into history books, let it be for heading up the only corporation too big for the Troaxian Cartel to tackle. Oswald Dillon associated himself with art and culture and kept his messy little corporate deals out of sight. Me—I want my corporation to leave behind it a swath so wide, they'll need spaceships to cross it."

From the corner of her eye Chelsea could see Zachery staring a warning at her. Deliberately she clenched her teeth together and said nothing.

Indigo steepled her fingers again, this time leaning her elbows on her desk. "If you want those records made public," she said, "what's it worth to you?"

Chelsea wet her lips. "I don't think you understand," she said carefully. "I'm not asking you to give me anything. I'm only suggesting that if you make those reports public—"

"Yes, yes, there will be a major outcry and my name will be bandied about," Indigo dismissed her, waving her hand as though to shoo away a tiresome pest. "My name is already bandied about. Give me a better reason."

"Because those people may still be alive!" Chelsea flared.

"Ah! Now we get to the heart of it!" Indigo exclaimed, slapping her desk in triumph. "You think Mummy and Daddy have been marooned on a deserted planet, and if only the rest of the universe knew, they'd be rescued. Well, then. How much is it worth to you to find out?"

Chelsea rose and leaned into the image of Indigo's desk—it was a threatening gesture to ignore the conventions of holoconferences. "I'm talking about people's lives!" she hissed. "Thirty-one people, stranded! It won't cost you a cent to intervene; it won't cost—"

"But it will cost you," Indigo shot back. "Sell me Terra Firma. Eighteen million redbacks."

Chelsea drew back as if slapped.

"Ms. Winthrop is not authorized to sell Terra Firma," Zachery spoke up. He rose from his chair, towering over both women. "Terra Firma is an asset of a limited partnership and not subject to disposition without the consent of the other partners."

Leaning back in her chair again, Indigo looked up at him with the same cold eyes and false smile. "Then she'd better convince her partners," she replied.

Shaking with controlled anger, Chelsea straightened up slowly and backed out of the desk image. "You are a reptile," she enunciated. "A cold-blooded, conscienceless social blight, and you're every bit as guilty in this as Derek Lujan."

"Lujan!" Indigo hooted. "And what has dear Derek to do with it?"

Chelsea stepped back, startled. "You knew him?"

"Met him once," Indigo admitted. "When he was a snot-nosed frat boy trying to make time with Judge Melhew's daughter. Let me guess—you think he's responsible for this mutiny, or sabotage, or whatever." She laughed. "That's almost worth releasing those records, just to see if you can prove anything on him. Slick as Castorian turnip juice, that one. He'd have you eating your own feces and saying thank you."

"You can make him burn," Zachery tried to tempt her.

"And you can sign over the ranch or find the door," Indigo replied.

Zachery looked to Chelsea, but her eyes had gone abruptly unfocused. Her mouth gaped a little; then suddenly she drew herself up with a flickering smile. "And you can fry in hell," she told Indigo with sadistic pleasure. "I don't need your bloody records. You've just given me the clue I've been searching for."

"All right," Zachery growled when the connection was dissolved and they were headed out toward his rental flivver. "What did she say that's got you grinning like a Cheshire cat?"

"I knew Lujan dated that girl in college," Chelsea told him. "But she was using her mother's last name, not her father's, and I never made the connection that it was Richard Melhew's daughter. *Judge* Richard Melhew."

"You mean the man who accepted our claim against the Dillon estate fifteen years ago?" Zachery asked.

"Exactly," she replied. "You said yourself you didn't know why he should; he had a reputation for straight dealing. But do you remember what he said at that first hearing? He said his daughter had interned at Dillon's museum."

"The connection," Zachery breathed. "She introduced Dillon to Lujan. But how can we prove that?"

"I don't think we need to," Chelsea continued. "You know that for some time I've been looking for a lawyer to whom Lujan might have entrusted his letter, since it would have more credibility if there were an unbroken chain of legal custody. A lawyer. It didn't occur to me to look for a judge."

"And you think Lujan went back to Judge Melhew and asked him to keep this letter?"

"It's possible," she replied. "Melhew's the kind of stalwart, upright person Lujan didn't come across too often. And it would explain why Melhew didn't deny our claim even though we had absolutely no evidence to support it. We didn't have it, but he did."

Zachery sighed. "Well, at least it gives us a new place to look," he admitted. "But Chelsea, if he does have it, why do you suppose he never opened it? What happened to the trigger that should have exposed its contents to public view?"

Chelsea gave a lopsided smile. "One mystery at a time, Zach," she pleaded. "Let's contact Judge Melhew."

CHAPTER TWENTY

Coconino froze, having caught movement out of the corner of his eye. His eyes turned first, slowly, then imperceptibly his head followed. But it was only a banded lizard clinging to the face of a rock. A fat green and brown lizard with a double collar and a striped tail, like the one in his dream. Fear tickled at Coconino's spine, but they were in a canyon surrounded by many trees, not on a high and rocky piece of ground. "Good morning, little brother," he greeted the lizard.

The lizard bobbed its head once or twice; then in the blink of an eye it skittered away into the forest undergrowth.

"Ah," One-Eyed Fox commented as the two men continued their climb upward along the river trail. "I see the northern People also talk to their fellow creatures."

"We are all children of the Mother Earth," Coconino replied. "Should we not greet each other in passing?"

They followed the river upstream out of the village, then took the right tributary where two rivers ran together to make one. It was cool and refreshing in the shady canyon, but as they toiled their way up the steep gorge, following the twists and turns of the watercourse through rocks and ravines, they soon grew warm from their labors.

The air was moister here than in the canyon of the northern village. The plants were very different, too, and Coconino eyed them cautiously, wondering which ones were dangerous. He was glad enough to let One-Eyed Fox take the lead when they left the stream and began to climb even higher up into the mountains.

Coconino noted the tracks of many animals he knew: squirrels, deer, raccoon, and, of course, coyote. But at one point they came across a spoor that was unfamiliar to him. "What creature makes this?" he asked his host.

One-Eyed Fox glanced at the droppings. "The ringtail," he replied, taking advantage of the pause to swallow a mouthful of water from his canteen.

"Ringtail?" Coconino puzzled. "You mean raccoon?"

"No, not raccoon," One-Eyed Fox said. "The ringtail is more slender, like a fox or a squirrel. It has a reddish-brown coat and a tail as long as its body. Sometimes they come into the village and steal food from us."

To Coconino, however, who had never seen a coatimundi, the description meant nothing. "Are they good to hunt?" he asked.

The older man laughed. "Always hunting, you! Yes, they have graced the cook pots of the People from time to time, and their hides make very nice furs, especially if you leave the tails attached. But you know what Father Nakha-a said."

"No," Coconino grunted. "What did he say?"

"He said, 'Let your bow remember that the four-legged creature walks that much closer to the Mother Earth.' "

Coconino drew back, nettled that anyone should think he needed reminding that all creatures were dear to the Mother Earth and that the People should respect that, especially the hunter. It was a lesson he had learned at his stepfather's knee and one he in turn had instilled in his half brother and in Phoenix.

Ah, Phoenix, he thought. What would you think of this place? Would you know what a ringtail is? You knew of many strange animals, ones from the Before Times and ones from the Sisters of the Mother Earth. What could you have told me of the bear? Did you believe that it, like the eagle, lived no more?

As they rose above the forest at midday, Coconino was dazzled by the sight of the intricately carved rock columns. Rank upon rank of chiseled rhyolite spires reared up to rake the sky. There were places where the stone appeared to be a wall that was gradually eroding and others where it seemed that only the will of the Mother Earth kept the precarious steeples from toppling. It was the same buff color of the Valley of the People where Coconino had been raised, yet it had none of the flinty, crumbly texture of that place.

"Father Nakha-a said," One-Eyed Fox quoted, "that Mother Earth must have made this place in the morning, when she was fresh and full of energy. She tossed the mountains high into the air, and gouged out deep canyons for the rivers to flow in, and filled them with wondrous animals and plants. Then, in the evening, when she was tired, she made the Sea of Grass."

Coconino was growing weary of hearing Father Nakha-a's views on anything and everything, but in this instance he had to admit that he agreed with his son.

His thoughts wandered back to the letter Phoenix had written him, one that had been handed down from generation to generation among the northern People until he had arrived to claim it. In it she had spoken of the three children he had left behind in that time. Nakha-a was Nina's son, but there were no stories among the northern People that called him by name after his birth. There were many that referred to "the son of Coconino," of course. Until now Coconino had assumed that the stories could have been about either of his sons—or neither, most likely. The ratio of truth to fiction in the stories about himself was decidedly lopsided.

But here among the southern People, stories that named Nakha-a abounded. It seemed that he and his mother had led a group that left the Northern Village and wandered for several years, coming at last to these mountains. Among the southern villagers, Nakha-a was honored as a prophet, the wisest of the People who ever lived. He was quoted constantly, apparently having imparted jewels of wisdom on every aspect of life and every living creature.

Were you so obnoxious when you lived? Coconino wondered. Or is it only since your death that the People have turned you into this font of proverbs?

I was glad to know, my son, Coconino thought, that you survived to a venerable old age. But what brought you south? The People in the north no longer remember why there came to be two villages. What drove you from the island canyon, and why did my Witch Woman not go with you?

They had now crested the saddle that had forced the river north of their route and were working their way along its top toward the south. Here one mountain peak rose higher than the rest, and Coconino saw that One-Eyed Fox intended to go up it. It was well after midday now, and Coconino hoped the older man intended to rest first. For all his bulk, One-Eyed Fox was a strong and vigorous man, and he climbed at a pace that even Coconino, fit as he was, found challenging.

Much to Coconino's relief, they climbed only to a shady spot on the north side of a rock face where One-Eyed Fox suggested they stop and eat. The trail food was welcome, if dry, and after they had eaten, One-Eyed Fox settled himself comfortably with his back to the stone wall. "Father Nakha-a said," he quoted, "that only children and old people know how to rest when their bodies require it." One-Eyed Fox winked. "I have spent a lifetime proving him wrong," he confided, and was instantly asleep.

But although he, too, was fond of a short nap during a hard day's labor, Coconino found himself unable to get comfortable. The rock beneath him seemed the hardest he had ever sat on, and that at his back the roughest. He, who had once dozed while leaning against the ragged wall of the Well, could not now find a spot that did not cock his lolling head at an awkward angle or pinch his ear. Just as he was about to give up and rouse his companion, he noticed that they were not alone on this rock shelf.

The banded lizard sat in the sun not two feet from his bent knees, watching him with a curious eye. A cold feeling crept along Coconino's spine, for now he was seated on a rock shelf, and here was the lizard. But there were no watching eyes, since One-Eyed Fox was sound asleep.

Still the lizard sat there, not an arm's length away from the man, watching him with a glittering eye. It was unusual for such a creature to come so close, but this one seemed to have no fear of Coconino at all. He wondered if it was the same lizard he had seen down in the forest, and if so, how it had come to be there. Was it following him? Coconino chuckled at the thought.

He was still chuckling when One-Eyed Fox shook his shoulder. "Come, my sleeping friend," he bade him, "we must go on if we are to reach the Thinking Place before sundown."

But I wasn't sleeping, Coconino wanted to protest. Yet the sun seemed to have moved perceptibly toward the western horizon, so he said nothing but rose and followed his companion on the trail upward.

There were still some trees at this altitude, but they were mostly stunted pines, with an occasional gnarled oak sending its feisty roots into rock crevices for nourishment. Yet there was vegetation aplenty: manzanita and buckthorn and sotol and agave. It intruded on the path and scraped and scratched at the two climbers as they struggled higher toward the rounded crest of the mountain.

On this last leg of the journey they spoke little, for it took all their breath to keep climbing. Finally, just as the sun was sinking behind another, more distant mountain range, they reached the peak. Coconino turned his face to the west, gazing out over the spires and forests of this range, which rippled in majestic splendor down to the fields of the People. Beyond them the tideless Sea of Grass rolled unchecked to the western mountains, which glowed now with a halo of tangerine from the setting sun.

"I can see," Coconino admitted, "why my son chose this as his Thinking Place."

"It is a splendid view, isn't it?" One-Eyed Fox agreed. "One's spirit soars like a hawk just to look out from this place. But to see why Father Nakha-a chose it, you must turn to the northeast.''

Curious, Coconino turned around and glanced in that direction. It was also a nice view but nothing spectacular. Beyond the dark forested tops of other mountains rose a ridge of whitish rock that glowed in the fading sunlight. To him it seemed quite unremarkable.

But One-Eyed Fox watched him with a curious smile, as though waiting for something to happen to the younger man. ''Well?'' One-Eyed Fox prompted finally. ''Do you not see it?''

''See what?'' Coconino asked.

''The Head,'' One-Eyed Fox replied enigmatically.

Coconino looked again but he could not imagine what the man was talking about. ''I see only mountains,'' he said, ''and trees. And good blue sky.''

''But do you not see your own face in the mountains?'' One-Eyed Fox asked.

Startled, Coconino stared at his companion. ''My face?''

''Yes, there.'' One-Eyed Fox laughed, pointing at the ridge of white. ''I must say, the resemblance is remarkable. Father Nakha-a spotted it at once, and that is why he told the People to stay in this place. They had wandered for three summers, you see, before reaching it. But once he saw you sleeping there, he knew this was the place where the People should stay.''

Coconino looked again at the ridge and then jumped as he finally saw what the older man was talking about. The rounded eastern peak of the ridge formed a forehead, and to the west of it another made a nose, while a third became a chin. There it was, the profile of a man lying on his back, standing out in white against the darker hills surrounding it. Coconino could only stare.

''The People call it Coconino's Head,'' One-Eyed Fox told him. ''Now you know why we did not think at first that you could be Coconino, for how could you be there and here, too? But I think that is what has happened, for it seems to me that you are who you say. I am not sure how, but I will think on it.'' He sat himself down on a small boulder beside the path, one worn smooth from such use. ''That is what the Thinking Place is for.''

Overwhelmed by the giant stone face, Coconino wandered farther along the path to the east. There was no doubt that the formation resembled a face and that it was a face of the People. Whether or not it was like his own he could not tell, for he had not seen his own face often or clearly enough to be familiar with it. Plunking himself down on a handy rock, he stared at it in the fading light.

Is that why you came to this place, my son? he wondered. Were you looking for me? Or were you, as I was, surprised to climb a mountain and find your father there? I have not thought of him since, my Man-on-the-Mountain father. Did you think of me often in this place? And who was there to tell you of me?

Coconino snorted. Three-Legged Coyote, that's who. My old uncle who seems to have delighted in telling the tales of my misadventures rather than my great deeds. Did he ever tell of my quest for Tala? Did he ever tell of my journey to the Witch Woman's home? Now not only do I have to prove to your descendants that I am in fact Coconino, I have to prove what kind of man Coconino really is! It may take me years.

Once again movement caught his eye, and Coconino was surprised to see another banded lizard perched on a rock not far from him. Another one? he wondered. Or the same one? "Have you followed me to this place," he asked in exasperation, "just to torment me?"

The lizard stared at him unblinking. "I was here before you," it said.

It did not surprise Coconino to hear it speak. Since he was a child he had heard the voice of the Mother Earth in many forms: the cry of a hawk, the whisper of wind through the sycamore grove. This was not very different. In the past he had always welcomed such voices as signs of the Mother Earth's favor.

But Coconino was in a poor mood, tired from climbing, weary of his son's proverbs, undone by the sight of a face in the nearby ridge. "It is bad enough that you haunt my dreams," he accused the lizard. "Must you haunt my waking as well?"

"It is you who haunt me," the lizard replied.

Coconino snorted in disgust. "I haunt no one," he said sourly. "I seek only to be left alone."

"That," the lizard replied, "is what haunts me."

Coconino glared at the snub-nosed little creature perched boldly on its drab rock pedestal. Its skin was beaded in texture, and a combination of striping and speckling made for camouflage of the subtlest kind. "Why should you care," Coconino demanded, "whether or not I live out my life in peace?"

"Your peace is of no concern to me," the lizard agreed. "It is the living out of your life that needs attention. The People of the north want your leadership."

"They want what I cannot give," Coconino snapped.

"They want what your Witch Woman promised them," the lizard pointed out. "She has created this expectation in them."

To that Coconino only growled, for it was true. None of the People could have imagined that he would come again after he had disappeared in the Magic Place. But his Witch Woman had known that it could bend time as well as space. She alone could have known where he had gone and known that he would return. Yes, his beloved Phoenix had set him up, and two centuries of embellishment had only heightened the People's expectations.

"Once you cared for them," the lizard reminded him. "You looked out on the People and loved them not as individuals but as a whole."

"That was my own People," Coconino objected, "in my own village. And I gave them all that I had to give." I gave them what was not mine to give, he thought. I gave them the lives of Juan and Falling Star. I gave them my mother to lead them. I gave them my Witch Woman.

"You have more to give," the lizard assured him, and its self-assurance irked Coconino. "It collects in your liver and your throat and your gut and your groin. It is what makes you restless, so that you sought this Southern Village. It will drive you to hunt the bear, if you stay long enough, and to do other things that do no one any good, least of all you. For yourself, Coconino, as well as for the People, you must go back to the north and lead them."

"I am not a leader!" he snapped. "I am only a hunter and a storyteller."

"You are a favored son of the Mother Earth."

For a long moment Coconino sat silent, watching as the light disappeared from the pale contours of the stone head. The songs of grosbeaks and warblers, which had heralded them on their way up the mountain, diminished in favor of the calls of owls and other nocturnal birds. A breeze stirred through the cypress and oaks below him, but it said nothing to him. "Am I?" he asked finally. "I don't know anymore. She does not speak to me the way She used to."

"She still speaks," the lizard assured him. "It is you who do not listen as you once did."

Listen? he thought bitterly. I have begged for Her voice! And yet he knew even as he thought it that he had done less begging than demanding.

"I know that my sacrifice was necessary," he said miserably. "I know that—that it was arrogance to think I might claim a Witch Woman for a bride. But when I had given all that I had, when I took a bride of the People as a dutiful son should do, why, then, did the Mother Earth take my child? Why does She still chastise me, I who have done so much for Her?''

In the great silence Coconino heard the echo of his own pride, could almost hear the Mother Earth demand, You? Have done much for *me*?

But the lizard did not chide him for his conceit, nor did it seem to be angry. If anything, there was compassion in its voice. ''Must you know the answer to everything?''

''*Is* there an answer?'' Coconino asked in anguish.

Again the echoing silence.

''Yes,'' the lizard replied.

''Then what is it?''

The lizard studied him a moment. ''If I tell you,'' it asked, ''what will you do? Decide if you think it is just? Will you pass judgment on the answer, measuring it against your own sense of right and wrong?''

The truth of those questions wounded Coconino, and he grew angry. ''You are a bold lizard,'' he growled, ''to sit so close to my hand. Be careful I do not snatch you up and cast you out from this mountaintop.''

In the growing shadows the lizard's tail did not even twitch. ''You will not do that,'' it replied calmly. ''You are still a son of the Mother Earth. A rebellious one, perhaps, but it is not in you to wantonly destroy any creature of Hers.''

''Rebellious!'' Coconino sat up straight. ''Do not tempt me, little brother. I will have your skin for a flint pouch and your fat little body in the stew pot!''

The lizard only wagged its head from side to side, giving the impression of laughter. ''Save your wrath, Coconino,'' it told him. ''There is one who deserves it more than I, and you have yet to meet him.''

Lujan. Coconino jumped to his feet and searched the trail behind him. ''Where?'' he demanded. ''Does he come now? Is this the place?''

''Does who come?'' asked One-Eyed Fox from his spot of meditation farther up the path.

''My enemy,'' Coconino responded. ''The lizard said he would meet—''

''The lizard?''

Coconino looked back to where the banded creature had been, but of course it was gone. ''It's nothing,'' he lied badly. ''Just a creature from a dream I sometimes have.''

"A *pi-ika*," One-Eyed Fox guessed. "A haunting dream."

"Yes," Coconino admitted. "But it is nothing."

The falsehood was transparent, but One-Eyed Fox had the good grace to say nothing.

Tomorrow, Coconino thought, I will descend into the forest and not venture up to the rocky heights again. If I stay away from the rocks, then I need never meet Lujan. I can stay here in the south, where it is peaceful, in spite of what the lizard said. I have nothing left to give.

And I have nothing I will allow to be taken.

Lujan bolted upright in his bed. "No, he's mine!" he shouted. "You can't take him away! He's mine!"

From her office in the Infirmary, Liza Hanson came running. In the doorway she stopped short, trying not to hate the patient in the bed. "Lie back down," she instructed from the relative safety of ten feet. "You'll tear out your stitches."

One blue eye turned on her with unfiltered madness, the other being covered by a gauze pad, and Liza wondered briefly if ten feet was far enough. But the man was too badly injured to be dangerous at the moment. "Mine," Lujan repeated. "He's mine. They can't take him away."

"Sure, sure," Liza responded carelessly. She had grown accustomed to his ravings. "He's yours. Now lie back down and rest or you'll start bleeding again."

Lujan looked down at the mass of bandages covering his abdomen. Bleeding again. Yes, there had been blood, lots and lots of blood, but there was something wrong. It was *his* blood. That wasn't supposed to happen. "That wasn't supposed to happen," he articulated, and slumped back against his pillow. Coconino's blood, that's whose it was supposed to be. Coconino's blood. Or that woman's, Phoenix's. No, she's dead, dead and gone. I can't get to her anymore. Too bad—that might be worse for Coconino.

But I can get to him, Lujan thought. Soon as they get these bandages off me. I'll find him. Only—who was trying to take him away? Just a moment ago there was someone else looking for him. . . . It doesn't matter; I'll get there first. I'll get there first. Then, Coconino, it will be your blood drenching me. Yours, not mine.

When I find you.

Though he no longer wore judicial robes, Richard Melhew had never lost his air of authority. It came from the very core of his being, from the belief that justice was an achievable goal, the law a finely crafted tool, and himself a master craftsman. As he invited the couple into his home study and gestured for them to sit, his mind was already probing their case like a diagnostician seeking what was sound and what was weak.

They had always been an odd couple, he so dark, she so fair. The years had made it an odder combination still: he was still an attorney on Argo, hub of the corporate and political universe; she was now a horse breeder from agrarian Juno. He had never forgotten the claim they had filed in his court. Though he had been removed from the case after the initial filing in favor of a judge more apt to see the government's point of view, he had watched it all the years he had remained on the bench.

Now he was retired, and it had surprised him when they called. But he had not forgotten. He had never forgotten.

"Thank you for seeing us in person," Zleboton was saying. An interesting character, this Zleboton; he'd stayed on in New Sydney as a criminal lawyer and made quite a go of it from all reports. "This isn't something we felt could be taken care of by telecom or even holoconference."

"Let's say that I'm intrigued," Melhew replied. "I was intrigued many years ago when you first filed your claim—an absurd claim, seeking to prove some connection between Oswald Dillon and the *Homeward Bound*. And I am intrigued that you come to me with it again now that I am retired and have no influence in the courts."

"As we told you in our message," Zleboton repeated, "we believe there is a connection between Oswald Dillon and the first officer of the *Homeward Bound*, Derek Lujan. I believe you knew Mr. Lujan."

"And do you think I can help you prove this connection?" Melhew asked coolly. "If so, you could have saved yourself a long trip." A very long trip, he thought, looking at the woman. What ever possessed you to come here all the way from Juno at a time when wise people are staying out of spaceports and away from warp terminals? The Troaxians gesture for peace with one hand and hold a dagger in the other.

"I believe I can establish the connection myself," Ms. Winthrop spoke up. She had been silent at their first meeting, letting her lawyer cohort do all the talking; now she displayed all the presence and command her father had been known for. "For fifteen years I've been collecting information on Derek Lujan, Oswald Dillon, and the *Homeward Bound*." She produced a set of storage globes, rather archaic-looking things; Melhew much preferred the new biosynthetic storage devices. But his equipment would still read this older kind.

"Be my guest," he replied, and called out to his computer. "Sushama: access for gum balls, please." A panel popped out of his credenza, and he gestured for Ms. Winthrop to install her globes.

Her presentation was concise but thorough. He had expected Zleboton to do the talking, but the big attorney was content to sit by, adding only an occasional comment. She showed the public information reports from the *Homeward Bound*. She showed the radio fragment received at Xerbus, her extrapolation, and the documentation of its credibility. She expressed their dissatisfaction with the cohesiveness of the story about plague.

Then she got into the saga of Camilla Vanderhoff. Zleboton became more involved at that point, but it was obvious they were both aware that the testimony of a madwoman did not carry much weight. Although Vanderhoff's assertion that Dillon had an agent on the *Homeward Bound* had consistency, the woman had been diagnosed schizophrenic—out of touch with reality—and none of it was evidence that he would have allowed in a courtroom.

Still he listened, for the theory was an interesting one and in retirement he had the luxury of listening to whatever he pleased. Even when it became obvious that they had obtained illegal copies of the *Homeward Bound*'s logs—"undisclosed source," indeed!—he did not stop Ms. Winthrop. And finally she presented her coup de grace: Vanderhoff's assertion of a letter documenting collusion between Oswald Dillon and his agent.

"I see," Melhew said, leaning forward on his desk and clasping his hands. "So you believe there is a letter somewhere that will verify your theory that Mr. Lujan and Mr. Dillon were in league to sabotage the *Homeward Bound*."

"Yes, sir," they chorused. Even in retirement, people still called him sir.

"And if there were and you could prove this conspiracy, would that bring back the dead?"

There was a moment of silence. Then the woman cleared her throat. "Sir, we believe there may be survivors of the *Homeward Bound* stranded on Earth."

Melhew arched an eyebrow in genuine surprise. "Survivors, you say!"

"Yes, sir," she continued. "Because of Derek Lujan's history and psychological profile and the fact that he must have had only

a handful of followers, we believe that he would have found it—"
She groped for the right word. "—cleaner to maroon the balance
of the crew than to destroy them. The story of plague would easily
have prevented anyone here from finding out."

"And may continue to do so." Melhew observed her. "Even
if you proved the likelihood of survivors, who do you suppose is
going to go pick them up? The Troaxians?"

He saw her wince behind her cool, professional demeanor. "If
we can finally substantiate our claim," she replied carefully, "Dillon's long-disputed estate will come into our hands. Then we can
carry out the rescue mission ourselves."

Outrageous! Did they expect him to believe that? Did they expect him to believe that with their hands on all that money and
property, they truly intended to mount a rescue expedition to the
planet Earth? Melhew studied their faces long and carefully. There,
though masked by the years and a raft of disappointments and
frustration, he found the same thing he had seen a decade and a
half before: an intensity, a passion that was not fired by greed.
They still believed, this odd couple. They believed they were right.
They believed there were survivors. They believed they could do
something about it.

"Well, I wish you great success in finding the letter," he said
finally. "It sounds like a noble cause. But don't you think it strange
that it hasn't shown up already? Wouldn't you think it was one of
those 'to be opened in the event of my death' kinds of things?"

"Yes, sir," Zleboton agreed. "But we believe there was another condition attached, beyond Lujan's death. Something that
hasn't been met." And his hazel eyes bored straight into Melhew.

"Perhaps . . . something that never can be," Melhew suggested, giving no acknowledgment of the knowing stare. "Such
as . . . if Lujan were to precede another party in death . . . when
in fact, the other party preceded him."

"That's right. Lujan would only have wanted to threaten Dillon," Zleboton realized, piecing it together, "to make sure Dillon
didn't have him disposed of. He would have wanted the letter
opened only if Dillon were still alive. 'To be opened in the event
that I precede Oswald Dillon in death.' But Dillon's death was
confirmed before Lujan's could be assumed. Camilla inadvertently
threw a wrench into the works by wreaking swift and immediate
vengeance on her employer."

Slowly Melhew rose from his desk and crossed to the wall.
"You're an attorney, Mr. Zleboton," he said. "You can appreciate
the ethical dilemma involved. The conditions weren't met. It wasn't

legal to open the letter, yet it wasn't prudent to dispose of it when your claim was still pending and it might indeed constitute material evidence.'' He palmed a particular square of tile, and a small wall safe popped open. ''Damned nuisance, paper documents,'' he said. ''But I suppose we'll never truly get away from them. Here.'' He withdrew an envelope and handed it to Zleboton. ''As one member of the bar to another, I entrust this document to you. I have no idea what's inside; all I ever knew was the condition that linked the names of Dillon and Lujan. You'll have to find someone who'll order it opened, of course; otherwise it won't be admissible as evidence. Try Judge DeMott; he's apt to be sympathetic.''

The big man's hand trembled as he accepted the letter.

There was relief in turning the letter over to someone else after so many years—relief and a sense of justice done. More than once in his career he had wondered if the best way to uphold the law weren't to sidestep it now and again, but he had never given in to that temptation. That was why he'd decided to wait until they put the case together themselves. A good case never hinged on a single piece of evidence. ''I always hoped you would come for this,'' he confided. ''Now that you have, I hope it says what you want it to say.''

Chelsea watched over Zachery's shoulder as he sliced open the envelope. They were still in the clerk's office; Judge DeMott had just signed the order giving them legal access to the contents.

There were three pages in a crisp, bold handwriting, and she skimmed them quickly. Her heart pounded; it was everything they'd hoped for. It told how Lujan had arranged the *Aladdin* disaster at Oswald Dillon's behest. The company that owned the mining asteroid had refused to sell to Dillon, so he wanted their finances impaired through the loss of assets. He'd tried first to bribe the captain of the *Aladdin*, but when the woman couldn't be bought, he'd arranged a berth for Lujan. Lujan had planted the explosives that took out the station and had gotten rid of the captain in the process.

Then the letter went into the arrangements for the *Homeward Bound*. It stated bluntly that Dillon had hired him to see that the mission failed. The ship was never to reach Earth, and in the event that it did, no encouraging reports were to return. He was to take any and all measures necessary to see that Dillon's control of the market in Terran art and artifacts went undisturbed.

Slowly Zachery folded the letter.

''Well,'' Chelsea said quietly, ''I suppose we should take this to the probate court now. I think we can finally make good on our claim.'' Fifteen years of searching, finally come to a close. But was that all? Could that be all?

"Yes, I think that's in order," Zachery agreed. "I have a feeling, though, that the court won't be very happy to see us."

Chelsea shivered. Not happy, indeed.

Ironwood Blossom watched her son toddle along behind his father as Coconino strolled to Green Willow's wickiup to chat with the old toolmaker. Juan had grown so rapidly this summer, she was sure she would have to make a new carrying pack for him to make the trip back north. He would not like it, either; he loved running about the village with the other children, tumbling in the grass, playing in the mud at the water's edge.

With a sigh, Ironwood Blossom realized that she, too, did not look forward to the journey back north. It had been a most pleasant summer, perhaps the most pleasant of her life. The women in the Southern Village were gracious, and they had been happy to teach her new skills: weaving, for one. She was not very good at it yet, but she understood the principles of it, and if Coconino would build her a loom when they got home, she could practice. The cotton harvest had been good, and she was sure that the southerners would allow them to take a travoisload back with them.

The corn harvest had been good, too, and she had helped bring it in. She had weaned Juan so she could leave him with Dancing Knife while she went down to the fields, and they had all sung harvesting songs while they picked the corn. Soon a second planting of beans would be ready, and she would help with that, too.

But there would be no time to help with the last of the squash and melons. Alas, they had to be on their way before that if they were to reach the Northern Village before the first snows arrived, and she did not want to risk being caught in a storm on that last mountainous leg of the journey.

Coconino came back now to where she sat spinning cotton into thread, another art she had yet to master. Hummingbird would be good at this, she thought. *Her fingers are quicker and more deft than mine. She can spin the cotton, and I will weave it.*

"You look happy, my wife," Coconino greeted her as he squatted near the fire and sniffed at the steam rising from their cooking pot.

"I am content," she replied.

He smiled at her, a smile she once thought would never be hers.

At times like this she could not believe her good fortune. "That is good," he told her. "I am content in this place, too."

Well, not quite, she thought. The restlessness was still written in him, the urge to find some great deed to do. He talked often of hunting the bear, and it made her afraid. But he was Coconino; surely no harm would come to him.

"Soon," he observed, lounging on the ground and watching little Juan finding twigs, "we will have to break down our wickiup and move down the mountain to set up the winter camp. The nights grow chilly here, and some of the farming families have already gone."

Ironwood Blossom caught her spindle and stopped dead.

"What is it?" Coconino asked, seeing that she had ceased her incessant working.

"My husband," she said. "We will not join the winter camp. When the village moves down the mountain, we must be on our way back north."

For a moment there was silence between them. Then Coconino rolled over on his back and gazed up through the opening in the trees at the pure azure sky. "I think not," he told her. "I think we will stay the winter among these People."

"And then the spring, and then another summer, and then winter again—no, Coconino," she said simply. "It will only grow harder. It is time to leave."

Now he rolled onto his stomach and lay braced on his forearms, entreating her earnestly. "Then why go at all?" he asked. "This is a pleasant place where seasons of want are few and the winters are milder and bring less sickness. Think of our son. Would it not be better for him to grow up here?"

Ironwood Blossom's lip trembled. It was not as though she had not thought of it. Oh, to live in this village forever and have Coconino all to herself! She had grown fond of having him sleep so close to her, of sharing her mat and no other's. What would it be like to go back now and have him spend half his time with Hummingbird? Would he still tease her and be playful with her, as he had been since they began their journey last spring? Or, once away from this place, would he become again the brooding young god who had taken her from pity but had other options?

Yet for Ironwood Blossom there was no choice and never had been. She looked at his earnest face and by chance caught sight of the blue-green bird stone dangling from his neck. It did not matter whether they lived in this village or the northern one; Coconino would never truly be hers. Though he seldom cried out in the night anymore, he still belonged to his Witch Woman, to the She Who Saves of legend. They could be good companions, she and the man Coconino, but his heart would be forever in the past.

"You must not think only of one child," she told Coconino firmly. "You have another child and another wife in the north. We must go back."

"In the spring, then," he urged. "If we go now, we will arrive in the north unprepared for winter. We will have no supplies of wood laid in, no meat dried, no plants gathered. It would be unfair to ask to share in the harvest we did not gather."

"We harvested here," she answered. "We will take cotton back with us, which we can trade for whatever we need in the north. And you are an excellent hunter. We will not want."

Coconino sighed and rolled into a sitting position, staring into the fire. Juan saw his opportunity and climbed into his father's lap.

Stroking his son's downy soft hair, Coconino was filled with remorse. She was right, of course; Hummingbird and Snow were in the north, and it was unthinkable to abandon them there. But to leave this place, to go back to where things were expected of him, where there were so many windswept rocky places—and to pass the camp of the Others—

"I will speak to Dancing Knife tomorrow," Ironwood Blossom said firmly as she returned to her spinning, "and ask her to ask Corn Grows Tall what we may take with us."

"Perhaps next year," Coconino suggested, "we will come back and bring Hummingbird and Snow with us."

Ironwood Blossom looked up at him in surprise. Could he truly abandon the People like that, the People who had waited generations for his return? Behind his dark, brooding eyes she saw the haunted expression, and suddenly she was filled with sorrow for her illustrious husband. My poor, poor Coconino, she thought sadly. No wonder you are restless and unhappy. I thought it was only your grief that made you so, but that is only the half of it.

In your heart you wage war with the Mother Earth.

Casey spotted Liza Hanson coming out of the old Johanneson shack and hurried to catch up to her. "How's the patient doing?"

I should ask how the doctor's doing, he thought. Liza looked worn and haggard. She had lived in Camp Crusoe less than two years, but she seemed to have aged ten in that time. Then again, what had she seen during those years? A madman arrived from centuries past, an arm burned off above the elbow, a man brutally mauled by a mountain lion . . . And politics. She'd seen all the worst machinations of Crusoan politics. Casey sighed. It was enough to age anyone.

But when she looked up at him, Liza managed a smile. "Oh, hi, Casey." She was still a pretty woman when she smiled, no matter how tired. "He's doing quite well, actually—worse luck."

He knew what she meant. Janine had suffered from the same mixed feelings when she had found out the man they'd been so patiently caring for for nine months was the mutineer who'd stranded the original settlers in Camp Crusoe. Now Liza had toiled for months with all the skill she possessed to restore to life and health a man who was undoubtedly dangerous to the inhabitants of her village. "He moves around pretty well now, doesn't he?" Casey observed.

"Remarkably well considering the manacles he's sporting," she agreed. That had been the Exec's decision, finally: Lujan was shackled to his iron stove with a fifteen-foot length of chain. It seemed inhuman to Liza, yet Lujan himself seemed more beast than man these days. Perhaps he would recover, as he had from his catatonia.

At any rate, he would recover physically: she had left the man doing calisthenics in spite of his shackles. They were moderate calisthenics, according to her orders, but grueling physical therapy for all that. He did them every day, relentlessly. Pain wrote itself across his face, sweat gushed from every pore, but he never stopped. He never stopped. "What do you suppose drives him?" she wondered aloud.

Casey shrugged. "I've been wondering that myself," he admitted. "When they found him up there in that old cliff dwelling— I mean, what do you suppose he was doing?"

"Up to no good, I'm sure," Liza growled.

"Yes, but why was he there?" Casey persisted. "With all those weapons? Was it just to escape us, or was he going somewhere?"

Liza gave a half chuckle. "Where would he be going?" she asked. "There's nothing up north."

"Except the primitive village," Casey pointed out.

Now Liza stopped short and studied him. "You think Lujan was headed for the primitive village when the cougar got him?"

Again Casey shrugged. "I don't know. But it's like you said: Something's driving him. Something powerful."

Did the man truly have a vendetta against the aborigines living to the north? Liza shuddered. She had seen them when they had come to trade: proud people, reserved, innocent. How could they cope with a madman like Lujan?

Perhaps better than we, she thought. Perhaps their solution would be more direct than ours. My ethics won't let me condone that, but dear God, how relieved I would be.

But she couldn't bear to say that. Instead, "He won't be getting loose again," she pronounced with more assurance than she felt. "There's not a tool in the camp that can break that chain he's wearing. And Tav Ryan has the only key."

CHAPTER TWENTY-ONE

Phoenix was just coming up from the river with a rabbit she had cleaned for their supper when a hue and cry went up from a group of older children who had been out gathering the first flower stalks of sotol for the evening meal. "A Machine is coming!" they shouted excitedly. "A Machine That Crawls is coming across the land from the west!"

In an instant Phoenix was running for the trail that crossed the creek and led up the canyon wall to the western rim. Others? she wondered. Or Men-on-the-Mountain, after all these years? All these—eighteen? No, nineteen years.

The minute she saw the truck, she knew it was no machine of the Others but one of the centuries-old relics she had once nursed to life on the Mountain: a 2247 Ford pickup truck with probably not an original part in it anymore. In fact, she was sure she'd machined half the sheet metal for this one herself. There were two people inside, but in the glare of the afternoon sun she could not see who they were.

The truck rolled and bumped to a stop about twenty feet from where she stood on the canyon rim. The engine coughed and ran on painfully after it was turned off, and Phoenix winced. Who was taking care of the vehicles these days? Reed would never let a truck out of the shop running like that. But then, Reed had probably retired, and Tommy Sakka, too. Retired or—

She tried not to think about that.

Now the driver's side door swung open, and a middle-aged man stepped out. Phoenix gasped as she recognized her ex-husband, Dick McKay.

"Debbie?" he called out to her tentatively. "My God, Debbie, it's you, isn't it?"

His words sounded odd, and it took her a moment to realize he was speaking in English, not the language of the People. She had not heard English in a very long time. "Yes, it's me, Dick," she replied, the words thick and strange on her tongue. "It's me."

He came toward her across the rough ground sprinkled here and there with purple and orange wildflowers. The years had been kind to him; his hair was stone gray and he bore numerous lines in his face for his fifty-nine years, but he looked fit and healthy enough. Trimmer than the last time she had seen him, she thought. He stopped uncomfortably an arm's length away from her. "We've been looking for you for days," he began awkwardly. "We stopped at Camp Crusoe to see if they knew where you were, and they told us a band of primitives stopped in there, oh, five years ago, headed south. But not you. You were still in the north, they thought, in some old cliff dwelling." He gave a wry smile and a shrug. "There are a lot of cliff dwellings up here."

Phoenix only nodded. Why had he come? Why, after all these years, show up now? Had something calamitous happened on the Mountain? Had people come back again from the stars?

"But there was one woman," Dick went on, "who seemed to know more than the others. She talked about an island. I checked my maps, and this place seemed to fit."

"Karen," Phoenix whispered.

"I never got her name," Dick admitted. "We came up the old highway till the lava flows obscured it completely, and then we—"

But Phoenix was no longer listening to Dick's ramblings. Her gaze shot past him to where a young man was climbing down out of the other side of the truck. The brightness of the sun behind him obscured the details of his face, but his chest was bare, his shoulder-length hair tousled and jet black—

Coconino! her heart sang. It's Coconino, he's come back, he's here!

But then the boy came closer, and she knew it was not he. The face was a bit too narrow, and the jaw not quite as strong. His shoulders were not as broad, either, though well muscled. He looked like Coconino but not like Coconino. Phoenix trembled.

Dick saw the flood of emotions cross his ex-wife's face as the lad approached. He remembered her defense of Coconino to the Advisory Board before she left the Mountain for good, her declaration of devotion and despair. It had surprised some people that Debbie would abandon the Mountain to live with the primitives, even lead them, but not Dick. He knew what a passionate woman she could be. "I brought someone," he told her gently. "Someone who wanted to come and live for a time with the People, as I did when I was a young man. Someone who wanted to learn more about his father. Debbie, this is Michael. He is Coconino's son.''

Michael extended his hand. ''I am honored to know the friend of my father,'' he said politely in the language of the People.

Tears sprang unwanted to Phoenix's eyes. His voice was the voice of Coconino, a rich baritone that rang with music. Numbly she lifted her hand to his; then at the last moment she grasped his arm in a hunter's greeting, forearm to forearm. ''You are welcome,'' she declared fervently, ''in our fields and in our village. Michael, son of Coconino, you are welcome among the People.''

At that a slow smile spread across his face, and Phoenix thought her heart would break. It is your smile, Coconino, she wept inwardly. It is your smile but not you. How shall I bear it? For nineteen years I have lived with only my memory, and now how shall I bear to see your smile and hear your voice and never touch you?

Michael peered over the edge of the canyon to the steep trail leading down toward the island in its midst. ''It doesn't look like we'll drive down there,'' he commented to Dick. ''I'd better get my knapsack out of the truck.''

Phoenix watched him walk back to the vehicle, a swinging, athletic gate that was familiar and yet different. It was the careless, carefree stride of a Mountain youth combined with the effortless, catlike grace of a hunter.

''I hope you don't mind,'' Dick said quietly as Michael moved out of earshot. ''Things have been . . . difficult for him on the Mountain. There are people who won't forget what Coconino did, and there are others who are just . . .''

''Stupid,'' Phoenix supplied.

''Not so many,'' Dick hastened. ''But I thought it might be good for him to spend some time in a place where he could be proud of who his father was.''

''He should be proud anywhere!'' Phoenix flared.

''And I think he is,'' Dick replied quietly as Michael came back toward them with a canvas duffel slung over one shoulder. ''But here it will be a little easier for him.''

For a moment Phoenix just looked at Michael: the eager face, the youthful body, the pack that was doubtless filled with things he'd never use here. Behind her she could hear the children whispering, hear other footsteps scrabbling up the path, feel the curious eyes of the People turned on Michael. What would they think of

Coconino having yet another son? Could they see the truth of his heritage in his face as she did, those who had known Coconino?

"Come along, then," she said finally, turning to face the growing crowd behind her. "This is Michael," she proclaimed to them, "son of Coconino by his Chosen Companion, a Witch Woman from the Mountain. And this is McKay, a Man-on-the-Mountain who once walked among us. They have come to visit us for a time. Let us make a great feast in their honor!"

"How long will you stay?" Phoenix asked Dick as they crossed a simple wooden bridge over the swollen creek and headed for the island butte.

"Myself?" he asked. "Just tonight. I'm getting old, Debbie; I like the comfort of a soft bed and a hot shower."

"It's Phoenix," she corrected him. "And you, Michael? How long will you stay?"

"A year, I think," the young man responded. "My mother only wanted me to come for the summer, but . . ."

"I talked her into letting him stay through the winter," Dick finished. "That's when the stories of the People are told, while the rain beats against the wickiups."

"Here it snows," Phoenix replied curtly. "And wickiups are only for marriage ceremonies."

Dick was silent for a moment, and Phoenix cursed herself. You didn't have to be so sharp with him, she thought. Whatever pain he caused you in the past is of no importance now. He's brought you Michael. At least you can be civil to him.

"I suppose you've had to make some adjustments," Dick said finally. "Because of the climate difference. No cotton, I see."

"And only one planting of vegetables," she replied. "But the forests in the canyon and on the rim are full of nuts and berries, and the lands to the east are home to the biggest antelope you've ever seen. Some kind of elk descendant, I think." But no unicorns, she thought sadly. At least none that fly. Tala was the last of those.

They had reached the first cluster of houses now, and two shy young maidens peered out at the strangers passing their door. Dick cleared his throat. "Do the People, uh, still extend the, uh, the Right of the Chosen Companion?"

Phoenix stopped short and turned an appraising eye first on him, then on Michael. "Ababba," Michael whispered in embarrassment.

Ababba! Suddenly Phoenix's jaw dropped, and she stared at Dick. "He calls you Grandfather?" she asked, stunned. Ideas whirled through her head, chaotic, nonsensical. Ababba? Dick? But if Krista was the boy's mother, then—

The truth slammed home, and Phoenix fought for breath, staggering back, grasping the empty air for something to hang on to. "You?" she gasped weakly. "You were—Two Moons'—"

Dick watched her struggle with the concept, war against the truth he had kept hidden from her while they were married. *How could I tell you?* he pleaded silently. *How could I tell you it was your dark hair and your piercing eyes that stirred me so? How could I tell you that I looked at you and saw not Two Moons but the People? All the People. And when you came back to the Mountain after your first summer among them, how could I tell you that the man who guided you, the man you followed with a devotion I had lost from you, was my son?*

"Yes, Debbie," he said now. "Two Moons was my Chosen Companion. I am Coconino's father."

Lies and treachery and betrayal and deceit! Phoenix raged. But even as the tide of wrath swept over her, she knew it was pointless. Dick had not concocted the lie to hurt her; it had been in place long before she had drawn his interest. Should he have told her when they were married? Was it wrong to keep the secret from her when he knew how she worshiped Coconino? In the long run it made not one bit of difference.

Still, her knees felt weak and her stomach churned uneasily. "Croaking Frog," she called to a boy nearby. "Show our guests to my house. I must find Fire Keeper and tell him to prepare the Elvira." Then she scrambled off the trail and up the steep side of the island, away from Dick.

"She's a tough old number," Michael observed in English as Phoenix disappeared around the island's curvature.

"She's had a tough life," Dick said gently. "Try to be patient with her. She needs lots of patience." *More patience than I could give her. Be better to her than I was, Michael. Be truer to the People. Be everything I was not.*

They were approaching the southwestern part of the island, where a series of five or six houses were built into a shallow limestone cave. "I'm sorry," Michael said guiltily, "if I gave something away by calling you Grandfather. I didn't know."

"It's all right," Dick assured him as their guide stopped in front of the second house. "The crime was mine, not yours, and after forty years I'm still paying for it."

"It's not a crime," Michael protested, "to have fathered a child on a woman who wanted it. Who expected it." His grandfather had explained the custom of the Chosen Companion to Michael, and its purpose. It had occupied his thoughts most of the trip from the Mountain.

But Dick shook his head with a sad smile. "That was not the crime," he said softly. "The crime was in leaving them."

The boy Croaking Frog pulled back a hide covering from the door and indicated that they should go into the house. Such shy, reserved people, Dick thought as he smiled at the boy and ducked inside. How welcome their reticence had been to the gawky, studious teenager he'd been when he had arrived in the Valley of the People. At Michael's age he'd had none of Michael's charm and poise, none of his cocky self-assurance with girls. The giggling, bashful maidens of the People had embarrassed Dick with their awkward attempts at flirtation. And to think that he was expected to *choose* one—

"Boy," he heard Michael call to the child in a voice hushed with awe. "Who is *that*?"

Michael was still standing outside on the ledge, so Dick put his head back out the low doorway to see what had drawn the lad's attention. A girl, of course. A strikingly beautiful girl with fine, sharp features and a slight upward slant to her eyes. They were arresting eyes, like live coals in a face framed by flowing black hair. She wore a leather breechclout, as Phoenix had, and a single band of leather circled her breasts and was tied in front. She was slender as a willow, graceful as a cat. No wonder Michael was taken.

"That is Sky Dancer," the little boy told them. "She is the foster daughter of She Who Saves."

She Who Saves. The name meant nothing to Dick. But the girl was obviously not a full-blooded primitive. Her skin was lighter, and her build, though athletic, was too slight. Yet she walked with the regal pride of one who was highly honored among the People. Across her back were slung a bow and quiver; in her hand was a brace of quail.

Sky Dancer spotted the two strangers at her mother's door and stopped. She had never seen an Other, but she knew one would never be allowed in Phoenix's house, so the older man kneeling half-inside must be a Man-on-the-Mountain. The younger one, by his strange clothing, must be one as well, but his face was like the faces of the People. Curious, she drew nearer.

He was tall, this young stranger, taller even than her mother. And his body showed that he was not soft and weak, as she had been told the Men-on-the-Mountain often were. No, this young man's body was well proportioned, lithe, and muscular. His face seemed oddly familiar, but Sky Dancer couldn't imagine why that should be. It was a handsome face with strong, even features and soft eyes. An arresting face. She came very close to him on the ledge.

Michael looked down into the girl's face—a bold face, he thought. With her eyes she asked—no, demanded—who he was who dared to stand there so and gaze at her. *I choose you*, he thought to himself. *When it is time for the Choosing, as my grandfather told me, I choose you.*

"Who are you?" Sky Dancer challenged. He was unflinching, this stranger. Over the past two years she had developed a cold gaze that could make any young man in the village back off, and she had wielded it like a knife. But this one would not give ground before her. "What are you doing here?"

"I am Michael," he replied, fascinated by her boldness, aroused by her nearness. "I have come from the Mountain." *Say that you are not already married*, he thought. *Say that when the fire dies down tonight I may take you to my bed.*

"Are you a Teacher, then?" Sky Dancer asked. Inside her, feelings stirred that had remained dull and dead since Dreams of Hawks had been laid in the frozen bosom of the Mother Earth. *Would there be a Choosing for this Man-on-the-Mountain, as there had been in the old days? How was a Choosing done? Must a maiden put herself forward, or did the man simply pick at random? What would her mother say, what would the People say, if after rejecting four suitors in the past year she put herself forward to be Chosen?*

"I am no Teacher," Michael confessed, "but a learner. I come not to offer my knowledge to the People but to beg theirs."

At the sound of his words, Sky Dancer's heart fluttered. He did not speak with the rich accents of the People, but there was a poetry to his words that was worthy of the best storytellers in the village. "My mother says that learners are the best Teachers," she told him. *Are you as profound as you are handsome, Man-on-the-Mountain Michael?*

A smile played at his lips, and Sky Dancer wondered what it would be like to kiss those lips. "And who is your mother?" he asked her. "She is blessed indeed to have so rare a daughter as you."

From the ledge behind them Phoenix's voice pierced the air, edged with warning. "I am her mother," she called. "Her foster mother. She, also, is the child of Coconino. Sky Dancer, this is Michael—your half brother.''

Coral Snake watched the fox come, stealing through the brush without a sound, ears alert, eyes watchful. Once more Coral Snake lifted his hands to his lips and made the sound, the perfect imitation of a quail's comic beep. Then, as the fox started to circle, Coral Snake fitted an arrow to his bowstring and poised himself to strike. In one motion he sprang up from his hiding place, drew back the bow, aimed, and fired.

The fox squealed only once and went down thrashing in a bed of wildflowers. Coral Snake approached slowly, less from caution than from self-assurance that his bolt had struck home and there was no need for him to hurry.

Indeed, the fox was quite dead. Coral Snake withdrew his arrow and inspected it carefully for damage. Finding none, he cleaned it with grass and returned it to his quiver. For a moment he considered taking the fox's pelt, but his wife already had more hides than she could tan. Of meat there was plenty, as well, for Coral Snake was one of the best hunters in the village; if he took the fox back, he would only have to give it away. So he turned his back on his kill and left it to rot in the desert sun.

What would you say, old man-woman, he wondered, if you knew that sometimes I hunt for no other reason than that it gives me pleasure? You would be furious, I know, and berate me mightily before all the village. And do you know what? I do not care. Your words cannot harm me, and you have no power over me. I discovered that long ago.

But I have power over you, old man-woman. The power to make you angry, to send you into fits of rage. It is so easy, I seldom bother anymore. I would rather torment your daughter, for she hides her anger better than you. There is more cunning involved in making her lash out. It is a great sport.

Coral Snake picked up the portion of his day's kill that he wanted to keep—two plump quail and a large hare—and started back toward the village. He would stop at a stream he knew of to clean them, but he would make no chants over the dead animals, no blood offering to the Mother Earth.

For the Mother Earth does not really care, he thought. When I was a child, I believed she did. I went through all the rituals, chanted all the chants, hoping she would hear my prayers and look upon me with favor. But for all my obiesance, for all my worship, did she elevate me above the children of Coconino? No. Though

I excelled in every way, though I was better at wresting and games than Nakha-a, though I am a better hunter than Sky Dancer, though I am clever in imitating the calls of animals which neither of them can do, is there any honor for me in the village? No.

Why did the Mother Earth not respond? Why have I never once even heard her voice? Did she not care? Perhaps. Or perhaps she did not hear. Perhaps she has no ears, and those who say they speak with her are only deluded fools. That would make Nakha-a the biggest fool of all.

In the end, he had decided it didn't matter which explanation was the right one. Either way, there was no point in him carrying on with meaningless rituals. In the company of other hunters, he mouthed the words, but they were a mockery in his heart. Alone, he simply did not bother. If the Mother Earth noticed, she had not struck him down yet.

When he returned to the village, he decided, he would take a nap on the sunny southern slope of the island butte. Maybe after that Dirty Face and Horned Lizard would be back from planting corn and they could exchange stories or practice their bird calls. Or perhaps he could think of some new way to tease the widowed Sky Dancer. They could try to convince old Sleeps By The Fire that he should woo her.

When Coral Snake reached the village, however, he found the whole camp in an uproar. "What is it?" he asked the first children he saw scampering down to the river to collect rushes for bedding. "What is going on?"

"Men-on-the-Mountain!" they chattered excitedly. "Two of them! And one is Coconino!"

Coral Snake drew back as they bolted off to finish their task. Coconino? Impossible! Coconino was not a Man-on-the-Mountain. Besides, he was dead and gone. Irritated at this gross untruth spreading through the village, he ground his teeth and stalked to his own house.

There he found his wife all in a dither, plaiting flowers into her younger sister's hair. "Have you heard, my husband?" she blurted as he ducked in and knelt on a skin near the door. "Men-on-the-Mountain have come to our village! And one of them is Coconino's son."

"Nakha-a?" Coral Snake scoffed. "That weak, womanish—"

"No, no, not Nakha-a," his wife interrupted. "His name is Michael. He is Coconino's son by a Witch Woman of the Mountain."

Another son! It struck Coral Snake like a blow. "What if he

is?'' Coral Snake growled. ''He is only a man. I am a better one. Am I not, my wife?''

The girl cringed and stopped her plaiting. ''Of course, my husband,'' she answered meekly. ''There is no better man in the village than you. He is only a Man-on-the-Mountain, anyway; he is not of the People.''

''But he is handsome!'' giggled the sister. ''And he will want a Chosen Companion. Don't you think?'' Her eyes taunted Coral Snake, flaunting his lack of control over her.

''He will want one who can give him a child!'' he snapped. ''Perhaps he should look to another family!'' Then he rolled deftly to his feet and ducked back out into the sunlight.

Furious, Coral Snake stalked along the trail to his mother's house. It had been two years since he had taken a wife, and though she grew rounder each day, it was not with child. How could she sit there and prattle on about Men-on-the-Mountain? She ought to be pleading to the Mother Earth for a child, doing penance for whatever wrong she had committed to be left barren. Even if the Mother Earth did not hear, at least the rest of the village would know how ashamed she was. But, no, his unrepentant wife sat there plaiting her sister's hair with flowers so that the girl could attract a Man-on-the-Mountain. And one of Coconino's get at that!

Castle Rock was inside her house, fussing with the fringe of an old cotton shawl. Why did she wear that thing, anyway? Did she not have perfectly good furs that he had provided her? She was an elegant woman in her middle years, round and comely, with smooth cheeks and long hair just beginning to gray. She looked up and beamed at him as he came in and knelt by her cook fire. ''My son, did you hear?'' she asked. ''Two men have come from the Mountain! And one of them is the son of Coconino.''

Bright anger flashed through Coral Snake's eyes. ''What is that to me, woman?'' he snarled, betrayed by this line of talk in his own mother's house. ''It seems sons of Coconino are as common as coyote turds.''

Accustomed to her son's temper, Castle Rock ignored his outburst in favor of her own thoughts. ''Ah, but this one . . .'' She shook her head. ''At first, when I saw him, I thought it was Coconino come back to us at last. We all did.''

''Coconino!'' Coral Snake snorted contemptuously. ''Coconino will never come back. Only that stupid old man-woman believes it anymore. Coconino is dead, burned by the fireshooters of the Others.''

''That is not true, my son,'' Castle Rock protested. ''He is only sleeping; Nina said so. But until he does return . . ." She approached her tall son—easily the tallest man in the village now—crawling across the low-ceilinged room to kneel beside him and stroke his powerful arm. "Here is what you must do, my son. You must befriend this new son of his. Become his *compadre*, his teacher—it will give you great status in the village. Then, when the son goes back to the Mountain—"

But Coral Snake pushed her roughly aside. "I am tired of your schemes, woman," he growled. "They do not work. You told me to woo Sky Dancer—ha! I would rather woo a rattlesnake; it has a warmer heart. Then you got this other prize for me, this dim-witted thing who eats and eats and makes no babies. I want no more of your meddling in my life."

"Hush, my son," Castle Rock said, turning on her habitual charm to soften his mood. "Any day now she will conceive. You will see. Perhaps now that the son of Coconino has come—yes, yes, that must be a good omen. Things will improve now. The corn will grow better, the winters will be milder, and your wife will conceive—"

"You foolish old woman!" Coral Snake barked angrily. "Why should that happen because the stinking get of an overrated storyteller has wandered into the village?"

Castle Rock sat back, finally taking notice of her son's deep wrath. "What are you saying?" she asked, mystified by his anger. "You do not truly believe such things, do you? My son, I knew Coconino, and he was the finest of the People."

"No, *I* am the finest of the People!" Coral Snake shouted at her. "I am the tallest, I am the strongest, I am the cleverest. Have you not told me so since I stepped out of my cradle basket? Who is this son of Coconino? Why should he have more honor than I?" A cold and wicked smile twisted his lips. "Am I not the son of . . . a Man-on-the-Mountain myself?"

Castle Rock blanched. "My son, I think you do not understand."

"Come, Mother," he admonished. "Everyone in the village knows whose son I am. How did I grow so tall? How did I get these blue eyes? Everyone knows."

Now a fire kindled in Castle Rock's eyes as well. "Your father was the Teacher," she replied stubbornly. "I was his Chosen Companion. It was a great honor and—"

"And you left his bed to sleep with the Other. With Lu-jan. My father."

"You must never say this," Castle Rock hissed. "You must

always say that your father was the Teacher. Let people think what they like—sometimes it is amusing to see the uncertainty in their eyes, to know that they wonder—but you must never say it. Never.''

"Why not?'' Coral Snake demanded. "Why should I not proclaim who my father is? Can anyone else make such a claim? I am the only one. I alone am the son of—''

"A Teacher, of a Man-on-the-Mountain,'' his mother insisted with growing ire. "It is one thing to tease, Coral Snake, but it is quite another to say it straight out! Now, listen to me. You must befriend this new Man-on-the-Mountain, this son of Coconino by his Chosen Companion. Then, when people see you side by side, they will say, 'Ah! Two fine young men with *linaje nuevo*.' And—''

"I will not besmirch myself by fawning on that son of coyote dung!'' Coral Snake said.

Suddenly Castle Rock's hand flew out and struck her son across the face. Coral Snake gasped, startled.

"Never call him that,'' she told him flatly. "Never call Coconino vile names in my presence. Never!''

"You hit me!'' Coral Snake stared at his mother in astonishment. "You *hit* me.'' Never in his life had his mother raised a hand against him or allowed his stepfather to do so. Shocked, he searched her face for some explanation of her behavior.

What he found there shocked him even more. Behind the anger, behind the cold rebuke, there was sorrow. Sorrow and regret. Regret? Why should that be? Yet there it was. Why should his mother defend Coconino this way after she had defied all custom and authority to sleep with his deadliest enemy? Was she not proud of that? He had always thought she was proud of that.

Slowly it dawned on him. "You loved him, didn't you?'' he asked incredulously. "You *loved* Coconino!''

"Yes, I loved him,'' she whispered intensely. "He was the finest man in the village, the handsomest, the noblest. But he wouldn't have me. If he had, do you think I would have slept with that grunting pig of a Teacher, who couldn't even get me pregnant? Do you think I would have sneaked off to be with an Other?''

"I thought,'' he replied coldly, "you were the only one with courage.''

"Courage!'' she said. "Stupidity. Oh, he was handsome and exotic, the Other, but what kind of man was he? His kind are violent and disrespectful of the Mother Earth, my son. They raise their hands in anger and take human life. They killed Juan, and Falling Star, and Always Hungry—''

Coral Snake's hand lashed out, and he returned his mother's blow with enough force to knock her to the ground. She screeched in pain and fright. "I am sick to death of those names!" he cried, leaning close and shouting in her ear. "I am sick to death of Juan and Falling Star and the other men who did nothing in their lives but become heroes by the accident of their deaths. And most of all, I am sick to death of Coconino."

With that, he bolted out the doorway and left his mother sobbing on the floor.

They built the Elvira down in the canyon by the stream, for the vegetation there was lush and green with the spring runoff and there was little danger of a careless spark setting fire to the area. Those who had known Coconino came to gape at this son whose visage testified so clearly to his parentage: Loves the Dust and Hair Like a Rope and Smooth Pebbles, and of course Flint. Older men now, in their late thirties and early forties. Men whose knees were growing weak from years of running. Women whose children had children who stared wide-eyed at the visiting strangers.

Cactus Flower, Juan's widow, waddled up to Phoenix as she sat in the shadows, watching the People watching the boy. "Is he not the image of his father?" Cactus Flower exclaimed. "When I saw him, She Who Saves, I thought it was Coconino come back to us at last!"

Phoenix smiled indulgently, but it was a hollow smile.

"Would that I had a daughter," Cactus Flower went on, "that she might be a Chosen Companion to Coconino's son!"

Nor was Cactus Flower the only mother to think such things, Phoenix knew. The maidens of the People had come eagerly to the Elvira, giggling and poking each other, washed and brushed and dressed in their finest clothing. Everyone knew there would be a Choosing, and every girl of marriageable age was praying to the Mother Earth that she would be the one Chosen. Now they understood why their mothers sighed when they spoke of Coconino, for if the son was like his father, the father had been a prize indeed.

In the dancing light of the flames, Sky Dancer sat beside her half brother to interpret the customs of the People for him. He lounged with easy grace, like the other young men, but she sat rigid and proud and proper, drawing around her the wall that she used to protect her from unwanted attention. The wall extended to Michael now, but he understood it and was not angry but grateful.

A wall was needed between them to keep the sparks they had known on the ledge from kindling a fire.

"Ababba told me of the custom of a Choosing," he said to her as he watched a group of five young girls whispering together and throwing coy glances in his direction. "You must tell me which maidens are available so that I don't make a fool of myself."

"Them," Sky Dancer replied simply with a curt nod of her head toward the group.

They all looked to be fourteen or fifteen, with shining round faces and firm, fleshy bodies. The prospect was a heady one to Michael; he tried to keep a hold of his reason, but it fled him like a lizard that dropped its tail to escape capture.

"Then tell me about them," he encouraged Sky Dancer. "If I must have the same Chosen Companion for a year, I want to make a wise choice, but—I'm not thinking too clearly just now."

Sky Dancer shrugged. "They seem a silly lot to me," she replied. "But they are sweet-tempered, for the most part, and will keep your house and liven your nights, I am sure. I do not see much difference between them."

No, you are the only one who is different, he thought. But you are forbidden. Help me, Sky Dancer. Help me choose one who will keep my mind off you.

But Sky Dancer was obviously not going to assist him in the selection. He could choose any one—as she said, there was not much difference between them—and satisfy his immediate lust, yet he hesitated. He had made a mistake with Cilla Thurston, and that had been a painful situation to get out of. Imagine a year of Cilla! And before that he had made an even worse mistake by falling in love with Hillary Martin, but that was over, it was over, she had married Darron, she had never really loved Michael—

"Well, I don't think I'll choose one tonight," he decided, stifling his body's urgent demands. "I want to see them in the daylight, at least, and talk to them. It's all right for me to talk to them, isn't it?"

"Yes, you may speak to them," she agreed, "but it is wisest to do so in the presence of others. There is . . . significance . . . attached if a man and a woman walk alone together."

Significance. Yes. In my culture, too, he thought. Then he turned mischievous eyes on Sky Dancer. "But I must bring no gifts to her door, eh?" Michael teased, trying to get a smile out of his sober sister. He knew such a gesture was an offer of marriage, not companionship. "No ram slung across my shoulder? No string of striped skunks as an offering?"

That finally got through to her, and Sky Dancer's mouth twisted upward in spite of herself. "We need not worry about that," she chuckled, "until you learn which part of the arrow fits onto the bowstring!"

At that he laughed, a joyous, musical laugh, and Sky Dancer broke into a broad smile. Laughter is good, she thought privately. I have not laughed in a long time. It is better than this tension, at any rate, that gnaws at me when you are near and I must remember you are my brother. If we laugh together, Michael, we will be all right. If we only remember to laugh, it will never get too bad.

Far to their right Coral Snake watched the pair with cold eyes, keeping his anger carefully pent within him. Are you your father's son? he asked silently. Do you do more than look like the great Coconino? I think not. You have never camped alone in the wilderness, or made a bow, or hunted so much as a field mouse. You know nothing of the Way of the People, yet see how they fawn on you! Why? Can you tell me why? What reason is there to show you honor, to feed and shelter you, to give you one of our maidens? What have you done to earn any of this?

Yet they heap praise and accolades upon you because of your handsome face. I have a handsome face, too; do they make a feast for me? No. Last winter I provided more meat for the village than even the great She Who Saves—was I rewarded? A polite thanks, that is all. They save their highest honors for the son of Coconino.

His eyes narrowed. Well, let us see if you can keep their respect, O Son-of-the-Great-Braggart. How will you react when you find a dead Gila monster in your sleeping furs? What kind of dance will you do when you hear the dry buzzing of a rattlesnake shaking in your ear? How will the People esteem you when they discover you are both a coward and a fool?

For I shall make you a fool in their eyes, Man-on-the-Mountain. I shall make you a figure of mockery and derision, and you shall be so glad to leave this village that you will never come here to trouble us again.

"Full extension on your arm!" Phoenix snapped. "Turn your elbow out—no, turn at the shoulder! You'll have a welt on your arm the size of a barn swallow's nest if you get slapped by the bowstring!"

Michael ground his teeth and corrected his form. Then he let fly the arrow and buried its point deep in the soft wood of the ponderosa pine.

"Not bad," Phoenix admitted grudgingly. "Practice a little

more, and tomorrow we'll take you out and see how you do on a moving target.'' She raised her own bow and, as a matter of pride, set her own arrow neatly in the tree beside his. ''You've got a strong arm. If we can get you close enough to a mule deer, you shouldn't have any trouble bagging it.''

''Why don't we go today?'' Michael asked as they retrieved their arrows from the target. ''There's still plenty of daylight left.''

''Because today,'' Phoenix snapped, ''I need to bring something back to eat, and I'm not apt to get it with you tramping through the underbrush like a wounded elk!''

''I'll learn!'' he flared.

''You'll have to.''

''You'd better go, Mother,'' Sky Dancer intervened from the sidelines, where she had been watching the archery lesson. ''I will spend some time today teaching my brother how to walk quietly in the forest.''

Phoenix drew back and looked warily from one to the other. Sky Dancer knew what she was thinking. ''Either he is my brother or he is not my brother!'' Sky Dancer snapped. ''If he is to be my brother, then allow me to treat him like one! You cannot walk on both sides of the trail.''

Still Phoenix hesitated. One part of her wanted to take Sky Dancer to task for her tone and her naiveté, but another part warned that she should not get her daughter's back up. *Stubborn child. Where did she acquire that trait? I wonder.* Finally Phoenix gave them one last measuring glance. ''Very well, then,'' she conceded. ''I trust the children of Coconino to honor the Way of the People as brother and sister.'' Turning on her heel, she trotted away through the trees to the south.

Mother Earth help her, Phoenix thought as she jogged away from the teenagers. *Sky Dancer lost one boy so tragically, and it has left an emptiness in her that aches to be filled. Does she know how strong the temptation can be? She is so young; does she have any idea? And Michael is so beautiful. Mother Earth, he is so beautiful. . . .*

''Your mother doesn't like me much,'' Michael complained as he and Sky Dancer turned their steps back toward the village.

''That is not true,'' Sky Dancer replied simply.

''I can't do anything right for her!'' he cried. ''I don't hold my bow right, I don't plant my feet properly—I hit the target, didn't I? What more does she want?''

''Perfection.''

''Is she that way with you?'' he asked. ''Does she criticize everything you do and make cutting remarks about your lack of experience?''

Sky Dancer gave a great sigh. "No," she admitted. "She has always been patient and encouraging with me, more so since Dreams of Hawks died. Though she can be harsh at times, she can also be most loving and supportive."

"Then why does she pick on me?" he wanted to know. "Why the short temper and the quick tongue?"

"It is only that when she looks at you," Sky Dancer told him, "she sees our father."

"Is that my fault?" he demanded.

Sky Dancer stopped in the shadow of a tall, ancient Douglas fir and studied her half brother, studied the striking face and the fiery eyes, and she understood her mother a little better. "No, it is not your fault, and you must tell her that," she urged. "Throw it up to her—it is the only way to deal with the mighty She Who Saves. You must be as strong-willed as she is or she will trample you without meaning to. Are you strong enough, Michael? Are you strong enough to take her on?"

"Yes," he replied unflinchingly.

Sky Dancer believed him. "Good," she said, starting once more for the village. "Now, pay attention, and we will walk from here as though we were stalking a Great Antelope." It is good that you are strong, she thought. We must both be strong to be children of Coconino. We must both be strong if we are to live as brother and sister for this year.

Michael worked the wet barberry shaft through the straightening tool, intent on making the perfect arrow. It was an absorbing task, like shaping a racquet frame, requiring both patience and dexterity. He was determined that Phoenix would have no complaints about the quality of his work.

But just down the path a group of young maidens was approaching. They all bore large clay jars on their shoulders, for they had the daily task of bringing water up from the river, but they took care to strut gracefully as they drew near, and their chatter diminished to whispers, then the whispers dissolved into sly smiles as they passed. Distracted, he stopped his work and watched them parade by, knowing they would be disappointed if he didn't, wondering if they would scatter like quail if he actually spoke to them. He decided to try it.

"Good morning, Younger Chick," he greeted the first one.

"Good morning, Sleeping Dove. Good morning, Beads in Her Hair and Willow Branch and Summer Sky."

"Good morning, Michael," they replied, suppressing giggles and blushing prettily. "The sun shines brightly today."

"Does she?" he asked. "I thought it pale beside the brightness of your faces."

At that they all tittered and nudged one another furiously.

Michael smiled to himself as they continued up the path toward their houses. He had narrowed his choice to two, but it seemed each day it was a different two. Beads in Her Hair was the loveliest, but she was painfully shy; he wanted someone more playful than that. Summer Sky seemed to be playful, but her older brother gave Michael foul looks every time their paths crossed, and Michael just didn't want trouble like that. As for Willow Branch—

The sharp crack of stone on stone caught Michael's attention, and he turned his face toward the sound. Down the path, just outside one of the adobe houses, a young girl knelt grinding corn furiously. Every once in a while her long hair would fall in front of her face, and she would twitch it aside angrily. The sharp sound had been her *mano* smacking against the *metate*, the sort of wasted movement even a girl of her age would not make unintentionally. He wondered what had upset her.

But the wood in his hand was drying. Michael dipped it again in the bowl of water beside him and slipped it through the straightening tool. Six arrows, Sky Dancer had told him. One for each finger of his right hand, plus one that was sure to get lost. Chipping the flint arrow tips was something best left to Strikes with a Stone, who was a master at it, but every hunter was expected to spend the tedious hours crafting his own shafts and fletching them with hawk feathers.

Suddenly the girl down the path leapt to her feet and marched in his direction. Michael looked up in surprise, and she stopped directly in front of him. She was obviously past puberty and coming into the pleasant roundness of womanhood, though she had not gathered with the other maidens at the Elvira or joined their group flirtations. On her face was a fierce pout, and it reminded him a bit of his half sister Linda when she had been denied her way. Michael was hard pressed not to laugh.

"It's not fair," the girl announced.

"What's not fair?" he asked. Hers was an ordinary face for a maiden of the People: round and open and unpretentious. Except, of course, that at the moment her brow was wrinkled by her petulance and her lower lip protruded a bit.

"This is my fourteenth spring," she declared, "and I am to have my womanhood ceremony when the moon is full, but that is not for two weeks yet. I don't think you should choose until after I've had my womanhood ceremony."

Michael's jaw dropped in a gaping half smile as he stared up at the feisty little maiden. Tradition might keep her from participating in the copious flirtation that preceded a Choosing, but it was not going to keep her from letting him know about it.

"And you think I should wait for you," he said with only a trace of mockery in his tone.

"I didn't say that you should wait for me," she contradicted. "I said you should wait to choose. There hasn't been a Man-on-the-Mountain in our village since the Time When Coconino Walked Among Us, and after you go there may not ever be another one, so I don't think it's fair that I can't be considered for a Chosen Companion just because the moon isn't full yet."

Michael wondered if she was always this brassy or if it had taken her days to work up the courage to say something. The latter, most likely. Yet there she was, standing defiantly before him and making her case. He had to admire her fortitude.

"Tell me what your name is, then," he drawled, "so I may know for whose womanhood ceremony I must postpone my Choosing."

That took some of the huff out of her stance, but she eyed him suspiciously, unsure if she was being teased. "Swan," she told him. "My name is Swan."

"Very well, Swan," he agreed. "I will wait until I can consider you with the other maidens. But that does not mean I will choose you."

For a moment they locked eyes, until Swan determined that she was not being made light of. Then, "That is fair," she told him. "That is all I ask." And she marched back to her grinding stone.

No, I cannot promise to choose you, little Swan, Michael thought as he watched her return to her work. But dear God, after a display like that, how can I not?

288   Catherine Wells

it. Plunking himself down on a handy rock, he stared at it in the

CHAPTER TWENTY-TWO

Coconino glanced over his shoulder and saw a wisp of cloud clinging to Father Nakha-a's Thinking Place like a tuft of cotton clinging to a woman's hair. Deep melancholy swelled within him to see those mountains turn dark and purple with distance and know that the cold, forbidding island canyon awaited them. The day was warm and dry, with only a trace of fall's crisp scent on the breeze, but it was already winter in Coconino's soul.

The two of them traveled largely in silence, he pulling the travois, she carrying Juan on her back. Fresh from her labors with the harvesters, Ironwood Blossom had no difficulty with cramps in her legs as she had on their previous journey. But there was none of the lightness of the trip south, none of the storytelling and playful antics that had taken the edge off long days of walking, walking, walking.

Every morning it seemed to Coconino that he could feel a coldness blowing down from the northwest. In his mind he saw the camp of the Others with its slick, ugly buildings and its smelly Machines. A knot formed in his stomach, and his steps began to drag. They would pass through much rocky, unprotected country before they reached the Northern Village. Often Coconino left Ironwood Blossom resting by the side of the trail while he scouted ahead, and at night he slept with his knife close at hand.

For her part, Ironwood Blossom seemed to grow dull and weary, lacking some of the dogged energy that was her stock in trade. She misses it, too, Coconino thought. She misses the Southern Village with its friendly faces and its easy pace. It is only because of her promise to her sister that she insisted we return, and it weighs heavily on her. "We can go back in the spring," he repeated reassuringly. "We will take Hummingbird and Snow this time."

The eyes she raised to his held no enthusiasm, however. "Did you ask Corn Grows Tall if we could come back?" she asked him.

The idea surprised Coconino. "It did not occur to me. Why should he mind if we join them? What are five more people except extra hands to help with the work?"

"And five less to help in the north," she replied tightly, turning her face again to the trail and plodding onward, right foot, left foot, right again.

"Do you not think we should go back?" he asked her bent head.

She sighed. "You will do what you will do, Coconino. Only . . ."

"Only what?" he prodded peevishly.

"Only what will you do there that you cannot do in the north?"

It stung him, though he could not say why. "Hunt the bear, for one thing," he said, then added quickly, "Not to kill it," for the words of the lizard came back to him. "But to see it, at least, as I saw Tala. I would like to see a bear."

For a moment Coconino ached inside remembering Tala, remembering the camaraderie and the sweet rushing sensation of flight.

"Why?" she persisted.

"Why?" he echoed, and found that he could not quite answer that. "Because I am Coconino!" he cried.

"To tell stories afterward."

There was no accusation in her tone, but he felt prickled nonetheless. "To earn honor and respect among the People!" he contradicted, though he knew that was only part of it.

"You already have honor and respect in the north," she pointed out.

But anger stirred inside Coconino at that. "No. Some stranger out of legend has honor and respect!" he retorted. "Half the stories they tell are not even true. More than half. In the south I must earn what honor and respect I get. If I am asked to serve on the Council there, it will be because of what I, as a man, am and have done, not because of some foolish expectation built up by generations of storytellers."

She stopped dead in the path and turned to him. "Then do that in the north," she said flatly. "Earn the honor and respect they want to give you. Show them the kind of man you are and the kinds of deeds you do. Give them a basis for different expectations if you do not like the ones they have. Is it not the same thing?"

The logic of her reasoning laid him open like a knife. "No!"

he objected. "It is not the same thing at all." But he could think of no words to refute her.

For a moment she regarded him with eyes that were uncharacteristically puffy and dark. Then, turning back to the trail, she trudged on. "The People of the Southern Village do not need you, Coconino," she said wearily. "They have Father Nakha-a. My people, the People of the north, need you. They have only Walnut Bark and Winking Star and my father."

The truth of that was bitter; there was no single leader among the northern People. The men she had named were those who pushed and prodded the Council into occasional action, but without consistency or plan. At the moment, however, Coconino did not care. "I cannot lead them," he repeated. "I have lost too much. I am only half a man." Then he, too, set his face to the dusty trail and spoke no more for the rest of the day.

That night he dreamed the *pi-ika*, the haunting dream. He stood on the unprotected rocky ground with eyes watching him, northern eyes, eyes that expected him to save them. On its rock pedestal the collared lizard bobbed its head, only this time it seemed a wagging motion, as though it did not approve of Coconino or his actions. The wind swept across him, cold and filled with dust, so that Coconino could hardly see. "Where are you?" he called out. "Phoenix, where are you?"

But there was no Phoenix, only Lujan coming toward him out of the wind, the sun a harsh glare at his back. "Would you take my life?" Coconino demanded of his adversary. "You did that already when you took me from my time and my Witch Woman. What more can you do to me?"

At that Lujan only smiled his cruel, cunning smile and lifted an arm to show the trophy he bore. It was a severed head, clutched by its long black hair. "Phoenix!" Coconino cried, but as the dangling head twirled slowly around, he saw that the face was not that of his beloved. It was Hummingbird.

With a shout of horror Coconino sat bolt upright on his bed of ferns. Dawn was just graying in the east, and a twitter of birds began in the mesquite trees around them. The air was still and cool and fresh.

Ironwood Blossom's hand found him in the darkness, caressed his arm soothingly. "You are dreaming, Husband," she whispered in reassuring tones. "It is only a dream."

Yet the horror of it clung to Coconino like a spider's web, and he could not shake it off. "Come, Ironwood Blossom," he bade her, struggling to his feet. "It is nearly daylight; let us get an early start. We have been too slow these last days; we should move quickly now and get back home as soon as possible.''

We must get home and make sure Hummingbird is safe, he thought. But he could not share that fear with her. It would only cause her needless alarm. So he buried it away in his gut, where it gnawed at him like a desert rat.

In the darkness of the mesquite grove Ironwood Blossom rubbed at her tired eyes and clambered ungracefully to her feet. She'd awakened earlier with her bladder feeling uncomfortably full and had been about to rise when Coconino had cried out in his sleep. Phoenix. After all these years he still called out for Phoenix.

It never used to bother me, she thought as she trudged off to relieve herself. It seemed he was not my husband anyway, only a god who took pity on me and favored me; what did I care if his heart belonged to another? That was beyond any hope I dared have.

Her stomach quivered sickeningly, and Ironwood Blossom leaned weakly against a tree for a moment. But this journey, she thought, has changed all that. Here I have known his laughter and his tenderness and his pride and his folly, and I have seen in him a most remarkable man. I can no longer detach myself from his desires or from his pain; they are mine. Once I thought that after I had a child, I would be happier to return to my mother's house and live there—but no more. I do not want to be separated from Coconino, ever. Is this love? It must be.

But it is a love he does not feel. This time together, which has been so life-changing for me, could not purge his soul. He still longs for his Witch Woman. Whether we stay in the Northern Village or return to the south, it will make no difference. In his darkest moments, in the suffering of his spirit, he will never find comfort in me, or in my sister, or in the children of his flesh.

He will always call out for Phoenix.

Coconino crept to the top of the hill and peered down at the activity on the other side. The Machines of the Others crawled across the fields, slicing down the tall cornstalks, devouring them whole, and storing the fat ears of corn somewhere in their bowels to be regurgitated later into granaries. In a single day one man and his Machine could do what it would take the sum of the People an equal time to accomplish. It was a marvel, indeed.

But Coconino did not feel awed. Not only had he seen such Machines before on his visit to the Mountain, he had a bitter disdain for the people who rode in them. How could they feel the life of the Mother Earth, tucked away in their metal monsters? They could not smell the richness of the soil, feel the bloated weight of the ripe corn in their hands, chant the praises of the Mother Earth as they harvested.

Not, of course, that Coconino was very fond of doing those things—sweating and bending his back in a dusty cornfield was not much to his liking—but he thought that those who harvested must benefit from the nearness of the Mother Earth. That was the sentiment expressed in the songs and stories of the People.

Wriggling back down the hill, he trotted to a willow grove beside the river where he had left Ironwood Blossom and Juan. His nightmare continued to haunt him, and the closer he got to the camp of the Others, the worse it was. "It is as I thought," he reported gruffly. "The fields of the Others are just ahead. We will need to go away from the river now to go around them and then loop back to make our way to the Valley of the People for the night."

Ironwood Blossom was mopping her forehead with a corner of her cotton skirt, a gift from Eyes Like a Deer. She seemed exhausted, though the day was only half-gone, but they had to keep going. They had to get back to Hummingbird. "Come," Coconino encouraged, picking up the handles of the travois, "put the baby here with our other bundles and I will carry him, too."

"He throws his weight too much," Ironwood Blossom objected wearily. "He will tip the bundles off."

"Then I will carry him on my back, as you do," Coconino replied irritably. "We must hurry if we are to reach the river again before dark."

But Ironwood Blossom's patience was overtaxed. "Why must we go around?" she complained, struggling to her feet. "If we are in such a hurry, why can't we just follow the river? The People have traded with the Others, north and south, for many generations, and they have never harmed us. Why can't we just go past their village?"

"I told you!" he snapped. "The man Lujan is there now, and he is very dangerous." The image of Hummingbird's severed head rose unbidden in his mind, and his stomach knotted fiercely. "It makes winter in my gut just to think of him there."

With a soft grunt Ironwood Blossom hoisted Juan's carrier and swung it onto her broad back.

"I said I would carry him," Coconino growled. Had he no travois to haul, no wife to slow his pace for, he could be back at the Northern Village in three days. With Ironwood Blossom it would probably take five.

"And how will you have your bow ready with a child on your back?" she asked. Her pack in place, she reached to take the travois handles from him as well. "If there is danger, let me take the child and the travois both so you can be ready for it."

But he shoved her arm roughly away. "You are slower than a mud turtle with it," he snapped. "If I must wait for you, hauling both a child and a travois, we will not be clear of their fields by dark!"

His rebuke was a slap in her face, and she stepped back, startled. Then her jaw quivered slightly. "I cannot help being slow," she said, wounded. "It is not my fault that—"

"If only you had stayed in the north as I told you to!"

He knew as he said it how foolish it was: then she would be in danger as well as Hummingbird, and without her prodding he would never have left the Southern Village to protect them. But the words tumbled out, and misery struck him deeply as he saw the tears spring in her eyes. She turned quickly back to the river.

"I'm sorry," he called quickly. "Ironwood Blossom, I am sorry. I have not been unhappy for your company on this trip. It is only that I feel a danger close at hand, and I long to be back where I can defend . . . what is mine." He still could not tell her of his fear for Hummingbird's safety. "I did not mean—"

But Ironwood Blossom turned on him with fiery eyes, her tears coursing down her cheeks. "Should I say I am sorry that I am slow and awkward?" she demanded. "Should I apologize that I am a hindrance and not a help when there is danger? I am not your Witch Woman, Coconino. I cannot run for miles like a hunter, or swim a creek, or use a bow. I tell you now that I have grieved much on your behalf, my husband. I grieved that you lost your friends and family in the Time That Was. I grieved that your tortured soul seemed to find no peace. But I cannot spare any grief for the fact that I am Ironwood Blossom and not She Who Saves. I am who I am, Coconino. If you grieve for that, you grieve alone."

Coconino staggered back, stunned. Grieve that she was not his Witch Woman? It had never occurred to him that she might do such a thing. Phoenix was an entirely different person from either of his wives, and his love for her was on a different plane from any other relationship he had known. "I do not want you to be like Phoenix," he stammered. "I do not ask you to change."

"No," she snorted, "only to walk faster." She hitched up her pack and set off along the river trail.

Coconino tugged at the travois and started after her. "Never mind about that," he said. "We will find our canteens and take our time and camp wherever night finds us. Think no more of it."

But Ironwood Blossom kept on at her dogged pace. "You go around through the fields," she said. "I will follow the river and meet you on the other side. I'm sure I can find the trail myself."

"No, no, you mustn't!" he protested. "It passes by the Camp of the Others and—"

"And I have always longed to see it," she cut in. "Every year since I was a little girl, when the traders came back from there, I thought, Oh! How strange a place it must be, and how wonderful! You have seen many things in your life, Coconino, but I have seen nothing remarkable except the weaving of cotton. I have never seen a Machine, or an Other, or the strange white wickiups that are not made of sticks. Once before you made me pass them by, but this time I think not. I think this one time I will do what I want and see the Camp of the Others."

Coconino caught at her arm and hauled her up short. "You must not go there!" he hissed, afraid for her. "Lujan is there, and he haunts my dreams, Ironwood Blossom. I fear him as I fear no other creature."

"Then you must go and face him!" she snapped. "For never did a man outlive a puma by turning his back on it."

For a long moment they glared at each other, and Coconino was shocked to realize that he faced not a docile, subservient wife but a woman whose will was equal to his own. How had he failed to see it before? She obeyed him if she thought that was the right thing to do, but on those points where she thought him wrong, she would not bend. This was one of those points.

Finally he relented, knowing that the only way to turn her from her course would have been to lash her to the travois with the rest of his burdens. "Very well," he growled. "We will go on the river path, and we will draw near enough for you to see this foul place. But if there is any hint of danger, any sign of a weapon, any hostile word or act, we will abandon the travois and flee. Do you hear me?"

She held his gaze with eyes that smoldered like a banked fire. "I hear you, my husband," she replied at last, starting back along her chosen course. "Only remember how slow I am."

Coconino noticed it as soon as he set his foot on the hard-packed road on which the Others ran their Machines. The sweet, living presence of the Mother Earth that he had always known in the soil faded and grew distant. He did not feel the utter abandonment he had known on the Sky Ship, far above the Earth's surface, but it was a most remarkable change nonetheless. It was as though She had formed a callus in this place to protect Her from a constant irritation.

Ironwood Blossom felt it, too, though it was mostly an uneasiness that crept through her as they approached the settlement. Although she had longed to see this strange place, the realization of her dream filled her with a queer sort of apprehension. The Machines in the fields gave off strange sounds and smells, and their speed was frightful—much faster than a man could walk. And the size of their wickiups was amazing: four or five times that of the brush dwellings they built in the south. Plus there were houses built of wood right out in the open—wouldn't the wind blow them down? And deeper into the village, far from the river's edge, was a long, lean building of shiny white that was as different from the faceted domes around it as a good stone house was from a wickiup.

But strangest of all were the people who stopped to gawk at the travelers making their way along the path. They were nearly all pale of skin and hair, and their clothing was of an odd design. The women all wore leggings, and they were built lean and angular, not fleshy and round. Were it not for the way their cotton shirts pressed against their breasts, Ironwood Blossom would have been hard put to tell them from the men.

Children playing at the river's edge saw them coming and passed the word back into the village. Soon a contingent of adults came down from the settlement, crossed the bridge, and stood in the path, awaiting the travelers. They were not armed that Coconino could see, but it was clear that they did not intend to let him pass unaccosted. He told himself it would be the same if strangers came to the Northern Village, but his heart began to beat like the drums during the Dance of Conflict.

Wordlessly Coconino passed the travois to Ironwood Blossom and loosened his knife in its sheath. His bow, however, he left slung across his shoulder; to do otherwise would have been to present a threat to the waiting Others. He did not want to provoke violence if none was intended; he was hopelessly outnumbered.

Some twenty paces off from the group he stopped, and Ironwood Blossom drew up behind him. He could feel her trembling at his back, as she had trembled the day they had approached the People of the south for the first time. "Good day," he greeted in the language of the Mountain.

"*Chee-eeya,*" a man replied. "Good day."

Relief washed over Coconino; they had greeted him in the language of the People. Perhaps they would be polite and let him go quietly on his way. "We are only passing through," he told them.

There was a slight pause. "Have you nothing to trade?" the man asked with some disappointment in his voice.

"No, nothing," Coconino replied, knowing how strange that must sound when he was pulling a heavily laden travois. "We have spent the summer in the south," he explained, "and are on our way back north."

That evoked a soft laugh from a woman in the group. "That's a little backward, isn't it? Summer in the south, winter in the north?"

Coconino appreciated the humor, but he could not laugh. "It is my wife," he said with some truth. "She wishes to see her sister."

"Ah." The man nodded wisely. "Well, you are welcome in our village even if you have nothing to trade. You may camp here by the river if you like, or take the high ground there—" He pointed across the stream. "—where there are fewer bugs." He glanced down at a small child who was peering out from behind his leg. "If the children become a nuisance, send them away."

Children are to be cherished, Coconino wanted to say. If they had no curiosity, how would they learn?

But instead he said, "We will not stay the night, thank you. We are only passing through."

The man shrugged. "As you wish," he said. "This is a safe place, though. You will come to no harm here." Then he turned and pushed through the group behind him, leading the way back across the bridge and into the village.

As they retreated, Ironwood Blossom tugged at Coconino's elbow. "What did they say?" she asked in a voice hushed with awe.

"They said we are welcome to stay, that we will come to no harm here," he told her.

"Good." Immediately she set down the handles of the travois.

"But we will *not* stay," Coconino objected. "We will go on to the Valley of the People tonight."

"I am tired," Ironwood Blossom replied. "Juan is hungry. If they say we are welcome, why should we go on? Do we not insult their hospitality if we do so?"

Indeed, Ironwood Blossom looked sorely fatigued, and the baby fussed in his pack. Alone, Coconino could have sprinted to the Valley of the People by sundown, but with his family . . .

"If we can find a protected place here by the river," he conceded. "A cave or a thick stand of willows. I will not sleep on the high ground." Where everyone can see me. Where there is no cover. Where Lujan may come.

They found a spot where high water had eroded the bank into a wall of sorts and a fallen tree provided additional screening. Here they stowed their travois, and Coconino built a small, smokeless fire while Ironwood Blossom cut up a squash and dumped it into their cooking skin with plenty of water. The water kept the skin cool enough that it did not burn while the squash inside simmered and filled the air with a savory smell.

While they rested in the shade of the western bank and waited for their supper to cook, Coconino became aware of someone watching them from behind a cottonwood tree some twenty paces downstream. Instantly his knife was in his hand and he was crouched, ready to defend himself, but the flash of movement back behind the tree was not at a height that threatened him. Coconino relaxed and stood up, keeping his knife in hand but down and near his body.

"Come out, little girl."

The child stepped out from behind the cottonwood. "I'm a boy!" it protested loudly.

Coconino surveyed the cotton trousers, the buttoned shirt, the heavy boots and straw hat. "You make enough noise to be a girl," he teased solemnly. "Did no one ever teach you to walk quietly through the trees?" And he dropped back down beside the fire, picking up a piece of deadwood and beginning to strip the bark from it with his knife.

The boy took a cautious step or two closer. "Nobody here knows how," he said.

"That I can believe," Coconino replied dryly.

As Coconino continued his whittling, the boy plucked up his courage and came closer yet. "My name is Nathan," he announced. "Nathan Johanneson."

"Nay-than," Coconino repeated solemnly. "And I am—"

He stopped. What would happen if he told the Others who he was, even this boy? Would they, too, have legends regarding his deeds? Would they, even after so many generations, desire revenge upon him for killing their Sky Ship?

"I am Say-ayka-pee," Coconino invented. "In your language, 'Keeps His Own Counsel.' "

"Say-ayka—"

"—pee. Say-ayka-pee."

"Say-ayka-pee," Nathan repeated. "Say-ayka-pee. I like that."

Ironwood Blossom threw Coconino a guarded, questioning look, which he ignored.

"Will you have some food?" Coconino invited the boy.

Nathan lost his fear then and came to sit cross-legged by the fire with Coconino. "I've never had primitive food before," he said, staring in curiosity at the fat little cakes Ironwood Blossom was shaping out of cornmeal and water and laying on a hot stone to bake.

"It is good food," Coconino assured him. "Food from the hand of the Mother Earth, rich and—" He couldn't translate "nutritious" into the boy's language. "Full of Her presence," he improvised. "It will make you strong and healthy, Nay-than."

The boy sniffed the air. "Smells like squash to me," he observed, wrinkling his nose.

At that Coconino laughed. "Yes, squash; I believe that is how you call this food. But here, have a tortilla." He handed the boy a cornmeal cake from the baking stone.

Nathan juggled the hot bread from hand to hand, blowing on it. "I thought tortillas were thinner than this," he said. "My mom says they're like leather except they crumble."

The child's honesty amused Coconino. "Some tortillas are thin like leather," he admitted. "They are good for holding frijoles or stewed meat or other things. But these are fat tortillas, and we eat them plain or seasoned with chilies."

"Are there chilies in these?" Nathan wanted to know as he bit gingerly into his corn bread. "My mom won't put chilies in anything. She says it's like eating fire and only primitive mouths are made to withstand the heat."

"Eating fire!" Coconino exclaimed with a grin. He lit the end of the stick he was whittling and then put it with its tiny flame into his mouth, sealing his lips carefully around the stick. Nathan's eyes grew wide with astonishment. In a moment Coconino withdrew the stick, which smoked but had no flame.

"Doesn't that hurt?" Nathan demanded.

Again Coconino laughed. "It is a trick, my friend. The fire needs two things to burn: the stick and the air. When I close my mouth, it cannot get the air it needs, and so it dies. All I must do is be very careful not to get my tongue anywhere near the flame before it goes out."

"That is a bad trick," Ironwood Blossom advised him, though she did not understand what he had said to the boy. "He will try it, or Juan will try it, and they will be burned."

Coconino looked down at his young son, clinging close to his mother while this stranger was in their camp. He watched his father with bright, perceptive eyes. "You are right," Coconino conceded. "I will be more careful." To Nathan he said, "My wife reminds me, and rightly so, that I should not show such dangerous things to children."

"I'm not a child!" Nathan protested. "I'll be eleven come the third of October, and this winter I'll go logging with all the men, and next spring I'll run the drill, not just the plow like the little kids."

Coconino did not understand about drills or October, but the tone of Nathan's voice was clear. "Eleven summers!" he exclaimed gravely. "Why, you should begin work soon on your bow for your manhood ceremony."

"A bow?" Nathan's eyes widened again. "You mean, like to shoot arrows with? Is that what your people do?"

"That is the Way of the People, yes," Coconino replied. "As a boy approaches his twelfth summer, he undertakes a task that will show he has the skill to take his place among the men of the People. Those who wish to be hunters, and even some who prefer farming, often choose to make a bow, though others make throwing clubs or farm implements or good flint knives. But among my friends and I it was thought that a bow was the best thing to show wisdom in the choice of materials, patience in the seasoning of the wood, and skill in the shaping and smoothing and polishing of the bow."

"Would you show me how?" Nathan asked eagerly.

Coconino considered that as he looked at the boy. He appeared rather ordinary, in the manner of Others and Men-on-the-Mountain. His hair was a dull brown, his face long, and his body lean but compact, for he had not come into the growth spurt that characterized adolescence. There was nothing to say that he should be a hunter rather than a farmer or that his hands would be clever in any way, yet he was eager, and Coconino found he wanted to share his knowledge with this boy. He glanced back at Ironwood Blossom.

"He wants me to show him how to make a bow."

His stalwart wife looked surprised. "Doesn't he have a father?"

"He spoke of one," Coconino recalled, "but I doubt that there are any Others skilled in making bows."

Ironwood Blossom seemed to ponder this a moment. "That is very sad," she said finally. "But I have heard that Others are quite ignorant."

Coconino looked back at Nathan's hopeful face, at eyes that

pleaded with him. "Well," he decided, "I can help you choose the right wood for the project. But I will not be here long enough to do more than that."

"Can't you come back?" Nathan urged. "Next spring, with the traders, can't you come back and show me then?"

Coconino's smile turned sad. "No, Nathan, I will not come to your village again," he told the boy gently. "There is a man here who bears me much hatred, and I think it would be better if our paths did not cross."

"Who?" the boy demanded. "Mister Aberjee? Mister Leoni?"

"No." Coconino shook his head. "It does not matter. Perhaps, when you are older, you can come and visit my village. Then I can teach you all manner of things: making bows and arrows, building a hunting shelter, finding the plants that the Mother Earth offers us though we have not planted and tended them—"

Suddenly Nathan jumped to his feet. "I know who it is."

A chill breeze stirred the fire and feathered Coconino's hair in wisps around his face. Nathan had grown pale, and his look of curiosity had been replaced by one of dead certainty. "It's the spooky man, isn't it?"

"Spooky man?" Coconino asked, not understanding the word.

"Spooky. Scary. Frightening. Crazy," Nathan elucidated. "It's the spooky man who hates you, isn't it? Spooky ol' Lujan."

Coconino flinched.

Nathan saw it, and his heart pounded with the revelation. "And you're not really Say-ayka-pee," the boy guessed. "You just said that 'cause you don't want anyone to know: you're Coconino."

Nathan tossed and turned in his bed, thinking about his encounter with the startling primitive. It was like meeting Long John Silver or Paul Revere or Madam Ying—suddenly all the stories took on a new meaning. Coconino had been so strong, so commanding, everything that legend said, yet he had not brushed Nathan aside. In fact, he had invited Nathan to supper and promised to teach him how to make a bow and arrows if Nathan could go to his village.

Imagine! Going to the primitive village! No one in Camp Crusoe had ever been there or even knew exactly where it was. Nathan would be the first, the first to be invited.

But they'll never let me go, Nathan thought. Even if I keep his secret, even if I never tell anyone he's Coconino. Mom and Dad will never let me go off to the primitive village. I'll run away. That's what I'll do. When I'm old enough to go to secondary school on the Mountain, I'll run away instead and go live in the village of the primitives. I'll live with Say-ayka-pee. I'll live with Coconino.

He would just never tell anyone that was who Say-ayka-pee really was. The primitive had grown surly when Nathan had identified him and had repeated that he was Say-ayka-pee, but Nathan knew. Who else could it be? The official history of Camp Crusoe said that Derek Lujan and the primitive called Coconino had disappeared from the warp terminal in the shuttle bay and that it was possible they had been thrown forward in time. Well, here was Derek Lujan, walking among them once more; Coconino had to be around somewhere. And who else would be so nervous about coming to Camp Crusoe?

For a long time Nathan pondered those early settlers and how they had been stranded here on Earth. They'd been upset, unhappy. Even today Nathan heard people speak in harsh tones of how Derek Lujan had cut them off from the stars and how wonderful things would be if only they could contact distant planets again.

For himself, however, Nathan was hard pressed to be sorry he had been born on Earth. He liked it here. He liked going into the fields to help his father and his uncles. He liked waking up on cold winter mornings and sitting in front of the fireplace drinking warm goat's milk. People on other planets ate food out of boxes, and they sat inside all day long, and there was something called divorce that broke families apart so that kids didn't see their father and maybe not their grandparents, either. Uncle Raymond had told him about that. Uncle Raymond had studied on the Mountain.

You were just trying to protect your people, weren't you, Coconino? Nathan thought. When you broke the spaceship so my ancestors couldn't go back, you were just trying to protect your people from boxed food and divorce and working inside all day. I can understand that. I don't mind what you did.

And I don't even mind what the spooky man did, telling other planets we had a plague here, except that he wasn't fair about it. And he killed people; that's what the official history says. It says that he most likely wrecked the aircraft that carried Captain Winthrop and Dr. Jim Martin and their pilot, and he didn't do it to protect anybody. He was just mean.

Coconino's not mean, though, Nathan thought as sleep finally crept over his dazzled mind. Coconino was really nice to me, and he didn't treat me like a kid, and he said he'd teach me how to make a bow . . . and a hunter's shelter . . . and take food from the Mother Earth's hand. . . .

Coconino was restless, too, and sleep would not come to him. Finally he slipped from his bed, satisfied himself that the place where his wife and child lay sleeping was virtually invisible, and crept over the bridge into the Camp of the Others.

All was quiet in the sprawling settlement as Coconino wandered from house to house, peering at Others through windows left unshuttered to catch the cool evening breeze, searching for the one face among them that he would never forget. Mostly the houses were dark, for like the People, these Others now rose with the sun and labored hard in their fields and at other crafts, so that when blessed darkness came, they went soon to their beds. Tomorrow the sun would rise again.

But in one little house a light burned brightly, and as Coconino drew near, he heard the soft grunting sounds of a man involved in physical exertion. It was a rhythmic sound, as though he repeated the same exercise over and over. Cautiously Coconino approached the window and peered inside.

A man lay on the floor, straining to raise himself time and time again by flexing only his arms. It seemed peculiar to Coconino, a most inefficient way to rise—and why keep trying it when obviously it could not get him more than two feet from the floor? Yet the man continued, grunting and sweating with his effort.

Coconino could not see his face, for his head pointed away from the window. But the hair, though longer, was the right coloring for Lujan, and his build was the same. Then, on a wall in the far corner, Coconino spotted the white uniform that Lujan had worn. It was as white and pristine as the day he had first met the handsome, conniving Other, yet it hung seemingly forgotten in an out-of-the-way corner of the room, a layer of brown dust collecting on the shoulders. The man exerting himself on the floor wore loose cotton trousers that were dull and grimy and rapidly becoming soaked with sweat.

Just then Lujan ceased his labors and rose wearily to his feet, stretching and flexing his body. Only then did Coconino notice the chain fastened to his leg. It clinked and clanked as Lujan moved, keeping him tethered securely to a large metal object near one wall. The Others are wiser than I gave them credit for, Coconino thought. They have seen the evil of the man and have undertaken to keep him from doing harm to them. It is a strange idea to tie a man thus, but I can see its merits.

Lujan clanked across the room to a bucket of water and poured its contents over his head. Now his hair clumped together in soggy ringlets that continued streaming water down his bare back. He shook his head like a coyote, sending droplets flying; then, in groping for a towel on a nearby chair, he turned toward the window.

Coconino shrank back in horror, and only his hunter's training kept him from crying out. From his right eye and across his muscular chest Derek Lujan was a mass of livid red scars. His beard scraggled and grew where it could, mostly on the left side of his face, with only grotesque wisps protruding from between the gnarled tissue on the right. His right eye was gone, its socket grossly shriveled and sealed forever with discolored flesh. The handsome, proud face of Derek Lujan had become a nightmare visage.

As he toweled his hair dry, Lujan's raised arms showed that the damage extended along the inside of his left arm, where he had thrown it up to protect his one remaining eye. Here the marks were clearly those of a puma, a vicious mauling administered by that fiercest of the Mother Earth's creatures. There was sweet justice in it, and yet Coconino could not rejoice. Who could, to see a man so mutilated? Even one's enemy.

Tossing the towel aside, Lujan peeled off his soaking trousers and brushed at the water on his hair-covered legs. Then he straightened up, reaching for the towel once more, and Coconino saw that the cat had exacted an even higher price than he had first thought. The scars extended across Lujan's lower abdomen and groin, and where his manhood should have been there was only a plastic tube.

Coconino was wracked by a sudden wave of nausea. He scrambled back from the house and sank to the ground at the base of a paloverde tree. For a moment he could only pant in shallow, ragged breaths, trying to keep his stomach from giving back its contents. This was your doing, wasn't it, Mother Earth? he thought. He spurned you and your children and your creatures, and you sent the puma to mete out your justice. There is Lujan, deprived of good looks, of half his sight, and of the wherewithal to ever father children.

And here am I with two wives, and two children, and the power to make many, many more. I have both my eyes and my hunter's wits, and the maidens still sigh when they see Coconino pass. The lizard was right; I am a rebellious son. I could see only what you had taken from me and none of what you had given. I felt I had been cheated and abused, when in fact you have blessed me more than my stubborn pride deserves.

Forgive me, Mother. I will go home now.

Lujan toweled himself carefully, for after six months the scar tissue was still tender. He had seen the face at the window, concealed though it was by shadows, and had known the shock in his enemy's face. Stare, Coconino, he thought. Gawk. Be repulsed. I shall be paid back for every pain, every disfigurement. As I have suffered, you shall suffer more. As I have been bereft, so shall you.

I heard, you see, that a primitive had come—just one, who didn't want to trade. Just one, with his wife and small child. I knew it was you, Coconino, even before I saw your face at the window. Who else would come for no other reason than to challenge the stronghold of the mighty and gaze in horror upon the face of his enemy?

You are a fool, Coconino. For six months I have pondered how to exact my vengeance, what I could do to you that would equal the suffering you have caused me. To carve your face as the cat carved mine? No, your people would still worship you. To cut out your heart and eat it before your very eyes? Not enough, Coconino, not nearly enough.

But you have given me the answer, my feckless adversary. You came here with your weaknesses exposed, flaunting your vulnerability to the world. You came here with your wife and child, and I knew the price to demand of you. I knew how to hurt you more than any simple twisting of a knife could hurt you.

Sleep, Coconino. Sleep cherishing the woman in your bed and the child who bears your visage and your genes. Sleep thinking yourself a lucky man, and in the morning go on your way believing you are safe and sound.

Tomorrow I will prove how wrong you are.

CHAPTER TWENTY-THREE

"Ho. Children of Coconino."

There was just enough mockery in the tone to raise Michael's hackles. He knew that tone from the Mountain, knew what kind of person used it. Slowly he turned to face the young man.

But Sky Dancer tugged at his arm. They were on their way out of the village to do some hunting, giving Michael much-needed practice in stalking. "Keep going," she whispered. "Ignore him."

Coral Snake had seen his quarry turn and stand, though, and he swaggered forward to engage it. They stood on the path that encircled the island butte, with the busy lives of the People going on about them on all sides. "Are you going hunting today?" he asked in the same mocking tone. "Perhaps you would let me join you. Or—" He leered at Sky Dancer. "—perhaps you hunt something only two people can find."

"Go away, Coral Snake," Sky Dancer told him bluntly. "You are not welcome here, and neither are your disgusting insinuations. Come, Michael, my brother."

Reluctantly Michael allowed Sky Dancer to pull him along the path toward the canyon floor. But Coral Snake was not so easily deterred. He followed only a pace behind them, in a swinging exaggeration of Michael's steps. "I would be willing to help you find your prey, Michael," he badgered. "I know this particular quarry. Sometimes it kicks and spits and—"

Michael swung around, but Sky Dancer stepped quickly between the two young men. They glared at each other over her head, eye to eye, blue to black.

"Go home, Coral Snake," Sky Dancer snapped, her throwing club resting warningly against his chest. She had slipped her wrist through its loop the instant she heard his voice, so that it sprang swiftly into her hand now. "Go home and ask your wife why you have no child yet."

Coral Snake drew back as though slapped, and Sky Dancer almost regretted her jibe. After all, her own foster mother was barren; it was not something one person should throw like sand in another's face. But hadn't Coral Snake asked for it? Suggestions of incest, like suggestions of rape, were not funny. As she had given him the broken arm several years before, perhaps it was necessary now to speak cruelly in order to make him keep his distance.

For a long moment Coral Snake continued to glare at them and it occurred to Sky Dancer that it was not likely she could break his arm with that club anymore. It was not likely the club was much of a threat at all, for he had grown tall and strong and lightning quick. She was relieved when a cruel smile twisted his lips and she knew he had chosen not to fight.

"Perhaps I neglect her," Coral Snake said, "because I am so smitten with your charms that you consume all my passions." He made an obscene gesture near his pelvis that needed no interpretation and, laughing, turned to walk away.

"Who was that?" Michael asked darkly as they continued down into the canyon, with more than one wary glance behind them.

"Coral Snake," she replied with unmasked disgust. "He has never had any love for the children of Coconino."

Like my two uncles on the Mountain, Michael thought. But it was not for my father they hated me, only for the time and attention Ababba showed me. "Why should he hate us for our father?" Michael asked. "He's too young to have even known him, isn't he?"

Sky Dancer shrugged. "My mother says it is because he comes from bad seed, but Nina told me once it was just the field he was planted in."

"His eyes are blue," Michael commented.

"Sometimes the People have blue eyes," she told him. "But his mother claims it is because his father was the last Man-on-the-Mountain to come to our village. *My* mother claims it is because his father was Lujan."

"Lujan?" Michael exclaimed in surprise. "Derek Lujan, the man who abandoned his followers down in the Verde Valley?"

"I do not know this valley you speak of," she said, "but yes: he was the Other who thought to leave his people behind and return to the stars. But our father put an end to his designs."

Michael was silent for a while as they took the river path up the canyon toward the headwaters. Over their heads birds twittered as they built nests for their young, and the rush of the creek through its narrow channel added to the soothing symphony of sound. "You know," Michael said finally, "I could almost feel sorry for Coral Snake if he is Lujan's son. I know what that's like, growing up in a place where people think your father was the worst kind of traitor."

"But you are not rude and obnoxious," Sky Dancer pointed out. "Coral Snake is. Even as a child he would bully Nakha-a and me. But Nakha-a is not like you; he would never stand up to Coral Snake."

"Who is Nakha-a?" Michael asked.

Sky Dancer looked at him in mild surprise. "Our half brother, Coconino's other son. Did no one tell you? His mother was Nina, the prophetess. We were raised together, he and I."

A half brother! Michael was thunderstruck. Why had no one thought to tell him about that before? Another boy who shared his father's blood . . . On the Mountain Michael had three half sisters, and here was Sky Dancer, but the notion of a brother was new to him. "Where is he now?" he demanded. "What happened to him? Did Coral Snake do something to him?"

"No, no," Sky Dancer assured him. "I do not think the Mother Earth would let anything happen to Nakha-a. He is a most favored son. No, he went south with his mother and some others from our village six years ago to find another place to live. I am waiting here so that when our father comes again, I can tell him where Nakha-a is."

"And where is that?" Michael wanted to know, wondering how far it was from them here. The people at Camp Crusoe had had no idea where the wandering primitives had gone. If he had his grandfather's maps—they had gone back to the Archives, though, for who had thought he might have need of them in this place? He tried to call them to mind now, wanting to picture where his brother was.

But Sky Dancer only shrugged. "In the south somewhere, I suppose," was her answer.

"How will you tell our father where it is if you don't know?" Michael protested.

"I need not tell him *where* it is," she replied patiently, "only *that* it is. Then we will find it together."

It irked Michael that she should be so blasé about knowing where their half brother was. "Maybe you and I could go," he suggested, "while I'm here. We could find our brother—" The word sounded foreign on his tongue. "—and then, when our father comes, we would know exactly where to take him."

Sky Dancer looked doubtful at the idea. It was one thing to go on such an adventure with one's illustrious father in the golden age When Coconino Returns; it was another thing to set off with an unschooled Man-on-the-Mountain who most likely could not talk to the Mother Earth and probably would injure himself on the journey.

"Oh, not right away," Michael said as he saw the doubts crossing her mind. "I need to learn much before we could undertake such a trip, but later, maybe in the fall. Or next spring. We could wait till next spring."

Her eyes narrowed. "I thought you were going back to the Mountain in the spring."

Guilt flushed over Michael's face. "Maybe." He looked away to the horizon, and Sky Dancer saw that it was something he had been thinking about for some time. "Maybe I'll stay longer than one year. I didn't promise, you know, to go back when Ababba comes for me next spring. I'm not saying I won't, but . . . I want to wait and see, that's all." It was a poor lie. He had known long before he had come that he alone would choose the time of his return. It was why he had applied himself so diligently to learning the Way of the People: not just because he was Coconino's son but because he was Michael and he might want to stay. He might just want to stay.

Suddenly he turned back to her with earnest eyes. "But I would like to find my brother before I go. If I can't see my father, at least let me see my brother. Don't you think that's fair?"

Sky Dancer was moved by the urgency in his voice. Knowing Nakha-a, she often longed to see him again, but not knowing Nakha-a, Michael longed for him even more. But Sky Dancer foresaw a problem, and a major one. She pursed her lips and stared thoughtfully at the trail ahead.

"I do not think my mother will sanction such a journey," she replied.

"She could come, too," Michael urged. "The three of us."

At that Sky Dancer shook her head. "My mother will not go farther away than the Red Rock Country," she explained. "She wants always to stay close by for the day my father returns."

"That could be centuries!" Michael protested.

"Never say that to her," Sky Dancer warned sharply. "You will get nowhere with such arguments. Michael, I, too, would like to see Nakha-a again, if only to see how he fares and what kind of land he lives in. But we must wait for the right moment to ask my mother if we may go."

"Must we ask her?" Michael pleaded, seeing his chance slip away in the turbulent waters of Phoenix's stubbornness and fear.

Sky Dancer looked startled. "We cannot go without her permission, Michael," she told him. "She is She Who Saves. She leads the People. And beyond that, she is my mother."

Phoenix took the arrows from Michael's proffered quiver and inspected them one by one, returning each when she was through. "Not bad," she admitted. "Not bad at all."

"Not bad?" He slung the quiver back on his shoulder. "They're perfect. They're as good as any you make."

They stood at the foot of the canyon's eastern wall, ready to head out for a day of hunting. Michael had already tried for smaller game such as foxes and squirrels, but they were too quick and too difficult a target for a beginning hunter. So today Phoenix had promised to take him in search of mule deer. Sky Dancer elected to stay behind, complaining that no one else in the family could grind corn properly and it was not going to grind itself, so she must spend the whole day at this tedious task while they went off to have a good time hunting.

But their good time was off to a rocky start. Phoenix's eyes sparked dangerously at Michael's tone. "I am not the model of perfection in arrow making," she told him.

"But my father is, right?" he challenged. "My father is the model of perfection in everything around here."

"That's right," she retorted. "That's what you came to find out, isn't it? Who your father was? Well, this is it, Michael. This is who he was. The day you walked into this village, you took up the responsibilities of being Coconino's son. With the glory comes the responsibility, Michael, and a whole lot of hard work."

"I have worked hard!" he snapped. "Flint told me he's never seen anyone learn as quickly as I do. No one else is unhappy with my progress, only you."

At that Phoenix drew back. "I'm not unhappy with your progress," she said quietly.

"You do a fine job of concealing that!"

For a moment their eyes locked, and Phoenix was surprised to see the anger in the young man. *Mother Earth, have I been that hard on him?* she wondered. *Or is this left over from his life on the Mountain?*

But in her heart Phoenix knew that she had been tougher with the boy than she needed to be, as she had been with his father when they had first met. Coconino had caught the sharp edge of her bitterness, of her frustration at being childless, of her anger at Dick for leaving her. What was it now that made her snap at the boy when it gave her such pleasure to see him learning the Way of the People, putting his hand to the tasks his ancestors had performed for centuries?

Abruptly Phoenix turned and started up the steep trail. In a moment Michael followed, and they moved rapidly toward the top.

Is this what I wanted? Michael wondered as they climbed. To come here and live as my father lived? To meet the people he knew, my relatives, his *compadres*? To fall in love with my half sister and be drilled by this woman who is so tortured by my resemblance to him?

"Do I look that much like my father?" Michael asked finally.

Startled, Phoenix turned and looked back at Michael. The openness of her countenance caught him off guard; for a moment he saw the wound on her soul—not old and scarred but fresh and bleeding with every sight of him. Her face closed quickly, though, and her feelings were once more veiled. He was afraid she would rebuke him, but instead her shoulders sagged and she plunked herself down on the trail in front of him. "When you smile," she said after a pause. "Especially when you smile."

Michael sat down just below her and studied the older woman. Her face was etched with fine lines, her hair more gray than black, yet at this moment there was none of the hardness that usually characterized her. She looked worn, weary. He tried to imagine what she had looked like as a young woman, when her skin was smooth and her hair jet black—like Sky Dancer's. For a moment he felt he could see her with his father's eyes—the fire of her spirit, the flash of her eyes—and he was moved. "Were you lovers?" he asked quietly.

A bitter smile twisted Phoenix's lips. "No," she said wryly. "I turned him down. I had my chance, more than once, and I turned him down. How's that for irony?"

It was a brand of honesty he had never seen in her before. Her truth was always harsh, but not now. This was nostalgia. This was like Ababba speaking of Two Moons or his mother trying to explain what was so special about Coconino. It was the kind of love Michael only hoped he could find someday in his own life. For the first time he looked on the surly Witch Woman and felt profound pity. "I can't be him," Michael whispered. "I know you're waiting for him to come out of a time warp or something, but you'll just have to wait awhile longer, because I can't be him.''

"That's not the problem," Phoenix told him, and the nostalgia drained away from her face, to be replaced by a look of haunted grief. The eyes she lifted to his were filled with tears that made him ache inside as she told him, "Don't you see? Look at me, Michael: I'm forty-nine years old. Oh, I'm spry and I'm strong, but I'm still old enough to be a grandmother—in this village, a great-grandmother. And if Coconino came back today, he'd still be twenty.''

"How much longer can they stall?" Chelsea fumed over the telecom connection. "It's been two and a half years since we showed them Lujan's letter. Just how much longer can they stall?''

"Not much," Zachery assured her. "Even Judge Maruzikan is getting impatient with the delays. And if they try to change judges on us one more time, I'm going to file a pecuniary delay suit; they'll have thirty days to put up or pay a thirty percent penalty—and with the corporate war threatening to turn military and the arms buildup, they don't want to put an extra thirty percent in our pockets.''

"Have they got the money to give us?" Chelsea asked sincerely. "Have they spent it all on warships and defense nets?''

"Fortunately, most of it is in art treasures," Zachery told her. "And as administrators of the estate, the government can technically spend only their fee, but no doubt there are lower cash reserves than there were nineteen years ago.''

Nineteen years! Chelsea sat back in her kitchen chair with a sudden weakness in her spine. Had they truly been at it that long? "Zach, finish it up," she said bluntly. "I know I wanted to be there for the ruling and celebrate at the New Sydney Hilton and all that, but I don't care anymore. I'm too tired. Just finish it up. I want it to be over with.''

"Me, too," he sighed wearily. "Me, too, Chels." Then he signed off.

Nineteen years! What hope was there now? Nineteen years on a hostile planet, under hardship conditions—who was she fooling? It just wasn't possible, not even for the intrepid Dr. Jacqueline Winthrop. It just wasn't possible—

"Hang on, Mom," Chelsea whispered. "Just a little longer. Just a little longer . . .''

* * *

Jacqueline didn't have to see the monitor's blinking to know that something was wrong. She could see it in the faces of the technicians, hear it in the crisp call, "Dr. Miori, to the delivery room, stat."

"What is it?" Jacqueline demanded. "What's wrong with my baby?"

"Just lie down, Dr. Winthrop," they told her. "Just relax."

"Don't patronize me!" she snapped. "Tell me what's wrong with my baby or I'll come around and read those monitors myself!"

"The best thing you can do," they replied, "is to stay calm and—"

"I'll stay calmer if you tell me what the hell is going on with my baby!" she shouted as Dr. Miori burst into the room, a nurse at his elbow explaining the situation.

"Nothing to be alarmed about, Jackie," he assured her. "We have a little problem, but nothing we can't handle."

"Don't use that oil-on-water voice with me," she snarled at him, "I know what it means! What's wrong with my baby?"

"It's in distress," he said then, knowing she was right. "It looks like the umbilical cord has gotten wrapped around its neck."

"Operate!" she snapped. "Now!"

"The anesthesiologist is on his way."

"Now!"

"Jackie, stuff it!" he snapped back finally. "I shouldn't have to explain to you what happens if you go into shock during this procedure! You picked me for an obstetrician because you trusted me, and don't think I don't know how many doctors you screened first! So now it's time to exercise that trust. Shut up and let me do my job!"

A contraction gripped Jacqueline, and she fell back against the pillows and tried to find her place in the middle of a breathing pattern, but it was too late; she was floundering—"Clayton!" she cried out. "Clayton, our baby's in trouble; he can't breathe. . . ." How many minutes till brain cells started to die without oxygen? Four to six. Where was the anesthesiologist? And where was Clayton? Clayton had been there, he had been there the first time—"

"Jackie! Jackie, wake up, you're dreaming."

Jacqueline started awake, staring up into the worried face of Rita Zleboton. How old Rita's gotten, she thought. Her hair is more gray than black now, and her face is all lined, like mine . . . like mine. . . .

"It's all right, Jacqueline," Rita soothed. "It's all right; you're okay now."

"The hell I am," Jacqueline muttered, reaching over for the glass of water she kept by her bed.

Hearing her friend sound more like her normal self, Rita relaxed and eased herself into a nearby chair. "Must have been some nightmare," she commented.

Jacqueline grunted, sipped at her water, and set it back down. "I was in labor with Cincinnati. He was in respiratory distress, and they couldn't find the anesthesiologist."

Rita rested her elbows on the arms of the chair and locked her fingers over her ample midsection. "Is that what happened?"

Jacqueline nodded and slumped back against her pillow, a duck feather pillow Cyd Ryan had made for her when young Shalli had the flu. It seemed thin and unsubstantial, and Jacqueline's neck ached a little. "Ah, Rita," she sighed, "I'm old."

A chuckle gurgled up from her companion. "That you are, Jackie," she agreed.

"I thought I was so smart," Jacqueline sighed, "marrying a younger man; I figured I wouldn't have to go on too long without him. But it's been a long time, Rita; it's been such a long time, and I'm tired. I'm so tired that sometimes I just want to . . ."

"Go home," Rita finished. "Sometimes I just want to go home."

The autumn sun was strong and warm, but the wind was chilly. Phoenix grunted as she squatted by the river to wash the grime from her hands. It had been a frustrating morning; though they had flushed a number of ducks from the ripening cornfields in the side canyons of this stream, she had been unable to hit even one. The cold of the water was painful on her hands, and she chafed them to drive away the chill, but that was painful, too. Arthritis? she wondered. Tendinitis? Or just age?

Downstream from where she had stopped, Michael and Sky Dancer also paused and squatted at the river's edge. Sky Dancer slitted the belly of a duck she had bagged and proceeded to gut the bird, chanting to the Mother Earth as she rinsed her prize in the flowing water. Like Phoenix, Michael had no kill to clean, but he watched Sky Dancer attentively, learning from her skill at this chore. You would be proud of him, Coconino, Phoenix thought. He is eager and bright, and before he leaves here next spring, he will be as good with the bow as I am—I, whose strength begins to ebb now, whose eye is not what it once was. . . .

A crisp breeze rustled the dried leaves of the oaks that grew here on the riverbank, and Phoenix shivered involuntarily. Mother Earth, will he truly leave us? she entreated. Will you let him go away again, this son of yours who has come at last to the People? It is so right to have him here in the village. It is *moh-ohnak*. At last, after all these years, I know what *moh-ohnak* is: having Michael here to follow in his father's footsteps. Can you truly allow him to go back to the Mountain?

In the trees overhead a jay began to squawk, and soon the air was filled with the angry cries of a hundred birds. No! they seemed to shout. No! Michael must never leave. Michael must stay in the village and be of the People. His life is here now; the old life must pass away, as yours has faded behind you. . . .

Is that you, Mother Earth? Phoenix wondered. Is that Your voice in the cry of the birds? Or is it only that the maidens have come just now to the stream to fill their water jugs and startled these noisemakers? I never know. I never know if it is truly Your voice I have heard.

On a nearby rock a collared lizard darted forward, paused, then slipped over the edge and scurried away into the underbrush. Phoenix never saw it.

Droplets of water spattered against Phoenix's cheek. Startled, she glanced up to see Michael grinning in her direction, but he was not the culprit. Sky Dancer held her dripping duck and was playfully swinging it in her mother's direction, intentionally sending stray water drops at her. Ignoring the cold of the stream, Phoenix plunged her hands in, locking them together and squeezing to send a spray of water squirting at her daughter.

Sky Dancer squealed and danced back behind Michael. "Don't hide behind me!" he protested laughingly. "Fight your own battles." But Sky Dancer crouched behind him anyway, peeking around his torso to laugh at her mother.

Phoenix pulled her hands out of the water and tucked them into her armpits, feeling as though little needles were running through them. "Like your father," she growled affectionately. "He thought it was great fun to drip cold water on me while I slept or splash me while we cleaned our kills together." Childish games. Adolescent games. What I wouldn't give, Coconino, to play them with you again.

But if Coconino came back today, this very hour, he would be more interested in playing games with his children than with her. He would be just their age, and they would hunt together and laugh together—

—and I would weep, Phoenix thought. Weep with joy at his return, weep with sorrow that we could never share a life the way we wanted to.

"Is that Swan?" Sky Dancer asked, nodding at the group of maidens starting back up the path with their water jugs.

"Yes," Michael answered, shading his eyes against the sun. "Oh, she shouldn't be carrying a heavy jar like that!" And off he sprinted to catch up to his Chosen Companion.

Phoenix watched him go, the image of Coconino sprinting along a trail. He is yours, beloved, she thought. In his movements, in his smile, he reflects your image. Even his speech grows more like yours, filled with the colorful images and turns of phrase that you wielded like an artist's brush. No one can doubt that the son of Coconino has come among us.

Behind her Phoenix heard the sound of splashing, and she turned to see Sky Dancer rinsing the duck one last time. She chanted a final phrase, shook the bird, and rose nimbly to brush the water droplets from her arms.

But she is mine, Phoenix thought. Karen may have borne her, but she is my daughter in every way. Even the painful loss of her husband has made her more like me. If Karen saw her today—

Phoenix turned abruptly from the stream and headed for the other side of the canyon. "Where are you going?" Sky Dancer called after her.

"To see how the harvest is coming in the Canyon of the Horned Lizard," Phoenix called back. "If the gourds are ripe, perhaps I will bring one home. It would be nice to have *something* to show for my day's labors."

But she knew it was to keep her daughter from reading the fright that had suddenly written itself on Phoenix's face and heart. For just an instant she had seen in her daughter's visage the one person she tried never to see there: Karen Reichert.

Has it been there all along? Phoenix wondered. Do other people in the village see it as plainly as they see Coconino in Michael? Is it only the long hair and the dark eyes that have blinded me until now? All these years I have only searched your face for its resemblance to your father, though I have found him more in your stubbornness and your pride than in your countenance.

I will never have him for a husband, Phoenix mourned, or even a lover. But I have you, my darling; I have his child. You must always be my daughter.

I never want to see Karen Reichert in your face again.

* * *

Michael overtook Swan just where the path began to circle the island toward their house. "Swan, let me take that," he protested, lifting the huge crockery jar from her shoulder. "You shouldn't be carrying heavy things like that."

Swan giggled. "Michael, I have been carrying jars like that since I was eight. Why should I stop now?"

A breeze sent autumn leaves skittering across the path in front of them as they walked together toward the house. "Well, because," he answered lamely. "You know. Because of the baby."

Swan beamed up at her Man-on-the-Mountain, her very own, and thought that the summer had only made him more handsome. After much protest whose source she could not comprehend, he had finally taken to wearing a breechclout during the muggy heat of the rainy season, and he had grown browner during days of hunting with his half sister and her mother. Except for the odd accent to his speech, which lessened every day, one could hardly tell him from a man of the People.

True, he still had some strange notions, she thought as she ducked through the doorway into the shade of their adobe home: such as this, not carrying a water jar. The baby inside her was still small and light. Why did he think she could not carry a water jar, too? Her mother carried a water jar and two babies, one on the inside and one on her back.

But by and large he was a most satisfactory companion. He cared for her and provided for her as one would for a wife, which was not required of Men-on-the-Mountain. Since She Who Saves had undertaken to teach him, he had become a most credible hunter, bringing home game at least twice a week. Yesterday he had brought home a fine pair of ducks, and everyone knew how hard it was to shoot birds in flight.

Yet it was his kindness that pleased her most. Had he not waited for her womanhood ceremony before he asked to Choose? And then had he not chosen her from among all the maidens, even those more coy and beautiful? And how tender he had been on their first night together, how careful and solicitous for her comfort and her pleasure—not that lovemaking had been very pleasurable that first time. But Michael was gentle and patient, and in the past few months Swan had come to enjoy, even seek, his caresses, although the baby was already made and growing safely inside her.

That was the best part, of course. Scarcely two moons had passed before she had conceived, and now the child of a Man-on-the-Mountain—the grandchild of Coconino—slept in her womb. Where were their taunts now, those girls who told her she was too young to be Chosen, that one of them would be in Michael's bed before the moon was full? Their pride had vanished with the palo-verde flowers, blown to dust on the wind. Her moment of boldness had secured her Fulfillment.

"What thoughts dance through your head, my pretty one?" Michael asked as he set the water jar down inside the house for her. "They make your eyes sparkle and flash like sunlight on the stream."

"I was thinking how lucky I am to be Chosen," she replied. "And that if my child is only half as handsome as his father, he will have his pick of all the maidens of the village when he comes of age."

Michael reached out to her where she knelt on the floor, touching her arms, her neck, her swelling breasts. Summer had kept him in a constant state of arousal, for all the women of the People discarded their warm leather shirts and went about in only yucca aprons or short skirts. Even Sky Dancer wore only her loincloth when in the village, although she complained it was uncomfortable to run if she did not bind her breasts.

Now the chill of autumn had moved them to don warmer cloth-ing, but the pungent aroma of drying leaves and smoking meats seemed to have the same effect on Michael. His mother would have laughed and told him it was a product of his hormones, not the sights and scents of the island canyon, but Michael was sure there was more to it. It was not just the casual nudity and the woodsy freshness of this place, either.

It was Sky Dancer. She was so beautiful! The more he saw of her, the more they talked together, the more attractive he found her. Why did you have to be my half sister? he wondered. I would have Chosen you in a minute. Half a minute. But you are what you are, and I must place my passions elsewhere.

So he reached now, as he always did, for Swan. She was a delightful girl, an enticing substitute, and was becoming quite randy herself. Even now she groped for the ties of his breechclout, having complained before about the scratchiness of its woven yucca fibers. She was as ready as he, though it was only midafternoon and people came and went on the path in front of their house.

I'm glad I chose you, he thought. You are the kind of girl I need, saucy and playful and adoring. There is no guilt with you, no need to apologize or make promises as I had to with the girls on the Mountain. There is nothing but the joy of the moment and the sweet knowledge that this will go on day after day after beautiful day. . . .

On a ledge farther down the mountain Coral Snake stood glowering after the young people who had disappeared into their house. What is the magic of Coconino and his progeny? Coral Snake wondered. Is their seed so strong, or do they just choose fertile women? First the father managed three children by three different women, and now— Spring had not become summer before the son's Chosen Companion conceived, and soon she will begin to grow round with her treasure, whereas my wife . . .

Coral Snake turned and stalked bitterly along the ledge to the river trail. How long shall I be a mockery in the village, he thought, a joke among my friends? "Can't you get your wife with child?" they tease me. "Shall we come and help you?"

What if one of these days, Michael, son of Coconino, you walk carelessly and slip from the canyon rim? Then I could give my wife back to her mother and take your Chosen Companion for my own. Once she had delivered herself of your worthless get, I would fill her with my seed and see the fruit of my loins grow and overtake your weakling child.

Below the angry young man, by the water's edge, workers moved among the mesquite trees, gathering the last of the mesquite beans in their sun-dried pods. There was laughter and singing, and small children played in the mud under the watchful eye of older ones. His sister's child was there, and his friend Basking Lizard's twins. Twins! What if that stupid girl of Michael's bore twins?

If the Mother Earth were kind and just, he thought, as the People say that she is, she would give me a child to bear my seed among the People. One who is as clever and as strong as I should give the People a wealth of children. But the Mother Earth mocks me by withholding her hand, and her voice.

If she has either one.

Just then Sky Dancer started up the trail from the river carrying her cleaned and washed duck, and Coral Snake followed her with his eyes. Now, there is a sign I would believe, he thought. If the Mother Earth were to give me that one to bear my children—oh, what satisfaction to bend her to my will, to make her repent her words of scorn over the years. Give me Sky Dancer, Mother Earth, and I will chant your praises all my days.

His lip curled in a sneer of anticipation. It was not likely that Sky Dancer would sing any praises at all.

Michael lay with his hand on Swan's belly, wondering how soon it would begin to swell, how soon he could expect to feel life fluttering within. When he was a boy, his mother had let him put his hand on her stomach like this to feel the baby kicking inside her. Then he was only mystified; now he was overawed.

I'm going to be a father. A father! What does that mean? Can I really go away after a year and leave this part of me behind? Can I really stay and take on the responsibilities of caring for it? What if it dies? What if it puts its hand in the fire when I'm not watching? What if I can't teach it all the things it needs to know?

How do I behave? he wondered. If it's a girl, how do I treat her? Like I've treated my younger half sisters? No, oh, no. I have to be better than that, more careful. Or do I? What if I'm overprotective, as Swan says that I am?

If Michael had been on the Mountain, he knew he could have gone to talk to his grandfather. Dick McKay had been through this, the father of a child destined to be raised among the People. But Michael wasn't on the Mountain, and he couldn't just go back for a visit. Who could he talk to in the village? His uncle Flint, whom he hardly knew? The other young men his age? They might laugh at him, at his concerns. They all expected to be fathers at eighteen—the idea had never occurred to Michael until he had come here, and even then it had never been quite real until now.

Sky Dancer? Sky Dancer was a fascinating young woman, edged by early grief and wise beyond her years, but she couldn't know how a man felt. Michael desperately wanted to hear from another man what it was like becoming a father for the first time. Becoming a father among the People. But who was there to ask foolish questions of, to confide his terror to?

Nakha-a.

Michael sat up and gazed out the doorway of his house at the bright sunlight on the far canyon wall. His half brother would not laugh at him, he was sure. He was probably a new father himself or just becoming one. Yes, Michael's half brother would understand, would be like Sky Dancer but with a male perspective. If only he could talk to Nakha-a.

I'll ask Sky Dancer again, he thought. I'll ask her to speak to Phoenix about us making the trip south to find him. I've never had a brother, never even had a close friend—I was always too different. God knows how often I wished for a brother to share with, to talk to. Nakha-a is my chance to have that at last.

Surely Sky Dancer and I can get Phoenix to understand.

Sky Dancer glanced sideways at her mother, then leaned pointedly on a stack of soft, well-tanned hides in a corner of their cliff house. "So many nice hides we have," she commented, "from last winter. With the two of us hunting and Corn Hair helping to tan them, we will have twice as many by next spring.''

Sunlight from the open doorway warmed Phoenix's face as she sat cross-legged by the fire, waiting for her tea to brew. The hide door covering had been tossed aside to allow the fresh morning air into the house, and Phoenix had draped an antelope robe across her shoulders against its chill. She looked up guardedly when her foster daughter spoke, wondering where the conversation was headed.

With a sigh and feigned nonchalance, Sky Dancer went on. ''They will overtake the house soon, these skins. What shall we do with them all?''

Sky Dancer didn't really want to know, Phoenix was sure, but she was also fairly sure she'd better answer. ''Michael and his family will need some,'' she replied. ''And there are others in the village who do not hunt as well as we; they will come trading their corn and beans for furs.''

''Yes, and you will give them more than their vegetables are worth,'' Sky Dancer remarked, joining her mother at the fire. ''You are a generous person, Mother.''

It was not criticism, Phoenix knew. Sky Dancer had always been glad to help out other families and was often more careful of their pride in such dealings than Phoenix was. No, Sky Dancer was leading up to something else. So Phoenix just watched the simmering brew and waited.

The teenager twisted her long hair idly into braids and fastened them with leather thongs. ''I can't help thinking,'' she continued in the same casual tone as her fingers twined the strands of hair, ''that if we could trade with people who have as much extra of something as we have of hides, then we could give away even more that was needful. Food, and shirts, and blan—''

''No,'' Phoenix cut her off, not even looking up from the pot.

Irked, Sky Dancer put her hands on her hips and scowled at her mother. ''I haven't asked you anything yet!'' she pouted.

''You were going to ask if we could trade with the Others,'' Phoenix said simply. ''The answer is no.''

''Why not?'' Sky Dancer demanded. ''Michael has been to their village—they know him. He could go ahead, dressed in his Man-on-the-Mountain clothes, and talk to them. Then, when he had made the way safe, the rest of us could come and—''

''No.''

Frustrated, Sky Dancer slapped her hands on the adobe floor, which only made them sting. ''You have not heard all I have to say!'' she protested angrily. ''Did not Nina warn you against snap judgments? And my grandmother? You give the decision you made years ago without thinking about it now. When the question of trading was asked before, we did not have Michael with us, who could make the way safe. So how can you make a wise decision for today when you have not considered this new condition?''

Now Phoenix raised her eyes to study her daughter's face. The eyes sparked with indignation and self-righteousness. To Sky Dancer it was all very simple. To Sky Dancer, who had never seen the power of the Others' weapons, who had never seen the burned and blackened bodies of her friends or known the hostility on the face of Tony Hanson, it was all so logical.

Yet there was some truth in her logic. Phoenix's decision had been made long ago in response to very real and very terrifying conditions, conditions that might have changed. After all, Dick had passed through the camp of the Others and heard of Nina's band visiting there. They had not apparently been met with hostility. If Nakha-a, then a boy of twelve, could speak to them and negotiate safe passage, even an exchange of goods, why not Michael? He had already been in their camp, and he spoke the language better than Nakha-a ever would. Things had changed, indeed.

Yet there was another fear that lurked in Phoenix's mind, and only now would it name itself. She looked across at her beautiful fosterdaughter and wondered why she had chosen to take up this issue now, after Michael had come to them. What was on her mind? Not the welfare of the tribe, no—not in truth.

It is she, isn't it? Phoenix wondered silently. It is curiosity about your birth mother that moves you now to press for a journey to trade with the Others. But the thought of it strikes terror into my heart. How can I ever let you go there? She would take one look at you and know who you are, for your looks are different from the rest of the People. All the Others would know, and what if they want you back? Or my greatest fear: What if *you* want to stay for a while and learn from them, as Michael has come here to learn from us? How could I leave you there? What would I do if you didn't come back?

Phoenix drew her gaze back to the fire, back to the crackling flames and the steaming pot. Yet that is my personal fear, she realized, and what right have I to rule the People to suit my own needs? None. Coconino taught me that. I must think what is best for them regardless of whether that is best for me. Do we need to be able to trade with the Others? We have done well without them so far. But the versatility of cotton, the chance to obtain more grain in those years when the harvest is small . . .

"I will think on it, then," she told her daughter finally. "You are right; it has been several years since I thought on it."

Sky Dancer looked relieved at that, but there was still something on her mind. Phoenix could tell by the way her eyes focused on the fire as she tried to put together her next ploy.

"What else?" Phoenix asked bluntly.

Sky Dancer looked startled, caught. "It is something that Michael suggested," she said hastily, as though wanting to put the blame for this on someone else, someone who might have considerable stature in her mother's eyes. "He would like to go look for Nakha-a."

Phoenix laughed. "Michael? Alone in the wilderness, trying to find Nakha-a?"

"Not alone," Sky Dancer protested. "I would not let such a babe go alone. No, I meant he and I together."

Phoenix's heart rose in her throat. The two of them? Alone together day after day— "No," she said quickly. She had seen the look that passed between them when they first met; she had seen it lurking in their eyes still, when they thought no one saw. They were always circumspect and polite; they always called each other "my brother" and "my sister." But it seemed they were constantly reminding themselves and each other of how things ought to be between them. Ought to but . . .

"No," she repeated harshly when Sky Dancer started to object. "You have no idea where Nakha-a is. I will not have you going off to wander in unknown country where you don't know the landmarks or the water sources." The unknown country of temptation whose power you do not comprehend. "It is foolish, Sky Dancer. No. Nakha-a will come back to us here in his own time. You will see."

"But—"

"No!" Phoenix barked. "Do not press me on this, Sky Dancer. I will consider the matter of trading but not of going to find Nakha-a. Speak no more of it."

With a fierce scowl Sky Dancer snatched up her polished throwing club and started out the door.

"Where are you going?" Phoenix demanded.

"To give Michael your answer!" she snapped. "Which you have weighed so carefully and expressed so eloquently!"

Then she was gone, leaving Phoenix with only the harsh sunlight and the morning chill.

* * *

Sky Dancer entered Michael's house and cut loose with a string of epithets that would have done a fleet captain justice. Michael looked up in shock. "Where did you learn to swear like that?" he gasped.

"From my mother," she replied tartly. "I do not know what the words mean, but I know they are to be used when one is very angry, and Michael, I am very, very angry right now!"

Swan shrank away into the corner. She had always admired Sky Dancer because of her exotic looks, but the older girl intimidated her as well. No other woman in the village had undertaken to become a hunter like She Who Saves, and none had the hot temper that mother and daughter both seemed to possess. Swan preferred quiet, gentle women for company. But this was her beloved's half sister, so she simply faded away whenever Sky Dancer indulged in one of her vociferous outbursts.

"Coral Snake again?" Michael asked.

"No." Sky Dancer dropped down across the fire from him and wrapped her slender arms around her knees. "That rank little viper may be sly and fiendish, but even he could never make me this angry. No, that honor is reserved for my esteemed mother."

Michael grimaced. "I take it she doesn't want us to go look for Nakha-a."

"She wouldn't even consider it!" Sky Dancer shrieked. "She said no, it was foolish, and not to bring it up again. I scarcely brought it up the first time!" She thumped the handle of her throwing club on the adobe floor in frustration. "Why is it so foolish to go on a journey to places one has never been?" she demanded. "Did *she* never do such a thing? Did our father never do such a thing? When they went together in search of Tala, they knew of the Black Lands only from stories. They ran blindly into the great eastern prairie, and it was only our father's twentieth summer, you know. She knew less of the wilderness then than you do, but she went along with him."

Sky Dancer wanted to pace, but the ceiling was too short even for her. "I am not so young and unskilled that I could not undertake an adventure such as this," she ranted. "If it were Nakha-a, or Tree without Bark, or one of the other young men, she would not say no. But me she must deny, and without even considering it! That is what angers me so, Michael—she did not even consider it!"

In the face of Sky Dancer's tirade, Michael's own disappointment seemed meager. In fact, he felt compelled to defend Phoenix. "It is only because she loves you," he pointed out. "She worries about your safety."

"I have kept myself safe on hunting trips for years!"

Michael shrugged. "Maybe she just doesn't want you to leave her. My mother wasn't very excited about me coming here."

That stemmed the tide of Sky Dancer's rushing emotions. "But she let you come."

"Only because Ababba reasoned with her. And even then she cried when I left. She's afraid I won't come back."

For several moments Sky Dancer sat scratching at the floor with her club. "I would come back," she pouted. "I love my brother, but . . . she is my mother. Since Dreams of Hawks died, she is all that I have."

Michael felt suddenly uncomfortable. He had heard of Dreams of Hawks from other relatives and of how devastated Sky Dancer had been. True grief was outside his experience, for he had yet to lose anyone he loved.

"I see you have your throwing club," he said to change the subject. "Shall we go hunting rabbits?"

"Yes," Sky Dancer agreed vehemently, rising to her knees. "Let us go for rabbits this morning. I will feel better if I can throw this stick at something."

Castle Rock spoke more carefully with her son these days. Since Michael's arrival in the village, he had become more surly and sensitive than usual. So she tried to broach her subject delicately.

"Oh, is this the Moon of the Rains already?" she asked in apparent surprise. "The summer is more than half gone, then. Soon we shall be dancing the Dance of the Survivors." The dance was traditionally done during the new moon between the Moon of the Rains and the Moon of Mule Deer.

Coral Snake only grunted. He was stuffing jerky into his leather pouch, the kind of jerky only his mother seemed able to make properly. He planned to spend the day hunting alone, far from his whimpering wife, his fatuous friends, and the ever-present aggravation of Michael and his pregnant Chosen Companion.

Castle Rock gave a soft chuckle. "Remember when you were a little boy, how you used to imitate the dancers?" she asked. "Which one was it that you wanted to be—Alfonso?"

Now he looked up sharply, cinching the drawstrings on his bag. "It was Chico," he replied tartly. "He Who Had No Faith."

"Oh, that's right," Castle Rock said. "Oh, you were so good

at it. You knew all the steps, and you said that someday you would dance the part of—''

''Jumping Turtle dances the part of Chico,'' he cut in. ''Do not start with your foolish ambitions to set me up for an honor that can never be mine.''

''Why shouldn't it be yours?'' his mother snapped, giving up on her charade of nonchalance. ''Jumping Turtle hurt his foot last week, he may not be able to dance the part so soon. Why shouldn't you take his place?''

''Because the Council would have to give me that honor!'' he snarled back. ''And She Who Saves controls the Council, and she will never give me any kind of honor while there is breath in her bony old body!''

''She does not control them,'' Castle Rock said. ''My friend Moon Without Shadows is on the Council, and she says they often disagree with She Who Saves. If I were to go to Moon Without Shadows and suggest you to replace Jumping Turtle—''

''Then I could become a laughingstock in front of the whole Council!'' he shouted. ''And from there it would travel throughout the entire village. Coral Snake, whose mother pleads with the Council for him. Coral Snake, who was turned down for the role of Chico. Coral Snake, who will never have any honor in this village.''

''Not so!'' Castle Rock cried out, tears smarting in her eyes. ''You will have honor; only you must be willing to please certain people, speak sweetly to . . .''

But her words were lost. Coral Snake was out the door and headed down the slope toward the path which led to the eastern canyon rim. In his anger, he did not notice the children of Coconino gaining the top of that trail just ahead of him.

CHAPTER TWENTY-FOUR

Janine tapped cautiously at the cabin door. "Mr. Lujan?" she called. "I have your breakfast."

There was no answer. After a moment she tapped again. "Mr. Lujan, you know I won't open the door myself. I'm just going to leave your food outside here; if you want it, you'd better come get it before the roaches and ants do." Janine set the basket down carefully and started to back away. She couldn't say why she always backed away from his door; he was chained, after all. But somehow the thought of turning her vulnerable back toward him gave her the willies.

Suddenly the door burst open, and Janine jumped back with a gasp. Lujan stood in the doorway, his single eye wild, his hair dirty and bedraggled, the scars on his face livid in the bright morning sunlight.

"Do you have a nail file?" he demanded.

After six months of bringing him breakfast every day, Janine still could not get used to his appearance. It was horrid. When he had been swathed in bandages, it hadn't been so bad, but when Liza had removed them, the black stitches stood out in strong contrast to the bright red weals of surgery and made him look like a monster. Even now, with the stitches gone and the scars fading to pink, his face was a nightmare apparition. Janine backed farther away, staring stupidly at him.

"A nail file," he repeated with tried patience in his voice. "An emery board. Anything of the kind."

Steeling herself, Janine recovered her voice and forced a reply. "No," she managed. The chain binding him to the stove in the cabin would only allow him to step outside the door and no farther. At this distance she was safe, provided that the chain held. Faced with his ravaged countenance, however, she was never inclined to trust in that.

"Get one," he snapped, and started back inside.

But Janine straightened herself up now. "No, Mr. Lujan," she called after him with only the trace of a shake in her voice.

Arrested in the doorway, Lujan turned slowly back and fixed her with his manic eye. "A nail file," he repeated, as though to an idiot child. "A simple device for wearing away—"

"I said no, Mr. Lujan," Janine reiterated more firmly. "I will get nothing more for you."

There was a deadly pause; then suddenly Lujan smiled, a grotesque twisting of his mangled face. "I only wanted to trim my nails," he said in a pleasant, persuasive tone that was incongruous with his horrifying features. "I've . . . let myself get a little ragged, I'm afraid."

It was absurd, the disfigured madman who melted into a disarming pose and wheedled with the voice of a debonair roué. Janine might have laughed were he not so terrifying.

"No," she repeated, but less sternly. "You have some evil purpose for it, no doubt, and I will not get it for you."

Lujan laughed, a charming, good-fellow sort of laugh. "Now, what kind of evil do you suppose I could do with an emery board?" he asked.

Janine looked on him and knew finally that all her care and effort in coaxing him back to health the first time had been for naught. Once she'd hoped that the charity the Crusoans had shown him would heal him, change him, make him better than he had been, but their kindness had been as water thrown on loose sand: it simply vanished in a waste that bore no trace of its passing. And with that realization a burden was lifted from Janine. She was no longer responsible for this man. His sickness was not her failure.

What kind of evil could he do with an emery board? "Mr. Lujan," she assured him, "you would find something." Then she turned on her heel and walked resolutely away.

As Lujan watched her go, his astonishment turned quickly to burning anger. Damn her! He needed that file. Had the lock on his leg manacle been any kind of electronic device, he was sure he could have deactivated it in a minute, but this was a mechanical lock. It required a key to turn an internal tumbler. Lujan had seen the actual key, a small tubular device with a tab on one end. Rummaging wantonly through his belongings, he had fixed upon a plastic comb as a possible substitute.

Breaking out all the spindly teeth, he was left with a piece of plastic with the ends bent at right angles. An end was about the right length and could be filed down to the right diameter. But filed with what? Though he searched the cabin high and low, tumbling things haphazardly out of drawers and cupboards in his frantic quest, he could find nothing that would work as a file. And now, was he to be thwarted again by this uncooperative woman?

Lujan slammed the cabin door and screamed in rage. Spying the stone doorstop, he picked it up and hurled it at the stove. It struck with such force that a hand-sized piece cracked off and flew across the room.

Suddenly Lujan stopped. Stone. Whetstone, grindstone. He picked up the sheered piece of stone and studied its rough surface. Oh, yes. Yes, indeed. Retrieving the comb, he dropped to the floor and began patiently scraping the plastic against the stone.

It was as though he had crossed the Sea of Grass again; Coconino felt as if a monster loomed at his back. But that was impossible—Lujan was securely chained, and the rest of the Others appeared, he had to admit, quite hospitable. What could be stalking him across the land?

Yet that was what he felt.

They had left the camp of the Others early that morning, slipping away while the settlement was just beginning to stir. Ironwood Blossom had made no protest; the place she had dreamed of seeing had proved to be more frightening than fascinating to her, and she seemed glad to put it behind them.

There was no need to rush now, since Hummingbird was obviously in no danger from Lujan. Yet Coconino felt an urgent need to put obstacles between himself and the madman. Instead of following the traders' path, which went through the Valley of the People and past the Sacred Well of She Who Saves, he continued following the river that ran through the camp of the Others. This route was longer, but only by a little, and it avoided the tiresome journey overland between the Well and the Dead City that crumbled on the banks of this selfsame river.

Several times, as his wife and child rested by the water's edge, Coconino climbed up to high ground and looked back along their trail. He saw no one following, nothing unusual. Yet as the day wore on, his uneasiness grew.

Evening found them at last in the Red Rock Country, amid the staggering beauty of the soaring buttes. Ironwood Blossom's mouth gaped open as the fire of sunset lit the majestic monoliths and they seemed to blaze with a life of their own. A host of stone sentinels stood between them and any threat from the south, yet the nagging disquiet drove Coconino to scale the butte at whose foot they were camped and watch back down the trail until the light was gone.

When he climbed back down, his fingers and toes searching carefully in the darkness to find the purchase his eyes would not have found, Ironwood Blossom had a savory stew waiting. It was filled with beans and chilies and dried meat, thickened with cornmeal. Coconino discovered he was ravenous and gladly wolfed down a heaping portion.

His wife, however, only picked at her food. "What is wrong?" Coconino asked. "Are you not hungry after such a long day?"

She smiled wanly. "My stomach is upset. It is nothing. Tomorrow I will look for a fernbush to make tea; that always helps me."

Ah, Coconino thought wisely, it must be her moonflow time. Fernbush tea was often used for cramps as well as stomachache. Knowing how easily she grew chilled at such times, he loosened a pack on the travois to get her an extra blanket. "Here," he said, draping it around her shoulders. "We must bank the fire down low lest the wind carry sparks to all the dry grass hereabouts, but that is no reason you should shiver through the night."

Ironwood Blossom tried to smile her gratitude for his thoughtfulness, but the discomfort she felt overshadowed the attempt.

In the morning Coconino woke to the sound of his wife vomiting quietly behind a nearby creosote bush. Distressed, he flung back his blanket and hurried to her side.

"I'm sorry," she whispered as his arm slipped comfortingly around her shoulders. "I didn't mean to wake you."

Wake me? he thought. When you are sick and I sleep like a stone.

Then suddenly it became clear to Coconino: the dullness in her eyes, her tiredness, the uncharacteristic snappishness she had shown as they approached the camp of the Others. . . .

"Are you with child?" he asked quietly.

Ironwood Blossom nodded. "I think so." She forced a smile. "Bad timing, no? I had hoped the morning sickness would not be great until I got back to the village, but . . ."

Silently Coconino enfolded her in his arms. "There is no bad time for a child," he told her, but in his heart he knew it would have been easier on them both had this joyous news been postponed by four days. Still he kissed her hair and her forehead and held her close. "We will travel more slowly, if that helps; my enemy is far behind us. We can take our time from here."

Ironwood Blossom shook her head, though. "Let us go on as we have," she said. "I long to see my village and my sister. How big her daughter will be, and I have not seen her grow."

Suddenly Ironwood Blossom was in tears. "Hush, hush," Coconino soothed. "Soon we will be there, and what things you have to tell her! There will be no peace in my house for days while the two of you chatter away."

That brought a laugh from his weeping wife. "And you will sit at the Elvira and boast of your prowess," she replied. "What other man has four children in three years?"

Coconino laughed, too, and cradled her close to him. The words of the ancient lullaby filtered into his mind as he rocked her gently, but this time they were filled with the reassurance they had engendered in his childhood. *Sleep, child, sleep in safety; no harm can touch you here.*

They were happier that day, hiking through the heart of the Red Rock Country, even as they passed by the grievous ruin that had been a town in the Before Times. Most of it had been swept away by rampant floodwaters, leaving the earth clean and smooth in the aftermath, but here and there the wind had laid bare a rusting beam, a mound of concrete. The traders' path did not come this way, and Ironwood Blossom had never seen such relics; they sent shivers down her spine, and she was glad to push on and into the deep cleft of a canyon.

The next morning they rejoined the well-worn trail and climbed a perilous stretch to the rim of the canyon. The air was cold and sweet there, with a hint of winter on the breeze. As they rested at the top, Coconino felt cleansed and purified, as though he had left a great burden behind. He stood on the brink and looked back over the blaze of autumn colors that lined the gorge, feeling the wind ruffle his hair.

Suddenly he froze, and the hair on the back of his neck raised in alarm.

Someone was following them.

He could see no figure at this distance, of course; even had he a hawk's eyes, the towering trees would have hidden any creature moving through the depths of the canyon. But a small plume of smoke drifted up from the far end of that forested cleft, and Coconino knew that they were not traveling this trail alone.

Ironwood Blossom did not notice it. She was watching Juan, who was out of his pack and playing in the thick carpet of leaves and pine needles that covered the ground nearby. He stomped his little feet in the crinkly, crackly stuff, inhaling deeply of the pungent, musty odor that arose.

"Do you know what I think?" Coconino said with all the nonchalance he could muster. "I think we should leave the travois here and hurry home to Hummingbird. I can come back for it later."

Ironwood Blossom looked up in surprise, but she could only spare a quick glance for her husband and his suggestion. Juan was off into the trees, headed for a clump of poison ivy. By the time she had scooped him up and came back to their resting place, Coconino was already at work hoisting the travois into a tree with their sturdy yucca rope. "But wait!" Ironwood Blossom objected. "I need the cooking skin and my poncho. We are higher up now; the mornings will be colder."

"Our blankets will serve," Coconino assured her as he hauled on the rope, which was slung over a branch some fifteen feet above them. With a nod he indicated the single light pack at his feet. "I have them here, and enough trail food for two more days. We can travel faster if we don't build any fires for cooking." He shinnied up the tree and secured the rope around its trunk some eight feet off the ground. The travois dangled just to his right. When he descended again, he handed his wife two full gourd canteens. "This should get us to the lakes. Come, my son, how would you like to ride on your father's back today?"

Ironwood Blossom watched suspiciously as Coconino deposited the wriggling child in the carrying pack and slung it joyfully onto his back. Coconino seemed almost too lighthearted, too happy. Yesterday he had brooded all day, checking the trail behind them, fearful of something. Today had been better, it was true, but why this sudden decision to abandon the travois? Hanging it in a tree would protect its contents from most creatures, but not all; the squirrels would undoubtedly find their way into the corn. Why risk that kind of spoilage unnecessarily?

She looked back over the canyon through which they'd come, but her untrained eyes saw nothing amiss.

I do not understand you, Coconino, she thought, and perhaps I never will. But if you believe we have cause to make haste, I will speed my steps. You have a strength of conviction that will not let me do otherwise. When you have made up your mind to a course of action, who can stand against you? Who would want to? I trust you, Coconino. Not even a Sky Ship could stand in your way.

Is that how she felt, your Witch Woman, so many years ago?

* * *

Phoenix fretted as she sat by the fire in her house, knowing she had done the right thing, knowing she had done it badly. *Sky Dancer doesn't understand,* Phoenix thought. *She doesn't know I'm doing it for her own good, hers and Michael's. I've been young. I know how easy it is to get involved in something you don't intend. There was that first boy, before Dick spotted me: it was harmless fun, exciting, daring, to go skinny-dipping in the catch basin. I never meant to do more than that; most likely he didn't, either.*

You don't know, Phoenix raged inwardly. *You and Dreams of Hawks were bound by the customs of the People: reserved, patient, knowing your Fulfillment would come in due time. Michael is like me; he knows no such restrictions. On the Mountain life is so different. . . . And you, my young, wounded daughter. You had only begun to explore the sweetness of conjugal love when your husband was taken from you. It was not only your spirit that cried out for him, it was your body, too. I know. I have been there.*

Now Michael is here, and he is handsome and dynamic and forbidden— No, Sky Dancer. He is like his father: conscientious, caring, but driven by male hormones. What guilt Coconino suffered because he lay with Nina but could not bring himself to marry her! Yet he returned to her chamber night after night. With you and Michael it is not just two teenagers responding to their drives—the taboos against incest are old and deep. If you slipped, if you ventured too near the edge of the precipice, it would destroy you both.

But I can't tell you that is the reason you must not go in search of Nakha-a. You would be offended and believe I thought too little of you and of Michael, too. You would accuse me of having no trust, of thinking vile and evil thoughts of you both. You would never understand how easy it could all be until it was too late.

I must distract you, then, she thought. *I will give my permission for us all to journey to the Camp of the Others, as you wished. In the excitement, in the rush to prepare for the trail, you will forget this idea of going off by yourselves, the two of you. Yes, that is the answer: we will make the trip to the Camp of the Others.*

Only there you will meet your birth mother, and what will I do? How will I bear to watch the two of you face each other after eighteen years?

Danger if we go, danger if we do not . . . Mother Earth, have you no words for me? What shall I do? Will you not speak to me this one time?

A collared lizard scurried into the doorway from the path outside and sat, staring up at her with one unblinking eye. In frustration,

Phoenix drew the blanket from her shoulders and shooed it back out the door.

Lujan gazed up at the travois hanging in the tree. He'd almost missed it, intent as he was on the trail. But a chance breeze had set it swaying, and the movement caught his eye.

Run, Coconino, he thought wickedly. Blow your ballast and run; it won't do you any good. I'd follow you into the jaws of hell to give you back a fraction of the suffering you have caused me.

Making the key had taken only a few hours, but Coconino and his family had been long gone when Lujan had freed himself and torn down to the river in search of them. He'd had only a knife then, one he'd stolen from Kenny Johanneson's house on his way. Seeing that his quarry had flown, Lujan had sneaked back up to the village and rummaged through the storehouse domes in search of food and equipment for the trail.

In Franz Johnson's house he had found his Collection, complete with knives and hooks and surgical laser. The thrifty Crusoans had destroyed nothing, which did not surprise Lujan. No doubt Franz thought that if he studied the things long enough, he could find out how to use them for constructive purposes.

Fully equipped, Lujan had headed quickly up the traders' path to the north, but when evening approached, he had still seen no trace of Coconino's passing. No master woodsman, Lujan still knew he should have seen some evidence along the way: a footprint, a loosened rock, discarded food.

When by noon the next day he had not found the remains of a camp fire, Lujan began to worry that they had taken some other route, slipped through his grasp entirely. He shouted and cursed and raged at the ominous red buttes surrounding him, but they kept silent, giving nothing back but his own words. Not knowing what else to do, Lujan pushed on.

When the trail finally reached the river whose ancestor had carved the red bluffs, he found the drag marks. They came along the river's edge, marking the way Coconino had taken. Lujan whooped and shouted with joy, having picked up the trail at last. Even when the marks disappeared from time to time along the stony bank of the creek, his joy did not abate. Now I'll find you, you feckless bastard, he gloated. You, and the woman, and the baby . . .

He'd worried about losing them again climbing out of the canyon, for the ground was solid rock and the drag marks were undiscernible to his untrained eye. But here, just at the top, was the travois dangling from a tree. Did you only now figure it out, Co-conino? he wondered, the unscarred half of his face twisting into a smile. Did you only now figure out I'm coming for you?

Husband, wife, child . . . An old holoflick danced through Lu-jan's mind, and he laughed out loud. "The last one to die will see the other two go before him," he cackled. "I'll get you, my pretty—and your little boy, too!"

He marched on up the trail, leaving the travois swaying slightly in the breeze, suspended from the tree limb.

Coral Snake loosed his arrow, but a squawking jay startled the woodchuck and it bolted to one side just before the shaft struck. A soft *click* marked its landing and Coral Snake cursed silently. He retrieved it only to find that the flint tip had indeed chipped on a stone. Furious, Coral Snake picked up the offending rock and pitched it far into the woods where it struck a fir tree with a dull thud.

The birds set up a clamor at the disturbance, but Coral Snake did not care. He tramped noisily through the trees, breaking every stick he could put his foot on and tearing small branches from their trunks. There was no joy in hunting today. If only his foolish mother would leave off her meddling . . . and his wife was no better. Telling him he should lead a party of hunters to the eastern prairie to hunt the Great Antelope. Ha! As though such an expe-dition would not immediately be taken over by Flint or Fox With Two Tails or the old man-woman herself. He would go alone, that's what he would do, and bring back a Great Antelope all by himself.

Somewhat consoled by the thought, Coral Snake began to walk more quietly. Yes, he would go tomorrow and not even tell his wife where he was going. Let her fret and worry when he did not come back at sundown or the next day or even the next. Let his friends wonder where he had gone and why he had not told them. Let them all wonder what dreadful thing had happened to Coral Snake.

Then he would return with the largest buck antelope any of them had ever seen. He would return and—and . . .

And what? he wondered. Would anyone but his closest friends notice? Would Fox With Two Tails come up to him and say, "*Aieee*, Coral Snake, that is the finest kill anyone in the village has ever made"? Not likely. Would the old women grinding corn say, "There is not a hunter to compare to that Coral Snake!" No. They would say, "Oh, it is a fine kill, but Coconino had a finer one." Then they would be off on their stories about the great Coconino and how he could shoot the petals from a poppy, send an arrow so high in the air it would come down on the other side of the forest.

All his comfort had gone when, near the edge of the woods, Coral Snake heard sounds. Laughter. At first, he thought someone was mocking him, but he realized that it was two people laughing together and that they probably did not know he was anywhere near.

Stealthily he crept forward, keeping to the shadows, until he could see the meadow at the edge of the forest. Two hunters stood in the knee-high grass, engaged in soft conversation, their heads close together. Michael and Sky Dancer.

Coral Snake's face clouded with disgust. Just his luck, to come across these two.

Just his luck . . .

A smile twisted his lips. They did not know he was here. They were so enamored of each other's company, they would not notice if Tala himself swooped down from the sky. Such fools! So ripe for the taking. But what game should he play with them? How to humiliate them, to show the rest of the People that they were not god-children?

Coral Snake touched the length of rope which he had knotted around his waist. He had thought he might need it to lash together a travois for bringing back a large kill. But there was something else he could do with the rope. Something which would give him far more pleasure than bringing a slain animal back to the village.

The ground sloped steeply downward, and Coconino braced his wife's descent by holding her arm tightly, hurrying her through the trackless high desert. Not much longer and they would reach the shallow beginnings of the river canyon that hid the Northern Village.

As they had followed the traders' path away from the lakes, Coconino had thought more than once that he should leave the trail, but that would slow them down, and what if Lujan simply followed the path up to the village? Then Hummingbird would be in danger, and many others as well. No, the best thing was for them to go as quickly as they could and give the warning. Then the men of the People could be prepared.

The men of the People. *I am a man of the People,* Coconino raged at himself. *What am I doing, running back to the village to let others deal with my enemy? What will I tell them? "This is a* bad man; see that he doesn't hurt you''? What if he carries one of the fireshooters? Who will stop his wanton destruction?

I will, Coconino decided. I will stop him here, today. I will put an end to this threat to the People, as I put an end to the Sky Ship, by killing it. I should welcome this challenge. It is a good day to die.

But it is not a good day for my wife to die, he thought. No, nor my son, nor our unborn child. My own life I will give, for how better should I spend it? But I will not surrender another life that I love to that monster—

Suddenly Coconino stopped dead in his tracks.

Do I *love* Ironwood Blossom?

Looking into her frightened, trusting face, he felt his heart swell with emotion. It is not the kind of love I dreamed of as a young man, he thought. It is not the kind of love I felt for Phoenix—I will never love another in that way! But in a different way, a quieter way, I have come to care about this woman. She has lifted me up and cut me down; she has made me both proud and ashamed of myself; she has shared her wisdom with me whether I wanted it or not. Were I to lose her to Lujan, to *anyone* . . .

"What is it?" Ironwood Blossom asked anxiously, looking up into his face with earnest eyes. "Why do you stop?"

He looked down at her, a woman with broad shoulders and a forehead that was too high and a heart that was greater than the whole of the Black Lands in which they lived—

A gust of wind out of the north caught him, chilled him. "It is nothing," he lied. "Come, we will reach the canyon soon. Just a little farther."

Coward! he cursed himself. You should have told her.

A gust of wind from the north blew the front door out of Susan Winthrop's hand. She knew it was blowing dirt into her clean house as well and she ought to shut it, but she stood there in the doorway, looking anxiously toward the stable.

Just then Chelsea bolted out of that building, leaving its door standing open behind her. She's scared, too, Susan thought. She's scared for all of us, but mostly she's scared for Zachery.

Chelsea flew past her at a dead run, into the kitchen, to where the antiquated wall screen glimmered with the light of an incoming transmission. Susan thought about going down to the stable to close the door, but she decided Ari would remember. He was a good boy. She settled for closing the front door and following her sister-in-law into the kitchen. No telling what Chelsea would drop or throw or break when she was in this state. But considering the circumstances, Susan promised herself that this time she wouldn't scold.

"Zachery!" Chelsea cried, both relieved and terrified to see his image. "Where are you? I've been trying to reach you for days!"

"My office," he replied, and it seemed to her the delay was longer than it should have been; someone was monitoring the transmissions. That didn't surprise her. Three days earlier the Troaxians had just warped into Darius IV with no pretext of it being a corporate takeover. It was a military maneuver, pure and simple; the corporate war was suddenly hot, and one of Argo's chief allies was under enemy military control. "Chels, I've got a court date tomorrow. Pulled every string I knew, called in every marker—"

"Zachery, listen to me," she interrupted, only marginally aware that Susan was watching her. *"Get the hell off Argo!"*

There was a slight delay, then a smile played across his lips. "Can't," he replied. "It took us nearly three years to get this hearing. I can't let a little war stop us now."

"Zachery, I don't want to find your mother alive only to tell her you're dead!" Chelsea barked. "Get your ass off that planet and back here to Juno! We may not be immune, but we're a damn sight safer than the capital city of the Centrallies!"

Again the smile, but now she saw how bittersweet it was, and his eyes were, oh, so sorrowful. "Can't," he repeated. "Don't you think every good citizen of this murky world is trying to get offplanet right now? You can't get travel permits for love or money. Well," he amended, "maybe money. But I haven't got any of that left."

"Zachery!"

"It's my own fault," he went on quickly, knowing her protest before it could even be warped to him. "I've been liquidating for eight months in anticipation of the war, but I made the mistake of banking it on Darius IV. I thought that would be safer. How's that for irony?"

"Draw on Terra Firma accounts," she snapped at him. "I'll authorize it. Get passage off that planet!"

"Two more days and I can draw on Oswald Dillon's accounts," he told her. "They can't deny us, Chels. Why do you think they stalled us for nearly three years? But they've run out of time. By noon tomorrow I won't need to buy a warp ticket. I'll buy my own spaceship. Shall I come by and take you for a ride?"

"It's not funny, Zach!" Tears were streaming down Chelsea's cheeks, but she hardly noticed. These last three days when she had been unable to reach Zachery, she had been beside herself with anxiety. Nineteen years of research, nineteen years pursuing the dream of finding her mother, were suddenly meaningless if she lost Zachery now. "Don't wait, don't wait for anything. Get out of there! Get out of there now."

But still he smiled at her, and had she been less distraught, she would have noticed the tears brimming in his eyes as well. For a moment she thought the connection was frozen, because he didn't respond, but then he lifted his chin, and she realized it was just that the delay in the signal had been longer than usual. "I'll be there soon," he promised. "The Troaxians aren't likely to warp in here tomorrow. It will take them a few days to digest Darius IV before they belch and look around for dessert. I'll be long gone before they—"

Suddenly the screen went blank. *"Zachery!"* Chelsea screamed. "Mazie: get him back! Get the connection back!" But there was nothing the computer could do. In a moment a printed message appeared: INTERGLOBAL COMMUNICATIONS HAVE BEEN TERMINATED. PLEASE ACCESS YOUR LOCAL NEWSNET FOR MORE INFORMATION.

Chelsea felt as though her oxygen had been cut off. She stood gasping, unable to breathe until Susan, alarmed, hurried over and put an arm around her sister-in-law's shoulders. But Chelsea didn't feel it, only the panic, the choking terror inside. Finally she sucked in one huge, wheezing breath that rushed right back out as a shriek. Sobbing, she crumpled to the floor.

Beware, Coconino! the raven cawed. He's coming, Coconino, whispered the pines. Hurryaway, hurryaway! clattered the tiny feet of scurrying lizards.

The cave seemed to leap out at him from the dappled shadows of the ledge into which it was carved. It was only a shallow depression in the rock, but it was deep enough for his purposes. "Quickly!" he told Ironwood Blossom. "Crawl inside." She obeyed without question as he slipped Juan's carrying pack from his back and handed it in to her. "Stay quiet. I will cover the opening with shrubs."

Ironwood Blossom clutched at his wrist as he started away. "Stay with us," she pleaded.

"No, my wife," he replied firmly. "I must turn back and find him before he finds us. It was a mistake to let him follow this far.

You were wise when you said that no man outlives a puma by turning his back on it.''

Tears brimmed in her eyes, but she said no more, only folded her child in her arms and made herself as small as possible.

Coconino drew his knife and quickly sawed off some manzanita and desert broom at their roots to lay across the opening to the cave. There was no wind, at least; the shrubs would stay and look as though they had grown there. In a crevice near the cave some dried leaves and other deadfall had collected; he scraped up some of them and strewed them at the base of the shrubs to look as though this bed of vegetation were as old as those around it. Then he cut one last branch of desert broom and dusted their footprints and other markings from the area.

''My husband,'' came Ironwood Blossom's voice from the concealed cave.

He stopped in the middle of his frantic activity. ''Yes, my wife?''

''You will defeat him, this evil one who pursues you.''

Would that I knew that! he thought. But the Mother Earth has made no such promise to me, and I no longer know how to ask for one. Only this do I ask of the Mother Earth: that She protect my family, both here and in the village.

''Will She do that for me?'' he asked a banded lizard that sat upon a nearby rock.

Coconino whisked a thin layer of dust into the crevice to camouflage the place where he had scooped out deadfall; then he hurried back the way he had come, dragging the branch of desert broom behind him to erase his steps.

He did not see the many bones that lay scattered among the junipers and agaves on that rocky, unprotected shelf.

From the shade of a velvet mesquite Lujan watched calmly as Coconino dusted his trail. He smiled and scratched gently at the itchy scar tissue on his cheek. Oh, you are good, Coconino, he had to admit. If I hadn't caught sight of you an hour back and been watching you ever since, I would never have found them there.

But there they were, and there was Coconino trotting quickly down the trail, bow in hand. A hundred yards or so from the cave the primitive cut to one side, leapt a small wash, and tossed the shrubby branch aside. Then he broke into a run and headed back in the direction he had come, but parallel to the trail. Hoping to circle behind me, Lujan realized. Hoping to get the drop on me. But you are too late, Coconino, as you will come to find out. Yes, you will come to find out.

Lujan leaned into the tree's gnarly trunk, shifting slightly to keep it always between himself and the young primitive until Coconino disappeared into the scrubby vegetation. Then he dropped to one knee and opened his heavy pack.

One by one he laid his glittering assortment of weapons on the ground. Which to use, which to use? The thin, two-foot blade that was used for butchering animals? The broad-bladed machete? The garrote with wire so thin that it would cut through flesh as if it were pudding? Hooks? Prods? The surgical laser?

The butchering knife, he decided at last. The long, sleek blade appealed to him. A dagger he tucked into his waistband, and a bola he draped over one shoulder. In case. Just in case.

Then he left the pack behind and started toward the cave.

CHAPTER TWENTY-FIVE

Michael held his breath as he raised the polished throwing club slowly over his head. The hare was motionless except for the twitching of his nose, thinking he was safe in his tawny camouflage. Then, with the deadly eye of a racquets player, Michael hurled the club and struck the feckless creature cleanly on the head.

"Another!" he cried in triumph, holding the dead hare up by its oversized ears for Sky Dancer to see. "That's two for me. Where is yours?" he teased, his eyes sparkling wickedly.

"Stealing your buck's doe, most likely," Sky Dancer grumbled. She'd had only one opportunity for a kill, and even then the distance had bordered on being beyond her. Her dexterity was a match for Michael's, but not her strength; the club might have bruised the hare, but the creature had bounded away to the safety of its warren. "Now keep quiet or he will not venture out again."

With that, Sky Dancer dropped into a crouched position some two yards from the hole where her quarry had vanished and began to wait.

Michael watched her for a moment, marveling at her patience. All the People had such great patience; even children would sit by an animal's hole for hours with a snare set, waiting for the burrow's inhabitant to poke its head out. Michael could not bear it; he much preferred stalking through the meadow, seeing what would break and run. Keeping his eye on the darting prey was like keeping his eye on the ball in a game of racquets. Where would it go next? Which way would it twist?

I miss racquets, Michael thought. I miss the intensity of the game, the absorption that allows no other thoughts to intrude, where nothing exists but me and the ball and the racquet, which is merely an extension of my body—

A hare bolted from its hiding place in a desert spoon, and Michael's arm snapped back, but it was too late. The hare was out of range, and he held his throw. Pay attention, he scolded himself silently. Phoenix would not have missed a shot like that. Nor would my father.

It perplexed him, the relationship between his father and Phoenix. What had he seen in her? To Michael's eyes she was hard and bad-tempered and unattractive. But she had been younger then. Perhaps before all the sorrow, all the responsibility of caring for the People, she had been different. There must have been something about her. After all, his grandfather had married her.

And divorced her.

He'd asked his uncle Flint about it. "Did my father love She Who Saves as much as she loved him?"

Flint had stroked his chin and pondered on that. "I was not privy to my brother's thoughts," he cautioned, "but yes, I believe he did. They were always together. The bird stone that she wears around her neck, that was his, a thing he prized dearly, but he gave it to her. That is not something he would do lightly. He called her his sister-brother, but I do not think he truly thought of her as a sister. I think, rather, that he could not find words to express adequately the closeness of their souls."

The closeness of their souls. Who on the Mountain would ever say such a thing? No one. The People had a way of speaking that stirred Michael, conveying concepts that had never occurred to him before. The closeness of their souls . . . Will I ever feel such a thing? he wondered. Someone whose very essence touches me so deeply—

An eerie trumpeting startled Michael from his reverie. He lurched around to see where it had come from, but nothing moved in the meadow or the forest beyond.

Nearby, Sky Dancer jerked upright at the noise, her face a picture of shock. "What is it?" Michael asked. "Is that an antelope? An elk, maybe?"

Sky Dancer only shook her head impatiently and gestured him to be silent. Eyes and ears strained for the source of the sound.

It came again, from the forest, followed by the sound of branches rustling. Recognition blazed in Sky Dancer's face. "Tala!" she exclaimed. "It is Tala!"

She took off at a dead run across the meadow toward the sound. Michael raced to join her. "I thought Tala was dead," he called to her.

"He is," she replied. "But that is the sound he made. I heard it two—no, three times as a little girl. Nakha-a said that he had many wives, that he might have a son who would be like him—'' She broke off as the sound came again, deeper in the forest.

Could it be? she wondered as she flung herself around trees and over protruding roots. Could it be that there is a son of Tala, or a daughter, who trumpets in this way, who shoots lightning from a single horn? One, perhaps, who flies as Tala did? They say that Tala and my father had *moh-ohtay*, spirit speech, and knew one another's thoughts. Could this offspring hear me or Michael?

Urgently Sky Dancer sent forth her thoughts: Are you there, my brother? Can you hear me? Will you speak to me?

But nothing touched her mind—no curiosity, no fear, no presence that she could detect at all.

Then Sky Dancer remembered that Tala had always shown disdain for her foster mother, that his bonding had only been with Coconino. Perhaps he would choose only one of Coconino's sons. Perhaps it was Nakha-a he sought—had he not come at Nakha-a's birth? Or perhaps . . . "Call to him!" she urged Michael. "Call to him with your mind, as our father did. Perhaps he will listen to you.''

Following behind his fleet sister, Michael was hard pressed to avoid all the tangles and branches that she seemed to glide around and through, but he was determined not to lag behind. Tala! He could hardly believe it. He had heard the stories of the giant antelope, what his grandfather had speculated was a *Celux nobilis* from the planet Searg, though no one could explain how one might have survived on Earth. Was it possible that such a creature was in the forest ahead of them?

Michael had no idea what Sky Dancer had meant when she had told him to call out to Tala with his mind, but he tried to probe the foliage ahead. Was that a flash of movement? A rippling of sunlight through the green canopy? Was it only the breeze that stirred that branch? How big would the creature be? Would he allow them to approach him? Could Michael truly ride upon his back, as they said his father rode upon the back of winged Tala?

The trumpeting sounded again, to their right. They were close now, very close; Michael could hear the crunching of twigs under heavy feet. Just ahead, just beyond that oak—

Suddenly, Michael's feet went out from under him and he found himself dangling upside down in midair.

Phoenix slowed her steps as she neared Michael's house. Swan knelt on the path just outside the door, grinding corn into a fine meal in the *metate*. She looked up as Phoenix approached. "Good morning, She Who Saves."

"Good morning, Swan." She was a child, just a child—could it really be that Castle Rock had been that age when Phoenix had first come to the People? But Swan was so innocent, and Castle Rock had always been so sly and coy, hadn't she?

"Do you want something to eat?" the girl asked politely.

"No, thank you," Phoenix refused. Coconino's grandchild is growing inside this child, she thought. When Sky Dancer was pregnant, it was *my* grandchild—oh, how different that was! *My* child. *My* grandchild. Karen Reichert can never change that, not anymore. She gave up her claim at birth.

"Is Sky Dancer here?" Phoenix asked.

"She and Michael went hunting," Swan replied.

Hunting. Alone together. A shiver ran through Phoenix. "Do you know where they went?"

Swan shrugged. "They had their throwing clubs, and they went down the east side of the island, not the riverside."

Phoenix gnawed at her lip unconsciously. A peculiar sensation welled up in her, a feeling of unease that seemed to rise from the ground and spread through her chest and head, making her face burn. "How long ago did they leave?"

"It was still early morning," Swan told her. Then she studied the Witch Woman's brooding face. "They will be back soon, I'm sure."

"Oh?" Phoenix was curious. "What makes you say that?" Like her father, Sky Dancer was given to spending most of the day away from the village, hunting.

Swan made a face. "Because I saw Coral Snake going off after them," she confided. "He is sure to spoil their hunting; he always does. Why is he so mean to Michael, She Who Saves?"

Bad seed, Phoenix wanted to say. A weasel for a mother and a snake for a father. But suddenly Nina's words came back to her: "He is only a child; his path is not yet chosen." I knew better, she thought bitterly. I could have told them he would turn out like this. I *did* tell them . . . and I told him. . . .

The hair rose on Phoenix's neck. "To the east, you say? I will head out that way. Perhaps I will meet them coming back."

Coconino's eyes darted back and forth across the horizon as he ran, searching for some sign of his approaching enemy. He had come only half a mile; it was too soon to cut back to the trail. If he could get behind Lujan, see how the man was armed, see whether he carried a fireshooter. . . .

The trees were thick here, dark green junipers and pines, tall oaks with their leaves turning to gold and littering the ground. If he was quiet and careful, he could easily get past Lujan. How much better to meet him here than in an open place—

—an open place!

Panic seized Coconino. He had left Ironwood Blossom and Juan on a stony tract of ground, one with no cover nearby. And Lujan was coming, and there was a lizard—

Suddenly Coconino darted back to the trail, the one he and Ironwood Blossom had dashed across only half an hour before. He searched the ground, found the leaves disturbed from their passing, found the print of his own bare foot in a damp spot, found—

Another print. Deep, as though the walker carried a load. Heavy at the toe, as though he trotted. Smooth, with a sharp outline—not the outline of a moccasin. The outline of a shoe.

His heart in his throat, Coconino raced back toward the cave.

Lujan stared at the clever tangle of weeds and shrubs that Coconino had woven to hide his family. Had he not watched the primitive at work, he would have passed it by without a single thought. Even knowing they were there, he might doubt it; not a sound came from the cave, not a whimper from the child, not a breath from the woman.

But they were there. He had seen her—drab and shabby by his standards, not much of a prize. That seemed to be the nature of these primitive women, though: they were all stocky and sturdy, built to work hard and bear children. Lujan remembered his visit to Coconino's village two centuries before, remembered the feast they had put on for him, remembered the dancing, remembered one young girl. . . .

She was not so drab, he thought. She was young and well formed, nicely rounded with smooth skin and glistening black hair. She had come to him in the moonlight, speaking no word of his language but making clear her offer to him.

Lujan clenched his fists and growled in fury. No more tender young maidens for him. No more sweet manipulation of the fairer sex, no more bending them to his will. He had been robbed of that, robbed of his sport, robbed of his pleasure, robbed of his way of life. Coconino had done this to him, sent him to this foreign place, stranded him among people who hated him, people who robbed him.

And behind those shrubs sat Coconino's wife, his pleasure, his sport, and with her was a child who had Coconino's eyes. . . . I will steal from you, Coconino, as you have stolen from me. But not quickly, no—I will make you an agony of their deaths, as you have made an agony of my life. Then, when you have come and seen the horror, when you have seen the bodies as mangled as mine was after the mountain lion jumped me, then will come your turn.

I will rob you, Coconino, as I have been robbed, and leave you to walk among your kind in shame and despair. They will say, There goes Coconino, who is a horror to look upon. There goes Coconino.

Coral Snake's laughter rang loud and mockingly through the forest as Michael twisted and flailed at the end of the rope. He had been snared as neatly as any rabbit, one foot caught painfully in the heavy cord, his head smarting from where it had struck the ground as the trap hoisted him up toward an overhanging branch.

Sky Dancer stopped her headlong dash when she heard the commotion of the trap being sprung behind her. Immediately she ran to him, surprised and confused, but Coral Snake's laughter distracted her temporarily from her brother's plight. The insolent young man lounged against the trunk of the tree whose branch served as pulley to the rope, his blue eyes glinting in the dappled light of the forest. Sky Dancer gritted her teeth, wondering briefly if he had killed the unicorn; then Coral Snake cupped his hands to his mouth and made the trumpeting sound again.

"You!" she said, furious at having been fooled.

"What great hunters you are," he laughed, mockery in every word. "How silently you stole through the forest, how carefully you walked—it would make your father proud."

Michael groaned, and Sky Dancer turned her back contemptuously on their tormentor. The branch was only ten or twelve feet off the ground, and Michael's head bobbed just above her knees. "Are you hurt?" she asked anxiously.

"I hit the ground pretty hard," he said, gasping. "It's—knocked the wind out of me. And my leg hurts, but I—I don't think it's serious." It seemed to require all his energy and concentration just to breathe. "Can you cut me down?"

Sky Dancer drew her knife and stretched upward, but she could not even reach as high as Michael's ankle. Looking around, she saw that the other end of the rope was tied off to the stub of a branch near Coral Snake. She nailed the bully with a look and marched resolutely toward the taut rope.

Coral Snake stepped in front of her. For a moment they locked gazes, he sneering down from his great height, she glaring up at him in contempt. "Your game has gone far enough, Coral Snake," she told him. "Let me pass."

But as she made to go around him, Coral Snake seized her roughly by the arm. "You give orders very well," he said coldly. "Why don't you try asking politely for a change?"

Sky Dancer tried to shake off his hand, but his grip was tight. "Why should I be polite to someone as rude as you?" she demanded.

A sour smile twisted his lips. "Perhaps because it is in my power to deny you what you want."

The hair at the back of Sky Dancer's neck prickled as she realized just how strong the grip was that held her. She put on a more patient and rational tone and addressed him again. "Coral Snake, we are not children anymore. What you have done is childish. Help me get my brother down and we will say no more about this." As she spoke, however, she shifted her knife carefully in her free hand.

But even that slight movement caught the skilled hunter's attention. With lightning swiftness he snatched her wrist and twisted until she gasped in pain and dropped the knife. "Would you use violence against me?" he hissed, his eyes dangerous now.

"You have used it on my brother," she gritted back.

Behind them, Michael saw the turn this confrontation was taking. With a mighty heave he swung himself toward Coral Snake, but the bully only laughed and danced back out of the way, dragging Sky Dancer with him. "Ho-ho, he twists like a worm!" Coral Snake cackled in cruel delight. "Twist away, worm. Let us see if you are man enough to free yourself without depending on a woman."

"Bastard!" Michael snarled in English, and he bent his body upward, trying to catch hold of the rope that bound him. But he was still winded from the blow and could not manage it.

"Let us sit here, Sky Dancer," Coral Snake suggested, forcing her down by the trunk of the tree. "We will watch your brother dance like a spider on its thread."

"I will not willingly sit with you here or any other place!" Sky Dancer growled, trying to twist free. "Cut him down, Coral Snake!"

"You don't want to sit?" he taunted. "Then why don't we lie together? You and I, Sky Dancer. Shall we lie together here in the forest?"

Panic welled up in Sky Dancer as she felt herself being forced
backward, felt Coral Snake's weight crushing down on her, pinning her. Surely he did not mean to—no, no, not even Coral Snake
would do anything so despicable. It was unthinkable.

Wasn't it?

Ironwood Blossom shrank back in the cave, shielding Juan behind her body. Knife in hand, she waited as the madman tore away
the flimsy shelter of her blind and stood panting before her. His
face was a horror, a twisted and scarred thing that would live in
the effigies of evil kachinas for generations to come. This was not
the sly and sensuous snake that Coconino had spoken of, one who
dazzled with the beauty of his eye and the eloquence of his words.
No, this was the bear of which the southern People had spoken, a
monster whose strength and ferocity were out of proportion to
anything she had encountered before.

Lujan wavered a moment, swaying back and forth, shaking his
shaggy head and making strange animal grunts. In his right hand
was the longest knife Ironwood Blossom had ever seen. Its blade
was longer than her forearm and it glinted as the sun hit its shiny,
metallic surface. Her own knife was of bone, good for cutting a
squash or scraping a hide, and its blade was not a palm's length.

If I die and I fall across the child, she found herself thinking,
perhaps he will not even see Juan. There is a madness upon him;
Mother Earth, let it blind his eye to the boy, at least long enough
for Coconino to return. Make his feet swift, Mother Earth! Let
Coconino fly like the raven and arrive in time, at least, to save his
son . . .

Suddenly Lujan was distracted by a blur of movement at his
feet. He lurched back, knife in hand, and stared down at the thing
that had darted between him and the woman.

It was a banded lizard, no more than twelve inches from snub
nose to tip of tail. Now it sat stock still, head raised, eyes unblinking, as though its beaded skin were armor and by its very presence
it would stop his advance.

With a snarl of contempt Lujan raised his knife and hacked the
lizard in two.

Phoenix slipped quickly behind the broad trunk of an ancient
Douglas fir. It had not been hard to track Michael and Sky Dancer;
they were out for rabbits and were unconcerned about leaving a
trail to the meadow. From there their headlong rush through the
forest had been even easier to follow. The sound of Coral Snake's

voice had caused Phoenix to grow cautious as she approached; she stole up on the trio and peered carefully through the foliage.

What she saw shocked her. Michael dangling upside down, trying desperately to reach up and free himself, and Coral Snake bearing Sky Dancer down to the spongy forest floor. Trembling slightly she drew an arrow from her quiver, fitted it to the string of her bow, and crept silently forward.

"This game of yours is not funny, Coral Snake!" Sky Dancer cried out. Her voice was edged with fear, something Phoenix had not heard in a long time. "No one will laugh at it, not even your friends."

"Game? This is no game," Coral Snake answered with deadly sincerity. Up till now it had been, but as Sky Dancer struggled beneath him, a fierce lust rose up in Coral Snake. She had always been so proud, so haughty—even now there was a wildness to her spirit like the wildness of the Great Antelope. Yet he had power over her. Try as she might, she could not stop him from doing what he pleased.

"It is a poor wife my mother found for me," he went on bitterly, his anger and his lust feeding each other. "She bears no children to carry my seed among the People. But I will have that legacy. I will get a child on you, proud daughter of Coconino, what do you think of that? Not as my father did to my mother, though, in secret. The whole village shall know who planted in your field."

"You touch her, you die!" Michael shouted, struggling in vain to reach the rope that bound him.

Coral Snake looked back at his captive and laughed. "And who is it will kill me, you? Your blood is too thin for such a thing. I am a hunter, though, accustomed to killing. Perhaps when I have done with your sister, I will think of something to do to you."

Phoenix drew back on her bowstring and took careful aim. Mother Earth, guide my aim, she prayed. He is pressed so close against Sky Dancer that the slightest slip . . .

Abruptly Sky Dancer stopped struggling. "You will not harm me," she said with sudden conviction. "You *cannot* harm me. The Mother Earth won't let you."

"The Mother Earth!" Coral Snake hooted. "The Mother Earth! What does the Mother Earth care whether I harm you or not? She has never taken an interest in my doings before."

"She will not let you harm me," Sky Dancer repeated stubbornly.

It only made him angrier. "And how do you know?" he snarled. "Did She speak to you? I tell you, Sky Dancer, She has wasted

Her breath, for if She wanted to stop me She must speak to *me*—
and that She has never done.''

Behind the fir tree Phoenix flinched, and eased off the tension
on her bowstring.

''She speaks to you,'' Sky Dancer assured him. ''Only you do
not know it is Her.''

Coral Snake did not notice that Michael had ceased struggling
to free himself. Instead he had drawn his bone-handled knife from
its sheath and was trying to stop the helpless twisting of his suspended body so he could take aim. Sky Dancer saw him from the
corner of her eye and knew what she had to do. ''Do not do this
thing,'' she urged Coral Snake sincerely, keeping his attention.
''It is not right that one of the People should do this evil thing to
another.''

''But I am not of the People,'' he replied grimly. ''Remember?
I am the son of the evil one, of Derek Lujan, the Other. Have I
not been told this often enough? Your own mother has proclaimed
it most loudly.''

Phoenix caught her breath.

''But the Mother Earth rules you nonetheless,'' Sky Dancer
insisted. ''And if you will not stop yourself from this evil, then
She will choose another instrument. Look up there!''

At her shout Coral Snake jerked his head upward to the trees
overhead. Michael saw his opportunity and threw the knife; but
he was weak and disoriented from dangling for so long, and the
blade went cleanly past Coral Snake to bounce off the tree trunk
behind them.

A murderous rage filled Coral Snake and he turned hate-filled
eyes on Michael. Pinning Sky Dancer with one powerful arm, he
drew his own knife and twisted in the direction of the helpless
young man. ''No!'' Sky Dancer screamed, renewing her struggles
and trying to keep Coral Snake off balance so that he could not
throw the blade. ''No! No, don't hurt him! Coral Snake, don't hurt
him—''

The shaft came whistling from the shadows as Coral Snake
raised his right arm to throw the knife. Its flint point tore through
the muscles of his shoulder before he could release his weapon;
he screamed in pain and let the blade drop. Sky Dancer twisted
free of his weakened grip and ran to Michael, shielding his unprotected body with her own.

But Coral Snake was no longer a threat. Phoenix advanced from
her hiding place in the trees, another arrow nocked and ready.
''Mother!'' Sky Dancer cried in relief.

Clutching his wound, Coral Snake looked up at the tall woman. He expected anger, scorn, or even triumph; what he saw was a face as ashen and grieved as his own.

"*Aiie*, Coral Snake," she whispered hoarsely. "Today you and I have both heard the voice of the Mother Earth. For you it was in the pain of my arrow, bidding you stop this wickedness. For me— it was in the truth of your words. And believe me, Coral Snake, I have been struck as deeply as you."

Coconino bolted down the path, bow in hand, arrow nocked. He saw Lujan in front of the cave, saw the bloodstained knife in his hand. With a howl of rage Coconino loosed his shaft at the villain, at the evil kachina that swayed and weaved like a snake raised on its coils.

But Lujan turned at the sound and saw his enemy attack. He dropped to the ground, and the arrow, shot from too great a distance, whizzed harmlessly over him.

Coconino charged toward the downed man, drawing another arrow from his quiver as he ran. But Lujan rolled to his feet and snatched up a strange-looking device from his shoulder. It seemed to be made of rope with rocks tied at both ends. Lujan began to swing one weighted end of it over his head.

"Coconino!" Ironwood Blossom called out.

Alive! She was alive. But there was blood on the knife— Coconino stopped short and drew back his bowstring, sending another deadly shaft flying toward the madman.

But Lujan launched his weapon as well. He had practiced long hours with the bola, and his aim was true. Even as he dived to the side to avoid the second arrow, the bola wrapped itself around Coconino's bow, hopelessly fouling the weapon.

Coconino did not stop to wonder what the strange thing was or how it had thwarted him. Seeing that his bow was useless, he cast it aside and launched himself at Lujan.

Lujan met his charge like an enraged bull elk, and the two crashed to the ground in a prickly, dusty bed of dried thistles. They thrashed and tore at each other, each trying to use sheer strength to gain an advantage over the other.

Once before Coconino had beaten Lujan in a wrestling match, pinning the slick first officer to the deck of his own ship. But circumstances had changed. Though he still lacked skill, Lujan possessed a madman's strength, and Coconino had not taken time to unencumber himself. His quiver snagged in the dried brush; it jabbed him in the back and ribs. Breathless from his frantic run, Coconino found he could not throw off his adversary.

Glee shone in Lujan's single eye as his hands fastened around Coconino's throat. Now he had him, this arrogant, swaggering primitive who had destroyed his life. He had intended to kill the woman and child first, but no matter. This was too sweet for him to even care that the plan had gone awry somewhere. What could be better than this, to take Coconino's life with his bare hands? It was justice, it was nirvana, to slowly squeeze the life out of him. Just a quick pressure of his thumbs would crush the larynx; that would have satisfied the old Derek Lujan. But it was not enough for this new one. He wanted to savor this moment, draw out Coconino's helplessness, revel in the power he had over his enemy.

Coconino felt his air being cut off and knew that he must do something quickly or all would be lost. *It is a good day to die,* he thought, *but only if I can take this monster with me. Only if I can rid the People of him forever.*

But Lujan's grip on Coconino's neck was unbreakable. Coconino's legs were pinned, his left arm growing numb as Lujan leaned on it, cutting off the circulation. Only his right hand was free, and he could reach neither his knife in its sheath nor an arrow from his quiver. Desperately Coconino groped around on the ground beside him for a rock, a stick, anything with which to strike his enemy. Mother Earth, send me help, he prayed. Send Climbing Hawk, send Tree Toad, send Phoenix, send someone—

Suddenly his hand touched something long and cylindrical. It was not rough like a stick and it seemed much harder than wood. It had the feel of bone, except that its surface was rippled and uneven.

Recognition flashed through Coconino's brain. In his dream there had been bones, old bones, the bones of his companions. Here now was the one relic from the one companion who, long after he had gone to his rest in the bosom of the Mother Earth, could still save Coconino. From the scattered debris that had once been a purposeful mound heaped over noble bones, from the dusty bed where it had lain unheeded for seven generations, Coconino caught up Tala's horn.

Darkness threatened to engulf him, but Coconino fought it back. The horn was firmly in his grasp now. To wield it as a club was risky; it might be fragile with age and break. But it was sharp. Mother Earth, it was still sharp. Twisting his arm around, Coconino managed to bring its point to bear, finding that spot on Lujan's side just below the rib cage where no bone would deflect it. Then, with a cry of rage and victory, Coconino thrust the horn upward, deep into Lujan's heart.

A hush fell over the village as the Council filed out of their chamber and called for Coral Snake. His mother brought him to them, trailed by his weeping wife. To everyone's surprise, the young woman had announced that morning that the Mother Earth had finally favored her—she was with child.

Coral Snake stood proudly before his elders, though he wavered a bit from the pain his wound still caused him. The healer had tended it well, however; there was no infection, and the muscles would soon grow back as strong as they had ever been. Phoenix was glad for that. Much of her contempt for the young man had been expunged.

Though she had sat with the Council as they had struggled with what to do about him, she had refused to suggest a punishment. "It was my daughter he tried to hurt," she had told them. "My daughter, and he whom I have treated as a son. My judgment would not be fair. But," she had added, "I will say that if Coral Snake is guilty of walking outside the Way of the People, perhaps he was pushed there. Perhaps I am one who helped push him."

Moon Without Shadows spoke for them now. "Coral Snake," she addressed him, "by your actions you have caused us great sorrow. From time to time, one or another of the People has walked outside the Way of the People; but you have erred too many times. In your treatment of your wife; in your attempt to force yourself on another woman; in your disrespect for the Mother Earth; and worst of all, in your unrepentant attitude. The Council makes no decision; you have made it yourself. You are not of the People."

Castle Rock gasped, and Phoenix felt sorry for her. Insolent and manipulative she might be, but she was of the People, and she was about to lose her firstborn son.

"Because your spirit is not of the People," Moon Without Shadows went on, "we will no longer tolerate you in our village. When your wound has healed, we will take you from here to the Camp of the Others. Their ways are different than ours; perhaps you will find your place among them."

A sob escaped Castle Rock and she began to tremble with weeping. But Coral Snake stood unflinching; in fact, his lips began to curl in the smallest of sneers.

Now Moon Without Shadows turned to the young man's wife. "This is most unfortunate for you," she said gently. "Were there no child in your womb, we would send you back to your mother's house, there to be wooed by a man of the People. But—''

"Send her back," Coral Snake barked. "I do not want this wretched woman or her child. I will go to the Others and find a woman there to bear me a child. I will learn to speak their language, and then do you know what I will do? I will go to the Mountain. I will go to the Mountain in search of a Witch Woman." His mouth twisted in a grim smile. "Is that not what Coconino did?"

Their looks of dismay gave him great satisfaction. "You do not punish me," he told the assemblage. "You free me. I am glad to go. I am a fool to have stayed this long."

For a long moment there was no sound but the call of the birds down in the canyon, the buzzing of insects nearby. To the People, their life as a community was everything. They could not conceive of being isolated from their village, from their way of life. To all but a few, Coral Snake's response was beyond comprehension.

To Phoenix it was not. Had she not cut herself off from her own community and adopted another? Perhaps Coral Snake could do the same. But like her, he could not change who he was or who she had helped make him. "At the new moon," she said quietly, almost sadly, "we will go to the Camp of the Others with goods to trade, and try to establish good will between us at last. I myself will give you into their keeping and ask them to deal fairly with you. But," she warned, "I will tell them why you are no longer welcome in this village. They will know the color of your stripes, Coral Snake."

"Yes, tell them," he replied with sarcasm. "Tell them I am not a field mouse who hides in a burrow, like the rest of you. Tell them I must be reckoned with. Tell them I am my father's son."

Coconino sat numbly, staring at the bones in the crevice: old bones, great bones. Tala, my friend, is it really you? And is she there with you, my Witch Woman? No, she went down to the Well. That is what the stories say.

Behind him there was a scuffling sound, then the whimpering of a frightened child. It was quickly hushed. Coconino did not look up.

After a moment Ironwood Blossom came and knelt nearby. He could feel her presence there, hers and the child's. Finally she spoke. "*Aiie*, what a face," she said softly.

He was so numb that it took Coconino several moments to realize she spoke of Lujan. His corpse lay with its ghastly face turned up, the single eye staring blankly at the brilliant blue sky. Once, Coconino remembered, this man's eyes had been as blue as that sky. Once he had been a striking man who strode with confidence into the Valley of the People, dazzling the maidens there. We should have granted him the Right of the Chosen Companion, Coconino thought. Though the path he followed was a crooked one, there was a greatness about him. The People could have been enriched by his seed. But I was too proud to see that then.

What happened to you, my enemy? he wondered, turning the ravaged face toward him. What happened to the shrewd mind, the cunning brilliance with which you beguiled your followers in the Times That Were? How were you robbed, that you became this thing? Truly your evil was monstrous, for the Mother Earth has wreaked great vengeance on you.

With an effort Coconino tugged Tala's horn out of the lifeless body. Blood trickled along the channel formed by its twining and dripped onto the dusty ground. Coconino did not attempt to cleanse the horn, but laid it gently in the crevice with the other bones.

The Mother had told him once that those whom the Mother Earth loved best, She chastised most severely. Perhaps that had been Lujan's greatest crime. Perhaps of him, too, had greatness been expected, so that his corruption was the all more vile. Perhaps that was why he had been broken in this way.

And perhaps, Coconino thought, it is my own reluctance to give of myself to the People of This Time that has made my life here seem so hard.

Again the quiet voice intruded on this thoughts. "What shall we do with him?"

Still dazed, Coconino lifted his eyes to look at his pragmatic wife. "Do?" he echoed.

"We cannot leave his body for the coyotes," she said. "He was a man, after all—though an evil one."

"Yes," Coconino agreed, gazing with sorrow on the mangled face. "Once, he was a man."

"We can put him in the cave," Ironwood Blossom suggested.

Coconino blinked. "Cave?"

"The cave, here, where I hid with the child," Ironwood Blossom elaborated. "We can put the body here, and block it in with stones."

"Yes." Coconino stirred himself and found that he was weak, exhausted. But Ironwood Blossom was already moving, taking Lujan's arms, trying to tug the corpse toward the shallow cave alone. So Coconino hauled himself to his feet and, with her assis-

tance, dragged Lujan the short distance to the cave. Then Ironwood Blossom began to gather stones.

Coconino found he could not move from the mouth of the cave.
He was beginning to feel the stinging of his many cuts and scrapes,
the bruises he had gotten on the stony ground. He struggled slowly
out of his quiver and cast it aside, not bothering to see if the
arrows in it had been damaged.

Nearby lay the carcass of a banded lizard, hacked cleanly in
two. Coconino considered it a moment, then picked it up and
placed it in the cave beside Lujan. Why the lizard was there he did
not know, but it must somehow have been involved in all this, and
he would not offend the Mother Earth by being careless with the
remains of one who had spoken to him with Her voice.

Ironwood Blossom soon returned with her first load of stones.
One by one Coconino picked them up and began to build the wall
that would hide Lujan from maurading animals. Dust from the low
ceiling drifted down to coat the corpse. "He lies now in the bosom
of the Mother Earth," Coconino said as Ironwood Blossom brought
yet more stones to him. "In the end, even the most recalcitrant of
Her children comes to Her."

Then together they sealed the mouth of the cave.

The flivver settled on the grassy landing field of Terra Firma,
and the whine of its engine faded into stillness. Chelsea stood
waiting for the hatch to open, her face composed, her peace made.
There would be no tears for what would never be, only plans for
what would, when the war was over.

When the war was over.

Finally the flivver door opened, and Zachery climbed wearily
out. My God, he's gotten so old, Chelsea thought. I've made an
old man of him with my crazy quest. No—time made an old man
of him. It would have happened anyway; it happens to us all.

Zachery looked at Chelsea and thought nothing had ever looked
so delicious to him in his whole life. She was windblown and sun-
browned, and her hair was streaked with gray, for she was no
longer vain enough to color it. Where has your vanity gone? he
wondered. With mine, with all the pretenses of status and style
and other conventions of the so-called civilized universe.

We are at war.

Chelsea walked forward to meet him, slid her arms gratefully
around his neck, and felt the warmth of his bearlike strength as he
wrapped his arms around her in return. We will keep each other
safe somehow, she thought, through this war and beyond. We will

keep each other, and Cin and Susan and the kids, and someday their kids . . .

"I brought you a present," he said.

"I know; I'm holding it."

He laughed. "Something else." Fishing inside his robe, he brought out a tiny statue of carved jade. "Twenty-first century. I think it's a Larson. Dillon kept it on his nightstand; I thought maybe you'd like it on yours."

Chelsea ran her thumb along its smooth surface, over the subtle facets of green. "The rest is waiting on Argo, I presume."

"Except for a nineteenth-century ring with a fire opal the size of my thumb," he told her, "which is riding in the pocket of the ship's captain."

"But he wouldn't sell his ship, eh?"

"No, he rather likes living," Zachery responded. "Captains who don't turn their ships over to the Centrallies for military use get blown out of the sky."

Chelsea slipped an arm around his waist, and they started back toward the ranch house, where Cin and Susan were waiting. "We had a hard time convincing Ari not to enlist," she told Zachery. "Boys are so gung ho when they're sixteen. But I think I have him talked into staying in school, at least until he's draft age. Maybe the war will be over by then."

"Maybe." Zachery wrapped his arm a little tighter around her shoulder. "What does he want to study?"

"Warp physics." She grinned a very genuine grin. "Cincinnati's so proud, he could bust. His son, a warp physicist. He wants Ari to develop a warp transmitter with pinpoint accuracy so we could just warp to—" Chelsea broke off.

"Earth," Zachery finished. "So we could just warp to Earth. Not a bad idea."

"We'll make it someday, Zach," she whispered. "Or our children will, or our children's children. Someday we'll get back there, and then we'll know. We'll know if we were right."

He glanced up at the sky and knew that out there, beyond the reach of Juno's atmosphere, a hundred battleships were orbiting, preparing to join the Centrallied fleet. And far, far beyond them a tiny blue-green planet spun on its axis, shrouded in clouds and mystery.

"Yes, someday," he agreed. "Someday she'll let us come home."

EPILOGUE

Chelsea and Zachery stood on the knoll behind the ranch house, looking back over the stables and kennels, the house and the yard. To the west the great prairie sprawled in all its grassy splendor, an endless tract of golden brown that rippled in the omnipresent wind. The sun was a ball of orange sinking into that golden sea, spreading its halo of pinks and ambers in the dark blue clouds.

"It's going to be a long war, isn't it?" Chelsea asked.

"Very long." Zachery stroked her hair, still as soft and thick and sensuous as the first time they had made love on this knoll. "And when it's over, there are going to be a lot of changes. Changes in the way things are done. Changes in the way things are owned. Our wealth may be very short-lived."

"But knowledge is ours to keep forever." She leaned her head back against his chest, savoring his touch, savoring his presence, thanking whatever gods might be involved that he had escaped Argo and returned to her. "I've started a history," she told him. "A record of what we've done for the past twenty years. Not just facts but—feelings. Why we wanted to do it. Who my parents were. What they stood for. I want you to tell me more about your mother so I can include her. I'm going to give it to Arizona and Verde someday. I want them to know what they're a part of."

He let his arms slide around her, thinking how warm and comfortable it was here, how satisfying to know that he needn't rush off again tomorrow or the day after. Even with a war raging around them, even knowing there would be precious little market for show dogs and prizewinning horses until it was over, even fearing that children like Arizona and Verde would be called up to serve as fodder for the insatiable appetite of greed and aggression—just knowing that these days would be spent with Chelsea was enough for his soul.

"Well," he suggested after a moment, "you could give it to *our* children, too."

She was quiet for a minute, then she turned her head slightly to look up at him. "That's a thought, isn't it."

It was on this very knoll that he had asked her the first time. What an intense young man he had been back then! So confident that once he decided on a thing, it would be so. Her refusal had frustrated him, shown him that the power of his will might move juries and judges and even mountains but would not move Chelsea Winthrop.

But here he was again, and he knew what he wanted for his life. This time, however, he knew with a sense of humility, with the intimate knowledge that there were some things he could never have. "Chelsea, marry me," he whispered.

She reached up and stroked his arm, cuddling her head closer against his chest. Below them Cincinnati's children burst out of the house, sixteen-year-old Ari on the run and thirteen-year-old Verde chasing after him with a menacing dish towel, trying her best to snap him in the same fashion he had undoubtedly just snapped her.

Arizona and Verde: exuberant, joyful, full of hope in the middle of a dismal universe. Chelsea looked back at them.

"There's just one critical matter we have to settle first," she told Zachery.

He chuckled. "Only one?"

"Only one worth talking about," she amended. "And that is: How do you feel about place names for children?"

Phoenix stood on the ledge outside her stone house and gazed across the canyon at the adobe ruins on the far wall. Someday, she thought, we will need those ruins for housing, too. Someday the People will be so many and so prosperous that we will spill off this island butte and wash up the other sides. Coconino's children would take them there: Michael and his children, Sky Dancer and hers. Perhaps even the child Coral Snake leaves behind will grow to be a leader of the People.

The fact of Coral Snake's apostasy had appalled the village, and his impending punishment hung on them like a palpable weight. While to most it was incomprehensible, to Phoenix, it was a frightening demonstration of how destructive her own feelings could be. After all, she was well acquainted with the pain of infertility and the frustration of a silent god.

In a community so small with each member so dependent on

each other, the failure of one was the failure of all. Each member of the village felt that in some way, he or she had contributed to Coral Snake's downfall. So, too, was his punishment their punishment. A life had been wrested from among them, the life of a provider, the life of one of the People. And Phoenix acknowledged her own guilt in the matter.

Yet standing here on the ledge, looking out across the canyon, she found that her guilt could not overwhelm her, as it might have in her younger days. In finding it possible to forgive Coral Snake, she found it possible to forgive herself as well. If she had played a part in the twisting of his psyche, so had Castle Rock, and his friends, and the many others of the village who either praised or scorned him. In the end, Coral Snake had made his own choices, as Michael growing up on the Mountain had made his.

Down the path she could hear Michael's voice, telling Sky Dancer a humorous story from his boyhood days on the Mountain. Swan laughed, too, but it was a naive sort of laugh because she didn't really understand the story. No wonder Michael prefers Sky Dancer's company, Phoenix thought. She is the only woman here who can appreciate the complexity of his spirit, the light and dark shadings of it. To her, he is an equal; to the others, he is a demigod with strange ways.

There was still that dynamic tension between them, the crackling magnetism she had felt at their first meeting. But Phoenix knew now that her interference would not be the sorrow or salvation of that relationship. Whatever did or did not happen between them was theirs to control, not hers. She could only promise to be here, without recriminations, if they needed her.

"They are your children, Coconino," she whispered to the emptiness. "Overall they have made wise choices. If they ask again to go search for Nakha-a, I will let them go. It is time, Coconino—I will let them go." And with them will go your legacy, the spirit and the essence of Coconino: wise, witty, proud, naive, and filled with passion for the People and the Mother Earth—

Was that a movement on the far canyon wall? Phoenix blinked hard and squinted at the shadowy ruins—but no, there was nothing there. My eyes are going, she thought, like the cartilage in my knees. Another five years, maybe ten, and I will want only to sit all day by the fire and let Sky Dancer provide for me.

Then I will dream of my youth as a Witch Woman, when I had the love of the finest of the People, when I walked by the side of Coconino . . .

* * *

Coconino stood before his adobe house on the canyon wall and looked back at the island butte. When he had returned to the Northern Village, he had rebuilt this dwelling with his own hands. Ironwood Blossom's second child had been born there, and her third and fourth and fifth and sixth . . . Hummingbird, too, had borne him more children, before the Mother Earth had called her to rest.

He had never returned to the Southern Village. Instead he took his place on the Council in the north, curbing his impatience, listening to the elders, admitting his mistakes as freely as his victories. With the help of his wives, he had even learned to laugh at himself.

It was his sons who had returned to the south—appropriate, he thought, since a child of his had founded that village. Juan had come back, in time, with a wife, but Howling Coyote had stayed. Soon White Fox would go, too—Coconino could see it in his eyes. He had only to talk one or two of his friends into coming along; it would be a great adventure for them.

But Coconino would stay in the north and counsel the People, and teach the young hunters, and watch his grandchildren increase in number. Each night he would hold at least one of them on his lap and watch their eyes grow round as he told them the stories of the People.

He could hear his daughter Snow now in the next house, singing to her youngest. ''Sleep, child, sleep in safety; no harm can touch you here. I will embrace you, as the Earth enfolds her own . . .'' He thought of his first child, whom he had laid to rest in the bosom of the Mother Earth more than eighteen years ago. How bitter he had thought the Earth's embrace that night! But she had cradled Ironwood Blossom and Juan when Lujan attacked, and had given into his hand the horn of his old friend Tala, which had saved them all. Even when he felt most alone, She had never abandoned him.

Suddenly something on the island across the way caught Coconino's eyes, and he strained to see what it was. Only a hawk, perched on a prickly pear that grew up near one of the many paths that circled the butte. You play tricks on me, Mother Earth, he accused Her gently as he touched the blue-green bird stone which he still wore around his neck.

For a moment I thought I saw Phoenix standing there . . .

About the Author

CATHERINE WELLS grew up in North Dakota, a product of her rural environment and the television generation. She obtained a Bachelor of Arts in Theater from Jamestown College (Jamestown, ND) and a Master of Library Sciences from the University of Arizona.

Ms. Wells currently resides in Tucson with her husband, two daughters, and a dalmation named Daisy. She is devoted to her church, her family, and U of A Wildcat basketball.

Ms. Wells's first novel was *The Earth Is All That Lasts*. *Children of the Earth* is her second novel.

DEL REY DISCOVERY

Experience the wonder
of discovery
with Del Rey's newest authors!

. . . Because something new is
always worth the risk!

TURN THE PAGE FOR
AN EXCERPT FROM
THE NEXT *DEL REY DISCOVERY:*

The Outskirter's Secret
by Rosemary Kirstein

On the evening before Rowan's departure from the Steerswomen's Archives, the air outside was sweetly cool, warm and faintly dusty in the northeast corner of the Greater Library. Three cushioned chairs stood close beside the snapping fireplace. Rowan sat in one, uneasily, on the edge, bending forward again and again to study one or another of the many charts that lay on a low table before her. In the second chair, Henra, the Prime of the Steerswomen, nestled comfortably: a small, elderly woman of graceful gestures and quiet self-assurance. Silver-brown hair fell in a loose braid down her breast, and she wore a heavy robe over her nightshift; she looked much like a grandmother prepared to remain all night by the bedside of a feverish child, an appearance contradicted by the cool, steady gaze of her long green eyes.

The third chair was empty. Bel sat on the stones of the hearth, cheerfully feeding the fire to a constant, unnecessarily high blaze. "Enjoy it while you can," she explained. In the Outskirts, open flame at night attracted dangerous creatures.

The charts loosely stacked on the table had been drawn by dozens of hands, and their ages spanned centuries. Each map showed a sweep of mountains to the left, a pair of rivers bracketing the center, and a huge body of water below all, labelled "Inland Sea." From chart to chart, across the years, scope and precision of depiction grew: the edge of the mountain range became delimited, the river Wulf slowly sprouted tributaries, Greyriver later did the same, and the Inland Sea began to fulfill its promise of a far shore by acquiring a north-pointing peninsula.

Each map also noted an area labelled "The Outskirts"; each showed it as a vague empty sweep; and each showed it in a different location. Set in order, the maps revealed the slow eastward shifting of the barbarian wildlands.

399

Bel regarded the charts with extreme skepticism. "I don't doubt that the women who drew the maps believed that that was where the Outskirts were. But did they actually go there? And were my people there? And a word like 'outskirts' might mean many things. Perhaps they just intended to say, 'This is the edge of what we know.' That would explain why it keeps moving."

"I don't think so. Look at this." Rowan had pulled one map from the bottom of the stack: a recent copy of an older copy of a now-lost chart from nearly a thousand years ago, purported to have been drawn by Sharon, the founder of the Steerswomen. On it, the Outskirts were improbably shown to begin halfway between the tiny fishing village of Wulfshaven and the mouth of Greyriver, where the city of Donner later grew.

Rowan indicated. "Greyriver, deep in what was then the Outskirts; Sharon knew that it was there. The term 'Outskirts' did not represent the limit of what she knew."

Bel puzzled. "How did she know it was there?"

"No one knows."

"Is it shown accurately?"

"Yes."

"She must have gone there."

"Perhaps. Most of her notes have been lost. Nevertheless, to Sharon, Greyriver was part of the Outskirts."

The Prime spoke. " 'Where the greengrass ends,' " she quoted. " 'the Outskirts begin.' Those were Sharon's words."

Bel made a deprecating sound. "Hyperbole," she said.

"What?" Henra was taken aback; Rowan was not, and she smiled over her chart. She had learned not to be surprised when the barbarian made use of sophisticated ideas.

"Hyperbole," Bel repeated. "Exaggeration. The greengrass doesn't just end. It runs out, eventually. Either your Sharon didn't know, or she wasn't talking like a steerswoman, because it's not an accurate description. Perhaps she was trying to be poetic."

Henra recovered her balance. "I see."

"Well." Rowan sighed and returned to her work, sifting through the charts before her, uselessly, helplessly. There was no more to be done; all was prepared, as well as could be, all packed and ready for the first leg of her journey. Nevertheless, she reviewed, and reviewed again.

Rowan was to leave first, and travel eastward cross-country to a small village on the far side of the distant Greyriver; Bel would go south to the nearby port city of Wulfshaven, there to attempt to maintain the illusion that Rowan was still at the Archives, and later to leave ostentatiously alone, by sea. The plan was designed to deflect from Rowan the passing attention of any wizards.

The wizards and the steerswomen had coexisted for long centuries; but the wizards, by blithely refusing to answer certain questions, had consistently incurred the steerswomen's ban. Their refusal had engendered in the steerswomen a deep-seated, slow-burning resentment that had grown across the years, eventually becoming as pervasive as it was ineffectual. The feeling was largely one-sided: for their part, the wizards tended simply to ignore the order entirely. But the previous spring Rowan herself had managed to attract their notice, and merely by doing what every steerswoman did: asking questions.

She had not known that her investigation into the source and nature of certain pretty blue gems, decorative but otherwise useless, would be of any interest to the wizards. But when she and Bel were first attacked on the road by night, then trapped in a burning building, then waylaid by a ruse obviously designed to divert the investigation, it became obvious that the wizards were indeed interested, and more than interested—they were concerned enough to take action, for the first time in nearly eight hundred years, against so seemingly harmless a person as a steerswoman.

In the course of what had followed, many of Rowan's questions about the jewels had been answered, although none completely. And the course of her investigations had gifted her with answers to questions unasked and unimagined.

The jewels were in fact magical, and were used by the wizards in certain spells involving the animation of inanimate objects; but what the spells were, and how they were activated, Rowan never learned.

The jewels' pattern of distribution across the Inner Lands, which had at first so puzzled her, was explained by a fact both simple and stunning: they had fallen from the sky. They were part of a Guidestar—not one of that pair that hung visible in the night sky, motionless points of light, familiar to every Inner Lander, but one of another pair, previously unknown, which hung over distant, possibly uninhabited lands, somewhere on the far side of the world. Why one had fallen remained a mystery.

That the wizards, jealous and mutually hostile, should abandon their differences to cooperate in the hunt for Rowan, seemed a fact as impossible as the falling of a Guidestar, until Rowan learned yet another secret: there was one single authority set over all wizards, one man.

She knew that his authority was absolute; the wizards had sought to capture or kill her without themselves knowing the justifications for the hunt.

She knew that they resented his control of them but were unable to deny his wishes.

She knew his name: Slado.

She knew nothing else about him, not his plans, or his powers, or his location, or the color of his eyes.

The belt that Bel wore was made of nine blue shards from the secret, fallen Guidestar. Her father had found the jewels deep in the Outskirts, at Dust Ridge, which the wizards called Tournier's Fault. It was the largest concentration of such jewels that Rowan had ever heard of. The description of the finding, and Rowan's own calculations on the mathematics of falling objects, led her to believe that at Dust Ridge she might find what remained of the body of the Guidestar. Knowing this, she had to go there.

A current chart in her hands, Rowan retraced the long lonely route across the breadth of the Inner Lands, to that little village past Greyriver, where she and Bel would meet again to enter the Outskirts together. It was the one part of the journey of which she could be certain. Beyond that point . . .

She set the map down, took up the top chart from the sequenced stack, and studied it with vast dissatisfaction. It differed wildly from all the others.

Gone were the western mountains, the two rivers, the wide sea; this map showed a single river at the far left, running south, then curving southwest to the edge of the paper. Intermittent roads tracked the banks, occasionally branching east to end abruptly in small villages.

A tumble of low hills ambled vaguely across the southern edge of the paper; a second river with a few tributaries began seemingly from nowhere and ended without destination; a short stretch of shore marked "Inland Sea" made a brief incursion, then stopped, unfinished. In the low center of the chart, a jagged line trailing northeast to southwest bore the notation "Dust Ridge (Tournier's Fault)."

Despite its size, despite its scale, the rest of the map was empty.

Rowan glowered at it. It was drawn by her own hand.

She had reconstructed it from one she had seen as a prisoner in the fortress of the young wizards Shammer and Dhree. While their captive, Rowan had freely given all information requested, as befitted any steerswoman; since neither wizard had yet lied to or withheld information from a steerswoman, they were not under ban. Rowan herself had carefully avoided courting the ban, by never asking Shammer and Dhree any questions she suspected might be refused, and by this means the conversation had been able to continue for the best part of two days.

But in their eagerness to learn, the wizards had inadvertently revealed more than they suspected. The opportunity to see a wizard-made chart of this section of the Outskirts had constituted one such slip. Their map of those unknown lands had been astonishingly complete, and to a detail and skill of depiction unequalled by the best of steerswomen. But despite Rowan's sharp eye and well-trained memory, with no chance to copy immediately what she had seen these few unsatisfying details were all she could recall.

She knew her point of entry into the Outskirts; she knew her destination; she knew next to nothing between the two.

She caught Henra watching her. The Prime smiled.

"You must add to the chart as you travel. And bring it back to us, or find a way to send it."

"When I return, I'll come out through Alemeth . . ." Alemeth was far enough south to suggest a straight-line route west returning from Dust Ridge.

"Then send it from there. After Alemeth, I think you ought to go to Southport and do some work in that area."

This was new. "Southport?"

"No one is covering Janus's route." Janus, a steersman, had inexplicably resigned the order, refusing to explain or justify his choice; he was now under ban. "And," the Prime continued, "Southport has no resident wizard."

"In other words," Bel said with a grin, "when you're done with this, lay low for a while."

Rowan made a dissatisfied sound. "Keep out of sight. Hope the wizards forget about me."

And, for the moment, they seemed to have. How long that might last, no one knew.

According to Corvus, the wizard resident in Wulfshaven, the wizards had decided that Rowan's investigations must have been directed secretly by one of their own number. They were now involved in mutual spyings, schemings, and accusations, trying to discover the traitor, and had effectively dismissed Rowan as having been a mere pawn.

Rowan had herself disabused Corvus of the idea. He had neglected to pass the information on to his fellows.

What Slado might do when the truth was discovered was impossible to guess. He had motives of his own behind these events, Rowan was certain. He had some plan.

Rowan shook her head. "We don't know why Corvus is letting his fellows search for a nonexistent traitor." She found a mug of peppermint tea on the floor where she had abandoned it earlier, and took a sip. It was long cold. She studied green flecks of floating peppermint, then used one finger to push a large leaf aside. "He must gain something by it, some kind of advantage."

"What might that be?" Henra prompted.

Rowan made a face. "That's impossible to guess." Certainly, Corvus had been as interested as she to learn that a Guidestar had fallen, as surprised that Slado had not made the fact known among the other wizards. Perhaps Corvus planned an investigation of his own, which confusion among his fellows would somehow serve to aid. Nevertheless, for whatever reasons, the result was that, for the time being, Rowan was again free to investigate as she pleased . . .

Because Corvus wished it so.

Rowan found that she was on her feet, her chart, forgotten, sliding with a rustling hiss from her lap to the floor. Shadows from the flickering fire ranged up against the walls and across the long room, shuddering against the stone walls and the motley ranks of bookshelves.

She looked down at Bel, a backlit shape seated on the stones of the hearth, and made her answer to those dark puzzled eyes. Her voice was tight with anger. "I'm the advantage. Corvus is using me."

The Outskirter took in the information, considering with tilted head, then nodded. "Good."

"What?"

"If he's using you, then he'll want to help you. He'll want you to finish your mission."

"I don't want a wizard's help!"

"Too late. You've got it."

"If Slado is trying to keep the Guidestar secret from the wizards," Henra put in, "then Corvus can't move, can't investigate it himself without attracting attention. Perhaps he can learn something by seeing how Slado behaves amongst the wizards, but for outside information, for—" She spread her hands, making careful, delimiting gestures. "—for an understanding of the effects of these events . . ."

"He needs me."

"He needs you. You might be his only source. You might be the only one able to discover why the Guidestar fell."

"And find why Slado wants to keep it secret," Bel added. She leaned forward to retrieve Rowan's fallen map. "Corvus himself didn't know, until you told him." She regarded the chart thoughtfully, her eyes tracing undrawn lines of unknown routes across the blank face of the Outskirts.

But what help could Corvus provide, across those empty miles? And at what price?

"Gods below," Rowan said quietly. "He's made it true. I am a wizard's minion."

The Prime spoke quickly, leaning forward, emerald eyes bright in the gloom. "You're no one's minion, not even mine. What Corvus decides to do is his own choice. Your business is to learn. He's under ban, and you have no obligation to tell him anything."

To be a steerswoman, and to know, but not to tell . . .

As she stood in that wash of firelight, Rowan felt the long room behind her, felt it by knowledge, memory, and sensation of the motionless air. She faced the warmth of the hearth, and the far unheated corner of the room laid a cool, still hand on her shoulder.

High above, all around, the tall racks and unmatched shelves stood like uneven measurements, staggered lines across and up the walls. The books they held had no uniformity: fat and narrow, with pages of parchment or pulp or fine translucent paper that would stir in the merest breeze, between covers of leather, cloth, or wood. Each book was the days of a steerswoman's life, each shelf the years, each wall long centuries in the lives of human beings whose simple hope was to understand, and to speak. And Rowan knew, without turning to look, where lay that one shelf in the southeast corner that held her own logbooks: five years of her eyes seeing, of her voice asking, of her mind answering.

Her books stood to the left on the shelf. The right-hand end was empty. And more shelves waited.

"I will tell Corvus," Rowan said slowly. "Without his needing to ask." And she sat.

Her cold cup of tea was still in her hand, and Bel shifted the stack of charts to clear a place for it on the table. Rowan set it down and composed her thoughts.

"Whatever Slado is up to," she began, "it looks to be bad not only for the folk, but for the wizards as well, else he wouldn't need to keep it secret from them. For some reason, he can't let his plans become known—so the thing that we most need to do is to *make* them known, whatever part of them that we can see; known to

405

everyone, even the wizards." She looked at the Outskirter, then at the Prime, and spoke definitely. "It will make a difference."

The Prime was motionless but for her gaze, which dropped once to her hands in her lap, then returned to Rowan's face. "So the truth becomes a weapon."

Taken aback, Rowan paused for a long moment. "That's true." It seemed such an odd idea: innocent truth, a weapon. Then she nodded, slowly. "It's always been true. Truth is the only weapon the steerswoman have."

"Look." Bel was holding two maps, Rowan's unfinished one and the copy of Sharon's. The Outskirter laid them one atop the other and turned to raise the pair up with their backs to the fireplace. Yellow light glowed from behind, and the markings showed through, one set superimposed upon the other. The viewpoints suddenly struck Rowan as uncannily similar.

Fascinated, she reached out and took them from Bel's hands.

On both charts: west, a small, known part of the world, shown as clearly as could be managed by the cartographer; in the center, a long vertical sweep labelled: "(Outskirts)"; beyond, emptiness.

Sharon's map, and Rowan's: the oldest map in the world, and the newest.

Bel's dark eyes were amused as she watched her friend's face. "You're starting over."

Rowan separated the charts again and, across near a thousand years, looked into the face of her sister.

She smiled. "Yes," she said.

From DEL REY, the brightest science-fiction stars in the galaxy...

Available at your bookstore or use this coupon.

_____**THE WHITE DRAGON, Anne McCaffrey**   34167   5.95
Ruth was a dragon of many talents. though almost everyone on Pern thought he was a runt that would never amount to anything. Vol. III—Dragonriders of Pern.

_____**RINGWORLD, Larry Niven**   33392   5.95
The Hugo and Nebula Award-winning novel...the gripping story of a ring-shaped world around a distant sun.

_____**CHILDHOOD'S END, Arthur C. Clarke**   34795   5.95
Clarke's masterwork reveals Mankind's newest masters: the Overlords. They bring peace and prosperity: and for all they have done. they will exact a price.

_____**INHERIT THE STARS, James P. Hogan**   33463   4.95
Scientists had finally found a Man in the Moon...wearing a spacesuit, fully human and he had been there for 50.000 years!

_____**GATEWAY, Frederik Pohl**   34690   4.95
The Hugo and Nebula Award-winner! Rich man or dead man—those were the choices Gateway offered. and Robinette Broadhead happily took his chances.

BALLANTINE MAIL SALES
400 Hahn Road, Westminster, MD 21157

Please send me the BALLANTINE or DEL REY BOOKS I have checked above. I am enclosing $ . . . . (add $2.00 to cover postage and handling for the first book and 50¢ each additional book. Please include appropriate state sales tax.) Send check or money order—no cash or C.O.D.'s please. To order by phone, call 1-800-733-3000. Prices are subject to change without notice. Valid in U.S. only. All orders are subject to availability of books.

Name_____

Address_____

City_____State_____ Zip Code_____

08   Allow at least 4 weeks for delivery.   3/92   TA-30